Praise for Jeri Smith-Ready and

WICKED GAME

**A nominee for the American Library Association
Alex Award**

"Smith-Ready's musical references are spot-on, as is her take on corporate radio's creeping hegemony. Add in the irrepressible Ciara, who grew up in a family of grifters, and the results rock."

—*Publishers Weekly*

"This truly clever take on vampires is fresh and original. The characters have secrets and questionable backgrounds, which makes them intriguing. The use of music as the touchstone for life is sharp and witty. Smith-Ready proves that no matter what the genre, she has what it takes."

—*Romantic Times*

"A colorful premise and engaging characters . . . a fun read."
—*Library Journal*

"Just when I think the vampire genre must be exhausted, just when I think if I read another clone I'll quit writing vampires myself, I read a book that refreshed my flagging interest. . . . Jeri Smith-Ready's *Wicked Game* was consistently surprising and original . . . I highly recommend it."

—A "Book of the Week" pick by Charlaine Harris
at charlaineharris.com

"An addictive page-turner revving with red-hot sex, truly cool vampires, and rock 'n' roll soul. Jeri Smith-Ready is a major new talent on the urban fantasy scene."

—Kresley Cole, *New York Times* bestselling author of *Kiss of a Demon King*

"*Wicked Game* is clever, funny, creative, and way too much fun. . . . A surefire winner."

—The Green Man Review

"Jeri Smith-Ready has created a set of strikingly original, fascinating characters, rich with as much style and rhythm as the music her vampires love. Lyrical and uncompromising, *Wicked Game* is a winner I'll be reading again."

—Rachel Caine, bestselling author of *Thin Air*

"Jeri Smith-Ready's *Wicked Game* is a wicked delight. Peopled with fantastic characters from across almost a century of American music, this is urban fantasy that makes an irresistible playlist and an irresistible read. I await the next book with growing impatience!"

—C. E. Murphy, bestselling author of *Urban Shaman*

"Sharp and smart and definitely not flavor of the month, *Wicked Game* is wicked good. Jeri Smith-Ready will exceed your expectations."

—Laura Anne Gilman, bestselling author of *Free Fall*

"Jeri Smith-Ready's vampire volume *Wicked Game* will make your corpuscles coagulate with corpulent incredulity. It's for young bloods and old jugulars alike. Whether you devour it on 'Sunday Bloody Sunday' or just before 'Dinner With Drac,' simply turn off the 50-inch plasma, lay back, and 'Let It Bleed.'"

—Weasel, WTGB 94.7 The Globe, Washington, D.C.

WICKED
GAME

JERI SMITH-READY

Pocket Books
New York London Toronto Sydney

Pocket Books
A Division of Simon & Schuster, Inc.
1230 Avenue of the Americas
New York, NY 10020

This book is a work of fiction. Names, characters, places, and incidents either are products of the author's imagination or are used fictitiously. Any resemblance to actual events or locales or persons, living or dead, is entirely coincidental.

First Pocket Books paperback edition April 2009

POCKET and colophon are registered trademarks of Simon & Schuster, Inc.

For information about special discounts for bulk purchases, please contact Simon & Schuster Special Sales at 1-800-456-6798 or business@simonandschuster.com.

Cover design by Melody Cassen
Cover photograph by Sydney Shaffer/Getty Images

Manufactured in the United States of America

10 9 8 7 6 5 4 3

ISBN-13: 978-1-4391-0134-6
ISBN-10:   1-4391-0134-5

To Donna and Ted, my first rock 'n' roll gurus.

Acknowledgments

Many thanks to my family, for encouraging my love of music despite my almost preternatural lack of talent.

Thanks to Rob Staeger, Cecilia Ready, Tricia Schwaab, Barbara Karmazin, Rob Usdin; William Parris, President, Radio Broadcast, Inc.; and Gerard W. Weiss, Lt. Col., U.S. Army (Ret.); for their story comments and research assistance. Any remaining errors are mine, and probably due to a momentary lapse of caffeine.

To the hardworking folks at Pocket Books for bringing this novel to life: Louise Burke, John Paul Jones, Josh Karpf, Lisa Litwack, Jean Anne Rose, Erica Feldon, Don Sipley, and Anthony Ziccardi.

Much thanks to my editor Jennifer Heddle, for her extraordinary vision and brilliant insights (and forbearance in overlooking the muscle shirt); and to my intrepid agent Ginger Clark, for believing in this series from the get-go. You both rock.

Most of all, thanks to my own guitar man Christian Ready, for his love and support, and for proving that some things don't burn out *or* fade away.

Playlist

"I'll Never Get Out of These Blues Alive," John Lee Hooker
"Read My Mind," The Killers
"About a Girl," Nirvana
"Flower," Liz Phair
"Hard to Handle," The Black Crowes
"Eight Miles High," The Byrds
"Blue Suede Shoes," Carl Perkins
"Helter Skelter," The Beatles
"Uncle John's Band," Grateful Dead
"I'm So Glad," Skip James
"Baby Please Don't Go," Big Joe Williams
"Gallows Pole," Lead Belly
"Dreadlocks in Moonlight," Lee "Scratch" Perry
"Three Little Birds," Bob Marley and the Wailers
"Ciara," Luka Bloom
"Two Hearts," Chris Isaak
"Drain You," Nirvana
"The Rain Song," Led Zeppelin
"Isis," Bob Dylan
"Fearless Heart," Steve Earle
"The Old Main Drag," The Pogues

"Rock 'n' Roll Lifestyle," Cake

"More Human Than Human," White Zombie

"God Given," Nine Inch Nails

"Melt!," Siouxsie & the Banshees

"She's a Rebel," Green Day

"Norwegian Wood," The Beatles

"10:15 Saturday Night," The Cure

"Running Dry: Requiem for the Rockets," Neil Young and Crazy Horse

"I'm No Angel," Greg Allman

"Girlfriend," Matthew Sweet

"Low," Cracker

"Human Touch," Bruce Springsteen

"A Thousand Kisses Deep," Leonard Cohen

"Sleep to Dream," Fiona Apple

"Mean Woman Blues," Elvis Presley

"(Don't Go Back to) Rockville," R.E.M.

"Crazy Love," Van Morrison

"Burning for You," Blue Öyster Cult

"It's Only Rock 'n' Roll (But I Like It)," The Rolling Stones

If a lie is told often enough, even the teller comes to believe it.
—J. R. "Yellow Kid" Weil, con artist

WICKED
GAME

1

It's Only Rock 'n' Roll (But I Like It)

Family curses never die, they just mutate. In Greek mythology, the curse of the House of Atreus began with some smart-ass making soup du jour for the gods out of his own son's meaty bits. Things went downhill from there. These days, though, the curse probably just makes the Atreus family forget to send each other birthday cards.

The curse of the House of Griffin, whatever sinister form it may have taken in the Old World, has left me with a gift for the persuasive arts. In the straight world, this means sales and marketing—or as I like to call it, S&M.

The slim, thirtyish dude across the desk scans my skimpy resume. Short dark hair flops over his forehead as he nods along with the blues squawking from a wall speaker. His fingers tap the wooden surface between us in unconscious synchronicity.

The tiny office's clutter of memorabilia would shame the Hard Rock Cafe. Near one boarded-up window, a life-size cardboard John Lennon peers into my soul; near the other, Jerry Lee Lewis peers through my blouse.

"So, Ciara . . ." David slips me an earnest glance. "Why do you—"

"It's *keer*-ah, not see-*air*-ah." I rattle off the pronunciation as politely as I can. "Not like the mountains."

"Sorry. I bet you get that all the time." He flips my resume to look at the other side. Blank. He lifts my portfolio folder, probably searching for another page. "Where's the rest of your job experience?"

I give him a wide-open smile. "In the future, I hope."

He blinks, then looks back at the resume. His eyebrows pop up. "Well, it's very readable."

Due, no doubt, to the sixteen-point font I used to fill up the page.

He inspects it again, green eyes flitting back and forth in a desperate search for an interview kickoff. "Ciara. Interesting spelling."

"It's Irish. It means 'dark and mysterious.'" I point to my tawny hair and studiously guileless eyes. "Even though I'm neither."

David's lips twitch up briefly, then he puts the resume aside and opens my portfolio. While he examines it, his thumb pumps the plunger on his ballpoint, creating a staccato of clicks that wears my nerves down to the nub. I resist the urge to wipe my clammy hands on my only interview suit.

The air-conditioning clunks on. Above my head, backstage passes begin to flutter in the breeze, hanging like Christmas decorations from the antlers of a peeved-eyed deer.

"This first project's dated six years ago," David says. "I take it you go to Sherwood College part-time?"

My shoulders tense. "I take sabbaticals." Oops, this was supposed to be an exercise in honesty. "I mean, I take breaks so I can earn tuition."

He nods in sympathy. "It's expensive. I gave the army four years of my life in exchange for a degree."

"The army, wow. Did you kill anyone?"

His gaze sharpens, and I wince at my nerve-induced idiocy. Usually when I botch an interview, it's on purpose. The fact that I actually want this job makes my stomach ache.

David's mouth relaxes into a smirk. "Shouldn't I be asking *you* questions?"

"Sorry. Ask anything." As long as it's not about me.

"Why do you want to work at WMMP?"

I knew that one was coming, and I've been working on a convincing answer ever since David found me through my college's job-match program.

"I love rock 'n' roll." Damn, that was cheesy. I rub my nose and look away. "I wasn't allowed to listen to it growing up, but I did anyway. I'd lie under the covers at night with my Walkman, listening to tapes I'd stolen—I mean, borrowed—uh, stolen." This truth thing is harder than I expected. "Anyway, I figured a radio station might suck my soul less than a corporation would. Plus it's already June tomorrow, and I'm desperate. I can't graduate without a summer internship, and if I don't get out of this town soon, I'll—" My mouth shuts, about three sentences too late.

David blinks, and blinks, until I wonder if the air-conditioning has dried out his contact lenses. He sighs through his nose, making a sound that says, *Why am I wasting my time with this girl?* I scramble for something else to discuss.

On the desk between us, a photo of a beribboned Chihuahua sits next to a calendar of 365 Oscar Wilde quotes. I squint to read, *I like persons better than principles, and I like persons with no principles better than anything else in the world.*

I glance up at David, then back to the photo and calendar. "Cute dog."

"Oh. This isn't my desk." He pushes his chair back a few inches. "This is Frank's desk, the sales and marketing director." He shifts the Chihuahua photo's heart-shaped frame. "I'm not, you know . . ."

I think the word he's looking for is "gay."

"Are you the owner?"

"I'm the general manager. The owner is—" David glances past my shoulder at a closed office door. "—absent."

I wait for him to elaborate, but he just tugs the cuffs of his sport coat and changes the subject.

"I'm also the program director. As I'm sure you're aware, WMMP broadcasts syndicated talk shows and paid programming during the day. But at night—" He gazes at the wall speaker like it's a holy relic. "That's when WMMP comes alive."

Huh. "Will Frank interview me, too?"

"I make all the personnel decisions. Frank would have joined us, but he hates the—" David's glance flicks to the stairway behind me. "He hates to work at night."

I check the wooden mantel clock above the bricked-up fireplace. 9:30. "Why interview me so late?"

"I wanted any potential intern to meet the DJs. This is the only time they're all . . . here."

Hmmm. My first act as marketing intern would be to suggest playing music when people are actually awake to hear it.

He shuffles my resume and portfolio, rapping their edges against the desk. The motion has a finality about it, as if he's about to thank me for stopping by.

Panic jump-starts my mouth. "I know my resume is a little thin, but I can explain."

"No need." He folds his hands, steepling his fingers and tapping his thumbs together. "Do you know why I called you for this job?"

I've been afraid to ask, and I hesitate to guess.

David continues. "Your history indicates that you're sympathetic to—how shall I put this—the outsider's point of view."

My gut plummets. He did a background check.

"What kind of outsider?" I ask innocently.

"The kind with a lack of regard for—" He spreads his thumbs. "—conventional morality."

I sit back in my chair, moving slowly, as if from a poisonous snake. "I've never been charged with anything."

"I know you haven't." David extends his hands palm down, as if to hold me in my seat. "My point is—"

"Thanks for your time." I stand and grab my purse from the back of the chair. "I've really enjoyed our chat, but I think another opportunity would fit me better." I head for the exit.

"Wait." He intercepts me, placing his hand on the door before I can open it. "What I'm saying is, I don't care about your past. Neither would anyone else here."

My mind calculates how much he could know. A legal background check wouldn't reveal anything too incriminating. My juvey record cleared when I turned eighteen, and in the six years since I've never been caught. Sort of.

"We couldn't pay you a lot, I'm afraid." He gestures toward my resume. "But judging by your address, you don't need much."

Did he just insult my neighborhood? Doesn't he realize I live above the best pawnshop in town?

"You'd work over there." He points to a smaller desk next to the fireplace, on the opposite wall from Frank's. Beyond it sits a copier so old I expect it to have a hand crank.

"Come." David moves past me so suddenly it makes me jump.

He descends a creaky wooden staircase between the two closed office doors. I follow him, trying not to get my hopes up. Maybe his hiring talk was hypothetical, as in, *you'd work at that desk if all the other intern candidates got eaten by a giant cockroach*. I force my mind away from the things I'll have to do if I don't get a summer job. Things I can't put on a resume.

At the bottom of the stairs, David rests his hand on the knob of a closed door. He takes in a quick, deep breath as if to say something momentous. The words don't make it out before he shakes his head.

"Probably best if you meet them without preconceptions. If they like you, the job's yours."

I nod. No pressure or anything.

David opens the door to let me pass into a small, dim lounge. A pervasive cloud of cigarette smoke gathers over the halogen lamp in the far left corner, muting the room's lurid shadows.

My stinging eyes take a moment to adjust. I strain to see a group of—

Freaks.

Exquisite freaks, to be sure, so soul-shatteringly beautiful, it's a tragedy that radio is for ears only. But they each look like they stepped out of a different time machine.

David squeezes past me through the doorway, where my feet have stopped. "Ciara Griffin, meet the pride of WMMP."

Three men and a woman are playing poker around a table scattered with plastic chips and open bottles. They examine me with a palpable distrust. Maybe it's the interview suit: navy blue makes me look like a fed.

"Spencer, Jim, Noah, Regina." David points from left to right. "And back there is Shane."

On the love seat at the foot of the lamp, a young man in faded ripped jeans appears to sleep, right arm draped over his face. One leg is bent, foot resting on the cushion, and the other stretches beyond the end of the sofa.

David touches my elbow to urge me forward a few steps. "I'm hoping Ciara will be our new intern."

The hostility fades from the faces of the four awake DJs, replaced with a patronizing politeness. I attempt a smile, encouraged by the slight thaw.

"Spencer does our fifties show," David says. "Birth of rock 'n' roll and all that."

A man in a white dress shirt and black pants stands to greet me, unfurling endless legs from under the table. His dark red hair is slicked back into a ducktail. He squeezes the hand I offer.

"Hey, baby, what's shakin'?" Spencer's southern drawl

and impeccable clothes give him a gentlemanly façade, which doesn't quite gel with the feral look in his eyes.

"Not much, Daddy-o." It just comes out. Rather than take offense, Spencer smiles and nods approvingly.

The next guy springs out of his chair, and I force myself not to retreat from his approach.

"This is Jim," David says.

"Man, I really dug your portfolio." Jim hugs me. His long brown curls and tie-dyed shirt reek of marijuana and patchouli. "I used to go to art school, too."

"Thanks, but I'm not an artist." Is he sniffing me?

Jim pulls back and regards me at arm's length. "Then how'd you get all those layouts to look so groovy?"

"For my class projects? I used the computer, of course."

His eyes crinkle with confusion. "The . . . ?"

David clears his throat loudly enough for my bullshit alert system to creep into Code Yellow. What the hell's going on?

Comprehension crosses Jim's face, and he snaps his fingers. "Right. Back in my day, we had to do it all by hand."

I squint at him. He looks just a few years older than I am. They all do.

"Back in your day?"

The third man scrapes his chair against the floor as he rises. I turn to him, relieved to slide out of Jim's personal space, which seems to lack boundaries.

"I am Noah." The man's voice rolls over me like a warm Jamaican breeze. "It is a pleasure to meet you, sweet lady." He reaches across the table, takes my hand, and draws it to his full lips. My eyes go all moony and unprofessional under his gaze, which is softened by a pair of dark-rimmed glasses lying low on the bridge of his nose. Noah's green, gold, and red knit cap perches atop a fetching set of chest-length dreadlocks. I'm relieved the seventies are represented by reggae instead of disco.

"Oh, please. Get the fuck off her, you wanker." Despite the Briticism, the punk/Goth woman—Regina, I presume—has a flat midwestern accent. Beneath a shower of spiky black hair, her face is a study in monochrome, with black eyeliner and lipstick setting off her skin's porcelain perfection.

Regina gives me a chin tilt and a "yo," before turning to Shane. "You can pretend to wake up now."

He slides his flannel-shirted arm from his face, then turns his head. I take my first full breath of the evening. His warm eyes and crooked smile make me feel like I'm really here and not just a stain someone left on the rug.

"Hey." Shane drags his battered Doc Martens off the couch and stands up slowly. Even with the grunge-cool slouch, he's taller than the others. As he approaches, he flicks his head to sweep a tangle of nape-length, pale brown hair out of his eyes.

When our hands touch, he starts as if I've shocked him. He pronounces my name perfectly, and so softly I wonder if someone else in the room is still sleeping. Then his gaze cools, and he half-turns away, hands in his pockets.

Aw, he's shy. How lovable, huggable, stuff-in-a-bag-and-take-home-able.

Or not, as I look at Regina, whose eyes are slicing me in half. Shane must be her boy. She could probably weaponize any of those six facial piercings in seconds.

An enormous stack of chips sits in front of her next to an open bottle of tequila. "Who's winning?" I ask, in an effort to get on her good side.

"I have two hundred ninety-two dollars," Regina says. "Jim has forty-six, Noah one hundred sixty-seven, and Spencer, ninety-eight. No, wait—ninety-nine."

"Shane bombed early," Jim says, "not that he had much to start with."

The flannel-clad man in question turns to David. "She'll be fine. Can I go now?"

"Sure. Thanks for coming in."

Jim fishes a set of keys from his pocket and tosses them to Shane. "Happy hunting. And remember, none of that low-octane shit this time."

Shane heads for the door, sparing me a cool glance of acknowledgment. My eyes shift to follow him, but not my head. I congratulate myself on my restraint.

"What do the rest of you guys think?" David says. "Should we hire her?"

They examine me like I'm a cow at a 4-H auction. I try not to moo.

The four DJs exchange looks, then nod, more or less in unison. David rubs his hands together and starts to make a declaration.

"Wait," Spencer says. "What about Monroe?"

David shifts his weight from foot to foot, then shakes his head. "I don't want to interrupt his program."

"Who's Monroe?" I ask David.

He points to a closed door in the corner with a glowing ON THE AIR sign above it. "He plays the *Midnight Blues* show."

"But it's only 9:30."

"It starts at nine, ends at midnight. That's when Spencer takes over, then Jim from three to six, on alternating nights. The other nights feature Noah, Regina, and Shane, same schedule."

The DJs make a point of picking up their cards again, dismissing us. David beckons me to the bottom of the stairs.

He shuts the door behind us and jerks a thumb over his shoulder. "Do you know what they are?" he whispers.

It seems like a trick question, so I shake my head.

"A revolution." David's eyes are googly with fanaticism. "They each dwell in a time when a new sound embodied the zeitgeist of a generation and knocked the world on its ass."

Code Yellow again. "When you say they *dwell* in that time—"

"Musically."

"So what's with the costumes? Was that for my benefit, or are they on their way to a cliché convention?"

David sends me a sly smile that says he thinks *his* name should mean "dark and mysterious."

"All will become clear." He trots up the stairs. "What's important is that you understand the music they live for and the history behind it."

I hurry up after him, my hand flaking white paint off the banister as I go. "I'm not exactly a rockologist, but—"

"Don't worry. Ignorance is the world's most curable affliction." He turns right at the top of the stairs and opens the door of a tiny corner office. A light flickers on.

When I join him, David is running his hands over a wall-size bookshelf. He yanks out one tome after another and stacks them on a small round table until the pile stands as high as my head.

"Oh." He puts his hand on the stack. "You never said yes. To the job."

I can't afford to suspect why they want to hire me after such a perfunctory interview. But the weirdness begs one question.

"What about the future?" I point to the framed handbill of a '69 Dead concert at the Fillmore West. "This place is like a museum. What about now? What about tomorrow?"

David sighs. "Have you listened to the radio lately? Honestly."

"No."

"Why not?"

I shrug. "Too many commercials."

"And?"

"The music is boring." I pull my MP3 player from my purse. "At least with this, I know I'll hear something good."

"Exactly. All the music sounds the same, because big corporations take over stations and make everyone play the same vanilla-flavored crap." He leans forward, voice low and calm. "You won't find crap of any flavor at WMMP. Here the DJs play what *they* want, not what some CEO or record promoter tells them to play. Do you know how rare that is?"

"I'll take a guess: extremely?"

He slides the top book from the stack—*The Rock Snob's Dictionary*—and caresses the worn edge of the spine. "This place is a gift to people who love music. I don't take credit for it. It's all them." He points to the floor. "But people don't know about them—yet. The owner just spent a fortune boosting our signal strength to reach listening areas in D.C., Baltimore, and Harrisburg."

"That's good, right?"

"Maybe not." He taps the spine of the book against the table. "She did it to make the station more attractive to buyers. A communications conglomerate called Skywave has spent the last decade gobbling up hundreds of radio stations."

"And WMMP is next."

He nods. "Our owner says if ad revenue doesn't quadruple by Labor Day, she'll sell to Skywave. And we'll all be out of work." He tosses the book back on the stack. "Frank needs another set of legs for our last-ditch marketing campaign. Based on your course work, your portfolio, and your energy, I think you'd be perfect."

Again, no pressure. I glance at the books. "Those are for me?"

"You have to know your product." He says the last word with a twist of his lips. It must pain him to speak of music as a commodity.

"You never answered my question about the future."

He looks away, face pinched. "If Skywave is the future, maybe we're all better off in the past."

Dubious but desperate, I reach for the stack of books. "Get the door."

"Wait." He holds out his hand. I reach for it to seal the deal, but he brushes my hand aside. "Uh-uh. Give me that." He points to the MP3 player protruding from my purse.

"Are you kidding?"

"Spend two weeks listening to the radio instead. With

your first paycheck I'll give you a bigger player, with more memory and more songs, courtesy of the station."

I hand it over. "One with video would be great."

He laughs and slides the player into an empty slot on the bookshelf. "See you at eight-thirty tomorrow morning."

I lug the books out to the parking lot, trying not to stagger too much.

"And lose the suit," David calls after me. "This is a radio station, not a savings and loan."

I send him a grateful grin as he waves and shuts the door.

The parking lot's tiny pebbles crunch under my feet, loud in the summer-night stillness. No traffic noise reaches me, since the station lies ten minutes outside the small town of Sherwood, Maryland, separated from the highway by a quarter mile of dense woods.

I balance the books against the fender of my worn-out car and fish for my keys. My purse feels light and roomy without the player, which I already miss. Maybe I could borrow my friend Lori's—

Footsteps scrape the gravel behind me. David with more books, no doubt.

"Honestly," I tell him as I turn around, "this is more than—"

The word *enough* dies in my throat.

No one's there. The only light bleeds from an orange porch lamp near the station's front door, turning my half of the parking lot a dull amber. The radio tower looms above, its winking red eye too high to provide illumination.

The other side of the parking lot lies in shadow, and

that's where I look—muscles frozen, eyes darting, like a baby rabbit hoping the predator won't see me if I just stand still.

Yeah, right. Anyone stalking me might think I've been replaced by a mannequin. Good strategy.

Since there are no other buildings within yelling distance, I should either drive away or run back into the station. The thought of whimpering to my new boss about a scratchy noise in the parking lot makes my decision easy.

Without turning toward the car, I fumble for the trunk lock, then insert the key. The trunk pops, and I shove the books inside before slamming it shut. My feet stumble backward to the driver's-side door.

A breath at my ear, too cold for a summer breeze. I spin to face—

Nothing again.

I stifle a squeak, open the car, and slip inside with a quick check of the backseat. My elbow mashes down the door lock as I start the car and slam it into reverse. Gravel spins from under my tires and clatters against the undercarriage.

The driveway forms a long, headlight-bright tunnel in the leafy darkness, and it's not until I reach the main road that my lungs release their pent-up breath.

No wonder Frank hates working at night.

My hands have stopped shaking by the time I arrive in downtown Sherwood. After checking my side street for suspicious characters—more than the usual, anyway—I grab half of David's books from my trunk and head up to my apartment, over Dean's Pawn Shop. It really is the best in town, as evidenced by the large red-and-white sign in the window: NO STOLEN GOODS. Dean might as well have written WINK WINK at the bottom of the sign.

I enter through a double-locked, street-level door next to the shop, then clomp up a dark stairwell—I've been bugging Dean for weeks to change the unreachable lightbulb—to another door, also double-locked, leading to my apartment.

The stale hot air chokes me. I hurry three steps down the hall to the bedroom, where my only air conditioner perches in the window. Soon my suit lies crumpled in the corner and I'm standing before the AC in my underwear, letting the frigid breeze dry every drop of fear-infused sweat.

Once cooled to the point of shivering, I switch on my computer and connect to the Internet, then run to the kitchen to avoid the modem's eviscerated-android screech.

I open the fridge to see one lonely beer looking for company. It finds its ideal mate in a piece of leftover pizza.

Back in my bedroom, my e-mail has finished downloading. At the top of my in-box sits a message from David, sent a few minutes ago:

ARE YOU LISTENING?

"Yeah yeah yeah." I switch my alarm clock to the radio function and search for WMMP's frequency. (Do they know that their call letters sort of spell *wimp*?) I scan the dial until a harmonica purrs from the tiny speaker.

Returning to my e-mail, I notice that one of the

in-box's subfolders is bolded. It looks like this: "M (1),"
which means I have one message from a person who gets
filtered into her own subfolder "M." She must have convinced the guards to give her computer access again.

The message crouches safely behind a wall of mouse
clicks. After a few moments of stomach-churning hesitation, I leave it there.

Just before midnight, I send my last "I finally got a Job!"
e-mail, this one to my former foster parents. Stretching to
crack my vertebrae over the back of the chair, I notice the
radio's gone silent. Did the signal die? I grab my beer and
cross the room to make sure the plug hasn't slipped out of
the ancient, fire-code-violating outlet.

Then a voice, soft and low, says, "I'll never . . . *never*
get out of these blues alive." For a moment I wonder if the
voice belongs to Monroe the DJ—I haven't paid enough
attention to know what he sounds like. Then a guitar eases
in, followed by light applause. The words must have been
the name of the song.

A slow, insistent drumbeat joins the hushed guitar,
mesmerizing me even before I hear the first lyrics. I sit on
the bed, gingerly, as if an abrupt movement could break
the spell.

His voice sweeps over me, crooning of black coffee,
cigarettes, and the futility of trying to sleep in the face of
heartache.

An impassioned piano joins in, defying the lyrics'
doom. I close my eyes and I'm there, in a dim, smoky bar
where loners sway, heavy-lidded, wrapped in thoughts of
those they've lost. I swallow the last warm sip of beer and
wish I had another.

The song ends. Applause erupts. I click off the radio before another voice can take the singer's place. His contagious restlessness prickles my skin and shatters my sleepiness. I can't lie down. Even the soft cool sheets would scour my nerves.

I draw up the shade and peer out my window. The quiet streets of Sherwood beckon, begging me to make one last run before this normal life tightens like a strait-jacket.

I tap my nails against the wooden sill in a quickening rhythm and wait for someone, anyone. But in a small town at this hour, the sidewalks and alleys are empty of prey.

Besides, I always hunt far from home.

2

Won't Get Fooled Again

My office desk is empty, inside and out. I shouldn't expect too much from my first day of work, but how can I achieve the American dream of enhanced productivity without a computer or, say, a pen?

David seemed relieved to see me when I showed up a few minutes ago, but then he had to run back downstairs to the studio to switch a program, leaving me aimless and penless.

A metal cabinet sits on the other side of my desk, supporting the antique fax machine and a box-framed fretboard from a busted Pete Townsend guitar. I head for the cabinet, my sandals slapping against the rough hardwood floor.

The cabinet door creaks open to reveal shelves full of supplies. Score. It's like shopping without paying.

As I paw through empty boxes, my enthusiasm dims. Now it's like shopping in Soviet Russia.

Footsteps trudge up the stairs behind me. "You can have any color pen," says a languid voice, "as long as it's black."

I swing the cabinet door aside to see a pale, pudgy blond man approach the other desk. He tears off the top page of the Oscar Wilde calendar and reads today's quote. "Hmph." Apparently not one of Oscar's funnier bon mots.

"You must be Frank." I walk over to him as business-like as I can, considering the sandal-slapping, and extend my hand.

The corners of his mouth turn down, which looks like their natural configuration. "It's Franklin, actually." He sets down the calendar. "Everyone calls me Frank, even though I don't want them to."

"I have the same problem."

He looks at me directly for the first time. "Everyone calls you Frank?"

His delivery is so deadpan, the joke thuds through the floor and into the basement before I remember to laugh.

"I mean, they say my name wrong."

Frank(lin) scans my resume, which David must have left on the desk. "What's so confusing about 'Ciara'?"

He says it right: *keer*-ah. We're going to be great friends.

Franklin finally shakes my hand. He's taller and younger than I first thought; the slump threw off my perception. He's about six feet, in his midthirties at most. His clothes are sharp enough—a business-standard dress shirt and gray jacket with a blue-and-black tie—but they lie listlessly on his form, as if he came to inhabit them by accident. Maybe he just needs caffeine.

"Can I get you a cup of coffee?"

He sighs and rolls his eyes. "Sit down." He gestures to the chair in which I was interviewed last night, then sinks into the seat behind his desk.

"Did I say something wrong?"

"Fine, don't sit." He looks up at me with gray eyes that combine a basic benevolence with a soul-deep ennui. "Ciara, you're here to learn about marketing and sales, and help this station avoid oblivion. You're not here to serve anyone." His slight drawl pegs him as a local. "You fetch coffee for no one but yourself, you make copies and send faxes for no one but yourself. Got it?"

"Got it."

"If one of those disc jockeys—" He points to the floor as if they live under the building. "—asks you to so much as loan them a pen, let me know. After you tell them to fuck off, of course."

I sit in the chair and scoot it closer to Franklin's desk. "So what's their deal? Do they dress like that all the time?"

He leans forward to reply, then clamps his mouth shut. "Did you read the books David gave you?"

"No, I just got them last night."

Franklin studies my face for a few moments, drumming his fingers slowly on the arm of his chair.

"Hang on." He gets up, then shuffles down the stairs, managing to look both perturbed and apathetic.

I barely have time to snicker at today's Oscar Wilde quote (*To get back my youth I would do anything in the world, except take exercise, get up early, or be respectable*) before David bounces up the stairs.

"Ciara." He nearly turns my name into three syllables before covering his mistake with a quick chin scratch. "Have you at least skimmed the materials?"

Right now the books are lying in my hallway where I dumped them last night. "Why is it so important?"

He crosses his arms and shifts his feet. "You need to understand what we are—I mean, who we are, and the challenges we face in today's, er, business climate." He rubs the side of his neck. "So you can be one of us."

I'm not one of them. I'm an intern. But I'll agree to anything to make him stop twitching.

"Which book, which page? I'll look it up when I get home tonight."

"Now." He nods at my empty desk. "Your computer won't get here until Monday, so go home and start reading. Call me when you find out—when you finish."

I picture the three-foot stack of text. "Finish all of them?"

"You'll know when."

Even David's cryptic comments won't make me turn down a paid day at the pool.

I'm halfway out the door when I remember something I wanted to ask him. "David, who does that song, 'I'll Never Get Out of These Blues Alive'?"

He turns a proud-papa smile on me. "John Lee Hooker. Monroe plays it last thing every night. You like it?"

I shrug. "It's all right."

David's smirk says he sees through my understatement. "You'll love your job."

I love my job. I've never been able to say that before, but now, lounging by the pool at my best friend Lori's apartment complex and sipping a peach iced tea, I love my job.

My timer beeps, and I flip onto my stomach and reset it with an extra ten minutes, since my back always tans more slowly than my front. At least I don't turn red and freckly like most Gaelic girls. My dad once said I have Gypsy blood, but there's no reason why that one statement out of all his others would have been true.

I slide the next book in my stack across the concrete. "The *Encyclopedia of Rock and Roll*?"

"How are you supposed to read an encyclopedia?" Lori asks from the next lounge chair.

"He said to skim." I thumb the pages as fast as a flip book. "I'm skimming."

"Ow." Lori sits up and rubs the back of her neck. "I think I'm getting burned."

"Slop on more of that SPF 40. You keep forgetting you're Nordic."

"Finnish."

"But I've barely started."

She groans and squirts her squeeze bottle at me. I jerk a corner of my towel to protect the *Encyclopedia* from flying iced tea. "Hey, watch out."

"Puns make you a legally justifiable target."

I turn back to the book, but the sun's glare against the white page tightens the corners of my eyes. I lower my face into the darkness of my crossed hands.

To keep myself awake, I ask Lori, "How's the ghost tracking?"

"SPIT's going to help raise funds for the Battle of Sherwood monument. The town officially thinks we're nuts, but they're happy to take our money. Besides, if we find out that Sherwood is haunted, it'll bring in more tourists. Everybody wins."

"Except the ghosts. Maybe they'd rather be left alone."

She laughs. "Don't patronize me, Skeptical Girl." She says it like it's the name of a supervillain.

Despite the constant urge to roll my eyes, I support Lori's obsession with Civil War ghosts—after all, she has to do something with that history degree. Besides, it's kept my best friend in town two years after graduation, here with me and SPIT, the Sherwood Paranormal Investigation Team, who really need a new name.

I remember my encounter in the parking lot last night. It feels silly in the bright afternoon light, but I have to ask. "Let's say there really are ghosts in Sherwood."

"There really are ghosts in Sherwood."

"Okay. But what would one feel like?"

Lori shades her eyes at me. "Is this a joke?"

As I tell her about the cold presence, her mouth falls open like her jaw has lost all muscle tone.

"I am so jealous." She picks up her iced tea as if to fire it at me again. "You don't even believe, and you get an apparitional experience. The most I've ever felt is a tingly elbow, and that turned out to be nerve damage."

"Come on. There must be an explanation. If you were investigating, what other causes would you rule out?"

She taps the tip of her squeeze bottle against her chin. "With the trees around it, the parking lot might have natural temperature fluctuations, which would explain the cold spot. That whisper could have been the wind in the leaves. And everyone knows radio towers are massive electromagnetic sources. Sounds like a perfect recipe for false creepiness."

"Good."

"I could get SPIT to check it out for you."

"No no. I don't want my boss to think I'm crazy." *I don't want* myself *to think I'm crazy*.

Lori picks up her watch and whimpers. "Time for work." She stands and folds her towel. It's good she's getting out of the sun—her face is the red of a marathoner who just crossed the finish line. "Stop by the bar later?"

"Definitely. Thanks for the ghostly insights."

"You *will* belieeeeve." She hums the *X Files* theme music as she flip-flops away.

I skim the mega-lopedia's highlighted entries. No unusual facts yet, nothing that clues me in to the grand purpose of Wimp-FM.

My beach bag bulges with unread volumes—two books on the history of radio, one on women in rock 'n' roll, and a battered coffee-table book on American roots music.

The last one has a lump, something stuck inside the front cover, something almost big enough to be a book of its own.

I pull it out, a thick pamphlet. The back is yellowed and contains nothing but the copyright date of 1954. I flip it over.

"Oh, that's cute."

The title reads, in poorly typeset block letters, *The Truth about Vampires*. It looks like a public service brochure, part of a government-sponsored scaremongering series including titles such as *Marihuana: Stepping-Stone to Despair* and *It's Not Just Big Dandruff: How to Spot Head Lice*.

It contains thirty pages of thin sheets, gathered into short chapters. I lean back on the lounge chair to read it. Not part of David's curriculum, I'm sure, but it'll take me ten minutes, tops.

Yeah yeah, feed on blood, okay, can't go out during the day, yada yada yada, super-seductive, whatever. Sounds like rehashed clichés to me, warmed-over Anne Rice, but hey, I scarf those trendy vampire novels like they were heroin-soaked potato chips, so I'll play along for entertainment's sake.

I page ahead, looking for the big bad "Truth about Vampires." Given the period, the "truth" probably means Communist infiltration of blood banks. This thing reeks of McCarthyism.

One heading says, "Temporal Adhesions." Hmm, that's a new phrase. I reach for my iced tea.

Which never gets to my mouth, because all my muscles have frozen. The words reverberate through my head in a documentary-style voiceover.

> *Vampires become "stuck" in the cultural period in which they died, what they refer to as their "Life Time." To maintain cognitive comfort, a vampire will continue to dress and speak in the conventions of his or her Life Time. For example, a female vampire from the 1920s will often display "flapper"-style clothing and claim that "makin' whoopee" with multiple partners is "copacetic."*
>
> *As modern life intrudes on a vampire's carefully constructed reality, he or she may rebel against these feelings of powerlessness. A benign response may take the form of obsessive-compulsive behaviors, which grant the illusion of control.*
>
> *Every effort should be made to provide the law-abiding vampire with a means to connect simultaneously with the past and present, thus extending their*

lives and preventing potentially disastrous unrest.
Many vampires of a certain age utilize our network
of protective custody homes, where they can "fade"
without posing a threat to themselves or others.

Typed in red ink, on a sidebar:

NOTE: Vampires with certain characteristics—
including mental instability as a human, extreme
youth or old age at the time of "turning," as well
as several unknown factors—are likely to react to
their changing world in a violent manner. Since
an agent's primary duty is the protection of hu-
man life, he should take all precautions, includ-
ing preemptive action (see Field Manual Chapter
Sixteen, "Disposal").

Huh?

This must be what David wanted me to read. He thinks the DJs are vampires. *They* think they're vampires.

No, nobody's that delusional outside a mental hospital. It must be an act. A joke. A joke without the funny.

I examine the pamphlet again. The paper doesn't just *look* old—it feels brittle and smells musty as an attic. So they used old paper—and a typewriter, since these sheets would disintegrate in a printer or copier.

Why so much trouble just to trick the new girl? Did they put on this farce for the other candidates?

My fist clenches, crumpling the booklet. Maybe there were no other candidates. David called *me* for the interview, not the other way around. Why? Because of my past, he said. But how much can he really know about my past?

And what the fuck does it all have to do with vampires?

Doesn't matter. If it smells like a fish, swims like a fish, quacks like a—well, it's just really damn fishy. We've skipped Code Orange and gone straight to stoplight Red.

I retrieve my cell phone and dial David, whose name and number are neatly printed inside the book's cover.

No answer. Easier that way.

"David, I'm sorry to leave this message on your voice mail, but I've found an employment opportunity elsewhere." Here's where I should say something nice. "Thank you for your consideration." Ugh. Try again. "I mean, thanks for the offer. I think it would've been fun."

I slap the phone shut before my voice reveals my ambivalence. Time to check the want ads again.

On the way out of the pool area, I stuff *The Truth about Vampires* into the trash where it belongs.

3

Run Like Hell

The Smoking Pig is filled with the usual Friday night bar crowd—mostly college kids who stuck around town to take summer classes or avoid their parents. The Pig is made out of pieces of old mills, which apparently used to dot the local countryside like spots on a Dalmatian. To add ambience, rusty machinery parts lie wedged in the dark wooden ceiling beams.

After an afternoon perusing the Help Wanted section (flipping burgers versus driving a cement mixer), I need a drink. I squeeze through the crowd to the brass rail and wave to Lori at the cash register. She holds up a finger, her lips reciting the drink order to herself as she rings it in. Then she trots over, pale ponytail bobbing.

"Your tan looks amazing," she shouts over the din of the crowd and the blare of the latest Killers song. She lifts her bangs and tilts her chin toward the light. "Can you tell I was wearing sunglasses?"

"A little." Her face looks like a negative version of the

Hamburglar. I shouldn't let her go out during the day. The thought reminds me of vampires, so I shove it aside.

Lori slides a napkin across the polished wood surface of the bar. "What can I getcha?"

"Something strong and straight up."

She scrutinizes my eyes, which I know are bloodshot from too many job ads. "Strong, yeah, but definitely not straight. You need more than booze." She grabs bottles of Kahlua and vanilla vodka. "Chocolate martini'll cheer you up."

"How'd you know I need cheering up?"

"Bartender's sixth sense." Her hands trickle over the bottles in front of her before pulling out Grand Marnier, Frangelico, and Bailey's Irish Cream.

"Looks expensive."

"My boss is out sick, so it's free. But it means we're short-handed, so I'm totally in the weeds tonight. It's crazy—two bachelorette parties." She shakes the martini, then pours it into a glass in front of me. "After the crowd thins out, you can tell me what's wrong." She winks and hurries away.

I scan the crowd for anyone I know—or anyone I'd like to know. A familiar face appears in my peripheral vision at the end of the bar. Before I can get a better look, a brawny brunette in a wedding veil lurches into view.

"Oh. My God. Ciara Griffin?"

And I thought my day couldn't get worse. I force a smile and snap my fingers, pretending to search for my old hallmate's name. "Joanne, right?"

She slaps my shoulder. "It's Jolene! How can you forget? We only had like every business class together." She snickers. "When you were there, I mean."

I rub my shoulder and remember how during sophomore year she and her sorority sisters would shove Kmart sales fliers under my door every Sunday to show their opinion of my clothes. In return, I would soak their towels in the toilet while they were in the shower. "So how are you?"

"Awesome! I just got promoted and assigned to a huge market research project. Plus I'm getting married." She points her chest at me, and I see that her white tank top has BRIDE 2B stenciled in black letters.

"I'm so . . . happy for you." Her designer shoes and tight leatherette pants make me feel like a schlub in my knockoffs and last year's miniskirt.

"What are you doing now?" she asks me.

"I'm—" Still in college, six years later. Unemployed and unemployable. No fiancé, boyfriend, or so much as a hamster to keep me company two nights in a row.

One of Bride 2B's gold half-hoop earrings catches in her veil. As she tilts her head to release it, the familiar face reappears.

Shane.

Suddenly I have an answer. "I work with him."

She peeks and gives a low whistle. "He's cute. Mysterious."

It's true—Shane seems to sit alone inside an orb of silence. The woman on the next bar stool rolls her shoulders and preens in his direction, but he ignores her until she gives up and turns back to her friend.

My former classmate examines Shane's appearance. His charmingly disheveled hair gleams almost blond in the overhead bar light. He wears a similar getup as last night, but with a different flannel shirt over a different T-shirt.

Jolene turns back to me. "So you work for a logging company?"

I pretend not to get her joke. "Radio station. He's a DJ at WMMP, where I'm the head of marketing."

Her bleary drunken look is replaced by a sly grin. "Introduce me."

"I thought you were engaged."

"And this is my bachelorette party. I'm entitled." With a deliberate gesture, she twists her engagement ring to face her palm.

"I think he has a girlfriend."

"Is she here?"

The thought of Regina hanging out at the hopelessly bourgeois Smoking Pig makes me smile. "I doubt it."

"Neither is my fiancé. How conveeeeenient."

The Bride lets out a braying laugh and drags me toward the end of the bar. Her marquise-cut ring digs into the tender webbing between my fingers. She's stronger than she looks, and she looks like she could bench-press a Buick.

Just before we reach Shane, Jolene holds out her index finger and pinky in a salute to her bridesmaids across the bar. The women hurl a group catcall worthy of the skankiest strip joint.

"Hi there!" she says to Shane's left shoulder. It tenses at the sound, but he makes no other movement. She fans her face with his bar napkin. "Woo! Is it hot in here, or is it just you?"

Still no response. She reaches to touch him, but at the last inch her hand jerks back, as if disobeying a direct order from her brain. Smart hand.

Finally she turns and shoves her lip out at me in a pout.

I frown back at her. "Just leave him alone."

At the sound of my voice, Shane's head turns, pivoting like a praying mantis's. With his hands together on his beer bottle and elbows propped on the railing, the resemblance to the insect is uncanny. I step back.

A moment after his eyes meet mine, they soften, losing the leave-me-the-fuck-alone aspect. "Ciara."

"Wow, you do know each other." The bride-osaurus smooths her veil. I wonder why she hid her ring if she's still got that thing on her head. "I'm Jolene. And you are?"

Shane gives me a quick scan, then shifts on the bar stool to face us. Face *me*, really. He hasn't looked at Jolene yet.

I give him an apologetic smile. "Sorry to bother you, Shane."

"Shane!" Jolene tries to plop her formidable ass on his lap. "Great name. Do you want to party, Shane?"

He glances at the cleavage she shoves toward him. His eyebrow twitches, and his gaze sticks there for a moment. I suddenly long to wrap Jolene's veil around her throat and pull until she passes out.

"We've got a limo and a hotel room in the city," she says—not to me, naturally. "There's plenty of room."

To my dismay, he stands and edges closer to Jolene, letting her press against his chest. I wish Regina would walk in and knock this girl's teeth out her ears.

Shane mouths *Help* to me over Jolene's head.

"Come dancing with us!" She gyrates unsteadily against his hip. "My friends would love you. I promise we won't take too many pictures." She finds this last statement hilarious.

I take a final loving sip of my martini and wait for a guy passing on the right to walk behind me. When he does, I step hard on his toe. He howls and pushes me forward, sending my drink—and all its chocolaty goodness—cascading over Jolene's fresh white tank top.

She shrieks. "Clumsy bitch! My maid of honor stenciled this for me."

"I'm so sorry." I wipe at her top, pressing the liquid into the material. "Go to the ladies' room and I'll come help you clean up."

"You better." She stumbles off toward the restrooms, shaking drops of martini out of her veil. "Hurry!"

The moment she's out of sight, I grab Shane's hand. "Let's go."

We duck out a side exit, which leads to a long hallway. I drag him halfway down at a trot, then realize we're running from a drunken bachelorette, not the Mafia.

When I try to let go of his hand, Shane takes my wrist and pulls me to a stop. "Thanks," he says. "I owe you."

I try not to look at the place where our skin is touching. "It was the least I could do."

"Is she your friend?"

"More like arch-nemesis. But I feel bad for the guy I stepped on."

"Collateral damage," he says.

"I didn't know how else to get rid of her. She didn't care that you were ignoring her."

"I considered glaring her away, but I have to be careful." He shifts his glance above my shoulder. "It sounds wacked, but some people get a little out of control when I look directly at them."

"Oh." I have just enough martini in me to say, "Because you're a vampire."

He drops my wrist and leans back against the wall. "So you know."

"I read the brochure."

"What do you think?"

"I quit."

"Oh." He nods, then turns and saunters down the hall toward the exit, his gait suggesting a contained swiftness, like a greyhound on a leash. I accompany him to see his reaction, and because the only other way out is through the bar.

After a few steps he says, "Did you quit because you don't want to work with vampires or because you don't want to work with crazy people?"

"You're not vampires, and you're not crazy. It's a good joke. I just found a better job, that's all."

"Doing what?"

"Working for an account exec at a PR firm in D.C."

"That's a commute from hell, but congrats, anyway." Shane opens the glass door at the end of the hallway, which leads to a painfully bright liquor store. He heads to the beer fridge. "Do you want to get something to go?"

"Go where?"

He opens the refrigerator, then looks at me through the door. His breath fogs a circle on the cold, clear glass. "Your place?"

Normally with someone who looks and moves the way he does, I'd purr, "The sooner the better." But even I have my taboos. Men who belong to psychos, for instance.

"What's the deal with you and Regina?"

Shane shuts the refrigerator and leans against a pyramid of twelve-packs. "Regina and I have a special connection."

"Does this connection include sex?"

Shane glances at the gangly guy behind the counter, who watches us without embarrassment, then turns back to me. "Not anymore."

"How long anymore?"

He squints at the ceiling as if the answer is written there. "Maybe two years."

He's telling the truth. I've learned a thing or ten about spotting a liar.

I don't trust him enough to bring him home, however. Not yet.

I step forward and open the refrigerator. "Let's take a walk."

We stroll down Main Street, in the general but not specific direction of my apartment. Sherwood's downtown measures only four blocks by three blocks, so we'll have to double back soon.

The night swelters and the popcorn we bought at the store parches my tongue. I'm dying to break out the beers, but every so often a cop car cruises by, slow and predatory as a shark. Aside from domestic disturbances and drunken students, the police don't have much to do here, so their presence is more annoying than comforting.

"So what were you before you became a vampire DJ?"

"Something much more monstrous. I was a wedding DJ." He pulls his wallet from his jeans, then hands me a tattered business card.

McALLISTER MUSIC, YOUNGSTOWN, OHIO. Aha—I thought I heard a hint of that distinctive Pittsburgh–northeast Ohio dialect.

"Do you still hear 'The Electric Slide' in your sleep?"

"Actually, I had a reputation as the DJ for cool couples. They knew I'd play what *they* wanted, not what their parents wanted."

I turn over the card. Small block letters read, NO CHICKEN DANCE.

"Problem was," he continues, "the parents usually paid for the weddings, so I also got a rep for being difficult."

"I can't imagine you in a tux."

"Neither could I, which didn't help."

We stop to sit on a bench in front of the library, where hedges and trees curve around pebblestone paths to form a little park. During the day homeless people hang out here while the shelter is closed, but right now the park is empty.

"So what is it with bachelorette parties?" Shane asks.

"You mean why do otherwise decent women turn into complete ho-bags? Because it's their last chance to be bad, and for some it's their first chance."

He makes a skeptical noise. "I've seen bridal narcissism from every angle. My sister made our dad take out a third mortgage to give her the same kind of wedding all her rich college friends had. It was bizarre, because otherwise she was so down-to-earth."

I catch the verb tense. "*Was* down-to-earth? Is she—still around?"

"She's alive, if that's what you mean." He creases the fold of the liquor store's paper bag. "I just don't see her anymore."

I give him a moment to elaborate, which he doesn't. "Is your family in Youngstown?"

"As far as I know."

"But you don't talk to them."

He rests his elbow on the back of the bench, in a studiously casual pose. "I could explain, but you'd laugh."

"The vampire thing again?"

He sets down the bag and shifts to face me. The tree beside us casts him in shadow, but his pale blue eyes seem to burn into mine. I recall the alleged power of a vampire's gaze.

Glancing away would make me superstitious, so I don't. I narrow my eyes, challenging him. He just keeps staring.

"I don't know what you think you're . . ." My voice fades. I forget what I was going to say. It doesn't matter. Slowly my face goes slack and my vision blurs, but I can't stop it. I don't want to stop it. I want to sit here forever.

Shane leans forward and dips his head close to mine. My skin heats, and my hand reaches for the edge of his shirt to pull him closer.

"Someone's coming," he whispers.

"There she is!" screeches a voice behind me.

I blink hard, then turn to see Jolene and a posse of Bridesmaids 2B. They stalk down the middle of the empty street, almost in formation, like Sharks preying on a lone Jet.

Swiftly and without a sound, Shane moves to stand between me and the small-town gangsta-ettes.

I scramble off the bench. "I can defend myself."

"Against nine of them?"

"What could they possibly—holy crap!"

Jolene wields a serrated knife, which I recognize as the one Lori uses to slice bar fruit. Chocolate still stains her wet tank top.

I turn to Shane. "Let me do the talking instead of your testosterone. I don't want to start anything that'll involve blood and prison bars."

He crosses his arms and stands with feet apart. "I'm here if you need me."

They stop in front of us. The bridesmaids copy Shane's defensive stance. I wonder if they're also packing bar-accessory weapons, like ice tongs or double jiggers. I wouldn't want to get whapped with a cocktail strainer.

Jolene gestures with the knife. "You ruined my bachelorette party. You're going to pay, all of you."

"I said I was sorry. What do you want from me?"

"I want your shirt."

My favorite red top? Fuck that. "It won't fit," I tell her.

She advances on me. "What do you mean, it won't fit?"

"It won't fit you because I'm too—" Dissimilar to a heifer. "—flat-chested."

Jolene examines my figure, doubt tingeing her eyes. "Give it to me anyway!" She brandishes the knife again, with less conviction.

"Give me yours. We'll trade."

She clutches the hem of her tank top. "But my best friend made this for me."

"I'll mail it back to you tomorrow."

"Why should I trust you?"

"You know where I work." I hope Shane isn't blowing my cover with a questioning look. "Besides, why would I want to keep a Bride 2B shirt? I'm not engaged. It'd be like a Red Sox fan stealing a Yankees cap."

My argument makes just enough sense for drunk logic. Jolene nods slowly, her eyes vulnerable. "Promise you'll mail it?"

"Yeah, express. Can we get out of the street now? Someone might want to use it for driving."

We move into the library's little park. I point to two groups of shrubbery, one on either side of the path. "We can change behind those. Shane's the go-between."

Jolene brightens at the idea of him seeing her half-naked. She hustles behind the bush on the right. I collect the beer and popcorn from the bench and retreat behind the other hedge to wait. The bride-goons keep watch.

A few minutes later, Shane appears with the white shirt.

"What took so long?" I ask him.

"There were conditions." He turns toward the street as a car approaches. "Cops."

Sure enough, a bright light sweeps over the library's brick façade, then halts. A car door creaks open.

I snatch the bags and dash around the library toward the parking lot. Though I can't hear his footsteps over the pulse in my ears, I know Shane is right behind me. His shadow keeps pace with my steps.

The pebbly sidewalk curves downhill around the building. I almost topple over a waist-high barrier that keeps skateboarders from speeding out in front of departing cars. Shane leaps the barrier with an Olympic hurdler's ease.

"Which way?" he asks.

I guess he's going home with me. I'm about to wave him to follow when I notice what he's still holding.

From the other side of the building, Jolene shrieks my name in a parade of profanities, culminating in, "Cheapass, double-crossing, shirt-stealing bitch!"

4

Just What I Needed

"We should let these beers rest." I stuff the six-pack in my fridge. "They got shaken up when we ran from the police."

Shane hands me Jolene's shirt, glancing around my apartment with the caution of a trespasser. I plug the kitchen sink and turn on the cold faucet.

"I hope she didn't already try warm water. That'll set the stain." I soak the shirt and gently rub the brown blotches. "This top's big for me, but I could sleep in it."

"You said you'd mail it back to her."

"I never got her address. Hey, what do you think she meant when she said, 'You'll pay, all of you'?"

Shane emits the vocal equivalent of a shrug.

I smooth my hair back off my neck, then let it drop behind my shoulders. "Sorry it's so hot in here. Only the bedroom's air-conditioned." I wonder if he thinks that's a come-on. I wonder if it *is* a come-on.

He doesn't seem to hear me as he scours my walls with a nervous gaze.

"I live alone, if that's what you're worried about."

Shane offers a sheepish half smile. "I was, uh, never mind."

"What were you looking for?"

He scratches his shadow of light brown stubble. "Crosses?"

I laugh. "Don't worry," I say in a stage whisper. "No crosses here."

He spots my bulging photo album on the coffee table. "Can I look?" he asks with a little kid's eagerness.

"Sure." No guy's ever wanted to see my photos before. I turn on a lamp and join him on the couch. He whips open the album as if it contains the secrets of life.

"Whose dogs are these?"

"Not mine. I volunteer with a mutt rescue group. I've sponsored these dogs, paid for them to stay at a local kennel. Gets them out of the pound where they might be put to sleep." I point to a photo of a giant white blur. "That's Banjo. Last week he went to his forever home."

Shane's eyes widened. "He died?"

"No, he got adopted. On Saturdays I'd go to the kennel and try to teach him manners so he'd be more appealing. These days it's not enough just to be cute."

He flashes me a look of amusement, and I wonder who he thinks I was referring to. "That's really noble."

"No." I let go of the album. "I only do it to convince myself I'm a good person."

"Bullshit. By the look of this place, you can barely feed yourself, much less a bunch of dogs."

"I always get what I need to survive."

This time his gaze is steady. "Working for a hotshot PR firm in D.C."

His X-ray eyes propel me off the couch and toward the fridge. "Those beers have probably settled."

I hear him flip through several pages of dogs while I pop the tops of two bottles. One of them fizzes over, but I catch most of it with my mouth. "You want a glass?"

No answer. I glance over the counter to see Shane lingering on a page of photos.

"Are these sunrises or sunsets?" he asks.

"Some of both." I move back to the couch and put the beers on the table, using two unopened pieces of mail as coasters. "My bedroom faces north, so in the summer I see the sun rise over campus."

"So you're a morning person."

"I'm a morning person and a night person. So I have to be a nap person, or else I'm a tired person." Great, now I'm rambling. That's the second time I've mentioned my bedroom with no reaction from Shane.

He doesn't pick up his beer, just stares at the sunrises. I take the opportunity to study his profile, at least the parts I can see beneath his hair. His jaw is sharp and defined, and his nose is like a ski jump—perfectly sloped with a little curve up at the end. If my nose were a ski jump, the skiers would all plunge to a tragic death.

I clear my throat. "If you stay here late enough, you can see it yourself."

He looks at me then, brows drawn together. "I can't stay until sunrise."

His show, of course. "You go to work at three, right?"

"Right. Work." He scans the living room. "Where's your music?"

This time I say it with all the casualness I can muster. "In my bedroom."

"Oh." He focuses on the photo album again, but his fingers are twitching, and as he turns the pages, he doesn't react to the pictures.

Here goes.

"Do you want to see what I have?"

He looks up.

"Music-wise," I add.

He studies my face for a long moment, as if he's not sure what he'll find. Something about me bothers him, but maybe in a good way.

His hand brushes mine, and a tingling spreads through me. I let out a breath that sounds half-cough, half-hiccup. Very attractive.

I stand and head for the hall. "This way," I say, as businesslike as a tour guide.

I move through the dark bedroom to turn on a soft bedside lamp, rather than expose my squalor to the harsh overhead light.

"No crosses in here either," I say with a nervous laugh.

He sits on the floor in front of my CD shelves and contemplates their contents. "Your collection's pretty kickin'."

I wince at the outdated slang, then step out of my shoes and stretch prone across the foot of the bed, my head near the spot where Shane sits.

"They're out of order." He grabs a wide handful of CDs.

"What are you doing?"

"Fixing it." He starts sorting them into stacks on the floor. "Alphabetical okay?"

"Really, you don't have to—"

"I'll start with alphabetical. Maybe later we can sub-group by genres."

Shane must have read the section of the *Truth about Vampires* pamphlet that said they're obsessive-compulsive. He's putting on a show for me, which would explain his use of the word "kickin'."

Suddenly he stops and holds up a CD. Foo Fighters.

I try to be helpful. "That goes under F."

"Dave Grohl's new band," he whispers.

"Not really new." Shouldn't he know that? "At all."

"He was the drummer for Nirvana."

"I know. I was alive in the nineties."

"So was I," he says with a touch of bitterness.

"Do you want to listen to that now?"

"No." He sets it aside like it might poison him.

"Put something else in, then. Something soothing." What I mean is, something seductive. Despite his idio-syncrasies, I can't stop watching him, wondering what he looks like from certain other angles.

He puts in Nirvana's *Unplugged* concert. After a mo-ment of applause, the opening acoustic chords of "About a Girl" pulse through my bedroom. Shane listens for a moment, then reduces the volume.

"You think I'm crazy," he says quietly, not looking at me.

"No, I think you're funny. But honestly, the joke is getting a little old."

"I don't blame you for not believing I'm a vampire." The last word comes out stilted, the way someone might pronounce a foreign phrase. "It sounds insane."

"Hey, I know: I'll tie you to my bedpost until sunrise. If you burst into flames, it'll prove you're not kidding."

He jerks his head toward me, and I swear for a moment I see genuine fear. Then he blinks and turns back to the CDs. "Give me a hand here?"

I sigh and slide off the bed. "Sure, what better way to spend a Friday night?"

"There's four stacks." He taps each one in turn. "A through G, H through N, O through T, and the rest."

"Is that a statistical thing based on the probability of band names, so that the piles end up exactly even?"

He looks at me with awe. "No, but that's a great idea."

I take a handful and start sorting. "So what system is it? It can't be the same number of letters, because four doesn't go evenly into twenty-six."

He hesitates. "It's stupid."

"Tell me."

"No, you'll laugh."

"I promise I won't."

He straightens out the CDs I just tossed onto the H–N pile so that their edges line up. "When I was a kid I had a magnetic play desk, Fisher-Price or some shit like that. The letters were in four rows, in different colors. I still see the alphabet in my head that way." He looks at me. "In case you had any doubt I was a freak."

Actually, it makes him seem more human. I hold up a CD. "What color was M?"

"Red." He nods at my choice. "Mudhoney. Nice."

Basking in the approval of a rock snob, I hide my smile and lean across him to put the CD in pile number two.

As I pull back, my arm brushes his knee—accidentally, of course. His sorting slows for a moment, then resumes.

Sitting together, our heights are closer, which means

he's mostly legs. Long as they are, he crosses them easily beneath him. I like a man with flexibility.

I also gather from the way he handles the CDs that he's left-handed. Probably right-brained, then, maybe a creative type. But odd that he'd fixate on letters, which is a left-brained thing. Makes me more suspicious.

"It's weird," he says. "I'm a big fan of the other DJs' music, but they don't get mine. It's like they can't hear it."

I attempt a light laugh. "Must be lonely, living among dinosaurs."

He doesn't smile. "I'm turning into one, too. Every time I flip on the radio—not our station, but one of the regular ones—I feel lost in the present." He frowns at my Limp Bizkit CD. "It doesn't even sound like music."

I take The White Stripes' latest release off the U–Z pile. "Let me play you something good. Then you can see—"

I catch myself. I'm playing right into his game, acting like his reality is the truth.

"Wait a second," I tell him. "If you're stuck in the past, how do you know it's the past? Isn't it like crazy people don't know they're crazy, and if they do, they're not really crazy?"

He leans back against the side of the bed and contemplates. "You know, you're right."

I grin. "See, I told you—"

"As long as it bothers me, I can't be too far gone." His voice is still serious. "The rest of them are so lost, they don't even know it anymore."

I sigh. "That wasn't what I meant." I lean past him for more CDs. This time I brush against him on purpose, and not just my arm. I risk a glance at his face.

Shane looks at me, then at the CDs, then at me again, and so on. Something's stuck. I keep watching him. The rhythm of his breath turns uneven.

"Let me help you choose." I seize his shirt collar and pull him to kiss me.

Our mouths meet, and his shyness dissolves. His arms snap me tight against him like a trap. The combination of his hands, lips, and tongue sends an urgent heat rippling through me, obliterating all thoughts but *must have* and *now*.

Shane presses me against the side of the bed while his hands roam down to my hips. With no effort, he lifts me onto the bed, where I'm crushed beneath his body. Our breath comes loud and fast against each other's mouths. The crowd on the CD applauds again.

His hand in my hair, he pulls my head to the side. His mouth moves to my neck, and I stiffen. How far will he take this vampire fantasy? His teeth slide against my skin, making me shiver, then travel down my shoulder.

I slip my hands under his shirts and peel them both over his head. He tosses them away, then unbuttons my top quickly, without fumbling. I stare up into his eyes, which have darkened in the low light. The confusion in them has vanished.

I pull him close. His flesh presses cool against mine, like an evening breeze. The music pulses around us, and I feel each pluck of guitar strings as if they were my own nerves.

Shane draws back a few inches and watches me closely as he runs a finger down over my rib cage, toward the top of my skirt.

"Ciara." From his lips my name sounds like a hiss. "Tell me what you want."

I slide my fingers through his soft hair and cup his jaw in both hands. "I want you to make me scream."

The rest of my clothes disappear, with maneuvers so deft they seem to slip off of their own will. I hold my breath and watch his mouth descend on me.

No teasing, no tempting, no taunting—he knows what I need and that I need it yesterday. As I ride one crescendo after another, my voice hits notes I thought were beyond my register. I yank the sheets loose from the mattress and wish for some other anchor to grab on this endless roller coaster, and then—

Pain.

My scream cuts off as my breath stops. Something bit me. My first thought, which lasts about a quarter of a second, is that someone put a scorpion into my bed. My next thought—another third of a second—is that I should warn Shane.

The pain spikes deeper into my thigh. I try to pull away, but his hand is holding me hard to his mouth, and that's when I realize—

"No!"

My free foot kicks him hard in the head. As he jumps away, his teeth tear at my flesh.

I slide back toward the wall and feel a thick, warm liquid on my thigh. "*What did you do?*"

Shane's face looms in the lamplight. Blood drips from his lips, which part to reveal a set of fangs that—

Fangs.

All my muscles seize into stillness. My mouth opens but emits no sound.

"Let me drink you," he growls, eyes glazing like a junkie's. "No one will see the mark there."

A second wave of pain turns my fear into blind, invincible wrath. "That fucking hurt! Get out!"

"Please . . ." Shane crawls up the bed over my legs. "It's so good, the way you taste when you—"

"No!" I whack him hard across the face.

In a pounce faster than I can see, he grabs my arms and pins me to the bed beneath him.

His face hovers an inch from mine, jaw trembling and nostrils flaring. "That. Doesn't. Help."

Stupid, stupid—I just provoked a wild animal. My brain flails for the rules of dealing with aggressive dogs. It's the only reference I have, but my life depends on it.

I force my body to stop struggling. My gaze goes beyond him, breaking eye contact.

I am not prey, I tell myself. I am not prey.

Shane's breath rasps against my skin. His hair drapes in tangles over his eyes, but I can feel them burn into me. His hands shake as they tighten on my arms.

I stare through the ceiling and try to will my heartbeat to slow. A drop of something warm hits my upper lip, and I hold back a whimper as I smell my own blood on his breath.

Finally Shane's grip loosens. He gives a long, slow exhale, then rests his forehead on my chin. "That helps. Thank you." He rolls off me with what seems like a mixture of reluctance and relief. His fangs have disappeared.

I start to shake. The air conditioner feels like it's pouring thousands of tiny ice cubes over my skin. I get up, slowly, to search for my clothes, keeping an eye on Shane without looking directly at him. He sits on the other edge of the bed, one hand holding his head as the other blots the blood on his mouth with a tissue. I eschew the tank top and pull a sweatshirt from my closet.

"Well." I swallow, to wet the desert in my throat. "It's not like I wasn't warned."

"I'm so sorry I hurt you," he says in a hoarse voice.

"You need to leave now." Before I pass out.

"I can't believe I did that." His breath comes fast. "I lost control. I swear it won't happen again."

"No. It won't."

With shaky hands, he pulls on his T-shirt. "Let me at least help you clean it up, get you a bandage."

"I don't think that's a very good idea," I say carefully, though I want to scream, *"Are you fucking kidding me?!"*

He stands, then snatches his flannel shirt from the floor. He hesitates next to the piles of CDs, as if he can't leave them like that.

"Just go," I say through gritted teeth, opening the bedroom door wider to hurry him. God knows what happens to people who faint in front of vampires.

As he passes me, he stops, and I wonder with horror if he's going to ask for a good-night kiss. Instead he pulls a clean tissue out of his pocket and gently wipes the space between my nose and mouth. I see a spot of blood on the tissue before he crumples it in his fist. Our eyes meet, and an unwelcome shiver runs up one edge of my spine, then down the other.

"Forgive me," he says.

I open my mouth to reply, but he cuts me off.

"Not now." He shoves the tissue in his pocket. "Later, when I deserve it."

As he turns to leave, he glances at my left leg, and the sight propels him faster out my front door.

I shut off the music (the concert has arrived at the unnervingly appropriate "Dumb"), then limp to the bathroom across the hall. A rivulet of blood runs from thigh to ankle. I swipe it with a scrap of toilet paper before it hits the floor. The wound looks bad, more from the tearing than from the punctures, which means that if I hadn't shoved him away, I'd be in better shape. But with less blood. Possibly none.

I grab some gauze from underneath the sink, then press it against the wound to stop the bleeding. Once it slows to a trickle, I clean the gash, accompanying myself with a string of "Ow"s.

Maybe I should get stitches, but how to explain my injury? I can barely convince myself it really happened. Even now my mind is forming a wall of denial.

Shane's fangs were fake. Not plastic, of course, but maybe porcelain. Very sharp porcelain.

I close my eyes and shake my head. The fangs were one thing, but his strength and speed, and the magnetic pull of his eyes—entirely inhuman.

No no no. *Not. Possible.* Except it is.

I quit that stupid job because I thought they were nuts, or making fun of me, or both. But everything in the booklet was true. The DJs aren't insane, they're "just" vampires.

I bandage the wound, then return to my room, afraid of what I'll see. My bed looks like a murder scene, which it almost was.

Or was it? Shane didn't seem like he wanted to kill me—he could have done it easily enough. Maybe he thought I'd be a willing "source." My body quakes at the thought, the sudden movement delivering new jolts of pain.

I carry my sheets at arm's length to the bathroom and place them in the tub, which I fill with cold water. Soon the water turns pink to match the tile. I feel like crying, but I don't. They're just sheets, after all, and my head is so . . . so . . .

I clutch the sink to keep from pitching onto the floor. My vision turns blurry and liquid. I ease myself down to lie on the fuzzy bath mat, then carefully place my feet on the toilet, wincing at the pain in my left leg.

The booklet didn't say vampire bites were poisonous, so this dizziness must be shock. I draw the other end of the bath mat over me for warmth, even though it smells like feet. Closing my eyes just makes the room spin, so I stare at the stucco ceiling and try to calm the whirlpool of my thoughts.

Calling me a skeptic is like calling a polar bear white. But this is huge. Huger than an alien invasion and the return of Elvis put together. If vampires exist, maybe anything could.

No. Must not go off deep end of Crackpot Canyon. Must cling to what's left of brain.

When the light-headedness subsides, I drain and refill the tub to let the covers soak, then drag my winter comforter from the hall closet and retreat to the living room for the night. I can't face the disaster that took place in my bedroom. Plus it's my only set of sheets.

As I lie bundled on the couch, memories of pleasure and pain slosh through my fogged-up mind. I hope my subconscious doesn't get the two mixed up. I'm not that kind of girl.

5

Crossroad Blues

I'm suffocating to death, but it's okay, because judging by the bright light I somehow made it into heaven. I never thought it would be so humid.

"Ciara?"

"Hi, God." Frankly, I'm disappointed He's really a man. I figured being perfect would preclude that.

He shakes my shoulder, an inelegant gesture for a deity. "Ciara, wake up."

"Hot up here. Can I have a Popsicle?"

Heavy sigh, very ungodlike. My mind starts to climb out of the quicksand that must be sleep.

But if I'm not dead—

I sit up and throw off the blanket, smacking into something solid that grunts.

David.

"What the hell?" I blink at him in the bright morning light while he grimaces and shakes his hand hard. A snap of knuckle signals his finger unjamming.

"Your doors were unlocked," he says. "You're not as smart as I thought you were."

His distracted glance tells me I'm also not wearing as much pants as he thought I was. I jerk the blanket back over my bare legs, one of which throbs with pain. "Sorry I hit you. I'm usually nice to men who wander into my apartment while I sleep."

"Shane said you needed help."

I should be angry at this invasion of privacy, but all I feel is hot and miserable in my sweatshirt. I tug at the collar. "I need to change."

"I should look at your bite first." He holds up a hand as I gape at him. "If it makes you feel better, I'm trained as an EMT." He opens a red vinyl bag on the coffee table to reveal a complete wound care set: bandages, antiseptic, gauze, flexi tape. I don't want to think what the tweezers are for.

The thought of the gash in my thigh makes my head sloshy again. I slump back against the pillow. "At least get me a clean T-shirt from my bureau. Top drawer."

He heads into my bedroom. A few moments later he appears with a T-shirt from last year's Warped Tour. He hands it to me, then steps into the hallway out of sight. "I'm sorry you got hurt. I didn't want you to find out the hard way."

"Technically I found out through the handy-dandy pamphlet you gave me." My sweatshirt sticks to my back as I struggle out of it. "I just didn't believe it."

"I know. I got your message."

I pull the clean T-shirt over my head, wishing I could wash first. "A glass of water would be great."

David crosses through the living room into the

kitchen. He pulls a glass out of the dish drainer and fills it from the faucet. "So what happened?"

"Met vampire in bar. Brought vampire home. Lost some blood. Oh, and I think I got someone arrested."

He brings me the glass.

"Thanks." I take a sip of water, which has that sitting-in-the-pipes-all-night taste. "Why didn't you just tell me the truth?"

"You wouldn't have believed me. You didn't believe the primer."

"Primer?"

"What you called the pamphlet. It's just a reference guide, not the full field manual. You should read that next, now that you believe."

I hold the cool glass against my face. "Hard to stay skeptical after a demonstration like . . ."

Hey, wait a minute.

Suddenly the day doesn't seem so hot anymore. In fact, it feels like ice cubes are surfing through my blood vessels.

"You sent Shane in as the convincer, didn't you?" My voice rises. "This was all planned!"

He holds his hands up. "Plan B, yes. But I didn't think he'd bite you. Obviously things got—" He gestures to my wound. "—out of control."

Anger pulses through me, and I want to get up to punch him, or at least shove him out the door. But the slightest movement brings a stab of pain, and I collapse back on the pillow.

"I'm so sorry." David puts his hands in the pockets of his khakis and stands there for a few uncomfortable moments. "I really should take a look."

"I'll call an ambulance."

"And you'll explain it how?"

"Dog bite."

"What was a dog doing down there?"

My jaw clenches as I contemplate tough questions in a small town—not to mention my total lack of health insurance.

I pull back the blanket to reveal the bandage on my thigh. Grimacing, I tug the tape from my skin and peel the bandage off the wound.

David bends over and hisses in a breath. "Oh my God."

"Are you this professional with all your patients?"

"I was expecting a couple of puncture wounds, but he really tore you."

"He pulled away when I kicked him in the head."

David straightens and turns away quickly, no doubt disturbed by the visual I just gave him. "I'll go wash my hands." He leaves without waiting for my reply.

In a few minutes he's back at my side, with a clean cloth, soap, and a mixing bowl for a basin. He slips on a pair of squeaky latex gloves and hands me a flashlight to shine on the wound.

I have to ask, "Will I turn into a vampire?"

"For that he'd have to drain you to the point of death, and then you'd have to drink his blood in return."

"I'm pretty sure I didn't do that."

"It's all in the primer." He kneels next to the sofa. "I thought you read it."

"Yeah, but there could have been advances in vampire technology in the last fifty years."

"Some things never change. Now hold still."

It hurts when he cleans it, almost as much as the original injury. I can't hold back a whine.

"I'm really sorry," he says.

"It's not you. I have a low pain threshold. I need sedation just to go to the hairdresser."

"No, I mean, I'm sorry he hurt you."

"You said that already."

"They can be very persuasive."

I start to protest that it was my idea to come back to my apartment, but then I remember it was Shane who first proposed it, in the liquor store. "His breath is warm," I tell David, recalling the way the refrigerator door fogged up when Shane spoke to me through it. "I thought vampires didn't have body heat."

"He's young, still has the side effects of humanity. Life and undeath, it's not either-or, it's more of a continuum."

"When did he, you know—"

"Die? April 1995. Regina made him."

I snort. *Special connection*, all right.

David plops the washcloth in the bowl, pats my wound dry with a soft clean towel, then gently applies an antibiotic ointment. My angry humiliation quenches any possible attraction to him. Ever.

"You need stitches," he says, and embarrassment becomes the least of my problems.

"No no no. I hate sharp things. Why do you think I kicked Shane's head away?"

"You won't feel it." He unwraps a syringe and pokes it into a little vial. "Lidocaine."

I try to scoot away, but I'm at the end of the couch, and my leg hurts worse than ever. "Is this standard issue for an EMT?"

"It's not the first time I've had to clean up after my employees."

Fear of the syringe has finally woken me up. "Time out. You owe me answers."

"Which I'll be happy to give while the lidocaine takes effect."

I cover my eyes with my arm. "Get it over with."

The needle slips under my skin. I bite the edge of the throw pillow until it's over.

I uncover my face. David puts the syringe in a red plastic biohazard bottle, then opens a suture kit. The sight of all that stainless steel sharpness makes my stomach pitch like I'm on a capsizing boat.

"Talk to me so I don't throw up."

"What do you want to talk about?"

Not vampires. "Did you learn medic stuff in the army?"

"Technically the term is 'combat lifesaver,' not 'medic.'" He takes off the gloves and smooths the front of his blue polo shirt. "And technically I wasn't in the army." He sits on the edge of the sofa cushion. "I was in a paramilitary group called the International Agency for the Control and Management of Undead Corporeal Entities. The Control, for short."

Right, because "IACMUCE" doesn't have much of a ring.

"You said, 'International.' So they're not affiliated with the U.S. government?"

He waves his hand dismissively. "Much older. Around for millennia, although it wasn't always called the Control. Its original name is in an unpronounceable dead language." He puts on a new set of gloves and starts arranging the torture implements on a clean towel. I'm going to trust a vampire hunter to stitch my leg? I check to see if the phone is within reach. Nope.

"Anyway," he continues, "those at the top levels of national governments are aware of them and even coordinate operations with them when it suits their needs."

"Does the Control kill vampires?"

"Originally, yes." David picks up a scalpel and looks at my wound. He changes his mind and puts it back in the kit, allowing my heart to start beating again. "But about a hundred years ago, their focus changed to management. Sign of the times, I guess, with the worldwide rise of bureaucracy. Besides, like wolves or bears, the vast majority of vampires don't kill."

I'm not surprised, given that Shane let me go. "Then they're not evil?"

"Like humans, some vampires are bad, some are good, most are in-between. Granted, having so much power and beauty does turn some of them into monsters." David's jaw tightens for a moment, then he seems to will himself to smile. "On the other hand, to protect themselves, they have to be model citizens."

"Why?"

"Police stations have windows."

I draw in a sharp breath. "Sunlight, of course. So where do they get their blood? Butcher shops?"

"No, it has to be human blood. They either get it from blood banks or from donors who like to be bitten."

"What kind of freak would want to be bitten?"

He looks away quickly, a spot of red flushing each cheek.

Oh. Ew.

He picks up the sickle-shaped needle. "You should be numb by now."

He has me lie down, then arranges the blanket to provide a semblance of modesty and keep me from seeing what he's doing. When the needle enters, it feels like it's poking someone else's skin. No pain.

I let out a deep sigh of relief. "Will I have a scar?"

"Not a bad one, if I can help it." His face is the portrait of concentration; you'd never know he's operating a few inches from my crotch.

"So back to the Control," I say to ease the tension.

"By the time I joined, disposal was the exception. We only eliminated a few vampires, the ones who went crazy and posed a threat to civilians."

"You mean when they started to lose touch with their Life Time, like the brochure said."

"Right. The primer and the field manual are for Control agents."

"Which you're not anymore?"

He pauses before answering. "I left to start the radio station with our owner."

"And the owner, is he—"

"She. Elizabeth." A muscle twitches near his left eye. "A vampire."

"Why would she sell the station? Won't her fellow vamps lose their jobs?"

"And their home, and probably their sanity."

My neck jerks. "Sanity?"

He stops stitching and looks me in the eye. "They'd lose what is, for their kind, a unique opportunity to function in this world in spite of—or rather, because of—their temporal peculiarity."

"The whole 'stuck in time' thing? Yeah, I guess Graceland only needs so many nighttime tour guides." I pretend I don't care about the answer to this question: "Will they die if the station's sold?"

"Not right away." He turns back to the operation. "Theoretically they could live forever, getting physically stronger. But psychologically, they start to decay."

"Can you tell by looking at them?"

"Not at first. If you compared, say, Shane or Regina to other vampires their age, you wouldn't see much difference." He carefully shifts my knee to spread my thighs farther apart. "But once they're twenty-five or thirty in vampire years, like Jim or Noah, they become . . . vacant."

"So how does the station keep that from happening to—" I almost say "our vampires" "—to your vampires?"

"The music links them with their past, and the news and weather reports they have to read link them with the present." He tilts his head. "At least on the surface."

"So where are all these other decaying vampires?"

"All over." He pulls a tiny pair of scissors from the suture kit. "But as far as I know, our six are the only ones in Sherwood."

I catch his use of "our." "Do they usually hang out in groups like the DJs do?"

"Some are loners, but most try to find a community of like minds." David makes a quick snip with the scissors. "There's a big group out in the hills about an hour from here, but they're pretty fanatical about keeping to themselves." He smooths an adhesive bandage over the wound. "All done." He hands me a tube of goop and a foil pack of antibiotics. "Start these, and keep the wound dry for at least a day."

I read the directions on the packages. "I'm an idiot. I didn't even think about infection last night."

"Shock makes people temporarily stupid. But don't worry—vampires are technically dead, so their saliva has no germs." He looks at my grimy couch. "Though it might have gotten infected overnight. Any questions or problems, my office door is—well, it's usually closed, but just yell."

I scoff. "I'm not coming back to the station."

"Yes, you are." He latches the red bag. "It's either that or go back to conning old ladies out of their nest eggs."

The freeze starts at my spine and goes upward and outward. How could he know . . . ?

The Control. A group like that would have access to more than an everyday background check and credit report.

I stare at him and wish words would come out of my mouth.

"But I think you're over that, Ciara. I think you're ready to put your talents to more legitimate use."

My voice is low. "I never stole from old ladies. Not once."

"All predators pick on the weak." David collects the gloves, bowl, and bloody washcloths as casually as if we were discussing the Orioles game. "Why should you be any different?"

I tug the blankets over me again, up to my shoulders. "Who else knows?"

"Just the owner and me." He carries the supplies to the kitchen sink. "So far."

I hold back a shiver. "So you're blackmailing me into working for you."

He looks up then, startled. "No. It's your choice. But you need a real job, and we need someone who can sell."

"Who can trick."

"Whatever." He turns on the water and scrubs his hands. "The point is, our interests coincide."

The "old ladies" comment ricochets around my brain, stinging me with each bounce.

"You think you know all about me." My voice stays as cold as my skin feels. "You have no idea."

"Maybe. But I never will, if you chicken out." He turns off the water, then towels his hands dry. "We'll call today sick leave, with pay, even though it's Saturday. It's the least I can do."

"The least you can do is leave."

"Before I do, can I fix you something to eat?" He opens the refrigerator. "Oh." His voice echoes in the emptiness. "Maybe I should get us some bagels."

My stomach growls without my permission, and I stuff the blanket against it. After the things he said, after what he's trying to manipulate me into—damn it, I'm hungry.

"Egg and cheese on sesame seed."

He rubs his hands together. "Good. Be right back."

"Cheddar cheese. And sausage. Sun-dried tomato if they don't have sesame seed. If they do, I'll take one of each. And a large coffee, three sugars. The Kenyan blend, if they have it."

I hear David murmur, "Students," under his breath as he leaves.

The moment he's out the front door, I limp to the hall closet. I yank my suitcase from beneath a fallen coat and unzip the flap.

"Shit on a stick."

Time was, I had a bag packed with all the essentials so I could skedaddle in five minutes flat. I was Ready. The

Department of Homeland Security would have held me up as the paragon of preparedness.

The suitcase still contains my important papers, of which a person like me has very few. But over the last year I've raided it for underwear, shirts, and crackers when I've run low on laundry and groceries.

Comfort begets contentment. Contentment begets complacency. Complacency begets carelessness. My folks taught me *that* family tree even before King David through Jesus. But the crowds only heard me recite the latter.

I haul the nearly empty suitcase into my room. A handful of clothes from each drawer should cover it. A trip to the bathroom with a wrinkled shopping bag gives me a month's worth of toiletries. I dash back to the bedroom, fast as the pain will allow. As my feet slip into my kindest pair of jeans, I'm suddenly glad there are no pets to leave behind.

My CDs lie scattered on the shabby rug, where Shane left them last night.

I remember the look on his face as he organized them, like something else had a hold of him. It wasn't his choice to put Peter Gabriel before Godsmack. He was in the grip of something that was carrying him farther and farther from this world.

I turn away from the stereo. Why should I care?

Car keys lie on my desk next to the computer monitor. As I grab them, something snags my memory. A small thing that shackles my feet.

If I leave now, I'll never get it back.

Without sitting down, I slam the space bar to wake the computer out of standby. The monitor blurts to life to show my e-mail reader, where the M folder stands in bold with a "1" after it.

I click.

> *Ciara honey,*
> *I told you they'd let me have Internet access again if I was a good girl. If there's one thing I excel at, it's being a good girl. I trust the same can still be said of you.*
>
> *Did I tell you about the picture I have of you? I keep it wedged into my cellmate's box spring so I can see it last thing before lights-out.*
>
> *In the picture you're seven or eight—when your hair was so blonde, it made a halo when you stood in the sunlight. You're wearing your pink Easter dress, showing off your new Bible. You remember the white one with your name in gold letters, the one with all the thous and thees in it? Back then, proper people still used the King James.*

My body grows heavy, but I don't sit down.

> *The picture's not square, because I had to tear out the legs of people walking by in the background. People ready for miracles.*
>
> *I miss the miracles, Ciara. We don't get many of them in here.*
>
> *Let me know if your father contacts you. Let me know if he doesn't. Please just let me know anything. That you're still okay, even though I know it's silly to worry. You always take care of yourself, don't you, Sweet Pea?*
>
> *Hope you're enjoying lots of fresh air this summer.*
> *Hugs and kisses and more hugs,*
> *Mama*

* * *

I sink into the chair and close my eyes. My con artist's caution is prodding me to run, protect myself, wrap my ass in anonymity. But that path is theirs, not mine. Not anymore.

The last ten minutes move in reverse, so that when David returns, my suitcase is back in the closet, empty. I'm sitting on the sofa in same place as before, but he seems to know something's different, besides the fact that I'm wearing pants.

He sets the bag of bagels and cups on the coffee table next to me. "I meant to ask, when was your last tetanus shot?"

"I had to get one for school." My voice rings hollow in my head. "Six years ago."

He opens his red bag and looks at me apologetically. "I have bad news for your needle-phobia."

I roll my sleeve above my left shoulder and look away, wondering how many other vampire victims he's treated this year. The needle drives liquid fire into my muscle.

Bitten, stitched, and pierced, all in less than twelve hours. Welcome to the straight life.

He picks up his bag and his own cup of coffee. "Are you going to be okay?"

His words remind me of my mother's, bringing a bitter smile to my lips. "I'm always okay." I finally look up at him. "I'll see you Monday."

6

That'll Be the Day

The phone jolts me out of my nap, late in the afternoon, judging by the sun's angle through the living room window.

Groggy-minded, I heave myself off the couch, limp to the phone, and pick it up.

"Tell me everything." Lori emphasizes the last word. "Starting from the chocolatini you threw down her shirt."

I hesitate. "That's pretty much where it ends. Nothing to tell after that."

"I'll buy you dinner and drinks."

"See you in an hour."

It turns out that dinner and drinks aren't just payment for my juicy story. My friend has tricked me into helping her sort costumes for some Civil War reenactment thingy.

"That guy you left with?" Lori hands me a musty uniform. "I've never seen him before."

I thump the blue woolen coat, raising a cloud of dust. I use my ensuing coughing fit as an excuse not to talk about Shane. "Can we open a window?"

Lori clomps across the wooden floor of the antique-shop attic. She pulls on the sill of the window at one end, but it's stuck. "Sorry. We're almost done."

In the light of a bare bulb, I regard the pile of old clothes, nearly as tall as we are. It looks like we've just started.

I wipe the sweat from the back of my neck and sigh at the dust covering my shirt. "Any restaurant we go to tonight better have a no-skank policy."

She gives me a sheepish smile. "I'll buy you Chinese takeout, a six-pack, and any DVD you want to rent." Her grin widens on the bottom, showing all her teeth. "Pal o' mine?"

I pick up a stack of hangers. "I needed to get out, anyway."

She hands me a long green-and-white dress. "So you don't want to talk about Mystery Man. Tell me about your radio station. Sounds cool."

"In the same way autopsies are cool. My immediate boss is like Eeyore in a man-suit, and the station manager is a fanatic. The DJs are—" I cut myself off. How to describe them without using the word "vampire"?

Lori folds a bonnet and stuffs it in a zippie bag. "They're what, party animals?"

"It's not that." I pin the bag to the dress. "Do you know any obsessive-compulsives?"

Lori drops a box of medals, which go skittering across

the floor. "Damn it!" She scrambles after them. "Why do you ask?"

I kneel to help her scoop up the medals, biting my lip at the pain in my leg. "I think I know someone with it."

"Me, too. My mom." She lays the medals carefully in the box without looking at me. "It started when I was six. She would go around the house at bedtime and make sure all the doors were locked."

"So?"

"So then she started checking windows, even in the middle of the winter when they hadn't been opened in weeks." She sits cross-legged on the floor, oblivious to the layer of dust and dead bugs. "Then all the smoke detectors had to be tested."

"Every night?"

Lori nods. "Over the years, she kept adding more, and she had to do everything in order. If you interrupted her, she'd start all over." She wipes her wrist across her forehead. "By the time she got help, her bedtime routine would start at three in the afternoon."

"What kind of help?"

"Medicine, therapy. At first they told us just to play along with her 'truth,' as they called it. We were already good at that. Then little by little, we helped her find a new truth." She smiles. "I know, it sounds all mystic and existential. But it worked, and we got her back. Mostly."

"I'm glad." I squeeze her shoulder. "How come you never told me?"

Lori tugs at the collar of her shirt. "I don't know. It's complicated." When I don't let her off the hook, she says, "I felt bad complaining about my mom when yours is, you know . . ."

"Yeah." I look away, blinking hard. She probably thinks it's tears, but really it's just the dust.

She clears her throat. "Have you heard from your foster parents lately?"

"Just a few days ago." I smile at the memory of the two normal years of my life. "They just got another new kid, which makes it eighteen total."

"Which one were you?"

"Number thirteen."

She laughs. "But you weren't unlucky to get them."

"I don't believe in luck."

"You don't believe in anything."

"Not true." I angle my head. "I believe, for instance, that you're sitting on a cockroach."

Lori squeals and leaps to her feet, frantically brushing her butt. She looks at the floor and sees nothing larger than a ladybug.

"Just kidding."

She smacks my arm. "Just for that, you're buying tonight."

"You'd make a poor little orphan girl buy her own dinner? Heartless wench." We get back to work, laughing.

Like all my friends, Lori thinks that when I was sixteen, my real parents died, when in fact they just took a ten- to fifteen-year hiatus from my life. I never thought I'd have friends long enough for Mom and Dad to inconveniently reappear, but the possibility looms.

Because there's always parole.

It's after sunset when Lori and I finally stumble from the sidewalk into my dark stairwell.

"Sorry the light is still burned out." I shift the Chinese takeout bag into the crook of my arm so I can hold the banister on my way up.

At the top of the stairs I unlock the door and push it open. The light in my bedroom is on.

I never leave it on.

I freeze. Lori runs into me from behind. "Ciara, what the hell?"

"Someone's here," I whisper, though it's too late for stealth.

"Oh my God, are you sure?"

From my bedroom comes a familiar rattle of plastic, along with the faint thrum of a Liz Phair tune.

"You have got to be kidding me." I stalk down the hall.

Shane sits cross-legged on my bedroom floor, an island in a sea of CDs. He brightens when he sees me. "Hey, Ciara."

I smack down my unwanted delight and try to replace it with indignation. "How did you get in here?"

His innocent head-cock is almost convincing. "You invited me."

"No, I—" I stop, realizing he means I invited him in a general sense, in a vampire sense.

I turn to Lori, who just crept up beside me. "Give us a minute."

She eyes Shane with surprise. "Hey, it's the guy from the bar last night." She scowls at him. "Why did you break into her apartment?"

"Lori, it's okay. It's just a misunderstanding." I hand her the food. "Chopsticks are in the silverware drawer."

She takes the hint. "Yell if you need anything."

I step into the bedroom and slam the door. "How did you really get in?"

"I picked your lock." Shane points to his head. "Sensitive ears hear the tumblers click."

"Fascinating. I don't want you here."

A skeptical look flashes across his face, then he glances at my thigh. "How are you feeling?"

"I had to get stitches and a tetanus shot. It hurts to walk."

"I'm sorry. I really am."

"Why are you here?" I fight to keep my voice down to avoid alarming Lori. "You only came to the Pig last night because David sent you."

He nods. "Usually I hang out at O'Leary's. Less pretentious, no students."

"You ran away from Jolene with me, came home with me, made out with me, just to prove that vampires exist." Indignation masks the hurt in my voice. "You set me up."

"That's not the only reason I came home with you." He stands and takes a step toward me. "As for why I'm here now, I had to finish what I started last night."

A stab of fear makes me reach for the doorknob before I realize he's talking about the CDs. "I can do it myself. I know the alphabet."

"What's the fourth letter after *M*?"

"I don't care."

"It's Q," he says. "I don't even have to sing the alphabet song to myself to figure it out. I know it the way I know the back of my own teeth."

"Is that supposed to impress me?"

He takes another step. "I couldn't sleep today, thinking about it."

"Oh, poor you. I'll have nightmares the rest of my life, not to mention a scar that'll be hard to explain to future visitors. But you lost a day's sleep over some out-of-order CDs."

He gives me a steady look. "I wasn't talking about the CDs."

My breath catches and quickens under his gaze, and he's not even using his mesmer-eyes on me.

I'm about to order him out of my apartment when I realize he might refuse. Then what? Lori and I together probably don't match half his strength.

"Wait here." I back out of my room, shut the door, then dash for the kitchen.

Lori's on the sofa, trying to work the TV remote. "Everything okay?"

"Fine, fine." I rummage through the fridge's vegetable bin, shoving aside a month-old bag of liquid scallions. Nope, not there. I open one of the cabinets and climb onto the counter to peer into the top shelf.

"Sure you don't need help?" Lori calls.

"Yep. Set up the movie."

Finally I find what I'm looking for, behind an unopened container of fennel seed. I climb off the counter, clutching the little plastic jar.

"Be right back," I tell Lori as I blur past her.

In my room I shut the door and advance on Shane, who's sitting among the CDs again.

"Get out!" I twist off the red cap and hurl the contents of the jar at him.

He sputters and spits, then wipes his mouth. "What the—salt? I'm a vampire, not a slug."

"Keep your voice down. It's garlic salt."

"It is?" He brushes the stuff out of his hair and sniffs his sleeve. "How old is that jar?"

I glance at the bottom, which bears a faded price tag (89¢) instead of a UPC code. "Maybe a decade, or two. It came with the apartment."

"I'd say it's past its peak freshness." Shane rubs his arm. "Although I am a little itchy." He stands up, and I step back. He holds up his hands. "Relax, I won't hurt you. If you wanted me to leave, all you had to do was ask."

"I'm pretty sure I did."

He points to a stack of CDs between us. "Here's A through Bowie, in order. That was as far as I got before you started throwing condiments."

I put the empty garlic salt jar in my pocket. "I was afraid if I told you to leave, you might try to hurt Lori."

"No, you weren't." He smirks. "You were afraid I'd convince you to let me stay."

His cockiness provokes my foot to reach out and kick A through Bowie, scattering them across the rug. Shane blanches, a breath hissing through his teeth as if I've rammed a cross of pure sunlight into his temple. I remember what Lori said about her mother, and immediately I regret my action. A little.

He heads for the stairs without looking back. I follow him down and out the front door.

He turns and glances over my head as I stand in the doorway. "Hope I didn't upset your friend."

"Please don't break into my apartment again, even if I can't stop you."

"I won't, I swear. If you promise to do one thing for me."

"I'll put the CDs in order tomorrow. You want me to take a picture to prove it?"

He brightens. "That'd be great. Thank you."

Before I can react, he grasps my face in both hands and kisses me quickly, as if in gratitude.

"Night." He turns and saunters into the shadows.

I double-lock the door, then climb the stairs to join Lori. She'll convince me I'm an idiot for even considering the possibility of maybe not totally despising that monster.

Hopefully before it's too late.

7

Everybody Knows This Is Nowhere

"Heard you got bit."

Franklin wastes no time with Monday morning niceties.

I refuse to glance down at my thigh as I cross the office to dump my purse on my desk. "Had nothing better to do on a Friday night."

"Tell me about it. This town is no place for the living." He seems more relaxed now that we share the station's Big Secret. "Ready to do actual work?"

"When you put it that way, how can I resist?" I sit across from him, carefully, keeping my knees together, since crossing my legs would be agony.

"Today's prospect," he says, "is a Sherwood boutique called Waxing Nostalgic."

"The candle place where people sniff the merchandise and never buy it?"

Franklin nods and stuffs a pencil into his electric sharpener. When the buzzing fades, he says, "Bernita Johnson wants to cut back her ads from five thirty-second spots a week to two." He gives me a level look. "This is bad."

"So we pay her a visit, threaten to flatten her kneecaps."

"Something like that." He sharpens another pencil. "That's just to get your feet wet dealing with clients. This afternoon we start baiting the hook for bigger fish. Now that our signal is reaching urban markets, we can get clients with deeper pockets."

"Cool." I check out today's Wilde quote: *A little sincerity is a dangerous thing, and a great deal of it is absolutely fatal.*

Franklin sharpens a third pencil, and I notice that he has a cupful of about two dozen on his desk.

"What's with all the pencils?"

"Protection." He drops another sharp one into the cup. "You should make your own cache."

"A cache? As in, a collection of weapons?"

"I made a holster. See?" He stuffs a sharpened pencil into a receptacle hanging from his belt loop. "I've got boxes of them stashed in every room of this building, in case you need to defend yourself."

"Have the vampires ever threatened you?"

"No, but it's good to be prepared."

"If you don't like them, why do you work here?"

"Marketing jobs are scarce in Sherwood."

"Why not work in the city?"

"I hate commuting."

"Then why not *live* in the city?"

Franklin glares at me. "If you must know, my boyfriend teaches at Sherwood College."

"Oh." I hide my surprise. Not that I don't think Franklin's boyfriendable. He's actually fairly cute. He just seems awfully grumpy for someone in a steady relationship. "So where would I leave something for one of the DJs?"

Franklin shakes his head slowly, as if he's just heard of my tragic death.

"If I'm going to market this station," I remind him, "I have to get acquainted with its lifeblood. So to speak."

He sighs. "Mailboxes are in the lounge downstairs."

I go to my purse and grab a red greeting-card envelope. "If I'm not back in five, send the Salvation Army."

The lounge downstairs is empty, and silent except for the whine of a Rush Limbaugh wannabe bitching about illegal immigrants. The speaker sits mounted on the ceiling in the corner. When I turn to glare at it, I see the row of putty-colored metal mailbox slots. I make my delivery.

On my way back to the stairs, I pass the door to the studio. The ON THE AIR light is off, so I quietly turn the knob.

I find myself in a narrow hallway. The studio sits behind a thick glass window. It's like a museum exhibit of twentieth-century-radio history: reel-to-reel decks and turntables sit beside CD players and a computer monitor with glowing green numbers.

No one's inside, since a syndicated show is playing, but I wonder why the vampires can't broadcast during the day. They'd be protected from sunshine down here. Then again, this is their sleepy time. Asking them to work during the day would be worse than asking a human to work the night shift.

At the end of the corridor to my right, a thick metal door reads DANGER: KEEP OUT in red block letters.

I step up to it and place my palm on its surface, just below the sign. It's cold and smooth, like a restaurant's walk-in freezer. The handle is heavy, a lever rather than a knob. It would take some effort to open it, which, being smarter than your average horror movie victim, I decline to do. But I notice that the door's bottom edge is made of rubber, creating a seal against the linoleum floor.

My hand whips off the stainless steel surface.

KEEP OUT is cold storage for the station's most valuable assets.

I back away, rubbing my hand against the rough fabric of my denim miniskirt. The chill takes a few moments to subside.

As I stare at the door, an idea awakens, twisting and groping for freedom like a moth trying to pop out of a cocoon a few days early.

I look at the studio.

Nah.

Then the door.

Maybe.

And back at the studio.

Why the hell not?

Waxing Nostalgic is the kind of store that makes you wish you'd been born without a nose.

Franklin and I stop halfway through the door, slammed by ten thousand scents that don't get along. Thick pillar candles, grouped by color family, line the wall shelves of the claustrophobic shop.

I urge my feet forward against their will, toward a front table Fourth of July display. Founding Fathers with wicks coming out of their heads seem to beg us to buy them, burn them, release them from their waxy hell.

Franklin lets the door shut behind us, jangling a cow-bell tied to the handle. A brown terrier lies on a mat near the register to our right. It blinks at us, and nothing more. No doubt its brain is fried from the olfactory assault.

"Be right out!" A shrill voice emerges from behind the curtain of a back room.

Franklin turns to me and says, "Don't act surprised. Just play along." He hastens to straighten his tie and his posture.

I nod, more bemused than confused. I work at a radio station with vampire DJs. What could possibly surprise me?

"Bernita!" Franklin swishes over to the woman who just came out from the back room. "Hey, girlfriend, it's been a million years." He gives her an expansive hug, complete with fluttery back-pat.

She beams, then pinches his cheek like an aunt. "Frankie, how *are* you?"

"I'm fabulous, thanks for asking." His voice is an octave higher than I've ever heard it. I struggle not to gape. "And you—" He holds her at arm's length, tilting his head. "—you look spectacular! Have you lost weight?"

She preens at the attention and pats her formidable girth. "Two hundred pounds the moment I got divorced."

"You are too rotten!" Franklin squeezes her arm and stamps his foot. His breezy manner makes him look fifty pounds lighter himself. Suddenly his clothes appear perfectly tailored, no longer drooping over his body like wet washcloths on a towel rack.

"Oh, just look at our little Reginald." He leans over to *koochie-koo* the dog. "I tell you, I could eat him up with a spoon."

I think a little piece of Franklin died as he uttered the last word with a lisp.

Bernita sweeps her arm toward the merchandise. "Need some candles? I have a few." She's smiling, but her eyes plead for business. Convincing her to give us more money won't be easy.

Franklin grins at me. "Ciara needs some for her bedroom."

"Ahhh . . ." The nearly round woman sidles over. "Expecting an evening with a special young man?"

I send my boss an arsenic-laced smile, then turn to Bernita. "Do you have garlic-scented candles?"

She brightens. "I do have pizza candles. Only eleven ninety-nine."

I follow her to a food-related display, hoping WMMP will extend me an expense account. She hands me, with an inordinate amount of pride, a glass container filled with red, white, and green-striped wax.

"Oh, I couldn't," I tell her. "It's too pretty to burn."

She fluffs her helmet of mahogany-dyed hair. "That's why you need two—one to burn and one to look at."

"Fabu," Franklin says. "She'll take three so she won't have to make another trip."

Great. Instead of buying food, I'll just buy objects that smell like food. Maybe my pancreas won't know the difference.

"Let me check in the back." Bernita sashays toward the curtain. "I think we have one with pepperoni scent."

As soon as she disappears, I turn to stare at Franklin.

"What?" he says.

I cock my head at him. "Paging Dr. Jekyll?"

"Oh, that." His voice flattens back to normal. "A good

salesman fulfills expectations. This is a small town, where people lack exposure to nonstereotypical images of homosexuals. So if I queer it up a little here and there—"

"A little?"

"—and act like those assholes on TV, then people are charmed rather than challenged. I make them feel open-minded because they have a 'gay friend.' People who feel good spend money." Franklin spreads his hands in a gesture of resignation. "I faced the truth long ago: with my real personality, I couldn't sell a bucket of water to a man on fire."

As I'm marveling at the discovery of a kindred spirit, Bernita returns and clonks two more pizza candles on the counter.

"No pepperoni, but sausage will do, right?" She rings them up without waiting for my answer.

Franklin leans on the counter. "You know what would bring in even more business?" He flutters a sweep of blond eyelashes. "Advertising."

Her glee fades as she becomes the sellee instead of the seller. "Times are tough. I've got to cut back on something."

I pull the glass lid off the pizza candle and inhale the ghastly aroma of artificial garlic.

Franklin presses on, smooth as milk. "But Bernita, it's during tough times that you need to get the word out more than ever." His eyes actually twinkle. "If more people knew about this amazing place, you'd be flooded with customers."

Bernita blushes, then stands up straight, as if she just remembered she has a spine. "I need to check my budget. I'll think about it and call you."

I reseal the candle. It'd sure keep Shane away, along with the rest of the world.

Wait a minute . . .

"There's no time to think about it," I blurt.

They turn to me with quizzical looks.

"That is," I add, "rates will be going up soon. Now's a perfect time to lock in the current prices."

"Why are rates going up?" Bernita asks Franklin.

"Ciara, why don't you explain?" he says pointedly.

"I wish I could, but it's a secret." I lean over the counter and give her my best conspiratorial whisper. "We're beginning a new marketing campaign that will blow the socks off this entire region. Everyone will be listening."

Bernita glances at Franklin, who smiles and nods in an Oscar-worthy performance. She doesn't look convinced.

"Forgive my ignorance," she says, "but how can a marketing campaign make that much of a difference?"

"We're going to make a significant announcement about the nature of WMMP."

Her eyes widen. "What is it?"

I bite my lip. "If I told you, it would ruin the surprise. All I can say is that it will show the world how unique the station really is." At least, I hope it's unique in that respect.

Bernita taps her polka-dotted fingernails against the counter as she thinks. Finally she drops the down-home façade. "You'd better not be bullshitting me, girl."

"I assure you, she's not." With the flair of a magician, Franklin snaps open his briefcase and whips out the current rate sheet. "We hired Ciara because she's the best at what she does."

Bernita clicks on her adding machine and taps out

some numbers, using a pencil eraser instead of her fingers. "I suppose I could do my usual five thirty-second spots a week for four weeks. When will the rates go up and by how much?"

Franklin clears his throat. "Well, that depends on—"

"They'll triple by the end of the month," I tell her. "After that, depending on demand, they could rise again."

She taps the pencil on the counter a few times. "I'll take eight weeks, then."

I peruse the merchandise while Bernita and Franklin draw up a contract. The many clearance items include holiday candles with candy facsimiles embedded in the outer surfaces. A two-inch-long wax Easter bunny stares at me, trapped like Han Solo in carbonite.

"You have a tremendous day now, 'kay?" Franklin calls to Bernita as he walks toward the door. She gives me a bewildered wave, which I recognize as a sign to retreat before she can think too hard about what just happened.

Once we're outside, a few shops down and out of Bernita's sight, Franklin's fingers wrap around my elbow.

"This idea of yours had better be good," he growls, "or I'll have your head in a chafing dish."

8

Get Up Stand Up

The vampires—all but Monroe, whose *Midnight Blues* show pipes in over the speaker—file into the lounge and gather around the poker table. I stand next to an overhead projector, pretending to put my transparencies in order, though I've gone over them so many times I could do this presentation in a coma. Franklin helped me put it together, but he declined to join us this evening because of his "allergies." Coward.

David stands beside me and addresses the skeptical-eyed DJs. "You all remember Ciara, our new sales and marketing intern. I hired her to help us turn things around. She has a big idea, but we need your approval and cooperation."

As David covers some old business, Shane pulls a familiar red envelope from his shirt pocket. He jigs the envelope on the table and gives me a secretive smile.

I look around to gauge the other vampires' moods. Regina studies her nails as if they contain a long-lost Dead Sea scroll. Noah looks like his mind is paging through a list of all the other places he'd rather be. Jim rotates his '69 Charger key chain—a miniature replica of his own blue sweetheart—over and over in his hands. Spencer listens attentively to David while using a Crazy Straw to sip from a bottle of cranapple juice. He sees me looking at him and grins, his gums a rich red.

Oh. It's not cranapple juice. The butterflies in my stomach vomit on each other's wings.

"And with that," David says, "it's on to new business. Ciara?"

I take a deep breath and try *not* to imagine my audience in their underwear.

"Today's commercial radio is a musical wasteland. Modern disc jockeys play what the suits tell them to play. The less they know about music, the better, because every second they spend enlightening their listeners is a second the corporation isn't making money off ads or promoters' payments."

Relishing their attention, I expand my gestures and let the words flow. "But you're more than a bunch of trained poodles. You each offer something unique—an intimate understanding of your Life Time and the music it gave birth to. *You* know that. *I* know that." I point to the walls. "But the world doesn't know that. And even if we told them, 'Hey, we've got the experts right here every night,' they wouldn't care. Unless we told them why." Insert dramatic pause, my mental note tells me.

They glance at each other, then Noah takes the bait. "Why what?"

"Why you are experts." I nod to David, who switches off the overhead lights. My first transparency is carefully positioned on the projector. I turn it on.

WVMP—THE LIFEBLOOD OF ROCK 'N' ROLL.

Above the slogan appears the new logo: an electric guitar with two bleeding fang wounds.

The vampires examine the image on the wall without comment, their eyes holding a guarded curiosity.

"Is that supposed to be us?" Jim asks finally.

I regard them one at a time, with more confidence than I feel. "We're going to tell the world that you are all vampires. That's why you know your era so well—because you were born and raised in it, because you live it. We're going to tell the truth."

I continue before they can interrupt. "You've spent your whole lives—your whole unlives—trying to blend in. But the only place you'd blend in is a Halloween parade. You dress differently, you speak differently, you have the facial structures of gods on Earth. I say, let's not hide it. Let's flaunt it."

"Wait a second, honey," Spencer drawls. "You want us to go on the air and tell everyone we're vampires? That's kooky."

"Not just on the air. Live. In public. Show the world your magnificence. They won't believe you're vampires, because that's insane, but they'll believe you're special. They'll believe you have something they want."

After a brief pause to let it sink in, I slap up the next transparency. "Let me tell you how they'll get it."

I detail the marketing plan, from the live gigs to the media interviews to the podcasts (the last one requires a lot of patient explanation and a certain amount of "trust me on this"). At the end, out of breath, I flip the original transparency—the one with the logo—onto the projector.

"If this campaign works," I remind them, "ratings and ad revenue will go up, the station won't get sold to Skywave, and you all get to keep your jobs. How does that sound?"

They stare at me a few moments longer, then everyone but Shane looks to Regina to begin. She clears her throat.

"So we could be like rock stars?"

"Exactly like rock stars," I tell her, feeding off the eagerness of her ego.

"Why would anyone come to see us?" Jim asks.

"Have you looked in the mirror lately? Wait—can you look in the mirror?"

"Of course we can." Noah strokes his smooth brown jaw. "How else would we look so good?"

Regina snorts. "Yeah, if you can see us, why can't a mirror? Is it because we have no sooooooul?" She rolls her eyes and basks in the derisive laughter of the other vampires— Shane excepted. He still wears the stony, pensive look that claimed his face the moment I unveiled the original slide.

I focus on the other vampires as their laughter fades. "I'm sure you have questions, all of which will be useful if and when we go ahead with the campaign." I lean both hands on the table. "But you need to tell me, is it an 'if' or a 'when'?"

Another long, silent moment.

Finally Spencer shifts in his chair and toasts me with his Big Bloody Gulp. "I think the sunnyside's got something here."

"Yeah." Jim taps his car on the table and bobs the top half of his body. "Sounds like a trip."

Noah agrees reluctantly. "Anything that helps us survive, we should try."

Regina regards them all, then nods. "We like it."

I let out a breath and give David a triumphant look.

"I don't like it." Shane straightens up from his trademark slouch. "We're not rock stars. We're DJs. Most importantly, we're vampires."

"Wow, thanks, Señor Grasping the Obvious," Regina snaps. "Will you write my resume for me?"

"This campaign is dangerous," he says. "We've always kept the truth hidden. Now you want to announce it to the world?"

"No one will believe it," I point out. "Sometimes the best way to hide the truth is to tell it."

He shakes his head. "There are people out there wacked enough to believe it, and they'd come after us. We'd be in danger for the same reasons we'd be popular. People would want to get close to us."

"And they can, by buying our merchandise." I reach into a bag at my feet and with a grand gesture unfold a black T-shirt featuring the logo. On the back it says, FEED THE NEED. A chorus of *ooh*s and *ahh*s greets the unveiling, with one exception.

"This crap trivializes what we do," Shane says. "Haven't we always resisted commercialization?"

David moves next to me. "Like it or not," he says to Shane, "the recording industry has always been about money, and money comes from images and marketing."

"That's bullshit." Shane glares at David. "It's not what we're about. We're one of the few places left that's still about the music." He gestures to the T-shirt, and me in the process. "This corrupts our mission."

Regina croaks a laugh. "Our mission is to stay alive."

"Yeah, Shane, it's easy for you to be idealistic," Jim says. "You're young. You can find other work. Hell, you still look human." He twists the last word into an insult.

"But I'm not human." Shane glances at me, then focuses on the other vampires. "None of us are. If we spend too much time in public, someone'll figure out the truth.

Next thing you know, late one night we'll find ourselves delayed on the way home. Then it's 'Good Day Sunshine,' and they'll be sweeping us into a dustpan."

I squirm at the image. Spencer sees my reaction and tilts his head. "What do you care, honey? Why wouldn't you be just as happy to see us go *poof*?"

They all turn to me. I put down the T-shirt. It takes a moment to decide how much to tell them.

"It may be hard to believe, but I'm not all that different from you. I suspect that's why David hired me."

He nods with half a smile.

"I used to prey on people, too, for money instead of blood. It's how I was raised." I've never said this out loud. "I liked it. I was good at it. I've made a career out of it for the last six years." I look at them, each in the eyes. "So I can't judge you for taking what you need to survive."

"If you're just as predatory as us," Regina says, "why should we trust you?"

"Because I said so." David steps forward, his posture straight and sure. "I've always protected you guys, and I always will."

Shane groans and runs his hands over his scalp. "You're not omnipotent, David, even with the Control at your back. And have you even thought about how other vampires will react? Some of them already think we mingle too much with humans."

"It's none of their fucking business," Regina says. "We do our thing, they do theirs, we keep to ourselves. That's the way it's always been."

"This is not keeping to ourselves." Shane points to the logo projected on the wall. "This changes everything."

Spencer taps his cup on the table. "Shane, I don't

see as we have much choice. It's either this or we end up homeless and out of work."

"Exactly," David says. "So do we have your support?"

"No." Shane looks at me. "Sorry."

Regina eyes him with disgust. "Then stay out of it and let the rest of us have our fun."

He meets her gaze. "I hope you live long enough to hear me say, 'I told you so.'"

"It's settled." David rubs his hands together. "Ciara and Frank and I will draw up more specific plans and let each of you know where you fit in. Meeting adjourned."

I turn back to the projector to gather the transparencies. Several of the slippery little bastards slide onto the floor, scattering out of order. Augh. Why can't this place use an LCD projector like the rest of the universe?

"I got it." A deep, soft voice at my shoulder startles me. Shane kneels and sweeps up the fallen transparencies.

"Thanks." Most guys would just stand back and watch me try to bend over in a miniskirt.

He stands and hands me the transparencies, then holds up the red envelope, the one containing a photo of my CD shelves. "I should be thanking you," Shane says.

I shrug. "It's pure alphabetical for now. Maybe later I'll subgroup them by genre. I hear that's fun."

He sits on the table and rests a foot on a chair. "Look, it was nothing personal, what I said about your campaign."

"You're entitled to your integrity. It'll enhance your mystique." I start sorting the transparencies. "By the time you come to your senses and join us, the masses will be rabid for the broody, reclusive Vampire Shane."

"It's frightening the way your mind works. And yet I cannot look away."

David walks up and hands Shane a three-page list of call letters and frequencies. "I thought you might protest, so I made a list of stations Skywave has bought in the last ten years."

Shane's eyes widen at the size of the list. He rubs his face as he scans the pages, probably alphabetizing the call letters in his head.

"Listen to their Webcasts," David says. "Ciara can help you find them on the Internet."

"I can do it myself." Shane sounds less than certain. "But why?"

I gesture to the list. "So you can hear what this station could become. Let's say Skywave hires you to do a night-time show. Which they probably won't because it's cheaper just to pipe in someone else's show from, say, Cincinnati, add a local weather report, and pretend it's a hometown broadcast. But if they do hire you, you'll have to play whatever they tell you. You'll be a human jukebox."

"This isn't about me," Shane says. "It's about the music."

"Exactly." David taps the papers. "Listen for a week, then tell me if those stations are about the music." He pats Shane's shoulder, then heads over to talk to Regina.

Shane rubs his eyes, which, I just realized, are looking kind of sunken. "You want to get a drink?" he asks me.

"Not really."

"Of alcohol, I mean. In public."

Seems safe, at least in the physical jeopardy realm. "One condition. You answer all my vampire questions. Honestly."

"Didn't David give you the field manual?"

"It's written in bureaucratese. Besides, I get the feeling most of it is propaganda."

He considers the ceiling for a moment. "I'll answer

general questions, but reserve the right to protect my personal privacy."

"Deal. Meet me at the Pig in half an hour."

When all the vampires are gone, David comes over to help me clean up. "Four out of five. Not bad."

"Four out of six. Don't forget Monroe." I take a last admiring look at the T-shirt before folding it. "Monroe does exist, right? He's not just a recording?"

"Of course he exists. But he won't talk to you."

"Why not?"

"Think about it. In his day in Mississippi a black man could be lynched for having a conversation with a white woman that wasn't bookended by 'Yes, ma'am.'"

"But that was then." I switch off the projector's fan. "I'm not saying racism is dead, but—"

"It's still 'then' in his mind, Ciara. He's old. Fossilized."

"And he can't change?"

"None of them can."

I look at the chair where Shane sat a minute ago.

"Including him," David says.

"I refuse to believe that." I stuff the transparencies in the folder. "You saw the looks in their eyes just now. They want to do more than survive, they want to have fun. Does a fossil crave fun?"

He shakes his head. "Remember, they're not human."

"I'm not only remembering it." I grab my bag and head out the door. "I'm milking it for all it's worth."

The Smoking Pig is nearly deserted, which makes the music seem louder than usual. Shane is already waiting at the bar, chatting with Lori.

"Ciara, look who's here." Lori grins as if she personally dug him up for me.

"It's just a business meeting." I point to the brown ale he's drinking. "Give me one of those."

"Our very own microbrew." Lori reaches for a pint glass. "One of my boss's basement experiments, but I swear it's safe. This batch didn't explode hardly at all."

I climb onto the bar stool. "Hey, Lori—Shane and I have a secret."

"Cool! What is it?"

Shane turns to me. "You're kidding, right?"

I pat his arm, which feels cold through his shirtsleeve. "Don't worry, everyone'll find out in a couple weeks. But Lori should get the best-friend scoop."

"Scoop on what?" Her brows pop up as she fills my glass at the tap.

"Shane, along with all the other DJs at WMMP, is a vampire."

She gives a little laugh and flicks her glance between us. "I don't get it."

"It's our new marketing campaign. You know how each of them has a radio show based on a certain time period? The idea is, each of them actually lived in that time. That's how they know the music so well."

Lori sets my beer in front of me. "Cool idea."

"It gets better. Have you ever heard of the 27 Club?"

"Isn't that the weird thing where all these famous singers died when they were twenty-seven? Like Jimi Hendrix and Janis Joplin?"

"And Jim Morrison, Kurt Cobain—"

"Robert Johnson, the Stones' Brian Jones, Al Wilson

from Canned Heat," Shane adds, his voice low and reluctant. "Pigpen of the Grateful Dead, Badfinger's Pete Ham, Wallace Yohn from Chase, Uriah Heep's Gary Thain, Helmut Koellen of Triumverat, Jimmy McCulloch from Wings, the Minutemen's Dennes Boon, Mia Zapata of the Gits, and Hole's Kristin Pfaff."

"Wow." Lori seems impressed and a little disturbed at his knowledge. She steps away and picks up a rag to wipe the sink. "So what about it?" she asks me.

"Get this: each of these DJs died and became a vampire when they were twenty-seven."

"Huh." She looks at Shane. "So how old are you supposed to be?"

He tries to smile. "I'm thirty-nine."

"It was my idea." I execute a pitch-perfect hair flip. "We even have T-shirts."

"That's brilliant. People will love that." She gasps and whaps the rag against the bar. "We should have a kickoff party here at the Pig. We'll dress up all Gothy and serve blood-red beer. It'll be like Halloween in June!"

I gesture to her and look at Shane. "Can you tell why she's my best friend?"

She high-fives me across the bar, then heads for the phone near the cash register. "I'll call Stuart and see if he'll go for it. It is his bar, after all."

When she's out of earshot, I turn back to Shane. "See? Everyone will think it's a gimmick."

He pushes his pint glass slowly against mine, gliding it toward the edge of the bar. "This is one of those moments when I ask myself why I like you."

I catch my glass just before it topples. "Do you have an answer for yourself?"

"Still looking, with hope." He slides off the stool and heads for the cozy corner table.

I join him with a basket of popcorn, which I place on the table between us. "You all live in the basement of the studio, right? Past the 'Keep Out' door?"

He nods. "That door leads to our underground apartment. It has a bedroom for each of us, plus a living room and a kitchen. Not exactly a Park Avenue penthouse, but it's free. Not to mention safe."

"Safe from what?"

"Fire, for one thing. Probably a comet impact. Definitely a nuclear blast." He tugs on the white threads fraying his sleeve. "But the sun is what we worry about most. That's why the station's front door is always locked and the windows boarded up."

"Curtains wouldn't be enough?"

"Even a little daylight bleeding in around the edges can hurt. So we use civil twilight times instead of sunrise and sunset."

I read about that in the primer, but my head is a jumble of facts. "Civil twilight is what again?"

"It's when the sun is six degrees below the horizon. Basically, when humans need artificial light to see. The extra half hour makes a big difference."

"What happens if you get caught in daylight?"

He thumbs the rim of his glass as he considers. "You ever get a splinter jammed under your fingernail?"

I wince. "Ow, yeah."

"It's nothing like that."

I give him the appreciative *ha-ha* that he was seeking, but refuse to change the subject. "Don't vague out on me. What happens when you're touched by sunlight?"

"The same thing that happens when we're touched by fire."

His gaze unfocuses suddenly, and he wipes his hand over his forehead.

I have to prompt him. "What happens?"

He jerks his attention back to me. "We burn."

"But everyone burns in fire."

He shakes his head. "Humans burn like wood, vampires burn like paper. We can heal from brief contact with sunlight or fire, and we can survive more of it as we get older. You wouldn't believe how many fingertips Regina and Jim have had to regrow because of their smoking habits."

"Yikes." I grab a handful of popcorn, which I notice Shane hasn't touched. "Do you eat?"

"If I have to, to fit in. But solid food's pretty bland when you're dead. Everything tastes British." He holds up his beer. "Liquids are good, though, if the flavor is intense, like a rich ale or a dry wine or strong coffee, and the drugs in them still affect us, just not as much as they do humans."

"So what's the deal with vampires and garlic?"

"Our sense of smell is really acute, so any food that gets into people's breath and pores can drive us nuts. You can't get blood without going through sweat." He sips his beer. "I don't mind garlic too much. Asparagus, though . . ." He makes a yuck face.

"What about blood from banks? No sweat there, so how does that taste?"

"Stale, like three-day-old pizza. It's also not as healthy. But that's just for when we're lazy or desperate."

I munch another handful of popcorn and ponder last resorts. "Do you ever bite men?"

"Sure."

"Is that after—I mean, when you bit me, we were . . ."

He looks away like he's scrambling for a nonanswer.

"You promised you'd be honest."

He takes another long sip of beer, then wipes his mouth. "Blood tastes better during an orgasm. Theirs, not mine."

"Oh." My neck warms. I pull my hair forward to cover it. "And the guys you drink, do you—"

"It depends."

"On what?"

"On the circumstances. On the guy. Some, I can barely stand to put my mouth on their necks, much less—" He draws his glass across the table like he's outlining a battlefield. "All things equal, I prefer women. But we can't afford to be picky. A totally straight or totally gay vampire will end up a totally undernourished vampire."

"How long can you go without drinking?"

He sinks back in his chair, looking like he has a headache with my name on it. "Old ones can go weeks. Brand-new vampires need it at least twice a night."

"What about you?"

He doesn't answer, just rubs the bridge of his nose with his thumb and forefinger, grimacing.

"You don't look so hot tonight," I tell him, then realize it sounds like an insult. "I mean, you look—" Hot as ever. "—like you don't feel well."

"I'm just thirsty."

"Okay, I'll get the next round." I raise my hand to signal Lori.

Shane grabs my wrist and pulls it back to the table. "No, I mean I'm *thirsty*."

"Oh." I yank my hand out of his grip. "In that case, I'm not getting the next round."

He opens his cell phone. "Sorry, I need to leave."

A Lois Lane–size curiosity (and possible stupidity) surges within me. "Can I come with you?"

He looks up at me from the phone. "You don't want to do that."

"Afraid I'll be jealous?"

"No, I hope you'll be jealous. But you could also be repulsed."

"I'll take my chances in the name of research. And we'll drive separately, so if I freak out, I can go home."

"There's one a few blocks away." He presses a button, then puts the phone to his ear. "One who likes to be watched."

A kinky thrill courses through me, along with a vague fear—or maybe it's a kinky fear and a vague thrill. Please let this donor be a guy.

"Hey, it's me," he says into the phone. "Can I come over? Yeah, now, if you're sure you have enough." His cryptic words remind me of a drug deal.

"I'm bringing someone," he tells the phone person. "No, never." Shane smiles. "Well, I don't think she'd like that word. Red is good, yeah. See you in a few." He folds up the phone.

"What word wouldn't I like?"

He downs the rest of his beer in one gulp, then slides his glass to clink against mine. "Virgin."

9

People Are Strange

"Don't say anything," Shane tells me on the short walk to our destination. "If you need to leave, do it quietly."

"Are you going to—"

"Please, Ciara, no more questions." He rubs a knuckle over the corner of his mouth. "I feel self-conscious as it is."

We turn up the walkway of a brick town house. The porch light illuminates a yard with cheery, tasteful landscaping.

He opens the screen door and knocks softly on the wooden one, even though a doorbell sits to the right.

"Why not just ring—"

"Shh." He wipes his hands against the sides of his jeans. "Not a word, unless she speaks to you."

She. Damn it. I'm about to back out of the deal when the door opens. A pretty brunette in her thirties stands there in a very red dress. Its tiny straps show plenty of skin, and its hem swishes just above her knees. I would look so cute in that thing. She wears no jewelry or shoes.

"Shane," she whispers. "It's good to see you."

By the way he's looking at her dress, I can tell the feeling is mutual. She sends me such a genuine smile that I can't help but return it.

She beckons us into her tidy kitchen, which is dark except for a light above the sparkling white stove. "Can I offer you something to drink?"

Um, isn't that why we're here?

Then I realize she's talking to me, not Shane. "Thanks, uh, ice water?"

She gets me my drink, then signals us to follow her. At the edge of the dining room, she says, "I just had the carpets shampooed, so take off your shoes and walk on the papers."

We do as we're told, stepping from one white sheet to the next, like stones across a stream. The air holds a hint of soap. Shane covers his nose. His enhanced sense of smell must make chemical cleaning products intolerable.

Luckily, the stairs and upper level seem to be dry already. We pass a darkened room with a door slightly ajar, then enter a large bedroom at the end of the hall.

What I see there makes me sigh with longing. A high, queen-size bed with an oak frame sits under a vaulted ceiling, which is painted a slightly darker shade of peach than the rest of the room. The tall floor lamp casts a soft glow from one of those expensive full-spectrum bulbs.

"Sit." She motions to the green velvet window seat. I obey and set my glass on a delicate wrought-iron table. Feeling conspicuous, I avert my eyes to check out the backyard. A vague structure sits in a corner near the flower garden, which is outlined by white stones.

"Are you going to watch or not?"

The woman's voice brings my attention back to the room. Her gaze on me sharpens. I sit back against the wall and stretch my legs out on the cushion. She smiles again.

"Just be comfortable. And quiet."

I suddenly wish this were all over.

She moves across the room to Shane, skirt lapping against her thighs. "Do the neck."

"No." His fingertips trace a line from her ear to her shoulder, making her shiver. "It's summertime. You can't cover it up. Better here." He runs his hand over her waist, to a spot above her left hip bone.

"Whatever you think is best." She moves to her nightstand. "I trust you."

With a flick of her finger she turns on a small CD player, releasing a sultry instrumental tune, heavy on the baritone sax.

Shane looks at me for a long moment, as if he's trying to store me in his memory, then turns back to the woman. Will he try to forget my presence, or will he revel in it, the way she clearly does?

Her eyes grow hooded as he approaches her next to the bed. He runs his hands over the fabric of her dress, up and down her back and her waist, inhaling the scent at the base of her neck. She moans and molds herself against him.

Shane slides down her body and pushes her skirt above her hip on one side. Without further ceremony, he presses his mouth to her bare waist.

She looks down. "What are you doing?"

He stops without raising his head. "What does it look like I'm doing?"

"Already?" She slips out of his grip and sits on the bed. "No preliminaries?"

Shane stands to face her, fingers twitching. "I'm thirsty." He seems to be trying not to look at me.

"I've seen you thirstier." She leans back on her elbows and runs a bare toe up the inside of his thigh. "Fuck me first."

Oh, shit.

He stares at the woman. "What about your fiancé?"

"We broke up."

Shane glances at me. "Not in front of her."

"You have nothing to be ashamed of." Her toes slip under his crotch. "Think of it as free advertising."

"No," he says, even as he spreads her legs and moves between them. "Just give me what I came for."

"I know you can steal my blood if you want. But you won't, with her here." She tilts her head in my direction. "Wouldn't want her to think you're a monster."

He looms over her, hands planted on either side of her body. "I'm not a monster."

Shane kisses her then, so softly I catch my breath. I jam my fist against my mouth and try to pretend I'm watching a movie.

The woman peels his shirt over his head and tosses it on the floor. He looks at it, then at me.

She yanks him down on top of her, then slides her long nails up his back, hard enough to leave red marks in their wake. His body seizes and he kisses her again, harder.

Her legs curl around his bare waist, making her skirt fall above her hips. I try not to watch myself watching, fingertips between my teeth, and just watch. Forget what he might mean to me, forget what he did to me last Friday night. Forget the future and the past and just dwell in the pornographic present.

Shane breaks the kiss and grits his teeth. "No."

"No what?" she says sharply.

"I can't do this." He pushes himself out of her embrace. "I mean, I won't." He unwraps her legs from his body. His face is contorted in what looks like pain.

"Because of her?" Frustration peaks her voice. She kicks out, and he catches her heel just before it connects with his balls.

"Don't get violent," he says.

She lets out a harsh sigh. "Girl, tell him you're okay with it."

I am, but I really don't want to get involved. "Uh . . ."

Shane cuts me off. "I'm not okay with it."

She laughs. "It's eleven o'clock on a Wednesday. Who else are you going to get at this hour?" She sits up and trails her fingers down his bare chest. "You're getting colder." She lilts the words like a taunting child.

He breathes hard, shaking his voice. "I can drink bank blood."

"Tonight, maybe. But maybe next time you call I won't be such a flexible donor."

He jerks away from her. "You call this flexible? Demanding sex, then threatening me?" He yanks his shirt off the floor. "I'm not your gigolo."

"Don't you dare make it sound cheap," she snaps. "You never used to say no."

I can't take it anymore. "Stop it, both of you. I'll leave." I get off the window seat and head for the door.

"I'm coming with you," Shane says.

"Don't be ridiculous." Looking back at him, I open the door. "You need to drink. I'm just in the way—ack!"

I grab the doorjamb to avoid trampling a little boy. He

stands just outside the bedroom, clutching a stuffed blue dog around its neck.

I look down into his wide dark eyes. "Uh, hi."

"Oh, dear," says the woman. The music shuts off. She comes over, straightening her dress and smoothing her hair. "Sweetie, Mommy has some friends over. We're just playing a game."

"I can't sleep." He looks at me. "Can I play?"

I lean back against the doorjamb and focus on the ceiling. It'd be really rude to barf on her freshly shampooed carpet.

The woman leads the child down the hall. After a moment's hesitation, I go back into the bedroom and shut the door behind me. Shane is sitting on the bed now, holding his shirt in his lap, a mixture of guilt and frustration on his face. We look at each other, then away, quickly.

Muffled noises of love and comfort come from outside the door, along with a short stretch of water running in the hall bathroom.

Shane and I say nothing. I sit on the window seat and look outside. Now that my eyes have adjusted, I realize that the structure I saw before is a swing set.

The woman reenters the bedroom and locks the door. She turns to Shane and tucks her hair behind her ear. "Maybe you should just bite me."

He looks relieved. "Yeah. Good. Okay."

Thank God. A quick chomp and we're out of here, then I can go home and scour my frontal lobe to forget that kid—

Shane pounces on her so fast, I emit a little squeak, echoed by the woman. He slides down her body until his knees slam the carpet. She runs her hands through his hair, sweeping it back from his face.

As he pushes her dress above her waist, his eyes open

and fix on me. My muscles lock into baby-bunny mode again. His triumphant smile skewers me a moment before his fangs pierce her creamy skin.

She cries out, and her hands tighten in his hair, as if to pull him away. Then they drop to the top of his shoulders, where her nails dig into his flesh as she hisses through her teeth.

His eyelashes flutter as he draws the first swallow. He groans, and the sound sends a hot, dizzy feeling creeping over my scalp from nape to forehead. A single drop of blood escapes to trickle down her waist. Mesmerized, I watch it disappear beneath the red silk of her bikini panty.

It lasts much longer than I expected. Pins and needles prick my feet, but I don't dare move. The atmosphere in the bedroom feels fragile, every object connected by sticky, weblike strands of energy. If I move an inch or even breathe too hard, the balance between his survival and hers could tip.

Her legs buckle. Shane lowers her to the floor in a smooth, controlled maneuver that looks all too practiced. Her hair splays on the carpet like a dark halo.

Shane's hair covers his face now, but I hear him breathe deep and long through his nose as he drinks. Though her body lies limp in his arms, Shane looks like the helpless one. His right hand clutches her thigh, knuckles pulsing in a kneading motion. He begins to rock back and forth to a rhythm only he can hear. Is it her heartbeat? Is it slowing?

Suddenly the woman's body bucks and stiffens against him. Her nails rake over his bare shoulders, drawing eight thin trails of blood, red as any human's.

With a thud, her legs and arms fall limp against the floor. A moment later, Shane rolls onto the carpet, panting and staring through the ceiling. Blood stains his gums, setting off the white of his fangs, which recede in the span of a few seconds. With their pupils constricted to dots, his eyes shine brightest blue.

Lying on her back, the woman stretches like a cat waking from a nap. She draws a finger down his chest in a lazy motion. "Good?"

Between gasps, he manages an "Uh-huh."

"Good." Under her eyes lie dark semicircles, accentuated by the new paleness of her skin.

Shane closes his eyes and groans deep in his throat, a noise that embodies sex and death. His back arches, and his fingers rake the carpet as if to pull it up like grass.

"Yes," the woman whispers. "It's all yours now."

Slowly his body relaxes as he returns to our plane of existence. He looks at me, blinks hard, and sits up.

"Hang on," he whispers.

He rises to his feet in a fluid motion and grabs a box of gauze pads from the dresser. Eyes glazed, he tears two pads open, then kneels and presses them to the wound on the woman's waist.

She sighs and places her fingers over the cotton squares. "I've got it. Thanks."

Shane glances at me again and wipes his mouth. "Let me clean up, then we'll go." He heads into the master bathroom. The door shuts, and soon I hear the mundane sound of toothbrushing.

The woman lets out a deep sigh. She seems content to remain on the floor.

"Can I get you anything?" I ask her.

She smiles dreamily up at me. "Smokes. By the window."

I fetch her a cigarette. She puts it in her mouth and motions for me to light it. Her first exhale sounds ecstatic.

"You look like you could use one, too," she says. "Help yourself."

"I don't smoke anymore." My hands are trembling. "But I think I'll make an exception."

She flicks her long fingernails in the direction of the bathroom. "What's he to you?"

I light the cigarette, then take a shaky drag. "I don't know yet."

"Shane's a good man. Almost too good. I bet when he was alive he was one of those guys whose female friends complained to him about their jerky boyfriends but never noticed he was right there waiting to make them happy."

I consider introducing myself, but decide I don't really want to know her name. The opportunity passes as she falls asleep. I snatch the cigarette out of her hand before it burns a hole in the carpet.

Shane opens the bathroom door and gives me an apologetic look. "I hate to ask, but—I can't reach." He motions behind him. I set the smokes in an ashtray and join him.

He hands me a moist washcloth, which I draw slowly over the cuts on his back. With the blood wiped away, his skin is perfect again. If anything, it looks more luminous than ever, like he's had a full-body seaweed wrap.

"Thanks." He takes the washcloth and rinses it in the sink. "I'm running out of shirts without bloodstains."

"Nice."

He wipes his face and body dry with a towel. "We'll talk in a few minutes. I need to make sure she's okay."

The woman moans when he picks her up—as easily as I could lift a kitten—and lays her in bed. With tender motions, he dabs iodine on the wound and covers it with a butterfly bandage.

As he draws the sheets over her, she mumbles, "Get my purse. On the dresser."

I grab it, but when I turn back to hand it to her, Shane signals me to stop. Too late. She takes it and wakes up enough to rummage through her wallet.

"Don't," he says.

"Let me pay you."

"I've told you, no. No fucking way." He picks up his shirt and jams his arms through the sleeves. "This is the last time you offer, or you'll never hear from me again."

The thought seems to frighten her, and she looks to me for help. If she hands me the cash, I'm keeping it as emotional restitution.

"Just go to sleep." The softness returns to Shane's voice. He kisses her forehead and smooths the hair from her face. "Remember, extra iron for the next few days."

"Eat my spinach. Promise."

He holds her hand and looks into her eyes. "Thank you. Again."

Outside, the night's humidity has dropped a notch, and a tepid breeze stirs the leaves of the small trees that line the sidewalk.

I wait to vent until we reach the main road. "Why didn't you tell me she had a kid?"

"He never woke up when I was there before." Shane clears his throat. "I'm sorry about what happened. Not just the boy, but before. If I'd known she would insist on sex this time, I would have called someone else." He rubs his stomach and winces, as if he has a cramp. "She thought I would do anything for the blood."

"How do you find these weirdos?"

"Anymore, it's easy, thanks to the Internet. Type 'mortals seeking vampires' into any search engine, and you'll see what I mean." He glances back at the street we just left. "This one moved from Baltimore to Sherwood to be closer to me. That and the better school system."

"But these mortals on the Internet, are they actually seeking real vampires?"

"Most of them, no. They think it's a fantasy, and they're bummed when we show up without capes."

"What happens when they find out you're real?"

Shane slows his pace, scuffing his Chuck Taylors against the sidewalk. "I've always been careful. Too careful, the others say. If I think a potential donor won't play along, I get out before things get—" He comes to a full stop. "If they don't want to be bitten, if they scream and fight back, it triggers our . . . instincts."

My face goes cold as the blood drains from it. I sit down hard on the curb before my knees give out. He sits next to me, a few feet away.

"What happens to them?" I ask without looking at him.

His voice flattens. "Usually they die."

I don't know why this shocks me. I slide my hands through my hair and hold my head. "Oh, God."

"I've never killed anyone," he says. "I swear."

"What about the others? Regina, Noah, all of them?"

"Not as careful."

I close my eyes. I've made it my mission to protect a bunch of rabid beasts. Does that make me an accomplice?

I stretch my scalp back and forth over my skull to ease the pounding inside. "David said you guys don't kill."

"It's rare someone dies," he says. "When it happens, we don't tell him. We call a Code Black and help each other cover it up, make it look like a suicide or accident." He moves closer and touches my arm. His skin is warm, as warm as mine. "Ciara, I need to tell you something."

"You've been telling me plenty, thanks. Stop any time."

"Last week, with you, was the closest I've ever come to killing." His words echo in my head, muffled by my internal screams. "David only wanted me to show you my fangs to convince you. I never planned to bite. But I got . . . distracted. I wanted you, in the human way. So I figured we'd just fool around."

Fool being the operative word, and me being the one operated on.

"Then you smelled so good." Pain infuses his whisper. "You tasted so good. And the way you screamed when you came, like a rabbit in the jaws of a wolf."

I jerk my arm away from him. "So it's my fault for being scrumptious? Didn't they have date rape back in your day?"

He pulls his hands back to his lap. "I'm not making excuses, just trying to explain. What happened was my fault, and I'm sorry."

There are few sarcastic comebacks for a sincere apology. "Why didn't you kill me?"

"Because you were smart. You stopped struggling, stopped acting like prey. It gave me a chance to remember who I am." He pauses, waiting for my reply, which doesn't come. "I promise I'll never bite you again unless you ask me to."

"Why should I believe you? How do I know you won't go all *grrr* again and rip out my throat?"

"You don't know that, and you'd be stupid to trust me now. I'll earn that trust, if you give me a chance."

I scoff. "You just told me you almost killed me. Now you want to, what—date me? I don't even want to be alone with you."

He looks around. "There's no one else here."

"We're on a well-lit street corner in the middle of Sherwood. You can't bite me in public, or even semipublic. If I scream, you're discovered—and all your friends, too." I jab the air with an imaginary stake.

"Thanks for the image." He stands and stretches. I can almost hear his muscles singing with new strength. "Let me walk you home."

"It's not that far."

"It is when the streets are full of monsters."

"David said you six were the only vampires in Sherwood." I get to my feet and stride down the sidewalk toward my apartment.

He catches up to me. "We are, but there are those from out of town who like to keep an eye on us. They think we interact with daytimers too much as it is."

"Daytimers. Sunnysides. What do you call us behind our backs?"

"Dinner."

This shuts me up until we reach my door.

I pull out my keys. "Well, thanks for defending my fluids, if not my innocence."

"You called me human."

"What?"

"You said if I worked for Skywave I'd be a human juke-box."

"Oh. Sorry. I guess *human* is an insult for your kind."

"Not to me." He pulls a folded piece of paper from his pocket—the list of stations. "I'll do what you and David asked, listen to Skywave's garbage. But you have to do something for me."

I step back. "Will it require medical intervention?"

"Listen to my show tonight."

"You want me to wake up at three a.m.?"

"Five forty-five. Just for the last few minutes."

I flutter my hand against my heart in exaggerated coyness. "Why, Mister McAllister, are you going to dedicate a song to me?"

"That would be unprofessional." He takes a step toward me. "Just know that the last song I play every night will be for you."

He takes my hand and draws it to his lips, closing his eyes as he kisses the gap between the first knuckles of my middle and ring fingers. Something wakes and squirms inside me.

He lowers my hand but doesn't let go. The barest tug moves me closer. My chin tilts up, and the kiss is sweet, promising rather than insisting. His mouth tastes like mint, with a faint coppery undertone.

The kiss ends when it should. We say nothing more, and I enter my home and go to bed, alone.

I'm awake long before 5:45. In fact, I'm awake at 3 a.m., listening to Shane's *Whatever* radio show. To my surprise, it's not just grunge—though that's heavily represented—but includes samples of cerebral indie/college rock, buoyant pop-punk, and even a little alt-country. The common denominator seems to be an almost pretentious lack of pretension.

When Shane speaks, I close my eyes and imagine him lying here behind me, murmuring softly. Not words of dark seduction, just whatever's on his mind, some fascinating fact about Nick Drake or the Hammond B3. His breath moves my hair, tickling my earlobe, but I don't brush my hand between us because it's tucked inside his. Our entwined arms lie on top of the covers.

I open my eyes. Yecch, boyfriend thoughts, the kind I haven't had since I was a teenager. It's one thing to imagine Shane naked and slathered in olive oil, but another animal entirely to picture us cuddling.

I roll over and tell the ceiling, "He's not human." The ceiling stares back, dingy and unresponsive.

5:54 a.m. arrives. I expect him to finish the show with a tune lambasting modern bourgeois society, with a particular dig at the commercialism I so ruthlessly represent.

"Time for me to crawl back in my hole," he says, "so I'll leave you with one last song to start your day—or end it, as the case may be. A lot of people don't know that Otis Redding wrote this. The Dead covered it, but this is the best-known version, and, I think, the most kick-ass. Good morning, and good night."

After a brief drum intro, a bass guitar joins a piano in a ballsy, bluesey series of notes.

I laugh and pull the pillow over my head, wondering whether The Black Crowes' "Hard to Handle" is meant to describe me or Shane.

Probably both, which could be the most fun of all.

10

Just a Girl

June 7
We embark on our mission to rock the world. I write press releases, contract a new Web-site designer, and order WVMP merchandise. Franklin divides our duties into sales (him) and marketing/promotions (me). I'm thrilled; marketing puts me at arm's length from my targets and feels less like a con job than sales. Besides, Mr. Hyde is the master in that department.

The sutures in my thigh itch like crazy, requiring several trips to the bathroom to indulge in unrepentant scratching.

June 12
David takes out my stitches and buys me more bagels.

June 13
I fire our Web-site designer.

June 14

I create fliers and hire a new Web designer, one who doesn't think spinning logos and cheesy Flash animations are still cutting edge. If I hadn't met the first one during the daytime, I would swear she was a vampire.

June 15

Friday night I wander into the lounge, where I find Shane, Regina, Spencer, and Noah playing poker. I gesture to the empty chair, currently occupied by Shane's feet. "Mind if I join you?"

They all gape at me, even Shane. Regina turns to him, on her left. "Did you invite her?"

He smiles and pushes the chair out with his heels. "I am now."

"I hardly ever play," I say as I sit. "You'll have to remind me how."

Their laughter has the force of an air horn.

Regina tosses down her cards. "Why don't we just write you a check and get it over with?"

I wave off her concern. "Not all con artists are good poker players. Don't believe everything you see in *The Sting*."

They all look at Spencer. His shadowed gaze pierces me, but not long enough. He nods. "I don't see any harm in letting the little girl play. Everyone knows ladies are bad at poker."

"Sod right off," Regina says.

"Not you." Noah kisses the air in her direction. "Jah have mercy on the man who dare to call you a 'lady.'"

Spencer's knuckles rap the table. "Back to the game, boys and girls."

They finish the hand, and I pretend not to watch their patterns.

Regina gathers up the cards to deal. She eyes me as she shuffles. "Which games do you know?"

I tick them off on my fingers. "Draw, stud, hold 'em—but I'm a little foggy on the rules, so I might need help." I toss this last word to Spencer.

She taps the deck against her chin. "Okay, seven-card stud, follow the queen, low Chicago matches the pot."

Everyone groans. I play dumb. "What's that mean?"

"It means we're not playing," Spencer says. "Regina, you know the rules. No wild cards, no random factors, none of that garbage. Don't turn it into a game of luck." He shifts in his chair. "I don't trust luck."

"Luck is our only chance against her." She jerks her chin in my direction. Receiving no sympathy, she sighs and deals the cards. "Fine. Seven-card stud. Period."

Faking cluelessness is easy; faking a clueless person faking a clue requires more finesse. The key is to ask dumb questions that aren't too dumb, and knit one's brows at the appropriate times.

I bet aggressively at the beginning of the first hand, but fold before it's time to show my cards. This bizarre behavior puzzles the guys, but Regina just scoffs.

"Nice attempt at incompetence, but you don't fool me." She lights a long brown cigarette and pulls a French inhale as she examines me. "What's your middle name?"

"Marjorie. Why?"

"Marjorie?" She snorts. "And you think *we're* in the wrong decade?"

"It's my mom's name. I like it."

Her eyes shift to a distant focus for several moments. "Hmm. You're a one."

"A what?"

"In numerology. And your soul urge number is five. Figures." She shakes her head at Shane. "Don't bother trying to tie this one down."

He ignores her and starts to deal. We play the next few hands in silence, and I fold early in each. I sense their frustration as they learn nothing about my style.

Finally I get a decent hand—a low straight—and decide to overplay it. On the next betting round, I raise by three dollars.

Everyone folds. I pout. "Doesn't anybody want to see my cards?"

"Sure, honey," Spencer says, "let's have a look."

I display the straight on the table like a kindergartner with her first finger painting.

"I folded a flush," Noah says. "The way you bet, I thought you had a full boat."

"But a straight beats a flush," I tell him.

"No, it doesn't," Regina says, then catches herself. "Come on, you knew that."

"It's statistically harder to get a straight than a flush."

"That's backward," she says. "In seven-card stud the odds of getting a flush are one-in-thirty-three versus one-in-twenty-two for a straight."

Shane pushes the chips in my direction. "You know, it does seem like it ought to be the other way around."

She turns on him. "You're already whipped, and you haven't even fucked her yet."

Spencer clears his throat. "Ciara, would you like me to make you a list of the hand rankings?"

One down, three to go. "Would you?" I ask sweetly. "And I could use a drink, if it's not too much trouble."

"I'll get it," Shane says.

"Of course you will." Regina sends him a glare, which he ignores.

The two nice vampires depart, leaving me with Regina and Noah, who look at me like I'm made of garlic. Trying to forget what Shane told me about their killer instincts, I turn to Noah. "David tells me you're from Kingston. What's that like?"

He folds his arms across his chest, resting his thumbs on his biceps. "We don't care you're a con artist." His dialect turns the I into an EE so it comes out "artiste."

"Actually, we kind of like it," Regina adds. "But don't ever think of turning your talents on us."

"I've given all that up." I hold up my left hand to swear.

"Why?" asks Noah.

"Yeah, you said you were raised to cheat." Regina leans forward. "Are you from a family of cons?"

"Sort of." I run my fingernail over the table's rubber edge. "I'd rather just forget about them."

"Yeah, wouldn't that be nice? Pretend our folks never existed, that we all create ourselves just the way we want to be." She tugs on a strand of black hair that dips over her forehead. "Sometimes I think rebellion gives them more power than they deserve."

"You should not deny them," Noah says to me. "When you deny your roots, you deny your soul. For example." He gestures to himself with a shrug. "I was Rasta in my life. Becoming a vampire did not change that."

"I thought Rastafarians weren't supposed to eat meat. Wouldn't blood be not, uh, kosher?"

"'*Ital*' is the word. You are right, but God want me to be a vampire, so I must drink blood."

"But he won't drink blood bank leftovers," Regina says, "because it's processed."

Noah nods once. "I do my best. It's all He require of us."

"Why do you think God wants you to be a vampire?" I ask him.

"Because it's what I am. It's how I bring light into the world. How I fight Babylon."

Contemplating his circular logic, I glance at Regina, who regards Noah with a warmth and admiration I've never seen her give Shane.

I remember that "Babylon" is the Rasta word for the oppressive economic and political system. "Skywave is part of Babylon," I tell him.

"I know this. Why do you think I help you beat them?"

"Because it's fun."

His chuckle is melodic. "That, too."

Shane and Spencer return, the former with a cold beer and a brief brush of fingertips against my shoulder.

Spencer hands me an index card. "I'm afraid my handwriting isn't the world's neatest. Can you read this all right?"

I look at the list of poker hand ranks, then pull it closer to make sure it isn't typed. His print is meticulous and precise, each letter the same size, in perfect formation across the unlined card. A chill zings down my spine.

The other vamps look away in discomfort. They must be aware of each other's compulsions.

"It's lovely," I tell Spencer, who pulls his chair closer and settles in beside me.

Shortly before midnight, Jim bounces in, singing "Eight Miles High" so off-key I barely recognize it. He dumps himself on the sofa and waves at me like my presence is nothing out of the ordinary.

"Deal you in next hand?" Spencer asks him.

"Nah." Jim accompanies himself on air guitar. "Can't concentrate."

I recognize his glow as that of a well-fed vampire. My tension should ease, since his state makes me less tasty, but it creeps me out to picture Jim and an unknown donor locked in the same embrace as Shane and the Mommy in Red.

"How's Janis?" Shane asks him.

Jim groans and runs a hand through his long brown curls. "Cranky bitch. Need to drain her before she starts making noise."

I stare at him, then at Shane, who can't keep a straight face. "Janis is his car," he informs me.

I swallow hard. "I knew that."

At midnight, Spencer leaves to do his show, so the rest of us take a break. As I watch Noah carefully avoid stepping on the seams in the rug, my chair suddenly slides to the right. I look down to see Shane's boot tucked under its rung, pulling me closer to him.

"Since we're both almost broke," he whispers into my shoulder, "why don't we get out of here?"

I answer his left ear, careful not to be sucked into his seductive gaze. "Are you coming to the launch party at the Smoking Pig?"

"Not if it's going to be all about the vampire schtick."

"It'll be about the music. Speaking of which, are you doing your homework, listening to Skywave's Festival of Crap?"

His lip curls. "It's been one of the most depressing weeks of my life. What passes for music anymore . . ." He swipes his hand over his face. "I just sounded like a fuddy-duddy, didn't I?"

"Not until you used the word 'fuddy-duddy.' Look, all the other DJs are coming to the party at the Pig—even Monroe, according to Spencer. You don't have to play. Just show up."

He glances at Regina, lounging on the couch, her head propped against Jim's shoulder and her legs draped over Noah's lap. They don't even pretend they're not listening.

"If I show up to watch," Shane says to me, "you'll all drag me onstage and turn me into a spectacle."

"So you're not coming."

"I told you, I haven't decided yet."

I set down my beer with a bang. "Shane, you've heard what this station could become. Maybe you've imagined playing the same fifty songs over and over until your brain turns to oatmeal. If you're supposedly so young and human, then why can't you see what the rest of them see? You won't survive if you hide."

"So what do you care?" he says in a tight voice.

"It's my job."

"You're awfully dedicated for a summer intern."

"That's because for the first time I'm helping people, not hurting them."

"We're not people, Ciara." He slides his hand over mine. "No matter how much some of us might try, it's too late."

He leans over and gives my temple a brief, cool kiss. A few moments later, he's out the door, no doubt on his way to a long, warm drink.

"It'll never work," Regina says, tossing her lighter in the air and catching it. "Shane Evan McAllister has an expression number of three, with a soul urge of nine."

As if I needed more proof they weren't human.

11

The Revolution Starts . . . Now

Lori would kill me if I told her that under her white make-up, tight black leather, and silver chains, she still looks like a Scandinavian pixie. Right now she's applying the same white pancake makeup to my face as we sit in the back office of the Smoking Pig. Strains of industrial Goth rock float from the bar. Between the music's driving beat and my anxiety over the party, I can barely hold still for her.

"Which accessory do you want?" she asks me.

On the desk lie a cross, an ankh, and a feather, all in heavy silver. I snatch the ankh. It goes well with my black leather miniskirt and green satin tieback bustier.

"So what's up with you and Shane?" she asks me.

"I have no idea."

"Don't talk." She dabs and smears. The makeup smells like paste. "Are the other DJs as hot as him? Blink once for yes, twice for no."

"Lori, there's something you need to know about them."

"Shh. They're vampires, I know." Dab. "Your brows need waxing, by the way."

"No, you *don't* know. They're vampires."

"I know." Smear. "It's the secret. You told me."

I push her hand away and look her in the eye. "There's a secret behind the secret. Don't be alone with them. Don't even look them in the eye."

Her eyes widen, innocent even within their painted black triangles. "Why not?"

"Because they really are vampires."

Her face contorts. "Don't make me laugh—it'll crack the makeup."

"Lori, I'm not kidding."

"I always knew you were crazy."

"This from the woman saving her pennies to start a Sherwood ghost tour business."

She shakes her head. "There's a metaphysical basis for ghosts. See, when someone dies—"

"He bit me."

"Who, Shane?" She brushes my hair from my neck. "I don't see any marks."

"Not there." I stand and lift my skirt. The fading scar features two purple punctures along the gash.

Lori leans forward and angles the hood of the banker's lamp on the desk to illuminate the wound. "Wow." She sits back in her chair. "Your brows aren't all that need waxing."

My fist clenches. "You'll understand when you see the older vampires. Deep in your gut, you'll know I'm telling the truth."

"The truth about what?" growls a voice behind me.

Regina shadows the doorway. She's magnificent. Her

teased hair forms a black corona around her luminous face. A studded black leather minidress slides like a second skin over a torn fishnet bodysuit, which has holes cut for her long, silver-ringed fingers. The only color lies on her lips, a deep, drinkable burgundy.

I turn back to Lori, whose mouth hangs open.

With the power of an opera diva crossing the stage, Regina glides forward on silver-buckled combat boots. Lori stands up suddenly, spilling the makeup on the floor.

"What the hell's wrong with her?" Regina asks me.

"I told her you're a vampire."

"So?"

"I mean, I told her you're a vampire."

"Aw, for fuck's sake, Ciara."

"She's my best friend. I won't tell anyone else, and neither will she."

"Damn right she won't." Fangs out, Regina advances on Lori, who squeaks and backs up against the filing cabinet. Regina traces a sharp black fingernail down Lori's cheek, then neck, then lower, no doubt following a major blood vessel. "They'll be the last words she ever says. Isn't that right, little bit?"

Lori jerks her head back and forth. "I won't tell, I swear."

Regina peers into her eyes. "Whose grave do you swear on?"

"That's enough." I only let it go on this long because Lori needs to be scared. Scared, not abused. "Let her go."

Without turning, Regina grabs the strap of my top and yanks me to her face. "I don't take orders from you."

"I bet you'll take orders from this." I snatch the silver cross from the desk and thrust it toward her nose. A flicker of fear dances in her eyes, then she laughs.

"That has no power wielded by an unbeliever. You might as well come after me with a spatula."

"Maybe I will." I realize that makes no sense and try to recover. "David doesn't want you harassing civilians."

Regina scoffs but lets us go, her fangs retracting. "I came to tell you I nicked some of Shane's CDs." Her foot nudges the backpack she dropped on the way in. "That way if he shows up, maybe one of you posers can convince him to spin a few tunes."

"Or maybe you can," I say.

"I can't play that shit. It's not as bad as some, but—"

"No, I mean, maybe you can convince him."

Her eyes lock on mine. "I don't have that kind of influence on him anymore," she says, more softly than I've ever heard her speak. "I bollocksed that one up a long time ago."

She slips out of the office without a sound, despite her heavy boots.

Lori grabs my arm with a cold hand. "She—she's—"

"A bitch and a half, I know. But one hell of a DJ."

Lori starts to hyperventilate. I sit her in the chair and push her head down between her knees.

"You were right." She sounds like she's trying not to cry. "I could feel it down in my blood." She looks up at me suddenly. "What do we do?"

"Do?"

"We can't let them mingle with the crowd. Someone might get hurt."

"They know how to handle themselves around humans. If they rampaged through every public gathering, you think they'd have survived this long?" I help her to her feet. "But don't hook up with any of them unless you want to get bitten."

She rubs her arms. "Why would anyone want that?"

"It's supposed to feel good—after the pain, that is."

Lori looks at my thigh. "Did it?"

"I never got past the pain. You know me."

She squats to gather the spilled makeup. "Shane didn't creep me out the same way that one did. He seems so normal."

"He's younger, so he's less of a freak." I pick up a runaway tube of black lipstick. "Plus, Regina just likes scaring people."

Lori takes a deep breath. "So you're going out with a vampire who bit you? That's pretty messed up."

"We're just friends." I consider the good-night kiss and the string of 5:54 a.m. songs. "With potential."

The packed bar is decked out like a Goth club, with metal— or a plastic facsimile thereof—covering wood wherever possible. The ceiling is covered with black balloons, which bop around in the air-conditioning breeze.

"I'm impressed," I yell over the music to Lori's boss Stuart, whose black cape subtracts years from his forty-something age. His dark blond hair is slicked back with at least two handfuls of gel.

"Thanks," he says. "Too bad I couldn't finish the bondage parlor in the game room. The cuffs kept falling off the foosball table."

I look past him at the tiny raised stage in a dark corner of the bar, where Spencer, Jim, and Noah are conferring.

They're each dressed in their usual charmingly outdated—and distinctively nonghoulish—outfits.

"Have you met the vamps?" I ask Stuart with an ironic twist on the last word.

"I'm serving them free liquor, which makes me their temporary best friend. They laughed at my cape, though."

I withhold comment and turn to the table holding our WVMP merchandise, which Franklin is hawking in fine barker fashion.

"Ciara?"

I look up to see David approach. He stops and does a doubletake at my outfit. I return the gesture. He's dressed all in black—jeans, boots, and a tight T-shirt covered with a leather jacket.

"Hel-lo." He scratches his head after hearing the inflection of the word. "I mean, hi. Spencer says Monroe's coming by when he gets off work at midnight." He pauses, no doubt waiting for me to ask about Shane. "No word from the other one. I'll try again." He pulls out his cell phone and steps into the kitchen.

I join an uncostumed Franklin behind the sales table, since a line of excited customers is starting to form. People actually want to pay for the privilege of advertising our business. Most radio stations have to give away T-shirts and bumper stickers; but most radio stations don't have vampire DJs (again, I'm assuming).

As Franklin delivers the goods, I take people's money and give them change. From the corner of his eye, he watches me handle the cash, probably making sure none of it finds its way into my pockets.

When the next customer walks away, T-shirt in hand,

I lean over to Franklin. "Relax. Con artists don't steal. We take."

"There's a difference?"

"Why go to the trouble of robbing someone's money when they're perfectly willing to give it to you?" I unzip the cash pouch and pull out a ten-dollar bill. "For instance, if I took this and turned it into twenty, with Stuart's help, that wouldn't be stealing."

Franklin frowns at the ten. "How do you turn that into a twenty?"

"I'll show you." I start to approach the bar, then stop, gesturing to the six-person-deep crowd. "He's too busy now. We'll just practice here." I step to the other side of the table. "Hey, mister, I'd like to buy one of those swell 'Feed the Need' buttons."

He hesitates. "That'll be a dollar."

I hand him the ten, and he gives me nine dollars in change. "Oh wait." I look at the cash pouch. "This won't work."

"Why not?"

"We don't have enough ones to do the whole trick." I dig into my pocket and bring out a wad of dollar bills. "Here, let me give you ten ones for that, and we can start over."

"Okay." He gives me the ten.

I count out some ones. "Why do people come to bars with big bills? It drives Lori batshit." I place the ten he just gave me on the bottom of the pile of nine ones, which I hand back to him.

Franklin recounts the money, eyeing me suspiciously. I wave my bare arms to show I have nothing up my sleeves.

"Hang on." He holds up the stack of bills. "You gave me too much. There's nineteen dollars here."

"Crap." I grit my teeth. "I'm so out of practice it's pathetic." I sigh and pull out another dollar bill. "Here, let me just give you one more and you give me a twenty to even it out."

"Thought you could outsmart me, heh?" He takes the bill and pulls a twenty out of his pile.

I smile sheepishly. "I wanted to impress you. You are the master, after all."

He slaps the bill into my palm. "Better luck next time."

I pick up my negative-nineteen-dollar button. "Buy you a drink?"

I decide not to add, "sucker."

The Goth music fades as a light comes up on the stage. Spencer steps up to the microphone, the light glinting off his slicked-back auburn hair. The crowd hushes to murmur level as he surveys them with dark, hypnotic eyes.

"Thank you all for coming out to hear our little show." He holds the mike in one hand and shifts the stand in a gesture of false bashfulness. "Along with playing some tunes to get you moving, we've been asked to tell our stories tonight. Stories of how we became vampires." The crowd emits scattered snickers, but Spencer's face bears such an earnest look of wild innocence that most people just stare.

"Some of us wanted to live forever," he says. "Some of us just wanted to live." His Adam's apple bobs once, and his eyes go far away for a moment so brief I'd have missed it if I'd blinked.

"But for all of us," he continues, "it was about the music. The music turned us as much as the blood."

At the last word, the crowd buzzes, titillated.

"Lotta people say rock 'n' roll is about goin' all the way, seeing as that was the original meaning of the term." From beneath his long, dark lashes, he sends the women to his left a look that says, *I wouldn't know anything about that, but maybe you could show me.*

"Rock 'n' roll is really about immortality," he continues. "Thanks to Mister Edison's invention, your great-great grandchildren can hear Elvis and Jerry Lee like they were sitting right there with them in that Memphis studio. That's living forever, folks.

"But immortality isn't just about not dying—it's about never growing old, never growing up, never *wanting* to grow up." He tosses off another self-effacing smile, as if surprised by his own conclusion. "You might say being vampires has given us the ultimate rock 'n' roll lifestyle."

He hits a switch on the turntable, launching into "Blue Suede Shoes"—the Carl Perkins version. Within moments the crowd is bopping and twisting and whatever else-ing the music inspires their bodies to do. Spencer eyes the line of adoring women again. I watch him for signs of bloodthirst, but instead of rubbing his face, he just runs a hand through his hair and smooths the front of his white T-shirt in a classic cool preening gesture.

"What do you think?" says a familiar voice in my ear.

I turn to see David. "I think Spencer slinked out of telling his story. Do you know it?"

He nods. "But it's not for me to tell."

"What about yours?"

"What about what?" He leans toward me, pushing the top of his earlobe forward.

"What's your story?" I yell.

He shakes his head, taps his ear, and shrugs, like he

can't hear me over the music. "Got a reporter to talk to,"
he says, and walks toward the bar. He moves differently in
this getup than his work clothes, like he's finally wearing
his own skin.

At the bar, David displaces a tall brunette who turns
away with her friend. They each hold a pint of blood-red
beer, the heads of which spill onto their meticulously mani-
cured fingers. The brunette scowls and turns back to grab a
bar napkin, her face illuminated by the overhead light.

Jolene.

My first instinct is to look for the closest red EXIT sign.
But I have a job to do.

"I'll be right back," I tell Franklin.

Jolene and her attendant move to the far wall, in front
of the silver-on-black cemetery tapestry. They sullenly sip
and watch the show. As I approach from an oblique angle,
Jolene's redheaded friend starts to groove a little to the
music, nodding her head and tapping her finger on the
outside of the pint glass. Jolene notices and jabs an elbow
into her companion's rib, spilling more beer.

With a deep breath, I tap Jolene on the shoulder and
speak her name. She looks at me without recognition,
probably because of the makeup.

"It's me. Ciara. Bane of your existence."

"You bitch!" She takes one hand off her glass as if to
slap me, then stops herself. "I got arrested because of you.
Public indecency."

"Plus drunken disorderliness and resisting arrest," her
friend chimes in.

"Shut up, Kendra."

"That's not my fault," I tell Jolene. "If you'd explained
to the cop—"

"I did."

"—in words he could repeat to his own mother—"

"I can't ever get that night back," she says.

I gesture to the wedding ring on her finger. "You still got married."

Kendra laughs. "Yeah, who knows, Jolene? If you hadn't gone to jail that night, you might've shagged some dude and given Jeff gonorrhea for a wedding gift."

Before Jolene can assault her friend with another sharp body part, I hold up a hand. "Just give me your address so I can send back your shirt."

Jolene opens her mouth, then gets a crafty look. "Send it to my office." She whips out a business card like a weapon and shoves it a few inches below my nose.

> Jolene Scoglio
> Marketing Associate
> Skywave Communications, Inc.

So that's what she meant when she said we'd all pay.

Crap.

"That's right, Miss Griffin." Jolene flips her hair. "Soon you'll be working for me. For the two minutes it takes to clean out your desk."

I flick her card with my fingernail. "You don't have that power."

"It won't be up to me to fire you, but that's how these things work. You'll all be let go after the buyout. The weak succumb to the strong."

"'Succumb'? Did you learn that whopper on your Word-a-Day toilet paper?"

"At least I'm smart enough to get a job with a company

that's on the way up. Even this retarded vampire gimmick can't save your station."

"How much do you want to bet?"

A strong hand lands on my arm. I expect to see David telling me to get back to work.

It's Shane.

"Can we talk?" His expression is inscrutable in the low light, but his voice is dead serious.

"Hello, Shane," Jolene says. "Shirt thief."

He turns to her. "Leave us alone."

She shrinks back like he's radioactive. He walks toward the kitchen. I steel myself and follow him.

Out of the frying pan and into the crematorium.

12

What'd I Say

"Thanks for the rescue." I beam up at Shane, which must look ridiculous with the undead makeup in the kitchen's fluorescent lights. "What do you think of the party?"

"Congratulations." He holds up a headstone-tipped cocktail stirrer. "You've turned us into a farce."

"The decorations were Stuart's idea. At least I kept him from calling it a 'spooktacular' celebration."

He points to the kitchen door. "No one out there cares about the music. They only care about blood punch, and blood beer, and blood salsa."

"I know the party trimmings are dorky, but they're a means to an end—namely, saving your asses from unemployment."

"If you change us, there'll be nothing left to save."

"How am I changing you?"

Shane glances at Jorge the chef, who doubles as a dishwasher since the Smoking Pig doesn't do much edible business. He ignores us as he bastes buffalo wings—or "bat wings," as we're calling them tonight—and bobs his head to the blaring kitchen radio.

Shane turns and heads for Stuart's office at the back of the kitchen. I follow him, though I should get back to work. But if I could convince Shane to play, that would be worth a lot more than a few peddled bumper stickers.

As soon as I enter the office, he turns on me. "Do you know how many taboos you violated by asking for stories of how we got made?"

"What's the big deal?"

He groans and rubs his forehead, where deep vertical creases have appeared. "That story, Ciara, is one of the few things that truly belong to us. A vampire only shares it with someone he trusts. Rattling it off in public cheapens everything we are."

"Spencer didn't do it, and maybe the others won't either."

"That's not the point." He brushes past me and shuts the office door. "Just asking was an insult."

"I'm sorry." A flush of shame creeps up my neck, which pisses me off. "I didn't know."

"That's the problem. You met us what, three weeks ago? And you think you can understand us and expose our secrets."

"They're not secrets if no one believes them. They're fairy tales."

"It doesn't matter!" He moves toward me, slapping aside the hanging ribbon of a black balloon. Suddenly he stops. "What's that smell?" He wrinkles his nose in my direction. "Did you fall into a vat of chemicals?"

I bring a lock of hair to my nose. "I touched up my highlights. You know, because I'm a big shallow phony."

"I didn't say that."

"You don't have to. Look, I know I have a lot to learn about you guys. But while I'm ramping up on the subject, Skywave is planning to put you out of work. Maybe *you* can find another job to keep yourself from fading. But what about your friends?"

"I don't want them boiled down to a bag of clichés."

Suppressing a sigh of frustration, I turn away to regroup. The office chair is full of papers now, so I sit on the edge of the desk.

Perhaps a softer approach is in order. "Shane, I understand you want to be free of commercialism. You want to be pure. I admire you for it. But outside of monasteries, this is how the world works."

"I know, but we should be better than that." He frowns. "We used to be better than that."

"Until I ruined everything."

"You didn't—" Shane lets out a harsh sigh. "Stop that."

"Stop what?"

"Making it personal, so I can't attack the campaign without attacking you. Which I would never do."

"Why not? This was all my idea. Except the 'Bite Me, I'm O-Positive' buttons. That was Franklin."

"I don't want this campaign to come between us."

A high-pitched "Us?" pops out before I can stop myself from sounding like an eighth grader. "There's an 'us'?"

"I'd like there to be." He looks at me—really *looks* at me—for the first time tonight. His gaze drops to my thigh, sparking a flame at the base of my spine. He clears his throat. "How's your leg now?"

I wait for him to look me in the eye again before saying, "It's better."

He swallows. "All better?"

I shift on the desk, keeping my legs crossed but now at the ankle instead of the knee. "All better."

The office seems to shrink as Shane takes another step toward me. "In spite of the spectacle, I was looking forward to seeing you tonight." He moves close enough to touch, his smile turning ironic in the green light from the banker's lamp. "But this makeup, it's not you."

"I look more like a clown than a vampire, don't I? Just say it."

He leans in and inhales, his face close to mine. "It covers your scent."

Plus it itches like a poison ivy facial. I tilt up my chin. "Then take it off."

He peels off his short-sleeved T-shirt, the brown one he's wearing over a white T-shirt with long, frayed sleeves.

"Let's start with this." He wipes the shirt across my lips, slowly. I close my eyes. He wipes again.

"Is it working?"

"No," he whispers. "Too dry."

His mouth brushes mine, just the barest edge. His tongue flicks over my upper lip, tasting, moistening. A little moan escapes my throat. He does the same to my lower lip. My ankles uncross.

He pulls away a few inches and draws the shirt across my mouth. "There. Red is better." He leans in to kiss me again.

"We really should get out to the bar." This definitely no longer counts as a work-related activity. "I told Franklin I'd be right back."

"We can leave if you want." His thumb grazes my

shoulder, then slips under the thin black strap of my top. My skin comes alive, every nerve begging for another touch.

"Then again, I've been working all day." I slide my arms around his neck. "I think there's some OSHA rule that says I get a break every eight hours."

"Wouldn't want to get David in trouble with the feds." His eyes turn serious again as they stare into mine. "I know you're not what you seem. You've probably got a hundred different layers under there." His fingertips glide across my makeup-caked cheek, then into my hair. "I want to peel them all back until I find the real Ciara." He insinuates his body between my thighs. "I want to get inside you."

The heat of his skin radiates against me, so much warmer than the last time I held him. I need to feel it within me.

I lock my legs around his. He gives a low growl and brings his mouth to mine.

The velvet shock of his tongue makes my back arch. I pull him tight against me with all my limbs, though it feels like it can't be close enough. As our kiss deepens and our bodies strain against each other, I hear only the rasp of our breaths, the creak of my leather skirt, and the roar of my own blood.

"Lock the door," I manage to gasp.

"Uh-uh." He scrapes his human teeth over my neck. "I want you to feel safe from me."

I get it: he bites, I scream, him and all his friends—dusted. "Then hurry."

His hand slides under my skirt. He breathes hard when he discovers I'm already ready for him. With one arm he lifts me off the desk while the other hand slips under the string of my thong and pulls it down.

As I reach for the button of his jeans, I'm slammed with the thought that thwarts. "Do you have any condoms?"

"We don't need them. I can't carry disease or get you pregnant." He wipes the side of his face, which is smeared with my makeup. "Remember, I'm dead."

He smiles like it's a joke, but a chill rips through me. My mind suddenly returns to rational-thought mode.

"Wait." I put a hand between us. "Won't that be kind of messy? I have to work the rest of the night."

"Don't worry. When I have an orgasm, I feel the sensations, but I don't, you know, produce anything." He goes to kiss me again, but I plant my palm against his chest.

"When you say, 'I don't produce anything'—"

"Not me personally." He takes my hand and shifts it lower. "Vampires."

My mouth goes suddenly sour, and my stomach twists into a knot, the kind only sailors and Eagle Scouts can untie.

I'm about to fuck a vampire.

A vampire's about to fuck me.

Uh-uh.

This is Shane, my brain reminds my body. *He's a good guy. More human than half the men you've bonked. Now de-quease yourself and unbutton his pants.*

My gut wrenches again.

"What's wrong?" Shane says.

"I just remembered—I need to—I should get back to work." I push past him and move for the door, hoping I make it to the bathroom in time. I'll come back for my underwear.

My foot catches on Regina's backpack. Ah, subject change to the rescue.

I pick up the bag and flash him a weak smile. "Hey, Regina brought some of your music. Maybe you can play after all?"

"Why are you so nervous now?" He takes a step toward me. The memory of his blood-drenched mouth flashes in my mind.

"Nothing!" I back away fast, bruising my spine against the doorknob. "I mean, I'm having—I think I'm coming down with the flu." That and a severe case of being an asshole.

His eyes widen, and hurt creeps in around the edges. "You're scared of me again."

"No, of course not." My voice pitches up, a sure sign of deception. What good is honesty when I can't lie to save his feelings? "Shane . . ."

"You are scared." His brows lower into a scowl. "You're looking at me like I'm a monster."

"It's not you, I swear. It's me."

"Damn right it is." He snatches the backpack from my hand, which luckily lets go before he can tear my arm off. "I'm not a monster. I've never hurt anyone. That's more than I can say for you."

My throat tightens. "What?"

"Your con artist days aren't exactly in the distant past, are they? David told me you were arrested for swindling just a few months ago."

A flush of heat runs up the back of my neck. "He did?"

"He said the guy—what do you call it—"

"The mark."

"Yeah, the mark was too embarrassed to press charges." He steps forward again, well inside my personal space.

"They usually are." I put my hands up. "Stop looming so I can explain."

"So you can lie?"

"No!" If he's so quick to suspect me, maybe he doesn't deserve an explanation. "First of all, I wasn't arrested, I was brought in for questioning. Second of all, it's not true you've never hurt anyone. You hurt me."

"I said I was sorry. Is that ever going to be enough?"

"Not when you judge me like you're some kind of saint. You drink blood. The way I see it, better an empty wallet than an empty vein."

His voice lowers to a rumble. "My donors give me what I need of their own free will."

"You tell yourself that, that your *donors* are happy to do it, that they're not hypnotized by the magic in your eyes, the way my *victims* were fooled by pretty promises."

"I do what I do to survive."

"So did I. But a part of me loved it, the way you love having the power of life and death."

He shakes his head. "Don't compare us."

"The one person I don't lie to is myself. I know what I was, and I know how far I have to go to be something better. That's why I took this job."

"So we're your little redemption project?"

"Maybe." His sarcasm inspires my own. "Or maybe I just need to pay the rent. Who can know with me? Like you said, I have so many layers." I smear the makeup on my cheeks. "What would you find if you peeled them all away? Maybe nothing at all."

"Don't say that." He drops the backpack and pulls my

hands from my face. "There's something more than nothing there."

My stomach flops like a hooked fish. I break his knife-sharp gaze to keep from puking.

He releases my hands. "Let me know when you figure out what it is."

Before I can summon a reply, he's gone, out the restaurant's back door.

A half-jar of cold cream later, my skin is makeup free. I stare at my reflection in Lori's compact, but the mirror's too small to see more than half of my face. I hold it at arm's length for perspective, but the reflection shakes and blurs.

I slap the lid shut on the disquieting metaphor and stuff it back in the bag.

13

I Forgot to Remember to Forget

By the time I drag myself out to the bar, Spencer has left the stage and Jim is playing the Beatles' "Helter Skelter." The crowd has switched from bopping to writhing. I'd join in if my body didn't feel so heavy and dull.

Lori approaches with a tray of empty glasses. "What's wrong? What happened to your makeup?"

I rub my eyes, which feel puffy, and give her the condensed version of what just occurred, leaving out the part where I'm a criminal.

She gives my elbow a squeeze. "I don't get it. You told me to stay away from them. You said they were dangerous."

"Shane's different." I take the tray from her and move over to the bar, where we start unloading it. "But if I could unmeet him somehow, make all this unhappen, I would." Lori raises her eyebrows. "Or maybe not," I admit.

"He does feel different. And even the rest of them, they seem decent—except Regina." Lori sends a darting glance over her shoulder. "She keeps looking at me."

"She's just messing with your head. Best not to show fear."

"Right." Lori wipes the tray with a damp cloth. "No fear."

Regina pokes her head between us. "Hi."

Lori squeaks and knocks her tray into the row of dirty glasses. With one hand, Regina grabs them before they fall.

"Careful now," she purrs to Lori.

"Um, thanks." Lori keeps her face turned from the vampire. "Gotta go." She scurries off.

"What happened to your makeup?" Regina asks me, then sniffs my shoulder. "Ah, yes, Shane likes his humans to have a more natural look." She tweaks my hair. "Someday he'll tell you to stop highlighting. He'll say it's the smell of the dye he hates."

"Get away from me."

She clicks her tongue. "Testy for someone who just got laid, aren't we?"

"Not that it's any of your business, but we didn't."

Her eyes go wide in mock surprise. "Well, that explains why you smell so horny."

"Fuck off!" I tell her, unfortunately just as the music fades. Half the crowd casts curious glances at us.

"Ladies." David appears on my other side. "What happened to your makeup?" he asks me.

I rub my eye again. "It itched."

"You have an itch all right," Regina mutters.

David stuffs his hands in his jacket pockets and looks around with pride. "Great party. Frank is schmoozing clients, so Ciara, we need you to peddle the paraphernalia."

Relieved at the distraction, I stride over to the

WVMP table, grab a size small T-shirt, and yank it over my head. The soft black cotton covers the top half of my Let's-Play-Vampire getup. My too-bare skin sighs with relief.

Work: the all-American cure for heartache.

I shill and hawk for two hours, until all the merchandise is sold except two broken buttons and one extra extra extra large T-shirt. I consider bestowing this latter item on Jolene, but she and her sidekick seem to have vanished.

I find David and Franklin near the bar and hold out the cash pouch. Franklin snatches it.

"You robbed me, you little witch," he says with a touch of admiration.

"Huh?"

"That trick you showed me earlier, the one you screwed up. You used ten of our dollars to demonstrate and never gave it back."

I put a hand to my mouth. "My God, you're right." I slip him a ten-dollar bill. "Thanks for keeping me honest."

David pulls out a bar stool. "Sit. Take the rest of the night off."

"Oh, no, I couldn't possibly." I climb onto the stool, and my tired feet shriek with joy. "On second thought, buy me a drink."

David sits to my right, signaling to Stuart, who plops a red beer in front of each of us. I reach for it, but my belly says no.

Franklin spies another client by the hors d'oeuvres table and shifts into his sales waltz without sparing us a glance.

David takes a long sip of beer, then sighs with satisfaction. "So how are you?"

"You mean, how am I after finding out you told Shane I was arrested?"

He blinks. "I never said you were arrested. I said they questioned you."

"Why did you say anything at all?"

"Because you both need eyes wide open going into this relationship."

"What we need is for you and Regina to mind your own businesses."

"It *is* my business when two of my employees are involved with each other. And believe me, you do not want to fall in love with a vampire."

"Who said anything about love?" I realize what he just implied. "Wait—are you speaking from experience?"

He glances away and doesn't answer.

"Not Regina, I hope."

David scoffs. "I value my life, if not my sanity."

He suddenly looks past me, then touches my arm. I turn toward the front door.

The crowd hushes in the middle of the Grateful Dead tune flowing from the speakers. All eyes stare in the same direction. Their stupor is caused by the fact that Monroe Jefferson is, by my best estimate, the most stunning man ever to walk the earth.

I imagined him old, simply because he is old. But he has the face and body of a young man, even as his eyes hold nearly a century of heartache.

The sly way Monroe regards the crowd from under the brim of his white fedora sends a shiver up our collective spine. He wears an immaculate white suit and tie, which contrast with the battered black guitar case swinging at his side. He steps up onto the stage like he was born and raised there.

David speaks in a hushed voice over my shoulder. "Ciara, this is unprecedented. You've done something here."

"I never even talked to him."

Monroe sits, then flips open his guitar case while Jim lowers the microphone.

"But your idea," David says, "bringing them out into the light. It gave him the chance to perform again."

With no warm-up, Monroe starts playing, with such speed and confidence I could swear it was more than one person. He sings the first line of "I'm So Glad," and the ancient voice bears as little resemblance to his baby face as a butterfly to a caterpillar. One hand flies over the fret board while his picking fingers form a blur. On the second verse, his voice soars up another octave as naturally as a bird taking flight.

I grip the bar's brass railing. Though I'm totally sober, the music puts me under a spell as strong as any drug.

The song is short, and when the last note shimmers away, the audience members finish the breaths they were working on before exploding in applause.

Monroe tips his hat. "How y'all doing tonight?" More applause. "That's just fine, fine." He tunes his guitar as he speaks. "Name's Monroe Jefferson, some call me Mississippi Monroe, since that's where I hail from, Natchez to be exact, but you can call me Monroe if it suits you. I was born in 1913." He smiles and strokes his smooth ebony chin. "I look good for my age." Applause and laughter. His smile fades. "That's because in 1940 I met a man changed my life."

I gasp and turn to David. "He's going to tell it?"

David puts a finger to his lips. On the other side of the bar, Regina and Noah confer with worried faces.

"Lotta people know about Robert Johnson, how he's supposed to met the devil at the crossroads at midnight, sold his soul to master the blues. Anyone who knew him, like I did, knows that ain't true. It was Tommy Johnson— no relation—who said he himself had done it. He's the one gave me directions."

Pluck. Strum. "I'd been playing the juke joints, oh about ten year. Little bit of money in it, kept me in whiskey and cigarettes, but not enough to buy me a ticket to Chicago or New York, places where bluesmen made it big. I was good—you can tell that right now," he says without a trace of false humility, "but not good enough.

"So one night I go to the crossroads—not the one at Highways 61 and 49, that's a lie. The real crossroads is a secret, and no, I ain't telling." He strokes the strings like they were the hair of a woman on the next pillow over. "I went on a Tuesday, so I wouldn't have to stand in line."

I look at David, who reflects my smile.

" 'Round about midnight, a man walks up, a tall man, a white man. Just like Tommy said the devil would be. Long hair so black, look like a river of blood in the moonlight. He come up to me and says, 'Son, you're not here to catch a bus, are you?' I shake my head no. 'Well, I reckon we got business, then,' he says. By this time I'm scared as a whipped puppy, but I ain't about to leave, so I pull out a cigarette and try to light up." He pauses while he does just that. The brief flame casts shadows over his face, giving his deep-set eyes an even more haunted look. "Problem is, my hands shaking so hard I can't hold the match. Then the man flicks his fingertips and there he is, holding fire in his hand. Cigarette falls out of my mouth, but he catches it and lights it himself. He takes a puff—" As Monroe does. "—and hands it back to me. I put it in my mouth and—" He holds the cigarette between his lips while he plays a few more notes. When he's done, the silence is deafening. "—it tastes like blood."

I steal a glance across the bar at Regina. She stares at Monroe, frozen, her own cigarette holding a two-inch ash.

"Didn't surprise me none. After all, I thought he's the devil. But then he opens his long black coat, and I see he's dressed like a preacher man. 'I'm not here to take your soul,' he says, 'I'm here to save it.' I get mad, I tell him, 'Saving is the last thing in this world I want, so if you aim to save me, you well's to kill me.'"

He puffs for a bit while he plucks a different tune.

When the notes fade into the air, Monroe says, "The man took my word. He took my blood, he took my life. He made me what you see here, and if I walk this earth a thousand year, I'll never master the blues." He takes a long drag and grins through the smoke. "But it'll master me forever, so I reckon that's something."

He launches into "Baby Please Don't Go," and the crowd applauds slowly and reverently.

I turn to David. "Shane said they never tell their stories."

He lifts his glass in a toast toward the stage. "Anything to please the crowd."

I wonder if Monroe's telling the truth. How could a vampire hold fire in his hand? Maybe he was a super-ancient one. But didn't I also read somewhere that it wasn't the soul-buying devil that blues players went to see, but a hoodoo trickster spirit?

Anyway, it makes a great yarn, and that's all that matters.

We listen to the next few songs without speaking. The weight of the music, made of pure emotion, sinks my mood into the cellar. I take a few forlorn sips of my beer. Finally David holds up two fingers to Stuart.

"Jack Daniel's," he says. "Leave the bottle." Stuart raises his eyebrows but obeys without comment, plonking the half-empty bottle in front of us, along with a pair of two-ounce shot glasses.

"That's more like it." I pour us shots and settle in for a long night of commiseration.

At the end of the next song, I say to David, "It's sad, huh?"

"Yeah, even the happy blues songs have that effect."

"I mean Monroe's story. Did any of them want to be vampires?"

He wags his finger at me. "No, you don't. It's not up to me to tell their tales."

"And no one else can tell yours." I tip the whiskey bottle into his empty glass and dribble out the amber liquid.

David just rotates the shot glass, fingertips on the rim. Monroe strums and croons, weaving his misty magic with "Gallows Pole."

Finally David gets tired of staring at the Jack and downs it. He wipes his mouth, then takes off his leather jacket. A trio of nearby women join me in admiring the contoured biceps revealed by his sleeveless black T-shirt, but he's oblivious to the attention.

"My father died suddenly when I was a college senior." He drapes his jacket over the back of the bar chair. "I was away at school and didn't get home to see him in time."

"I'm sorry," I say, because I'm supposed to.

He nods. "He was Control. Growing up, I hated all the secrecy and the moving around. I just wanted a normal life."

"I know the feeling," I mutter.

"I majored in broadcasting and was managing the college radio station when I was only twenty years old. But after Dad died, there was no question what I would do. I signed up for the Control as soon as I graduated. On my first day I met Elizabeth." He falls silent after saying her name, confirming my suspicion.

I pour him another shot for strength. "So she was human at the time."

"Human, all right. We were in love." He slams back the whiskey. "She'll never admit it now." He takes a long sip of beer, then swishes the glass in the condensation puddle left behind. "When she was turned, she—"

Applause and hollering erupt as Monroe leaves the stage. Rather than stay for drinks and adulation, he grabs his guitar case and heads out the front door without a word for anyone.

Noah takes the stage and slides his smile over the audience, clearly relishing the whispers of female admiration. "I am Noah. N-O is 'no,' and A-H mean 'pain,' so Noah mean no pain. When I bite, you don't feel a thing but happiness."

"It's true," David says. "I don't know how he does it."

The crowd rises and falls to Scratch Perry's "Dreadlocks in Moonlight." I guess Noah's not telling his story, at least not yet.

Despite the change in music and my compulsive foot-tapping, the mood at the bar stays dark. "So Elizabeth was turned . . ." I remind David.

He frowns. "It happened on a raid in the Ozarks. A cadre of older vampires had gone rogue and started preying on a little town in the tail of southern Missouri. We went in, captured a few of them. But we were underdeployed." He leans his head on his fist and forces out the next sentence. "The lead vampire's name was Antoine. Some say he was a century old, but he looked maybe fifteen or sixteen. I think Elizabeth was fooled by his apparent youth, couldn't bring herself to neutralize what appeared to be a kid. He dragged her off." He clutches the empty shot glass. "She showed up at my place the next night." He closes his eyes for a long time.

"She bit you."

"She was so strong. I thought I was going to die, and after a while I didn't care, because it felt—" He glances at me. "Well, you know how it feels."

"Only the stabbing pain part." I lean closer, knowing the liquor is loosening his tongue. "What's the rest like?"

His eyes unfocus. "Like the far side of an orgasm. You feel complete, like you found something you never knew you needed."

I wonder what kind of power it would give someone who could make you feel that way. "So then what happened?"

"When I was almost unconscious, she tossed me aside and told me that was the only way she'd ever touch me again." David's lip curls into an expression I've never seen on him before. "Revenge was the only thought that kept me alive. I went against orders and hunted Antoine, alone. One night in a Memphis alleyway, I staked the fucker." He puts his head in his hands. "I never meant to hurt her."

"What do you mean?"

"When you kill a vampire's maker, you kill a part of

them. She came to me that night in agony. She said it was like someone had ripped out her heart and stuck it back in upside down."

"Did you confess?" I ask him.

"Eventually. She looked at me like she was the one I'd staked."

"But she'd bitten you. She hurt you."

"It wasn't her fault. Brand-new vampires can't control themselves. She should've been better supervised."

"No, David," says a low, female voice that makes my neck hairs stand on end. "I should've ripped out your throat."

We turn slowly to see a woman in a long black silk dress. She looks maybe a few years older than me, but much taller. Blonder. Everything-er.

"Elizabeth," David says in a hoarse voice. "I didn't—I didn't know—"

"I was here?" Her blue eyes flare with a controlled rage. "Didn't know I was listening to you tell my story to a stranger?" She doesn't even look at me—not that I want her to.

He clears his throat and meets her gaze. "It's my story, not yours."

"Antoine is mine." Her fingers slip around his forearm. "Not yours. Not ever."

"I wanted to make Ciara understand." His voice has steadied. "She deserves the truth. She's one of us now."

At the moment, I'm not sure I want to be one of them. In fact, I'd like to be one of the people walking out the door. Not that anyone is leaving.

"Pleased to meet you." I hold out my hand so she'll have to take hers off David's arm or be incredibly rude. "Ciara Griffin, marketing intern."

She looks at my hand like she thinks I just wiped my nose with it. "This is your party?"

"It's the station's party. What do you think of it?"

Without turning her head, she glances around at the humans dancing, drinking, and falling over each other. "I worry about the vampires losing control around so much fresh blood."

I pull my hand back. "What about you?"

She twitches a thin, arched eyebrow. "I always keep my thirst in check with blood bank leftovers."

David gives a harsh laugh and pries her hand off his arm. "Then why are you so cold right now?"

"The ratings are bound to go up," I say, trying to turn the conversation in a more professional direction. "David did interviews with all the major local media tonight."

He gives me a grateful glance, then turns back to her. "And on July first," he says, "we'll start replaying the DJs' shows during the day in place of some of those annoying paid programming bits whose contracts are up."

I nod vigorously. "Because who wants to wake up at three a.m. to listen to music?" Besides me, of course.

Elizabeth stays silent for a few more moments, then extends her hand to me. "Good luck," she says without smiling.

I try not to grimace at her icy grip. "Join us for a drink?"

"Not right now." She tilts down her chin and widens her eyes at David in what looks like a questioning, almost pleading gaze. He juts out his jaw and turns his head away from her, glaring at the floor behind the bar with narrowed eyes. She doesn't move, and I suddenly feel like I'm eavesdropping on an intimate negotiation.

Finally David rubs his chin and gives a jerky nod without looking at her. She lets out a deep breath and appears relieved.

"Now if you'll excuse me," she says, "I have to confer."

She glides away and approaches a broad-chested man standing against the wall observing the crowd. He's dressed casual like everyone else, but straightens into an official bearing when he sees Elizabeth. They converse, nodding and watching the partiers with wary eyes.

I turn to ask David who that guy is, but he's not even watching Elizabeth, he's just staring into his whiskey again, lips tight and brows pinched. The overhead bar light casts shadows on his cheeks in the shape of his long, thick lashes.

I touch his arm, and he looks up quickly. Disappointment crosses his face when he sees it's only me.

"Who's Elizabeth talking to?" I ask him.

He glances over. "Control goon."

"But—wait a minute. She still works for them?"

"As one of their contractors. She gives the Control information in exchange for money and protection."

A vampire rat. Glad she has a sense of honor.

The Control ogre bends to speak in Elizabeth's ear, and I notice a bulge in his black leather vest.

"Is he armed?" I ask David.

"Not with anything that hurts humans."

I watch them monitor Noah, who's lounging against the wall by the stage, chatting up a group of hotties. "So I take it you quit the Control after the Antoine incident," I ask David.

"They kicked me out with a general discharge. But I didn't care, because I finally had a chance to follow my dream."

"Running a radio station?"

He nods. "And in the process, helping a few vampires avoid the Control. Elizabeth and I gathered half a dozen DJs and musicians and gave them a chance to stay in the present and in their Life Times simultaneously." He gestures to our surroundings, by which I think he means Sherwood. "We gave them a safe, quiet place to achieve self-actualization." His whiskey-numbed lips struggle with the seven-syllable word. "A place where they wouldn't end up like Antoine."

I fill our shot glasses and lift mine in a toast. "To redemption quests."

We clink and drink. From the speaker, Bob Marley assures us that every little thing's gonna be all right, but somehow, deep down, I wonder.

14

Bad Company

When I arrive at the office Monday morning, Franklin punches the hold button on his phone. The other line is ringing.

"Get that, would you?" he says. "It's probably an advertiser."

"Advertisers are calling *us*? Did I come to the right office?"

"Put your smart-ass in a sling and answer the phone."

The caller is a local Italian restaurant I've been able to afford exactly zero times. They want to buy ad spots, and I find sadistic pleasure in telling them we'll try to squeeze them into our crowded lineup.

When we're both off the phone, Franklin holds up the *Washington Post* and the *Baltimore Sun*'s Sunday style sections, one in each hand. "Page four and page two, respectively."

"Nice work, Mister Hyde."

"You know what I realized in the shower yesterday

morning?" His phone rings, and he points at me as he reaches for it. "You conned me out of nine bucks."

"Consider it overtime pay." I turn back to my computer and pull up a spreadsheet of WVMP merchandise. We need to order more before the next gig this Friday.

Regina clomps up the stairs and snatches the papers from Franklin's desk. He manages to scowl at her even as his voice lilts over the phone.

She comes to my desk and sits on the edge while she examines the article and the accompanying photo. "I looked good, didn't I?"

"Mmm-hmm." Maybe more of the red-on-black T-shirts this time.

Regina flips through the newspaper's pages. From the corner of my eye I see her perusing the comics.

She grunts. "I swear I read the same fucking *Mary Worth* strip twenty years ago."

I look up at her. "Did you want me for something? Ridicule? Harassment?"

"Oh." She chews the inside of her cheek as she runs a black-lacquered fingernail over the edge of my desk. "I wanted to tell you, I thought the other night was pretty cool."

"And what's the punch line?"

"I've spent too many years cooped up in that little studio. Having us all play live in one place—it felt like I was doing the clubs again." She sniffs. "Complete with some preppie wanker bugging me to play 'Bela Lugosi's Dead.'"

"It's the only Bauhaus song the average person knows." Which made me an average person before I started listening to Regina's show.

"The weird thing was, people liked me. Even though I glared at them." Her dark eyes—cosmetic free for the first time since I've known her—glance away almost shyly. "I'm not used to that."

"Really? I'd think you'd be popular in any circle." I open a box of paper clips and a file folder of merchandise receipts.

She ignores my sarcasm. "We have something else in common besides shagging Shane."

"I told you, I'm not—"

"People mispronounce my name, too."

I squint at her, confused not only at how anyone could mispronounce "Regina," but also by the vampire's awkward attempt at nice-making.

"I grew up in Saskatchewan," she explains, pronouncing the province with three syllables.

"You're Canadian?"

Regina scowls. "What, I'm not nice enough to be Canadian? What is with that stereotype?" She tempers her voice again. "Anyway, do you know what the capital of Saskatchewan is?"

I sort and clip receipts as I think, the *Jeopardy!* theme song playing in my head. "Saskatoon?"

"Ignorant Yanks." She heaves a sigh. "No, the capital of Saskatchewan is Regina." She pronounces it to rhyme with "vagina." "So living there, everyone thought my name was pronounced like the city, but it's not."

"And that's why you moved?"

"I moved because it blew chunks. Imagine North Dakota, but colder."

"Yikes. Where did you go?"

"London, of course. Then New York, then L.A."

"I've never been to any of those places. Except North Dakota."

As I close the folder, its corner knocks over the box of paper clips, spilling them across the floor. I bend over to pick them up, but Regina knocks me out of the way.

"I'll get it!" She scrambles for the paper clips, counting them under her breath as she collects them in her palm. I look at Franklin, who spares the vampire an impassive glance.

When she's finished, Regina stands and cups the paper clips back into their box, which she sets on my desk with shaky hands. "Fifty-three."

I look at the box, then at her.

Her eyes pinch into a glare. "One crack about *Sesame Street* and I'll snap your neck like a twig."

My phone rings, saving me. "WVMP, the Lifeblood of Rock 'n' Roll. Can I help you?"

A short pause, then a smooth male voice. "I attended your party Friday night."

"Wonderful." *Give us money.* "Did you enjoy yourself?"

"No, I'm afraid I did not enjoy myself. In fact, I think it is the beginning of the end for our vampire friends."

I give a nervous laugh. "Seriously. What did you think?"

"It was an abomination."

An icy fist closes over my spleen, despite my sense that it's a prank. "But a rockin' fun abomination, right?"

I look at the others. Franklin is still on his call. Regina is angrily scanning *Rex Morgan, M.D.*

"Anonymity brings safety," the voice says. "Exposure brings danger."

"What kind of danger?"

Regina looks up at me.

"If you don't end this campaign," the voice replies, "sooner or later someone will get hurt. We'll make sure it's sooner."

"Hold, please." I mute the call just as Franklin finishes his conversation. "Someone's threatening the station," I tell them.

"Who?" Franklin asks.

I sigh. "He neglected to state his name. Shall I ask?"

"I'll handle it." Franklin picks up the phone and taps the line. "Franklin Morris, manager of sales."

"Did the guy sound old?" Regina whispers to me.

"No, his voice was young."

"Spencer's voice is young, and he's in his seventies."

"Oh, you mean vampire old." I shake my head. "My bet's on Skywave. Jolene probably put him up to it."

Regina frowns. We turn to watch Franklin jot notes on a legal pad. He nods and *mmm-hmm*s again and again. Finally he gets a chance to speak.

"Well, I'm terribly sorry, sir, but I'm afraid you've reached the one person here who absolutely, positively doesn't give a shit. Ciao!" He hangs up and turns to me. "We've got problems."

David reads Franklin's notes from the phone conversation, then sets the page on his desk.

"That's quite a list," he says.

Franklin crosses his arms and leans against the door-way. "You think they'll do one of those things to each vampire, or all of them to just one vampire?"

"Bugger off." Regina paces the worn gray rug in front of David's desk.

Franklin sighs. "Alas, not during business hours."

"Who do you think it is?" I ask David, stepping quickly through Regina's path before she treads on me.

"Gotta be Gideon," she says. "Sounds like his isolationist bullshit."

David shakes his head. "Gideon and his people just want to be left alone."

I raise my hand. "Uh, who's Gideon?"

"Old fart vampire living out in the boonies." Regina glares at me. "He thinks your kind shouldn't interact with us except as food." She points to the list on David's desk. "Only a vampire would know all the ways to kill us. Them or the Control, and Elizabeth's supposed to protect us from those brownshirts."

"Hey, I was one of them once," David says. "We wore black shirts." He looks at me. "I agree with Ciara—it's probably Skywave. This list includes things that don't kill vampires. Like silver, and running water. Those are myths."

"So what do we do?" I ask. "Go to the police?"

"No!" they all say in unison.

"We can't have the cops sniffing around the station," David says. "What if they look downstairs and find a fridge full of blood?"

I grimace at the thought. "We're not dropping the campaign, are we?"

"Hell, no," Franklin says, together with Regina's "Fuck that." They share a frown, clearly unaccustomed to agreeing with each other.

David plants his palms on the desk. "No matter who

it is, we won't cave. I'll talk to Elizabeth. She can ask the Control to deploy a security detail to the station."

"You think they'll do it?" I ask him.

"Over one phone call? Probably not." He folds the list in half and tucks it into his top desk drawer. "So everyone be careful."

June 29

Early polling results knock us on our asses; based on call volume and surveys, our listenership has increased by ten-fold less than a week after the party at the Smoking Pig. David takes me and Franklin out for happy hour, and for an hour even Franklin exhibits something close to happiness. As I warned Bernita the Candle Lady, our ad rates have tripled.

I snag some more gigs for the older vamps at a few clubs in Baltimore. The mystique surrounding the reclusive Vampire Shane is beginning to build, just as I'd hoped. I can relate to the public on that one, because I haven't seen him since the night of the Pig party.

So far, no more threats. Maybe that call was just a practical joke, or Jolene's lame attempt at intimidation. But I remember the cold feeling of being watched the night of my interview, and I never walk alone after dark.

15

Just Like Heaven

The phone wakes me too early on Fourth of July morning. Grumbling, I flop over in bed to answer it.

"What are you doing tonight?" Shane says, turning my crankiness into confusion.

I sink back onto the pillow, wanting to tell him about my elaborate plans for the evening with all my cool friends, except I don't have any. Plans, that is.

"Lori's still up in Gettysburg for the battle anniversary, so I'm going to bed early. It's my first day off since I started this job."

"You can sleep during the day. I do it all the time."

The thought of him in bed spreads a warmth through the bottom of my belly. "Why are you asking?"

"Let me make everything up to you."

"Huh? What everything? I started our fight."

"And I called you a liar. I'm sorry."

"Sorry you called me a liar, or sorry you think I am one?"

He sighs. "You're not making this easy, are you?"

I stretch and sit up, knowing I'll never get back to sleep after this call. "What did you have in mind for tonight?"

"Fireworks. Food."

I wait for him to add anything else that begins with F. "I can get those in Sherwood."

"You can't get in Sherwood what I'm going to show you tonight. Trust me."

"Trust you?" I let out a little laugh. "That's a work in progress."

"I'll take that as a yes."

Just after dark, Shane's knock comes from the bottom of my stairs. Nice that he didn't barge in this time.

I start to pull open the door to the sidewalk when he catches it, trapping me inside.

He holds out his other hand. "Give me your car keys."

"Why?"

"I have stuff to load in the trunk. Surprise stuff. It's good to see you, by the way." He keeps his firm grip on the door, which I can't open any farther.

I hand him the keys. "If we need my car, how did you get here?"

"Jim dropped me off on the way to his gig. Stay there." He backs away, holding up a warning finger.

A few minutes later, we're driving out of town, making small talk. Every time Shane speaks, my foot presses the accelerator.

A pause in the polite bullshit gives me a chance to set things straight. "I'm sorry I freaked the night of the party, after we—I mean, before we—you know."

"I can't blame you, considering you saw me at my worst the last time we hooked up." He shifts his legs, as if the fact that they don't quite fit under my dashboard has just now made him uncomfortable. "If you're afraid of me, why are you here now?"

"To prove I'm not afraid." I smile at him. "Plus, a college student never turns down free food."

"I remember."

"Where'd you go to school?"

"Ohio U for music theory." He points up to the left. "Turn there. And before you ask, no, I didn't graduate."

I turn onto a poorly paved country lane. "What would you have done with a bachelor's in music theory?"

"Enjoyed it." He looks over at me. "It's been two decades since I asked someone this question. What's your major?"

"Business, with a concentration in marketing."

He nods without comment. Nothing like total educational incompatibility to stall a conversation.

"Where are we going?" I ask him.

He shifts his legs again and sighs. "Hell if I know, Ciara. I hoped we'd figure it out if we spent some time together, like normal people."

"No, I mean geographically, where are we going? How can we see fireworks this far out of Sherwood?"

"It's a different display."

I take my foot off the gas. "These better not be metaphorical fireworks."

"These are the realest fireworks of all," he assures me.

The car lurches as the road turns to dirt. We come out of the woods next to a huge wheat field. The stalks sway under the lingering twilight and undulate in the breeze like sheets on a clothesline. A few fireflies dot the landscape.

"Pull over at the top of the hill," he says.

I ease the car to the side of the lane and turn off the ignition. "We're alone."

"I wasn't sure we would be. It's a popular spot for fireworks." He eyes me with regret. "We just won't touch each other. That way we won't do anything that will lead to screaming and piercing."

"You already promised you wouldn't bite me."

"But you don't really believe it yet. Pop the trunk and stay here."

As he busies himself with his grand setup, I check the surroundings for complications: cops, angry farmers, a posse of thirsty vampires. Everything appears copacetic, so I start to relax.

Shane knocks on my window, and I nearly hit my head on the ceiling. Guess I'm not that relaxed after all. He beckons me out of the car into the humid summer evening.

A large blanket lies spread on the grass, anchored at each corner with a jar candle. One half is covered with food and drink: barbecued chicken, a bread-and-cheese plate, tomato salad, chocolate-covered strawberries, and a bottle of wine.

He bows, motioning for me to sit.

"Shane . . ." I kneel on the blanket next to the brimming containers. "You're feeding me. No one ever feeds me."

His foot taps the other side of the blanket. "Sit over here."

"Why?"

"It's part of the show."

I do as he asks, putting my back to the wheat field. He opens the wine—red, of course—and sets it aside to breathe, then heaps a plate high with food and hands it to me.

"You're not eating?" I ask him.

"It won't taste good. Besides, I have something more important to do." He pours two glasses of wine, then takes a long sip of one. "Soon as I get up the nerve."

I'm intrigued. But also hungry, so I start eating.

He goes back to the open trunk and pulls out something long and dark. As he comes closer I realize it's a guitar case.

"Surprise." He lifts the instrument out of the case and sits cross-legged with it in his lap.

I'd guessed he played, since the fingernails of his right hand—the one that holds the strings on the fret board— are trimmed much shorter than those on the left. But instead of telling him that, I send him a smile of genuine excitement.

His gaze goes distant as he tunes the guitar, testing each string with the pick.

"Okay." He clears his throat. "I'll start with a song by this Irish guy named Luka Bloom. You've probably never heard—"

"Luka Bloom, are you kidding? He opened for the Violent Femmes at my first concert."

"Wow, cool. My first concert was Night Ranger and .38 Special, but don't tell the other DJs. They think it was Black Flag."

"Ooh, Shane McAllister's darkest secret, revealed at last."

He puts a finger to his mouth with a playful warning glare. "When you saw Luka, did he play your song?"

"My what?"

"You'd know if you'd heard it." He takes a deep breath and blows it out slowly. "I apologize ahead of time for fucking it up."

I set aside my food. When the first slow, tentative chords come, they transform the field into an arena. Instead of absorbing the sound, the landscape echoes and releases it back, as if reserving it just for me.

Shane starts to sing, with a voice I didn't know he had but feels like his true voice: soft, deep, and slightly tortured. His tongue curls around the R's to create a faint Irish brogue. He doesn't look at me; when he's not watching his fingers on the fret board, his eyes are closed.

I barely notice the words until he reaches the first chorus.

It's my name.

My gasp is audible even over his voice, which reaches higher and sweeter now. With a name like Ciara, I never hoped to have a song of my own. As always, the sound of my name from Shane's lips sends a warm sensation up my neck and over my ears.

I listen closely to the lyrics of the second verse and realize I'm nothing like that Ciara. She's virtuous, unreachable. An "angel."

My eyes grow hot around the edges, and my chest feels like it's in a vise. I cross my arms on my knees and bury my face in them. As the tears well up through my sinuses, I pinch the tender insides of my elbows to distract my mind.

The song builds to what sounds like a final chorus,

pairing my name with the word "angel." As the last few chords march toward silence, I gulp deep breaths, struggling for control.

Too late. The last note cuts off when Shane sees me. "Was it that bad?"

I try to say, "No," but it comes out as a strangled "Nyuh." The effort to speak chokes out the first tears, and it's all over.

"What's wrong? Ciara, what happened?" With blurred vision I see Shane reach for me, then change his mind. The No Contact Rule, keeping us safe and sane.

I shake my head, but can't speak. My breath heaves in a series of humiliating high-pitched sobs.

"No hurry." He tunes the instrument some more, while my tears slow to a steady drizzle.

Finally my lungs give me a break. "My father used to call me 'Angel.'" Sniffle. "Some joke, huh?"

"I'm sure it wasn't a joke." Shane hands me a paper napkin. It's the soft kind, the kind you buy for fancy parties.

"It is now." I try to laugh as I dry my face. "You should play in bars. Drive everyone to drink more."

He's silent for a moment. "Where's your father now?"

"In prison. With my mom. Not *with* my mom, obviously—they're in separate places, but for the same thing."

"What thing?"

"Guess."

"I'd rather not."

I sigh. "They were 'faith healers.'" I make the requisite air quotes. "They traveled all over the Midwest, turning believers into chumps. People threw money at them, money they couldn't afford."

The corners of Shane's eyes turn down. "They taught you."

"I played along with their routines. Sometimes I was a crippled child miraculously healed by them. Sometimes I was a shill, shouting out 'Amen!' or 'Thank ya, Jesus!' at just the right moment."

"You were a kid," he whispers. "They used you."

"It was fun. Besides, I thought we were—" My voice cuts out. We both sit and wait a moment for it to come back. "Mom and Dad told me the scams were all part of doing God's work."

He draws in a breath. "Holy shit."

"I believed it. My folks didn't smoke or drink or dance— and as far as I knew, never had sex except on their anniversary. So I thought they were good. The fakery was just a way for us to spread our goodness." I fiddle with the toe of my sandal, where the sole is coming loose. "One day when I was fourteen—not cute anymore, just gawky—I came late to the revival tent. My parents had already started. I walked up from the side and saw the people watching, how happy they were, how much they believed." My lips press together. "I saw them for what they were. Suckers. Clueless as cows on the way to the slaughterhouse."

"How'd your parents end up in jail?"

"They were arrested for fraud when I was sixteen. I testified." I put my face in my hands. "I betrayed them."

Shane is silent for a few moments. Then he says, "Hey, don't feel bad. Every teenager dreams of sending their parents to jail. My dad could've been convicted as a first-degree jagoff."

I snort—not quite laughter, but further from crying.

"I'm sorry I judged you." He hands me another napkin. "Can I do anything?"

I blow my nose. "Play a happy song."

A long pause. "That *was* the happy song."

I laugh, and then I can't stop laughing, even when my belly and cheeks start to ache.

"What's so funny?" he says.

"You. I like you. I like being with you."

"Yeah, that's hilarious." He points behind me. "Dry your eyes and turn around."

"The fireworks?" I spin on the blanket and search the skies. "I don't see—oh my God."

The field is ablaze.

Dancing, flashing fireflies cover the landscape as far as I can see. Half of them loiter within the wheat while the others swoop and dart above, creating a 3-D display, like a mile-wide Christmas tree. The field sparkles in every hue of green, from aquamarine to chartreuse.

"It's boy meets girl times a thousand," Shane says. "Or ten thousand."

"How do they know when they've found the right one? Or do they just pick the first firefly they see?"

"If it were that spontaneous, it'd all be over in five minutes. They each look for a specific signal that tells them, this could be the one."

"I've never seen anything so beautiful." I hear the goopy sincerity in my voice. "Much better than Sousa and gunpowder, at least."

"I thought you'd like it. Which means I'm not completely wrong about you."

The guitar is in his lap, but it'd be so easy to crawl

around it and kiss him, to remove it so I can pin him to the ground and press every inch of my body onto his. The look in his eyes says he wouldn't stop me.

"Play a song for the fireflies." I sweep my hand toward the field. "Something to get them in the mood."

He watches me closely for a second, probably rewinding my words to check for a double meaning, then turns back to the guitar. "I think 'Two Hearts' by Chris Isaak would be appropriate."

"Never heard that one. But Chris Isaak? A little straightforward for your tastes."

"You're not the only one with layers."

The song starts off slow and sad, lamenting the struggle to find love in the dark night. Then it pauses, and he gives me a mischievous glance. A moment later, it bounces into a jaunty, hopeful tune about life's burdens being too much for just one person (or insect) to carry. He hits an admirable falsetto on the chorus, and I start to realize how damn good a singer he is.

My feet start tapping of their own will. During the brief solo, Shane gestures with his chin for me to get up and dance. I kick off my shoes and hop onto the cool, soft grass. Then it's me and the fireflies, jamming, falling in love with the summer night.

I look back to see Shane watching me. He misses the high note and breaks into laughter without losing the rhythm. He starts the last chorus again when it comes around on the guitar.

When it ends, he applauds, and I bow, then clap for him with outstretched arms like a prima donna thanking her conductor.

Shane raises his wine. "To the fireflies." He empties

the glass and tosses it aside. "Here's one for the mosqui-toes."

He slams into Nirvana's "Drain You," squashing the sentimentality like a rolled-up newspaper on a—well, a mosquito. The harsh, growly parts of his voice take center stage to sing of a love based in disease and craving. I return to sit on the blanket.

Shane looks at home in his body as he returns to the music of his soul. With every strum, his pale brown hair swings against the sharp bones of his cheeks and jaw. I watch his fingers fly over the fret board and grow warm imagining them on my skin.

The solo alternates between a low, steady thrumming and wild bursts of intensity. As it builds to a crescendo, he glances at the landscape around us, probably deciding whether or not to do the scream.

Just when I think he's going to cop out to save his voice, he lets loose with a feral howl that sends a hot electric blast to the tips of my fingers and toes. It's all I can do not to run away, or rip off my clothes.

He shifts to the chords of the third-verse-same-as-the-first, snarling the lyrics like it's a personal anthem. His voice and the guitar build a noise that could tear the leaves off the trees.

The last chord soaks into the thick, humid evening. Shane sends me a feral gaze through a curtain of tangled hair. For the first time tonight, he looks like a vampire.

I clap slowly, though the gesture feels shallow in the face of such power. "I didn't know that song could be done acoustically. Those years of music theory really paid off."

"Not years. Months." He refills his wineglass without looking at me.

Clearly his abbreviated college career bothers him. I change the subject. "I have a new nickname for your kind. Mosquitoes."

"Nice." He takes a long sip.

"When was the last time you drank?"

He holds up his glass.

"I don't mean wine."

"I know." He stares into the red liquid depths. "I'm not an animal. I can control it."

"But you'd rather not."

"I'd rather do whatever it takes to get you and keep you." He puts down the glass and focuses on the guitar. "That's what I'd rather do."

The evening progresses, through Led Zeppelin and Bob Dylan and Steve Earle and The Pogues and some people I've never heard of. Though I started the night nursing one glass of wine, the music, food, and absence of vampire attacks have relaxed me enough to have a second, then a third.

The fireflies wink out one by one, as they either find their mates or give up for the night. I realize that if I were one of those bugs in the field, I would have turned off my blinky butt the moment Shane struck the first chord of "Ciara."

Finally Shane sets the guitar back in its case and shakes out his stiff fingers. He frowns at the empty wine bottle. "How are you going to drive us home?"

"You could drive."

He looks away. "My other dark secret is that I can't drive stick."

"Then I'll teach you."

"I can't learn new things the way a human can."

"Don't listen to that Control propaganda. You learned the 'Ciara' song, didn't you? You didn't just happen to have it in your repertoire when we met."

"True." He sighs and pulls the guitar out of its case. "One last tune, a eulogy for your transmission. How about 'It's the End of the World as We Know It'?"

"No, play my song again. Please? I promise not to cry."

He shrugs. "Cry all you want. As long as I know I'm not the cause."

He plays "Ciara" again, his voice softer, fatigued from so many songs. It strains to hit the chorus's higher notes, giving it a plaintive sound, as if he'll never reach that angelic Ciara, but he'll keep trying.

This time, I don't need to cry.

16

Twilight Zone

I wake at 3 a.m. Friday morning to Cake's irony-laced "Rock 'n' Roll Lifestyle" and decide I'm too restless to listen to Shane's program alone.

Soon I pull into the radio station lot, parking less than ten feet from the front door. Before getting out of the car, I check my surroundings—nothing but shifting shadows of trees and the hesitant chirps of a few early cicadas.

I step out of the vehicle. Immediately a cold presence permeates the humid night. Its gaze on my body feels like a hand with too many fingers. As I stride toward the building—not running, no matter how much I want to—I almost wish I could wield a cross with conviction.

Once inside, I shut and relock the front door behind me, then hurry downstairs.

Sitting around the poker table, Regina, Jim, Noah, and Spencer greet me with varied amounts of enthusiasm.

"Happy to take your money, honey." Spencer pulls out a chair for me to sit in.

Regina shakes her head at him. "Sucker."

I don't sit. "Gideon lives an hour from here, right?"

They share nervous glances. "Yeah, out in the mountains," Regina says. "Why?"

"Twice I've felt something watch me in the parking lot." I rub my arms at the lingering chill. "Something cold."

"I knew it!" Regina slams the deck against the table. "Skywave didn't make that threatening phone call after the party. It was Gideon, the skeevy son-of-a-bitch."

"Or one of his flunkies," Jim adds.

"Let's not jump to conclusions," Spencer says. "He's always kept to himself."

"Who else is old enough to have that kind of aura?" Regina stands and stalks over to me. "When did this happen?"

"The night I interviewed for the job, and again just now."

"Then he could still be outside." She turns to the door. "If Monroe were here, the five of us could take Gideon."

"Wait." Noah turns to me. "You said this happened the first time you come here." I nod. "Then it cannot be Gideon. Before your campaign, we kept our secret. He had no reason to stalk you, or the station."

Regina huffs out a breath. "Then there's another vampire besides Gideon after us?"

"Maybe it's Gideon now," Jim offers, "but a different one that other night."

"If there's more than one," Spencer says, "then we don't know what's out there right now. We could be outpowered *and* outnumbered."

I scratch my neck to subdue the prickling. "What's to keep them from coming inside?"

"Besides the locks on the doors? Nothing." Regina

paces, looking ready to bite the head off a chipmunk. "The Control won't give us extra security based on one phone threat, and they won't change their minds over an intern's goose bumps."

"You don't have any weapons?" I ask them. "Stakes and stuff?"

They look aghast at the mere suggestion. I guess it's no different than humans who won't keep a gun in the house.

"Not unless you count Franklin's pencil stash." Regina crosses to the credenza next to the sofa, opens the top drawer, and pulls out a white box. "You might stop one of us with a handful of these, but they wouldn't even make Gideon sneeze."

I suddenly wish I'd stayed in bed. "So what do we do?"

Regina puts the pencils back. "We know he's there, but he doesn't know we know."

"That's our advantage, then." I sit in one of the empty chairs. "We know we can't beat him by confronting him, so we act normal and wait for him to slip up."

Regina gives me an icy look. "That's what I was about to say." She comes back to her seat and picks up the cards.

I pull my chair closer to the table. "Tell me more about Gideon."

Regina deftly shuffles the cards without looking at them. "He and all the other geezers live out in the sticks where no one'll confuse them."

"Confuse them?"

"When we get old, we get freaky," Jim says. "Gideon runs a kinda sanctuary."

"How long can a vampire live?"

Noah answers this time. "Most live about eighty years after our turning." He straightens his pile of chips. "But a lucky one can live centuries."

Regina says, "I hear there are a couple two-hundred-fifty-year-olds working down in Colonial Williamsburg."

"That's a myth." Spencer points to the cards. "Let's go."

They deal me in, and my chips start to trickle away. We don't speak much, even between hands, each of us listening for signs of encroachment from outside. To distract myself, I focus on learning the vampires' various styles of play.

Noah is as conservative as they come, while Jim is at the other extreme, betting expansively and impulsively. I'm coming to realize his hippie veneer is just that; beneath the serene trappings of peace, love, and happiness lies a wild animal. Of the five, he probably has the highest body count. The fact that I can even speculate on such a topic gives me the chilly willies.

Regina plays according to the numbers, calculating the odds of each hand with the speed of a supercomputer. Spencer is a poker genius, surprising me with flashes of superhuman intuition. Sometimes his eyes go eerily vacant, like a shut-down robot, but maybe he's accessing some kind of collective card-player unconscious.

After an hour without incident, Regina goes to their apartment and returns with three beers. She hands one to Spencer and one to me.

"If you're such a good con artist," she says, "how come you're so poor? Did you ship all the scam money to Switzerland for your retirement?"

"No one uses Switzerland anymore—too strict." I

shuffle the cards, ineptly. "New Zealand is the hot new place for offshore accounts."

"Is that where your money is?" Jim asks.

"What money? I'm small-time. I only use scores to pay off student loans." I set the shuffled deck in front of Regina to cut. "I'm allergic to debt."

"Smart," Noah says. "Debt is a kind of slavery."

"It's a commitment." Regina taps the deck in an off-hand show of trust. "Con artists are afraid of commitment, aren't they?"

Instead of answering the question, I start dealing five-card stud, which automatically cuts off conversation, per Spencer's rules. The cards feel crisp and slick; I bet they use a new deck every night.

After the hand, I change the subject. "How are your podcasts coming?" In response to their blank looks, "That's the thing where I record you yammering for fifteen minutes, then people can download it onto their computers and listen to it anywhere in the world."

Regina recovers first. "I thought I'd talk about Sunday matinees at CBGB, the big hardcore scene and the fights that broke out with the pigs in uniform."

"I'm gonna do rock trivia," Jim announces. Everyone else rolls their eyes.

"Of course you are," Noah says.

Jim's head hoards useless knowledge like a hamster's cheeks hoard granola. He pulls a folded piece of paper from his pocket. "Ciara, you're a typical civilian, I'll test my trivia on you. If you know the answer, the question's too easy."

"Gee, thanks."

"First category, real names. Ready? Robert Zimmerman."

I snap my fingers. "Bob Dylan."

"Just a warm-up. McKinley Morganfield."

"Um—"

"Muddy Waters," he says without giving me a chance to think. "Famous quotes category: Who called rock 'n' roll 'the most brutal, ugly, degenerate, vicious form of expression it has been my displeasure to hear'?"

I shrug.

Jim arches one brown eyebrow. "Frank Sinatra."

"Hoser," Regina adds.

Jim flips the paper over. "Bonus question: What Flint, Michigan, band generated the original members of Grand Funk Railroad?"

Noah and Regina groan. Spencer furrows his brow.

Jim looks at the other DJs. "Terry Knight and the Pack. You guys didn't know that?"

"No one gives a shit about Grand Funk Railroad." Regina fake-spits on the floor.

"That's the point. The more obscure the trivia, the better."

"You need a mix of easy questions," I tell him. "You can't talk down to people if you want them to tune in again."

"Excuse me." Regina slaps the bottom of her cigarette pack against the heel of her hand. "How long have you been a DJ?"

"That's not the point."

"You think you know everything because you're from the so-called present, but you can't even get your boyfriend to join you there."

"Shane's not my boyfriend."

"Does he know that?" We lock eyes as Regina pulls

a cigarette from the pack with her teeth and lights it. I hear the others shift in their seats. Finally Regina looks at them. "Leave us."

Spencer looks at his watch. "Almost bedtime, anyway." He and Noah stand up.

Jim stays seated, gathering the cards. "I want to see them fight."

Noah gives Jim's hair a yank. "You heard Regina."

"Ow. Douche bag." He gets up and slouches after them, rubbing his head. They enter the hallway and leave the door open behind them.

I turn back to Regina. "Shane said you broke it off years ago, so what do you care?"

"We stopped screwing, but he'll always be my progeny, however freakishly oedipal that sounds." She puffs smoke in my direction. "Either start taking him seriously or end it now."

"I do take Shane seriously." I inhale her cloud of smoke without wrinkling my nose. "I would never hurt him."

"You wouldn't say that if you knew how easy it is to do." Her eyes turn sad around the edges. "It's like saying you won't step on ants."

The music fades from the speaker over our heads, and Shane's voice comes on.

"WVMP 94.3, five fifty-four on a Friday. Weatherman says it's another hot one, high of ninety-five and humid, so wear as little as you can get away with today." His words reach thousands, but I feel like he's speaking to me. "If you aren't awake by now, a little White Zombie'll fix that. Good morning, and good night."

The first throbbing chords of "More Human than Human" strain the ceiling speakers.

Regina looks toward the stairs. "It's light out by now. Safe for you to leave."

Sounds like a hint. "I've got work to do. Think I'll just head to my desk."

She folds her arms and leans back in her chair. "Be careful."

"I will." I know she's not talking about my safety. I put my feet up on the next chair and sip my beer, which tastes odd considering it's almost six in the morning.

Regina finally sighs, shoves her chair back from the table, and slinks through the doorway to the hall.

When her footsteps fade, I walk to the door and peer around the corner into the studio. Shane is inside the control room jamming to the schlock-metal riffs as he programs the system to play an hour of paid programming after his broadcast. He's facing the other direction, so he doesn't see me watching.

I pull back and shut the door, then turn for the stairs.

Figures. I've finally convinced myself he won't hurt me, and now I have a bigger, more realistic worry.

That I'll hurt him.

17

Waiting for the Miracle

"We'll start with the bands you liked when you were alive."

I lower my voice at the end of the sentence. Probably not necessary, given the volume of the new Nine Inch Nails CD grinding out of the store's speakers. Record & Tape Traders is holding a midnight madness sale, thus allowing me to bring Shane here for an after-dark lesson.

His gaze wanders over the selection of T-shirts and posters on the store's wall. He won't look at the CDs in the bin next to us. The major bands are in alphabetical order, but the miscellaneous ones at the beginning of each letter are all mixed up.

I guide him over to the G's. "You remember Green Day, right?" I hold up their first major release, *Dookie*, feeling like a remedial math teacher with a flash card.

"One of my favorites. 1994." He takes the CD case and caresses it like a Ming vase.

"In 2000 they came out with *Warning*, which got critical acclaim, though some of their fans thought it wasn't punk enough. But everyone's got to grow up sometime, right? Except you, of course."

The notion makes Shane smile a little, as I figured it might. Staying young and surly is probably the only thing he truly loves about being a vampire. He doesn't reach for *Warning*, though.

"But the big one," I continue, "was *American Idiot* in September 2004." I display the CD, which features a hand grenade in the shape of a bleeding human heart. "One of the most important releases of this millennium."

Shane hesitates before reaching for the CD. "Why?"

"First of all, the music is amazing. It's a rock opera."

"Hmm." He turns it over and smooths the plastic wrapper—carefully, as if it might be covered in anthrax.

"But its influence was more than musical. It was released right before the elections. Green Day was part of this movement in pop music trying to mobilize young people to vote. And it worked. College kids lined up at the polls on Election Day—at your old school, some waited as long as eight hours in the rain."

Shane continues the blank look he began around the middle of my speech. "Is Bill Clinton still president?"

I stare at him, the severity of his fossilization finally slamming my gut. Then the corner of his mouth twitches.

I huff in relief. "You son of a bitch."

"Psych," he says. "I'm not that dead. Yet." He taps the CD against his palm. "Also, I heard Green Day did a rock opera but never bothered to check it out. I'll try this, but don't expect miracles."

I beckon him down the aisle, past a group of multiply

pierced teenage boys arguing over whether AFI is a true emo band.

Shane shoots past me, toward the P's, and picks up Prince's *Purple Rain* CD. "I used to have this on vinyl. That movie inspired me to learn the guitar." He gazes through the far wall. "I took my first girlfriend to see it."

His faint smile makes me wonder what Prince's royal hotness inspired Shane's girlfriend to do that night. I pick up another copy and check the issue date—1984. I was still in diapers.

Back to the nineties. I lead him to the M's. "I've heard you play Morphine on your show."

His face lights up. "You like them?"

"Baritone sax, two-string bass, and a drum. Their sound is detached and ironic yet somehow sensual." Ew, I sound like a rock critic. "1993's *Cure For Pain* is some of the smokiest, sexiest music I've ever heard." I pull out one of their newer CDs, and this time Shane grabs it, handing me the others to hold.

"Are they still together?"

"The lead singer died in ninety-nine."

Shane looks at me, stricken. "Mark Sandman died?"

"Heart attack during a concert in Rome."

"That sucks." He frowns as he examines the track list. "I liked him."

I inch closer. "Why does it bother you that he died?"

Shane scrunches his face at me. "Shouldn't it bother everyone when someone dies?"

"Last night a car crash killed four people outside of town. Does that bother you as much?"

He shakes his head. "I didn't know those people."

"You didn't know Mark Sandman."

"It's different." He runs his thumb over the corners of the CD. "I felt like I knew him from his music."

"What else bothers you about it?"

Shane scratches his neck and looks away. "The world lost something when he died."

I point to the Morphine sign in the bin. "We haven't lost him. We can listen to him any time we want."

"We can't hear the stuff he hasn't written yet. Everything he never did, it all died with him."

"Yes!" I clasp Shane's hand. "Listen to what you just said. You're thinking about all the Morphine albums that will never happen. As if you could learn to care about new music. As if you could learn, period."

He curls his thumb around my hand. "Why do you care so much about what I care about?"

"I don't want you to live like this forever, stuck in 1995. You're not happy now, and as time goes on you'll be less happy." I tighten my grip. "I don't want you to fade."

Even under the fluorescent light his pale blue eyes seem to glow when he looks at me that way. The music growls above us as he leans over to kiss me.

For some reason, I keep thinking the kisses will become routine, that each one couldn't possibly be better or different than its predecessors.

I am wrong.

I like being wrong.

I thread my hand through Shane's hair and pull him into a deeper kiss. One of the teens behind me murmurs, "Yeah, dude, hit that." We ignore him.

An adult voice beside us says, "Please tell me you're off the clock."

We break apart to see Elizabeth. I almost don't recognize her in casual wear, though even in jeans and a V-neck T-shirt, her body could make a moldy cadaver sit up and beg.

"I'm tutoring Shane on new music."

"He looks like an attentive student." She winks at me, which I take as a positive sign.

"Good sale, huh?" I tilt my head to read the CDs in her hand. The top one is a collection of Rodgers and Hammerstein show tunes. "Franklin and I are about to close a cross-promotional deal with the store. They just have to work it out with headquarters to make sure they can align with more than one station."

Shane and Elizabeth, instead of listening to my fascinating speech on radio business, are giving each other flat, steady glares, like enemy cats separated by a window.

I try to make nice. "So, Elizabeth, thanks for giving the va—the DJs a chance to survive."

Her eyes narrow, still locked on Shane's. "They'd survive without the station. Someone will always take care of them. I'll make sure of it."

"Make sure we rest easy in the arms of the Control?" Shane looks like he wants to rinse his mouth after the last two words.

She waits for a pair of magenta-haired college girls to pass. "Many humans would long for such a comfortable retirement."

"Comfort? In one of their prisons, feeding off blood bank leftovers until they're so weak they can barely walk?"

"They're not prisons, they're refuges."

"What kind of refuge locks its residents inside?" He smacks his forehead in mock surprise. "Oh, wait, I forgot.

The doors unlock during the day in case anyone wants to shuffle off their immortal coil."

She glares at him and speaks in a tight, hushed voice. "Without the Control's retirement program, where would all those poor old vampires go when the world is too much for them?"

"Please. Save it for someone who doesn't know better. And this Skywave takeover threat had better be about money, not about finding an excuse to 'retire' the six of us."

"Of course. It's just business."

"So when the station turns a profit," Shane says, "you'll leave us alone."

She laughs and runs her fingers through her shaggy, Jennifer-Aniston-second-season-of-*Friends* hair. "We're so far in the red, it would take a miracle to bring it back by the end of the decade, much less the end of the summer."

"A miracle, huh?" Shane takes the CDs from me and loops an arm over my shoulder. "Guess we'd better get to work on that."

On the drive back to the station, Shane doesn't speak, just stares out the window, turning his new CDs over in his hands. Even in a stack of three, they're in alphabetical order.

His silence gives me a chance to ponder our encounter with Elizabeth. Shane said that a steady diet of bank blood weakens a vampire, but Elizabeth seems awfully vibrant for someone who claims to follow the Red Cross Plan.

As we pull onto the long gravel driveway, I finally break the silence. "How do you know so much about the vampire retirement homes?"

"I lived in one for two years," he says without turning

from the window. "Maybe 'lived' isn't the right word. I existed there, in a special rehab ward for young vampires who aren't too crazy about their new way of life. That ward's locked twenty-four seven." He gives me a little smirk. "Which was why I learned to pick locks."

"And it explains how you got out."

"But not why I left at night."

"Why?"

"I wanted a life. A purpose. The music gave me that. This place—" He gestures to the ramshackle building appearing ahead of us. "—gave me that."

We pull into the parking lot and get out of the car. The air feels warm and stalker free.

Shane stands with me next to the car and takes my hand. "Tell me what I can do to save the station."

I gasp. "You mean it? You want me to exploit you for the greater good?"

"Maybe you shouldn't put it that way, but yeah."

"Thank you!" I can't resist hugging him. "Your public is dying to meet the mystery vampire. You should see all the speculation on the blogs."

"On the what?"

"You've gotten more press than the other five put together, and you haven't even shown your face."

Shane tries to look like he doesn't care. "Why didn't you tell me?"

"Guys hate pressure. They want to believe everything they do is their idea."

"This *is* my idea, to . . . go along with your idea."

"The problem is, I'm not sure Elizabeth wants to sell the station to make money or retire the six of you. I bet she wants to get away from David."

Shane sighs and looks off into the woods. I can tell he wants to share gossip.

"She still bites him, doesn't she?" I ask.

He hesitates. "He's the only human she's ever tasted."

"Then no wonder she wants to cut ties. I'd hate to be so dependent on an ex-boyfriend. It's just not healthy. And why would David let her bite him when she makes him miserable?"

"You've obviously never been in an addictive relationship."

I put up my hands. "Ugh, no. Not into the whole needing thing. But if this is all about Elizabeth and David, it might not matter how many ads we sell or how much the ratings increase." Shane doesn't reply, just keeps staring into the woods, so I answer myself. "Then again, maybe it's only one factor in her decision."

Shane opens the driver's-side door. "Get back in the car," he says quietly.

"Why?"

"Casually. Now."

Once we're in the front seats, he says, "Someone's watching us."

I glance out the back windshield but see nothing. "Twice I've felt like I was being stalked in the parking lot. Regina said it was an old vampire named Gideon."

"I smell human." He rolls down the window. "A human who smokes Marlboro Light Menthols."

"You can tell all that with one whiff?"

"I'm kidding about the brand, but the rest, yeah. It's on his breath and in his pores."

"Where is he?"

"In the woods, I think. The wind makes it hard to tell

until he gets closer." He pats his leg. "Put your head in my lap."

"Huh?"

"If he thinks I'm distracted he might get bold." He puts a hand on my shoulder. "Go on."

I lean over and rest my cheek on his thigh. At first it seems like a nice place to be, except, "The emergency brake is in my stomach."

He slides his hand between the brake and my waist, creating a cushion. "Better?"

"Yes, thank you. Hear anything?"

"Just you talking."

I clamp my mouth shut. His other hand strokes my hair, soothing and stimulating at the same time. I understand now why dogs like having their heads petted.

Shane looks suddenly to the right. He adjusts the side-view mirror with the manual control knob on the door. "He's behind us, but not close enough that I need to start faking an orgasm."

I can feel Shane's nerves on alert. He focuses on the side mirror, leg muscles tensing. His hand slides down the armrest toward the door handle.

He lunges forward. "Move."

I sit up. Shane opens the door and jumps out of the car. I lean out to see him race across the parking lot and into the woods near the radio tower. A few moments later, the high-pitched rev of a small engine shatters the night's silence, then recedes quickly into the distance.

Shane reappears from the back of the building and returns to my car's open passenger door. "Son of a bitch had an ATV hidden back there. Almost got him."

"Did you get a good look?"

"Dark hair, mustache. Nothing special."

"But you didn't recognize him."

"Why would I?" He props his arms on the roof and peers in at me. "Could be one of your old boyfriends."

"I'd never date a smoker. Especially not menthols, yuck."

He chuckles. "Hypocrite. You had a cigarette with Deirdre."

"Who?"

"My donor, the one we visited."

"Great. Now I know her name. Now if I see her in the produce aisle, I can say, 'Hi Deirdre, how's your torso? Any new holes?'"

"You sound jealous." Shane sits in the passenger's seat and tugs me into his lap without a struggle. "You sound like a girlfriend." He strokes my cheek with the back of his hand. "I'd like you to be my girlfriend."

My stomach flips, but I remember Regina's warning about hurting him. "That's sweet, Shane, but can't we just enjoy each other? Going steady is so old-fashioned."

He sighs. "I hate the new millennium."

"Now who's the hypocrite? You put your hands all over those women you bite, yet you expect me to sit at home in a sackcloth."

"It's different. I have to drink, you don't have to see other guys." He runs a finger down the side seam of my camisole. "Besides, you'd look damn sexy in a sackcloth."

I push him away, a few inches. "It's not different. You would have slept with Deirdre that night if I weren't there. In fact, drinking blood is probably a great excuse to get laid, not the other way around."

"What if I stopped drinking women? I could make

some trades with the other vampires. Would that change your mind?"

"You'd do that for me?"

"I already did." He brushes the hair out of my eyes. "The last woman was Deirdre, the night you came with me to visit her."

My chest constricts, and I wipe my hand over my forehead. "Shane, I can't be your girlfriend."

His face falls. "Why not? I thought we were over the whole Beauty and the Beast issue."

"Not when I'm still a beast."

"I don't get it."

"You want the truth? It's not pretty."

"It usually isn't."

I move clumsily out of his embrace, back into the driver's seat. "You remember that guy, the one David told you about? The one who wouldn't press charges after I conned him?"

"Mark, right?"

"That wasn't his name. That was his function."

"Whatever."

"It's not whatever." I take a deep breath. "He was my boyfriend."

He blinks hard. "You conned your last boyfriend? Out of how much?"

"He only thought he was my boyfriend." I run my hands over the steering wheel. "Okay, rewind. I've always scraped by on short cons, the kind that take a few minutes or a couple hours. Bar bets, card tricks, pool hustling. Sometimes I'd join up with another con to do pigeon drops or the badger game." I pause, waiting for him to ask what those are. He doesn't. "But I was tired of scraping by. I thought if I did one long con, I could take off the rest of the year, live like a normal person."

His voice hardens. "Ciara, how much?"

"Thirty thousand."

"Thirty thousand dollars?"

"A year's tuition, plus living expenses."

"Holy shit." He takes several moments to digest this fact. "How'd you do it?"

"I convinced him to invest in a get-rich-quick land deal. I made out like it wasn't quite legal, so he'd give me cash and so there was no way he could check up on it. They say you can't cheat an honest man."

"But why would he trust you?"

"Lust can make a fool out of anyone. He would've bought the Brooklyn Bridge from me." My face heats. "I did things his wife wouldn't do."

"His *wife*? Did you know he was married?"

"That's why I chose him, because I knew he wouldn't jeopardize his marriage by pressing charges and making it all public." I can't look at Shane, so I focus on the nicks in the steering column. "I was right. He told her he lost the money at the craps tables in Atlantic City. He had a gambling problem, so she believed it." My throat tightens around the rest of the truth. "I didn't know he had kids."

Shane pulls in a sharp breath. "Did his wife ever find out?"

"Not that I know of. I took his money and disappeared. He called the cops, but dropped the charges when he found out he'd have to testify against me."

"Did you give the money back?"

"I couldn't, not without his wife knowing he'd lied. And technically I didn't break any laws. I never used the postal system, so they couldn't charge me with mail fraud. Everything was in person. They couldn't prove the money wasn't just a gift from a lover. His loss, my gain. Of course, most of my gain was re-gifted to my attorney, so I still had to take out a loan for school last year."

"This is bullshit," Shane says suddenly.

"No, I'm telling the truth."

"And you're right, it's not pretty. But what does it have to do with me? I have no money to steal. You're with me because you like me."

"Yes. I like you too much to see you get hurt."

"How do you know you'll hurt me?"

"I betrayed my parents. I betrayed—" I still can't say his name. "—that guy. Someday I'll betray you. I don't know how or when, but it's in my nature."

"Again, bullshit. You're using this as an excuse to keep us apart."

"Why would I do that?" I take his hand, against my better judgment. "I want to be with you, more than I've ever wanted anyone. When I'm with you, I feel . . . decent."

His eyebrow twitches. "Decent. Not a goal for most guys."

"And indecent, too." Again ignoring my inner voice of reason, I lean forward and give him a deep, passionate kiss. He pulls me as close as he can, given that the emergency brake is still between us.

It all seems so simple, at moments like this, as if nothing else matters but the heat between us and the perfection of the kiss. But moments like this last only as long as a pop song, and bear just as much truth.

Which is to say, none at all.

* * *

I lie in bed later listening to the end of Regina's radio show, *Drastic Plastic*. Sleep tugs at me, but I want to hear Shane's intro.

The Siouxsie and the Banshees song fades, replaced by Regina's voice. "94.3 WVMP, the Lifeblood of Rock 'n' Roll. It's two fifty-nine on a very special night for all you vamps and vamp lovers. One of our own is finally coming out of the closet."

"Thanks for spoiling the surprise," Shane says.

"What surprise? Like VMP would let a ninety-eight-point-sixer have his own show."

His warm laugh makes me curl into a ball around my spare pillow.

"So what changed your mind, Shane?"

"A couple of blondes."

"Two at a time now? You're such a dog."

"No, it's not like that. See, one represents the past, and the other, the future."

"Ooh, how mystical. You haven't been dropping acid with Jim again, have you?"

"I always keep an eye on my drink around him, after that last time."

"Yeah, after that last eight times."

"Anyway, where was I?"

"Blondes," she says with exaggerated distaste.

"Right. So I've started thinking about the future, for the first time since, you know—"

"Since I turned you into a glorious beast."

He scoffs. "Whatever. I realized that I need to move on, get over the past. Time to take a few risks, and one of them is admitting to the world that, uh—"

"Repeat after me. 'I'm . . .'"

"I'm a vampire."

"You did it." Regina applauds softly. "That was totally brill."

"And I'm going to start playing gigs like the rest of you."

"The babes will ooze off their chairs when you break out that guitar."

"And now for the big news: I'm announcing a change in format to the first hour of my show, as of tonight."

She hesitates. "What kind of change?"

"I'm going to play new music."

I sit up straight in bed and stare at the radio. Regina obviously shares my shock, because she allows four or five seconds of dead air (so to speak) to pass before she reacts.

"Why?"

"There are a lot of good bands out there that don't get enough airplay in today's radio wasteland, and some of them have inherited the spirit of the nineties. Also, some bands that got their start during my Life Time have gotten better."

"Like who?" Her voice drips with disbelief.

"Like Green Day, for instance."

"*Green Day*? Bunch of bleedin' posers! They wouldn't know real punk if it crawled up their arses and burst out their colons."

"Are we allowed to say 'arse' on the air?"

"It's three o' clock in the effing morning, I can say anything I want."

"'Arse' is one of those cute British profanities, so I guess it doesn't count. Anyway, Green Day is a different kind of punk. They're not trying to be the Sex Pistols or the Stooges. They're pop-punk, like the Buzzcocks."

"They're crap is what they are," she says.

"Because they can actually play their instruments, they're crap. Whatever. This song's for you, Regina, to keep you from slitting my throat. Friends, wish me luck."

A quick, stabbing chord introduces Green Day's "She's a Rebel," off the very same *American Idiot* CD he bought five hours ago. Though I should be sleeping, I throw off the covers, stand on the bed, and jam at the top of my lungs for two solid minutes of triumph.

18

One Way or Another

July 11

Shane goes "on the road," playing his first gig as an acknowledged vampire DJ at a Sherwood coffee bar called Legal Grounds, next to the county courthouse.

Curious onlookers flow out of the café, past the outdoor tables, and onto the sidewalk. I make a note to investigate the price of a private security detail. Before leaving the "stage," Shane plays a short set on the guitar, ending with "Ciara."

July 12

Though perhaps only a hundred people can fit into Legal Grounds, today on the blogs approximately two thousand people claim to have seen Shane's first show, making it proportionally the most inflated gathering since Woodstock.

Some reviews complain about his "eclectic" tastes,

how they didn't know what to expect from one song to the next. One reviewer was pissed that Shane didn't look enough like a vampire *or* a grunge-head, as if they expected him to show up in a full-length flannel cape.

July 15
We begin podcasting. Each DJ will do a weekly fifteen-minute interview about the music and culture of their Life Time, supplying anecdotes known only to those who lived in the Way Back.

To keep the casual listener's interest, we'll include a few details about life as a vampire—a small fraction of which are actually true.

July 22
The week two WVMP podcasts briefly appear on today's Top 100 Most Downloaded list on one popular site. The T-shirts go back for a third, quadruple-size printing. Our Web site crashes under the load of too many visitors.

I get a whopping four hours of sleep in one night, the most I've had all month. I consider taking a sledgehammer to my alarm clock, if only I had time to buy a sledgehammer and the strength to lift it.

July 23
David notices my preternatural paleness. He orders me to spend tomorrow outside before I come down with a case of rickets.

July 24
I become one with the sun.

Lying on a lounge chair beside Lori's pool, I inhale

motes of light and beams of heat. Sweat tickles my back as I convince each muscle in my body to forget about my job.

Lori creates a soothing background noise, telling me about SPIT's efforts to help raise funds for the town to erect a Battle of Sherwood monument.

The battle's details are a little fuzzy to me, but the basic gist is this: Some Union guy with a magnificent mustache led a charge against some Southern guy with a magnificent beard. The beard guy had the skinny on Union troop movements, but because of the scuffle in Sherwood, he didn't get to Gettysburg in time to deliver the intelligence, so the Confederates didn't know what they were getting into. And that's why Martin Sheen lost the Civil War.

Or something like that.

"So what do you think?"

I realize she requires words from me. "Huh?"

"You're not even listening, are you?"

"Sorry. I was thinking about the battle. Sad, all those guys dying."

"It was two soldiers. Just two."

"Oh. Good, then."

"I was saying it would be cool if we could find one of their ghosts." I hear her tear the wrapper of a bag of chips. "Or if we could make one."

"Make a ghost?" I sit up and squint at her just as my cell phone rings. I open it to see an unfamiliar number on the caller ID. I slap it shut again, hushing the sound, and turn back to Lori. "You mean kill someone?"

"No, we get a vampire from Civil War times to pretend to be a ghost. Then when investigators ask them questions only someone from that time would know, it'll make it more believable." She waves her scarlet barbecue chip. "So what do you think? Can you make it happen?"

I think it's the nuttiest idea I've ever heard. Luckily I have a better reason for saying no. "None of our vamps are even close to that age."

"What about others around here?"

I shake my head. "Even Gideon isn't that old, and he wouldn't cooperate, anyway. Besides, wouldn't that be fraud?"

"Only in the short term." She licks the red salt off her fingers. "It'd be like telling a lie to create a greater truth."

"Do I know you?"

"It's no different than what you're doing with the vampires."

I shake my head. "Lori, you should know by now not to use me as a role model."

"Why not?"

The phone rings again. Needing to escape the conversation, I answer it.

"Hello, Ciara," says Elizabeth. She pronounces it with three syllables—kee-*ahr*-ah—as if I'm Italian. "I wanted you to be the first to know. Due to the station's recent success, I feel disinclined to sell it."

"Really?" A surge of pride—or possibly heartburn—erupts beneath my ribs. "You're giving Skywave the blow-off?"

Lori's eyes widen, and she raises her arms in a silent *Score!*

"Not exactly," Elizabeth says. "The company has become more aggressive in their buyout efforts. They're offering me a tempting amount of money, but they want my decision sooner."

"How soon?"

"I meet with them next Friday."

I'm confused. "So what are you going to tell them?"

"It depends. Remember those end-of-August ad revenue goals I established?"

"Of course." I've only built my entire summer around those numbers. "We're right on target to reach them."

"Not anymore. If you can reach those goals before my meeting, I won't sell the station. Otherwise, I'm afraid I'll have no choice. Their offer's too good to turn down."

She can't mean what I think she means. "You want us to meet the end-of-August goals by next Friday?"

"Yes."

"In ten days."

"Yes."

"That's not fair."

Elizabeth clicks her tongue. "Grow up, Ciara. It's business. I have a very long future to think of."

I sink back against the lounge chair, heat pounding my temples. "So we might have done all this work just so you can make more money?"

"Don't worry. If I sell, I'll make sure it trickles down to your friends. Some sort of pension arrangement should set them up nicely for a few years."

"A few years? They're immortal!" I check my surroundings to make sure no one heard that last part except Lori. "They need the station to keep from fading."

"Then you make sure they don't lose it." She hangs up.

I slap the phone shut so hard, it flies out of my hand and skitters across the concrete.

Lori clears her throat. "That didn't sound good."

I stare at the clear blue sky as I bang my head against the back of the chair. I'll give Franklin a few more minutes' peace before I tell him we have to cram six weeks' worth of work into ten days.

So much for being one with the sun.

19

Steal My Sunshine

"I'm considering violence," I tell Shane as we wait in line at Legal Grounds. The crappy mandolin trio in the next room makes enough noise that no one will overhear us. "A tag team of Regina and Jim could scare the Skywave executives out of buying the station. A corpse-a-day-till-they-go-away campaign." I hop a little on my toes. "What do you think?"

"I think you need sleep."

"I need coffee." I crane my neck to see the cash register. "What's taking so long? Anyone who waits until they get to the counter to pick what they want should be sent to the end of the line."

A gaggle of college-age girls drifts by. "Hi Shane!" they coo in unison. He offers them a friendly wave and smile. I sway enough to stumble into him.

"Sorry, so clumsy tonight. And tired." I rest my head on his biceps until the girls have passed. Not that I feel possessive or anything.

"Like I said, you need sleep."

"Not until the sales goals are met. Elizabeth's meeting is in less than a week, and we're not even halfway there. If she sells the station, Skywave's juggernaut of soul-suckery will trample everything you and the other DJs have worked for."

"Don't worry." He rubs the stiff part of my shoulder. "Sometimes just when things look hopeless, that's when everything works out."

"That doesn't sound like something you'd say."

"No, normally I'd say that when things seem hopeless, it just means you have no idea how much worse they're about to get. But I'm trying to calm you down." He rotates me toward the counter. "I recommend chamomile tea."

I stagger forward and give the barista a shaky smile. "Gigante mocha, organic two-percent milk, one-and-a-half shots of coconut, no whipped cream. Please." The last word comes out like Oliver Twist asking for more gruel.

Shane gets a black-no-sugar coffee, then I let him drive us back to the station so I can gulp my drink more quickly. He shifts gears like a natural, never racing the engine or coming close to a stall.

"After this is all over," he says as we pull into the parking lot, "I want to take you out to dinner. Like a real date."

"I hear people do those things."

We get out of the car. "Maybe even a movie," he says. "I hear they made a sequel to *Wayne's World*."

I laugh, not caring whether he means it as a joke. "Wait, you left your coffee." I bend over inside the car to reach it.

When I straighten up and turn around, Shane is looming over me, fangs bared. His hand covers my mouth, cutting short my shriek.

A cold presence seeps across my skin, making me shiver. Oh God, all along it was Shane.

I squeeze the coffee cups in fear, sending hot liquid down the front of my shirt.

Then I realize he's looking over my head into the woods. His nostrils flare and his jaw trembles. "Something's out there," he whispers, dropping his hand from my mouth.

"It's what I felt before."

Suddenly Shane jerks his head to look behind him, a moment before a spark of white light flashes from the other end of the parking lot, followed by a very human-sounding profanity.

A beastly growl rumbles deep in Shane's throat. Footsteps pound away toward the back of the building. Shane takes off in swift and silent pursuit.

As I follow them, I hear the muffled sounds of a struggle, topped off by a metallic bang. Then Shane calls, "I got him."

I tiptoe around the corner of the building and see Shane crouched next to the Dumpster, poring through a leather wallet. A dark-haired young man with a mustache lies crooked and motionless on the gravel beside him.

I step back. "You killed him."

Shane glances at me. "Of course not. He hit his head. When he comes around, I want to know more about him than he knows about us." He hands me the man's digital camera. "See what pictures he has. I can't make it work."

I flip to the last image, which causes me to almost drop the camera. He must have taken it just before Shane grabbed him, because there's my dude, frozen in his fanged glory, reaching toward the lens with a red rage.

"You take a scary candid." I delete it. The next few shots are of the station, time-stamped earlier this evening. "Who is this guy?"

"Name's Travis Tucker, according to his driver's license." Shane stuffs it back into the wallet and rifles through the other cards. "He belongs to Triple A, the Olive Garden frequent diner club, and a fan club for—who the hell is Jeff Gordon?"

"This Travis Tucker's been spying on the station for weeks." I flip faster through the old photos. "Hey, that's not a bad shot of me in my car. I'd keep it if it didn't give me the heebie-jeebies."

"I think I know why he's spying on us." Shane hands me an official-looking card. "Because it's his job."

The card features the colorful insignia of the State of Maryland, right above the words "Private Investigator."

"Son of a bitch." I squint at the fine print. "Probably shady. His license expired years ago." I kneel beside Travis Tucker—if that is his real name—and sift through his jacket pockets, turning up a pair of sunglasses and a cell phone.

"Business cards." Shane drops the wallet on the ground to shuffle through the stack. "Maybe one is his client."

"Does he have any money?" Not that I would steal it.

Shane opens the billfold. "Thirteen bucks and a check."

I try to access the cell phone's contact list, but it's password-protected.

"Uh-oh." Shane hands me the check. "We'd better call the others."

* * *

"Skywave is spying on us?"

Regina's hair stands on end even more than usual. All the DJs except Monroe, who's on the air, are gathered in the lounge to hear what happened.

"Where is this detective now?" Noah asks from the middle of the sofa, where he sits, arms crossed.

"In the Dumpster," I say as I pace past him for the third time, "with a rock on the lid no human could move. We gagged him so he can't scream when he wakes up."

"Which should be any minute." From his position near the door, Shane gives the clock a worried glance. "I hope."

At the table, Regina exchanges pensive looks with Jim and Spencer. "It's better if he doesn't wake up," she says quietly. "Or if he does, that he goes back to sleep forever."

I turn to her, positive I heard wrong. "You want to kill him? In cold blood?"

"I bet it'll be pretty warm." Jim tilts back his chair, his bare feet propped against the edge of the card table. "Unless you already did him in."

"We didn't," Shane snaps. "So let's quit jaggin' around and figure out what we're really going to do about Travis."

Regina shoves back her chair and stands up. "We have to get rid of him. It's better that way."

"Better for who?" Shane and I ask in unison. I'm glad he thinks they're just as cracked as I do.

"Better for the station," Regina replies, "better for all of us, but especially better for you." She glares at Shane. "You could be charged with assault."

"Assault is one thing," I point out, "but first-degree murder is a whole other ball game."

"Don't worry." Regina stretches her shoulders and neck. "You won't have to watch. I'll take care of it."

"I want to help." Jim gets up to join her. "I never killed someone on purpose before. Sounds like a trip."

"'*A trip*'?" My hands form useless fists. "You people are sick!"

"Honey, we're not people." Spencer follows Jim and Regina toward the door. "You keep forgetting that."

Shane blocks their exit. "Don't do it."

"You think that little leech," Regina points back at me, "cares what happens to you? She'll get off with a slap on the wrist as an accessory, and you'll go to jail. A jail with windows."

For perhaps the first time, Shane pulls himself up to his full height, towering over his maker. "What did you call her?"

Regina wavers under his simmering stare. "I'm trying to protect you. That's a hell of a lot more than she'll do."

"This isn't about me." I step forward and hold up Jolene's business card, the one Shane found in Travis's wallet. "I have a better idea, one that doesn't involve bloodshed."

"As if that's a plus," Regina says. "Come on, Noah."

"Can't we at least discuss it?" I fight to keep the panic out of my voice.

"If we let him go," says Noah, who hasn't moved from the couch, "Skywave will know the truth about us." He folds his arms tighter and hunches his shoulders. "But to kill him, it's wrong."

"It's not even necessary." I hold up Travis's camera. "I can delete the pictures."

"There could be others," Spencer points out.

"None of it is proof you guys are really vampires. We could say Shane put on plastic fangs for fun."

"It doesn't explain why he's so fast and strong," Jim says, "or why he had to knock this guy out to hide fake fangs."

Shane bristles. "So I overreacted. You would've done the same thing."

Jim shrugs. "No, I would've just killed him."

"Right." Regina shoves Shane aside with astounding ease. "Time to finish your half-assed job." She reaches for the door.

I open the credenza drawer and grab Franklin's box of sharpened pencils. I rip open the box and advance on Regina.

Before the others leap to defend her unlife, I fling the pencils, dozens of them, onto the floor. They spin and scatter across the rug and under the furniture.

Regina freezes. She stares at the pencils, then at me, with more hostility than I thought a Canadian could possess. A strangled cry escapes her throat as she fights the compulsion. Her hand tightens on the doorknob, then lets it go with a jerk.

She falls to her knees and crawls across the floor, gathering pencils and counting under her breath. Noah looks on, immobilized with indecision. Spencer and Jim shake their heads in sympathy and move toward the door.

"Don't you dare go without me!" Regina clutches the pencils so hard, most of them snap in two. "Bugger all! Where was I? Twenty-seven or twenty-six?" Her hands shake with rage as she drops the broken pencils and sifts through them again.

I turn to the others. "Listen. If we play our cards right, we can use this guy Travis to our advantage."

"Stop talking!" Regina is almost in tears. "I can't concentrate."

"If we can outwit Skywave," Shane says, "beat them at their own game, I say let's do it."

The others eye him, then Regina, as if trying to determine who's in charge.

Finally Jim shakes his head. "Too big an 'if.' Let's waste the bastard."

"Not without me!" Regina crawls under the table to retrieve the rest of the pencils. "Thirty-three, thirty-four— I'm almost done. Thirty-five—"

Jim opens the door. "What the hell?"

The detective is slumped on the bottom stairs, his head against the banister.

I step back. "It's Travis."

Regina blurs past me and pounces, grabbing the detective by the front of his shirt. Without waiting for him to scream or beg, she plunges her fangs into his throat. Shane moves to stop her, but before he gets there, she hurls Travis to the floor and starts to gag and cough like a cat with a hairball.

"He's already dead." She swabs the inside of her mouth with her finger. "Yecch. It's like biting Jell-O."

"No way." Shane kneels beside Travis. "He hasn't had time to get cold, unless he was—" He turns Travis on his side, revealing two other puncture wounds in his neck. "—drained."

"You said you didn't kill him," Spencer says.

"I didn't. I definitely didn't bite him." Shane looks at me. "You were there."

True. But in the dark I might not have seen Travis's wound.

Shane catches my dubious expression and stands to face me. "Ciara, I couldn't have done this. There wasn't time, and besides, I don't kill people."

I back away, hands out, trying to speak in a soothing voice. "You felt threatened. He fought back, right?"

"How can you believe I'd do this and then lie to you about it? Don't you know me better than that?"

"Guys? He's not dead." Jim is examining Travis's face. "Unless we stick an 'un' in front of it."

He turns the man's head to reveal a mouth full of blood. The teeth and gums are stained red like in a denture commercial.

I take a step closer. "Couldn't that just be from—"

Travis's eyes pop open. We all jump, but I'm the only one who screams when his fangs appear.

He starts to twitch and flop, shrieking with what sounds like pain. Jim tightens his hold on his shoulders. "Shh, don't freak out, man. We're here to help."

Travis breaks out of Jim's grip with the ease of a bat from a spiderweb. He leaps at me. I have time for one step backward before he knocks me to the ground.

"No!" My heels pedal the thin rug as I try to scramble out of his hands, one of which tightens around my waist while the other flattens my shoulder against the hard floor. Quick as a snake, his mouth slashes forward. I use my last breath to scream.

Shane's face appears above us, his arm looped around Travis's neck, barely holding him off me. I shove against the detective's chest, but Shane and I together can't match the strength of such a desperate hunger. In Travis's watery green eyes I see that it's a struggle for his survival against mine.

"Someone help me!" Shane shouts, but no one responds. "For fuck's sake, she's our friend!"

"And he's one of us now." Regina appears in my field of vision, arms crossed. "He needs blood."

"He'll kill her!" Shane's face is red from the strain. Travis is drooling now, bloody saliva dripping onto my neck.

"Maybe not," Spencer says. "And he'll die if he doesn't drink."

"Man, that is not cool," Jim observes, "turning someone, then leaving them to starve."

I hurl pleading gibberish through a gurgle of tears.

"I swear," Shane gasps, "if one of you doesn't pull him off right now, I'll—"

Suddenly Travis is jerked away from me. I hear a crash against the far wall, then lift my head to see Travis collapsed on the sofa, stunned.

Monroe stands next to us, looking down at Shane. He puts his hands in his pockets. "You'll what?"

Travis lunges again, but Monroe grabs him with a deft gesture and suspends him off the ground, feet kicking. For the first time, WVMP's oldest DJ looks straight at me.

"Run."

I stumble to my feet and launch myself up the stairs.

At the top, I freeze, staring at the front door. Whatever killed Travis is out there.

I lock the door, grab another stash of sharpened pencils from Franklin's desk, then scramble into David's office.

The lock's not enough. I slide two chairs and the small table against the door, then huddle beneath the desk.

For a minute or maybe longer, I hear nothing but my own unsteady breath. I clutch the pencils and take a few practice stabs at the air.

Footsteps approach the door. I hold my breath.

"Ciara?"

Shane. My voice sticks in my throat. He's one of them.

"Ciara, I know you're in there. I followed your scent. I'm alone, I swear."

"Where is he?"

"They took him to our apartment to give him some bank blood, just to take the edge off. Then they'll go visit a donor, one of the experienced ones."

"Brilliant idea." I spit out my words through the tears clogging my throat. "Why didn't they think of that before, instead of waiting for him to eat me like he was their pet python?"

"I don't know." He hesitates. "But I think they feel bad about it now."

A scoff is all I have to say about that.

"Can I come in?"

I shrink farther under the desk. "I don't think I like vampires anymore."

"Yeah, me neither."

He waits in silence, though he could easily pick the lock and shove aside the furniture to get to me.

Finally I go to the door and listen hard against its wooden surface for other presences. Nothing. I pull back the table and chairs and open the door.

Shane moves slowly, as if I'll spook and run away again, then puts his arms around me. I tremble, teeth chattering so hard it brings on an instant headache. The feeling reminds me of our first night together, when he nearly took my life. I should push him away, go home, pack my bags, and drive far out of the range of his perky, super-sensitive nose. Instead I pull him closer and let what little warmth he has seep into my skin and soothe the shivers.

We stay like that for a long time, saying nothing, until I state the obvious. "You saved my life."

"Monroe saved your life. And Noah, who went to get him."

"But you started it."

"Then I guess you owe me."

My knees go weak, literally. The adrenaline of the attack has worn off, and so has the triple mocha with organic two percent milk and a pump-and-a-half of coconut syrup. I need to lie down, but . . .

"Come home with me," I tell Shane.

He eases me out of his embrace far enough to look into my eyes. "You don't owe me that much."

"I don't want to be alone tonight."

He lets out a deep sigh, then brushes the hair from my forehead to kiss it. "Are you sure?"

"I've never been so sure of anything. But then again, I'm suffering from shock and sleep deprivation." I blink at him. "Which actually shrinks the list of things I'm sure of, so this seems like a safe bet."

"It is safe. I promise."

He takes my hand and leads me home.

20

Fragile

By the time we arrive at my apartment door, my mind has cleverly locked away the terror of the recent past to focus on that of the immediate future, on what awaits us at the top of these stairs.

I avoid Shane's eyes as we ascend side by side. Sex was probably implied in my invitation, but after what just happened, I'm not sure I'm ready. I wish I had wine, but one drink would snag my last scrap of consciousness. Even now it's just nervous energy keeping me awake.

I stop outside my room and turn to Shane. "Why don't you get something to drink while I—I mean, not drink. Yes, drink—from the fridge. I'll have iced tea." I step back into my bedroom, trying to muster a seductive gaze. "Give me a minute to put on something a little less Almost Got Killed In." I start to close the door.

"Ciara?"

"Yes?"

He rubs his face and hesitates a moment. "Nothing red, okay?"

Ah. I see. Deirdre wore red the night he drank from her. He told her on the phone, *Red is good*. Good, as in, thirst-inducing.

I shut the door.

Damn his feral instincts, I look hot in red. I sift through my lingerie drawer. Tiger stripes? Leopard spots? Definitely not—should probably downplay the wild-animal aspects considering I was almost eaten alive less than a half hour ago. If only I'd had a bridal shower—without a wedding, of course—I'd have a collection of demure yet alluring white teddies.

My mind and my eye arrive together at the solution. I slip into said solution, then light a few candles and turn off the lamp before lying on the bed. When Shane knocks, I invite him in.

He opens the door and sees me. The force of his laughter sends him halfway out into the hall.

"Thanks," I tell him. "That really sets the mood."

He approaches, all caution and tension gone, and sits next to me on the bed. "You're like a warrior, wearing the mantle of her fallen enemy."

"Jolene's far from fallen."

"You'll take care of that soon." He traces the edge of the letters on the white tank top. "I can't imagine you as anyone's 'Bride 2B.'"

"Because I'd look ridiculous in virginal white?"

He takes his hand away and sets my tea on the night-stand. "Because you don't like to be tied down."

I'm too tired for that discussion. "But hey, if I ever do

get engaged, I'll already have the shirt. They say that's half the battle." I rest my increasingly heavy head on the pillow. "Come here."

He stretches out on his side facing me. "I've dreamed of this, your hair spread across a pillow." He strokes it, making my scalp tingle. "I wish I could see it in the sunlight."

"I'll get you a picture. You can put it next to the one of my alphabetized CD shelves. Have your very own Ciara Griffin gallery."

This remark seems to spark a thought. "Is Griffin your real last name?"

"You think I made it up? Playing on the word 'grift' to laugh at the world?"

"Did you?"

"Pretty much. Hold still." I reach out and ski-jump my finger off the end of his nose. "I've been dying to do that ever since we met."

He snorts. "You're a very kinky girl."

"I'm a very tired girl."

"So what's your real last name?"

My goofy smile fades. "It's not important. I'm not that person anymore."

"It's exhausting, isn't it? Trying to outrun the past?"

I don't answer, hoping this thought will lead to his story of how he became a vampire. Yet I'm not sure how long I could stay awake listening to his soothing voice.

When he doesn't continue, I say, "What were you like when you were alive?"

"Probably not your ideal mate." His fingers trickle down my neck to my shoulder. "I had depression. Pretty bad at times."

"Did it go away when you turned?"

"It's part of who I am, so not entirely. Becoming a vampire doesn't give you a personality transplant. But it helped the chemical part. It ended the medical causes, the same way it would cure me if I'd had diabetes or a drug addiction." His voice stays nonchalant. "Which I did."

"Wow. That's rough."

"The way I treated myself, it was a miracle I made it to twenty-seven with all my extremities intact." He gives a wry smile. "If I hadn't died, I would've died by now."

"I'm glad you didn't die. I mean, I'm glad you did. I mean, I'm glad you're here." I touch his chest. "Really glad."

"I think we're done talking." He draws his finger down the neckline of the tank top, between my breasts. I close my eyes to savor the sensation, and suddenly feel like I'm plummeting, then tipping over like at the bottom of a carnival ride.

I jerk my eyelids apart. "Do you want some music?"

He shakes his head. "All I want to hear is you."

Aww, he's so roman—

The next sound *I* hear is that of my own snoring. I rub my eyes and see Shane lying on his back next to me.

"God, I'm so sorry. How long was I asleep?"

"About three minutes. Plenty of time to have my way with you. You liked it, judging by the way you flopped around."

I giggle like a drunk girl. "Can we try this again?"

"Maybe tomorrow." He tugs at the sheets, sliding them out from under my body, then pulls them over me. "Tonight, just sleep."

"Don't go."

"Nothing but the sun will make me leave."

"Set the clock so you don't catch fire," I mumble.

"I did, plus the alarm on my cell phone as a backup."

I hear him blow out the candles, then take off his jeans and shirt. I want to open my eyes to see him, but exhaustion has glued my lids together.

Shane slides under the sheets and pulls me close. The feel of his skin against mine should start my blood racing, should yank me into instant horniness. But instead it just makes me think how right and safe it feels to have him in my bed, and makes me think how much I love him.

Wait . . .

Oh, crap.

My alarm cries out, echoed by a beeping across the room. Darkness shrouds the bedroom window. An arm reaches over me and silences the clock. I close my eyes again, hoping sleep won't let go.

It doesn't. The last thing I feel is a kiss on my bare shoulder, then the emptiness of an unshared bed.

My eyes open to a yellow glow around my window. The reawakened alarm clock says 7:30. I smack the snooze button and turn over, where my arm flops onto the other pillow and hits a piece of paper.

Lying on the indentation from his head is a note from Shane:

> *Ciara,*
> *I set your coffee to start brewing at 7:20, so it should be ready by now. I put three sugars in the bottom of*

the mug, so just pour and stir. I know you like it strong
and sweet.

    Shane

P.S.: The Dave Matthews Band should be filed under
D, not M. I'll fix it tonight.

The smell of fresh-brewed coffee drags me out of bed by the nostrils. Though the seven hours of slumber barely made the minimum payment on my sleep debt, I'm refreshed and alert enough to walk in a straight line toward the kitchen. I realize with no small shred of astonishment that I slept better last night next to a vampire than I have in years.

My feet stop. I stare across the room at the coffee-maker, whose orange light glows with pride to signal the brewing of another satisfying pot. But I'm not looking at the coffee. I'm remembering my last thought before I fell asleep in Shane's arms.

That I love him.

The coffeemaker plops one last drop into the carafe, to accentuate my epiphany.

It's a delusion, an emotional mirage, a by-product of exhaustion and gratitude. He did save my life, after all.

My feet unfreeze and take me to the pot. Three sugars sit at the bottom of the beagle mug. I reach for the pot and realize I'm still holding his note. Instead of throwing it away, I transfer it to my left hand, which, against orders, clutches it like a sacred relic. I stare down in annoyance.

The phrase "Bride 2B" mocks me from my chest.

Hmm . . .

Jolene.

Travis.

As I pour the coffee, I realize that the man who tried to kill me could end up saving us all.

Franklin greets me at the office door with a stack of plates and forks. "It's about time. I've had to sit here smelling that thing for fifteen minutes." He sees the thermos in my hand. "Good, you brought some decent coffee."

"I need to talk to you and David right away." I glance past him at my desk. On it sits an object with a large clear, plastic lid. "What the hell is that?"

"An olive branch, apparently. Hopefully a chocolate-flavored, butter-cream-icing olive branch."

I go to my desk, expecting the strange item to explode any moment. It's a large sheet cake with white icing and a label from a local all-night supermarket. Scrawled across the surface in green decorating-tube frosting is one word: SORRY. Four initials, T, S, J, and R, appear at the bottom, penned with a thinner decorating tube. Off to the side is a roughly drawn frowny face with tiny fangs.

I can barely lift my jaw to speak. "They stood there last night while I almost got eaten, and to make up for it, they buy me a *cake*?"

"Can we eat it now? I didn't have breakfast." Franklin pops the lid. "Do you want a corner piece?"

"I don't want any piece! I don't want anything from them."

David opens his office door. "What's going on? Ooh, cake."

"You won't believe what's going on." I relate last night's harrowing events.

Franklin displays his typical lack of wonder. "I told you those pencils would come in handy."

David shakes himself out of shock. "Why didn't you call me when it happened?"

"Hey, I was too busy trying not to be ground into human hamburger meat, okay?"

My phone rings, from the basement line. Shane's checking in on me—how sweet. I pick up the receiver. "My hero!"

"It's just a twenty-dollar cake," Regina says. "You did get it, right?"

"You—" Every profanity in my arsenal strives to be the first out of my mouth, leaving me speechless.

"Shane said I should apologize directly instead of through baked goods."

"How could you—"

"So I'm sorry for almost watching you die. I got caught up in the moment. The way you were screaming—"

"Stop—"

"—you're lucky we didn't all fall down and take a slurp."

"After all I've done for you, you would've let that thing tear out my throat. I thought you were my friends!"

"We are," she says calmly. "We're also vampires. We look out for each other."

"What did you do with—" I can't say my almost-killer's name. "—with him?"

"He's here, under our care. Poor kid's tired and cranky, like a baby switching from breast milk to formula."

"Pardon my lack of giving a shit. Put him on the phone." I don't want to talk to him now or ever, but I need answers about Jolene and Skywave.

"He's not ready to interact with people. Monroe and Spencer and Jim are taking him to find his maker tonight."

"Let me guess: Gideon?" I give David a pointed look.

"Yep, the scuzzbag," Regina says. "This was the first shot from his camp. They want us to stop the campaign."

"If he's so dangerous, why take Travis to see him?"

"They belong together, at least while Travis is young. It's a vampire thing. But more importantly, it's time to negotiate. Gideon told Travis to tell us that next time, he'll leave a dead body where the police can trace it back to us."

"Won't that defeat Gideon's goal of keeping vampires a secret?"

"It would defeat everything, but us first. Reminds me of the Cold War. We've got to lower tensions without totally capitulating." A moaning comes in the background. "I better go take care of Travis. Tell Elizabeth to meet the guys at Gideon's place tonight."

"For what?"

Regina sighs. "For détente."

21

Bigmouth Strikes Again

I've never ridden in a Mercedes before, not even an old one like this. Even the tan vinyl of the backseat feels elegant. I try not to stroke it too much.

"Our file on Gideon is pretty slim," Elizabeth says to David, who sits in the passenger's seat. "We know he's well over a hundred, probably American, and that he runs a compound out in the Catoctin Mountains, not far from Camp David. It's sort of a sanctuary for old vampires who can't hack reality anymore. Until now he's been content to leave the rest of the world alone. In fact, he seems fanatical about keeping his vampires free of human influence."

"Why?" I ask.

"Notions of purity, I suppose. Superiority."

"What about you? Do you think vampires are better than humans?"

"Certainly not." She looks at David. "Really, I don't."

I lean forward. "Let me make sure I have these factions

straight: The Control protects humans from vampires, right?"

"When necessary," Elizabeth says. "But we also protect vampires from themselves."

"Sometimes at the cost of their freedom."

"Only when—"

"Let me finish my thought. Gideon's gang also wants to protect vampires, but they want more than just to survive. They want isolation and absolute freedom, and they're willing to kill humans like Travis to get it."

She frowns at me in the rearview mirror. "So it would appear."

A faint queasiness spreads through my gut. We're about to enter the domain of a vampire survivalist, escorted by the embodiment of everything he hates.

It starts to rain as we take the exit for Thurmont, Maryland. As we enter a valley between the mountains, WVMP's signal and Noah's reggae tunes crackle and fade to static. Elizabeth switches off the radio.

"I've been thinking about this all day," she says, "and I've come to a decision." She pauses and looks at each of us, clearly relishing our curiosity.

Finally David says, "A decision about what?"

"I'm not going to sell the station."

I don't dare believe my ears. David gasps and says, "Why not?"

"It's exactly what Gideon would want. I sell VMP, the campaign ends, and he wins." Her hands tighten on the steering wheel. "I can't have that. We're going to make it the best damn radio station ever—*with* vampires."

"What if he comes after us again?" David asks her.

"Now that he's made a move, the Control will dispatch

a security team to protect the station until he's—until the threat has been neutralized."

I scoff. "So someone had to die before the Control would protect us? Travis could've killed me, you know."

"I'm sorry." She shakes her head. "But no law enforcement agency sets up round-the-clock guard just because of a threatening phone call. Look at all the battered women killed after a lot more warning than Gideon gave us. There aren't enough resources to make the world safe for everyone."

"Hey, Ciara?" David turns in his seat to face me. "Congratulations. You did it."

"No, Gideon did it."

"Not entirely," Elizabeth says. "I wouldn't keep the station just to spite Gideon. If it were still hemorrhaging money, I'd sell it in a heartbeat."

"Oh. Good. I guess." I'm glad no one mentions that without the campaign, Gideon would still be a happy hermit, and there'd be one less dead detective. "Whatever the reason, thank you."

David's gratitude—and abject adoration—requires no words as he gazes at Elizabeth. I wonder what her change of heart means for their twisted relationship.

She slows the car and peers through the wet windshield at a group of mailboxes, the only ones in sight on this dark and wooded road. Elizabeth glances at a sheet of paper taped to the dashboard. "This is it, according to our files."

We bumble up the steeply sloping lane, which becomes gravel, then dirt, as it enters a thicker patch of woods. I see nothing but trees blurred by sheets of rain.

We come to a gate in a high chain-link fence topped

with barbed wire. Elizabeth pulls up to a small white box. She rolls down her window and pushes a button under a round speaker. "We're here to see Gideon."

After a moment of static, a raspy male voice says, "Front door." It's hard to tell from only two words, but I don't think it's the same guy as the threatening caller.

The gate swings open, and we continue down the lane, which ends in front of a long white rancher. On the porch sits a single empty rocking chair, nodding in the blustery wind. The yard is about two acres large, with what looks like a playground toward the back.

Several antique and classic cars, including Jim's blue Charger, gather on the grassy hillside to the left of the house. We pull in among them.

Elizabeth leans over and opens the glove compartment. In the process, her arm slides against David's knee. His face goes all blissy. Yuck, just when I thought he was over her, she reels him back in. But at least he still has a job.

She sits up and offers two wooden stakes. David takes one.

"I'd rather go unarmed," I tell her, "than carry something I don't know how to use. Besides, they're bound to search us."

"That's the point," Elizabeth says. "I want them to know we mean business." She pulls my wrist forward and slaps the blunt end of the stake into my palm. "It's not complicated. One hard jab to the heart."

"I know, I know." I want to drop the thing, but her hand surrounds mine.

"That's only half of it. You have to pull the stake out again."

"Why?"

"Because that's where—" Elizabeth turns her head. "Tell her, David."

He looks away, out the window. "That's where their life flows out."

"Don't whitewash it." Her voice is sharper than the thing I've got in my hand.

"After the stake is pulled out," David says, "their bodies go through the hole."

"Where?" I ask.

Elizabeth titters. "That's the eternal question for all of us, isn't it? Heaven? Hell? The never-ending void?"

"No, I mean, do they go through the hole and splatter all over the room, or do they just disappear?"

David and Elizabeth look at each other. His face is etched with guilt; hers, with bitterness.

"Something in-between," he tells me. "Pray you never have to see it."

The music hits us even with the door closed. Standing on the porch, we can hear the thumping of a swing rhythm and the high calling of trumpets. Through a bay window to our right, thin curtains show shadows dipping and swaying with acrobats' ease.

Elizabeth knocks hard. A wind gust drenches us with rain and scoots the rocking chair across the porch.

The door opens to reveal a tall dark man, powerfully built enough to make his magenta zoot suit look macho.

"I am Lawrence," he says in a voice as deep as a foghorn. I notice that it doesn't match the one on the phone or the security gate. Apparently Gideon likes to spread out his flunky work.

He tips back the brim of his felt hat and examines us. "Us" meaning Elizabeth. The look he gives me and David is the kind you give dog shit to avoid stepping in it.

Finally, after submitting her to a gaze more penetrating than an MRI scan, he nods at Elizabeth. His large, dark palm unfolds. "Give up the tree bits."

I pull the stake out from under my shirt and hand it over with relief. I'd be more comfortable packing an Uzi.

The living room just inside the front door is larger than I expected; the wall between it and the adjoining dining room must have been knocked down to create one huge space. A space filled with vampires.

Some bop and jump to the wild, pulsing music; others stroll the perimeter with drinks of wine or blood, smoking cigarettes through long, silver-tipped holders. Judging by their dress, all are at least as old as Monroe. The epochs mix and mingle: a bob-haired woman in a red flapper outfit fox-trots with a man in a dirt-brown bowler hat and morning suit.

"Excuse me." A plump young woman with curly red hair nearly steps on my foot. She brushes past in her cigarette girl outfit and edges around the room with her tray, delivering smokes and drinks. I'm pretty sure she's human, judging by the way she wobbles in her high-heeled pumps.

Despite the vampires' aura of cool, they all look faded. They glance at us with empty eyes, moving, dancing, and speaking as if they're going through the motions of an endlessly repetitive existence, the meaning or purpose for which they've long forgotten. I hate the thought of the VMP vamps getting those cold, dead eyes. Better to be weird than catatonic.

"They're waiting for you downstairs," Lawrence tells us as he opens one of the doors in the hallway to our left.

The stairway is so dimly lit, I can't even see to the bottom. Elizabeth steps in front of me and starts to descend. I grope for the banister and follow, willing my knees to keep their strength. David comes up behind me, with Lawrence bringing up the rear.

At the bottom of the stairs lies what looks like a typical basement family room. The only light comes from a large TV in the corner with a tiny black-and-white screen. My eyes adjust to see Spencer, Monroe, and Jim lounging in a set of armchairs.

Someone's pacing behind the love seat with shaky steps. He sees me, and his hands fly to his mouth.

Travis.

For one moment, as I look into the eyes of the creature who tried to kill me, I wish I had that stake back in my hand. But his trembling fingers and tight face tell me that like most wild animals, he's more afraid of me than I am of him.

Jim stands and takes Travis's arm. "Go on now," he says, "tell her you're sorry."

"No time for this jive," growls Lawrence. "Gideon is waiting."

Travis jolts at his maker's name. His expression changes to rapture, like someone about to meet a celebrity. I notice he's lost the mustache—for easier slurping, I suppose. He looks younger and halfway cute now.

I look around, expecting to see Gideon in another corner, but we're led to yet another staircase, beneath the one we just descended, and I realize this is no ordinary house.

We descend the stairs to the next level. Though the

basement above held a musty smell, this second one feels dry and clean. I peer down the hallways lined with closed doors. The recessed ceiling lights provide an almost human amount of illumination.

Before turning to descend the next flight of stairs, Jim and Elizabeth stop on the landing and sniff. Her eyes narrow in anger, while Jim looks intrigued. I tap Elizabeth's elbow.

"It's the farm," she whispers to me and David. "Just like we suspected."

Odd, it doesn't smell like a farm—no animal manure or straw or . . .

Oh. They don't keep animals here.

"Disgusting," she mutters.

"But convenient," Jim points out as we continue down the stairs toward the next level. "It's like having room service instead of eating out."

"You want to live here?" she snaps. "Go ahead."

"I'm too young for this place." He lowers his voice. "It's full of squares."

I glance at David beside me to see if we should worry about turning into livestock. He looks pissed rather than frightened, so maybe these people are volunteers. Food and shelter in exchange for blood might be a good trade-off if a person came from rough circumstances. But it feels like prison, a reverse image of the Control's vampire retirement homes. I have a strong desire to be somewhere altogether else.

Behind us, Travis mumbles to himself like a toddler. "Ice train. Slowly and carefully. No, I don't want chicken." At least I think that's what he says.

At the bottom of this longest staircase, our guide leads

us to the right. This looks like the bottom floor—not that I can see much in the nearly nonexistent light.

We head down a narrow stone corridor, past open bedrooms containing writhing, moaning figures in candlelit shadows. Even my limited human nose smells blood. My pace slows until Travis bumps into me from behind. He gasps and leaps back.

Someone takes my hand. David. I sigh in relief and squeeze hard. His skin is warm with life that comes from eating hamburgers and salads and Nutty Buddys, and that's all that matters.

Ahead to the right, near the end of the corridor, firelight dances against the wall. Our guide ushers us through a door on the left, which is flanked by two beefy guards who look like sewer rats on steroids.

A massive man sits cross-legged in the corner behind a campfire, his back to the wall. His face is hidden under the rim of a battered light gray fedora. The flames illuminate what must have once been a high-fashion morning suit and waistcoat. His posture is slumped but so perfectly motionless it gives the impression of rigidity and control.

Lawrence shuts the door behind us, blotting out all sound but the crackling logs and Travis's shaky wheezing.

The man raises his head. David and I step back. The chills skipping among my vertebrae make my first reaction to Monroe seem like one long yawn.

His wide, ink-black eyes wield a movie-star magnetism beneath low, brooding brows. The look reminds me of Orson Welles in *Macbeth*, with just as much sanity. His dark hair, slicked back, sets off the flawless ivory of his skin, the color of piano keys in candlelight.

"Welcome," he says, without a trace of it in his voice.

At the sound, Travis flings himself on the dirt next to the man who must be Gideon. Oblivious to the fire a few inches away, the detective presses his forehead to the ground next to his maker's knee and utters a rapid, incoherent plea.

In response, Gideon pats him on the head, causing Travis to shudder and moan. Then the older vampire gives what seems to be, from his end, a light shove. This small effort sends Travis tumbling across the room to crash into the opposite wall. The other vamps gasp and hiss.

"Bastard," Elizabeth snarls to Gideon. So much for détente. "First you turn him and leave him without food, then you reject him? What kind of vampire are you?"

"If I don't conform to your code," Gideon says evenly, "it's for a good reason."

"And what might that be?"

"He's an example, a demonstration, if you will." Gideon extends his arm toward Travis and crooks his finger once. Travis scuttles to him like a broken-legged crab. When he gets close, Gideon flattens his palm in a stop gesture. Travis freezes, staring at his maker with pleading eyes. I want to look away, for fear that Gideon will order Travis to stick his head in the fire. The detective would do it, happily—their connection is that palpable.

"Very nice," Elizabeth says. "A demonstration of your sadism, like we needed further proof."

"A demonstration of my power." Gideon keeps his unblinking gaze locked with Travis's. "And of what will happen again if the chicanery doesn't stop."

A corner of my stomach begins a cold burn.

"This WVMP foolishness," he continues, "telling the truth disguised as a lie. Duping people with their own skepticism. The slickest grift is no grift at all." He shifts his eyes to me. "Isn't that right, Ciara?"

I stammer, my throat pinned shut. It feels like he's inhaling me with every breath.

"It must end before someone gets hurt," he says.

"With all respect, sir," Spencer says as he kneels beside the trembling Travis, "somebody already got hurt."

"Then help him if you feel charitable." Gideon waves them away. "The life of any one vampire is not my concern. My duty lies with us all." He regards David, Elizabeth, and me. "Some humans won't be fooled by your gimmick. They'll come to understand that vampires truly exist. Then we'll have a war." He spreads his hands. "Or a curious person might want to see what happens if one of your friends meets the rising sun, or gets a taste of fire." He lifts a log out of the flames and waves the burning end at the vampires, who jump back. "Just to jazz up a Saturday night."

Maybe he has a point. Maybe this campaign has put them in mortal danger. Maybe things were better before. Safer.

Then I think of Shane's transformation over the last month, the way he's learned to love new music, learned to drive a stick shift—the way he's learned to *learn* again. How he looks happy to exist in this crazy, wide-open, scary-as-shit world of Today. The Today that makes him look forward to Tomorrow.

"You're right," I say.

Gideon's eyebrows pop up, then scrunch together, as if he's surprised and confused to be addressed by a mere human.

"All of that could happen," I continue, "despite our

precautions. They could all go *poof*, either by accident or design. But a vampire's life—a human's life, for that matter—is always a precarious thing." I look at the walls of his cave. "Better to hide in the light than hide in the dark."

"This is not a hideout," Gideon says. "This is a fortress."

I keep my voice soft. "And what's a fortress for? Keeping out the things that scare you."

"The things that *threaten* us." His eyes narrow on Elizabeth's face. "I've seen what they do"—his voice shakes with rage—"those Control humans and their vampire whores."

Elizabeth maintains a stony demeanor. "The Control protects vampires."

"By keeping us in line," he says with a snarl, "by serving the goals of humans. We have a right to live in peace."

"You call this peace?" She points at the ceiling. "Holding humans captive?"

"Our guests choose to be here," he says.

"Because you've turned yourself into a cult leader, like Jim Jones or David Koresh." She stops and shakes her head. "You have no idea who those men are. You have no idea how backward this all is, because you're still stuck in World War One. Which is why you and every other vampire need the Control."

This undead *Crossfire* episode is getting us nowhere. I step forward, closer to the flames than any of the vampires will dare, and speak to Gideon again. "If you've been spying on us, you know how happy the DJs have been this summer. They're truly in the world. They're living."

"Perhaps living at the price of survival," he says.

"Isn't that their choice to make? You talk about freedom from the Control, but you'll never be free if you let fear make all your choices." I can hear my mom and dad speak through me, and in my mind the tiny room turns into a crowded tent full of lights and music and hallelu-jahs. "I saw people who couldn't walk because they were afraid to fall. I saw them rise out of their wheelchairs, throw away their crutches, and dance a jig, the moment they let go of that fear."

"Your mind tricks may work on weak humans," Gide-on rumbles, "but vampires are not human."

"You're wrong." I point at the three DJs. "Humans still live inside them, whether they admit it or not."

Gideon looks amused. "And how long have you known them?"

"Long enough to know they believe in things. They believe in the music with every scrap of their souls. They believe in finding a balance between today and yesterday. Hell, they even believe I'm a crappy poker player."

"Why should that impress me?"

"Because believing is what being alive is all about." Daddy would've liked that one. I move in for the close. "Gideon, just let go of that fear, tell it to pull its poi-sonous claws out of you." I gesture to the fire. "It's fear keeping you crammed into that corner because you don't trust anyone with your back. Fear made your neighbors in Camp David build bombs so that they have to hide under-ground like moles from a hawk. And it's fear, in the end, that'll kill us all."

Imaginary *amen*s reverberate in my mind as I turn to Elizabeth. She nods slowly and smiles. I step to her side to create a united front. Yeah, sistah.

After a long moment, Gideon speaks. "You think you know all about fear, little girl?"

He holds out his hand to Lawrence, who slaps a stake into his palm. Gideon keeps his focus on me as his arm flicks back, then forward. The stake blurs through the air.

I look down to see my shirt dripping with blood. Holy shit, did he just stake me? I wish I'd answered my mom's e-mail.

My knees turn to gelatin as cries of dismay echo from a distance. Someone sobs the word "no" again and again.

My hands grab at my chest to pull out the stake, which, I realize, isn't there. The drops of blood all point from the same direction.

Elizabeth.

22

Darkness on the Edge of Town

I turn to see her crumpled on the floor, head and shoulders in David's lap, legs skewed to the side. The bottom half of the stake protrudes from her chest, which is blanketed in blood. She clutches David's shirt.

"P-pull it out. Please." She coughs a spurt of blood over her chin. "It hurts, it hurts so bad."

David's face is soaked in tears. "I can't."

"Please." Her voice pitches up to a spine-grating octave. "Pull it out, oh God, make it stop, David."

He leans over her and grips the stake. The muscles of his arm tighten, then release. "I can't do that." He lowers his head. "Not to you."

I kneel next to them and wrap my hands around the stake, covering his.

His grip tightens as he stares at me. "You don't understand."

"David!" Elizabeth lets loose a gurgling scream. She tries to cough again, but only pulls more blood into her lungs. Her eyes roll up to show pure white, and her hands flail at us, nails scratching my bare arms.

"David, she's in pain. We can stop it." I plant my feet under myself for better leverage. "On three, okay?"

His gaze meets mine with agony, then returns to her face.

"One," I whisper. She's looking at me instead of him. "Two." Come on, Elizabeth, give him one last look. Don't waste your final sight on my silly mug.

Her eyes close, and when they open again, they focus on David.

"I love you," he whispers.

"Three!"

I fall backward, the stake clutched in my fists. One of Gideon's door guards snatches the weapon from me. I sit up to see David cradling Elizabeth in his lap, stroking her hair. Blood gushes from the wound, but nothing else happens. Maybe Gideon missed her heart, or maybe she never was a vampire. Come to think of it, I've never seen her fangs.

Suddenly she begins to tremble, but it's not like any spasm I've ever seen. It's like every atom is vibrating, ready to trade places with another one at the opposite edge of her body. David lays her gently on the floor and backs away. He puts an arm around my shoulders and covers my eyes with the other palm. "Ciara, don't look."

I swipe his hand from my face but don't push him away. The others, except for Travis and Gideon, have already turned their heads. I clutch David's arm with both hands and watch.

The blood runs back into the hole, trickling like rain

down a windshield. Maybe the wound is healing itself, the way the scratches on Shane's back disappeared.

But now her flesh is being drawn toward the hole, flesh from her chest, her stomach—oh God, from everywhere, muscles stretching, bones creaking and snapping, all moving toward that single two-inch circle in her heart. The speed of the disintegration builds, but not fast enough to keep me from seeing her face stretch and tear, pulled downward as if it's melting off her skull.

I don't know if Elizabeth's collapse makes a noise, because I can't hear anything over the siren of my own shrieks. David clamps my mouth shut, and only then do I remember not to scream around vampires.

Elizabeth's not screaming, because her throat is slipping into the void, followed by her teeth, then her nose, then her eyes, staring into nothingness with what I hope is relief. Her hair rasps as it slides against her blouse and into the hole. Finally, limbs flop and flail against the dirt floor, fingers scraping trails in the dust as they're dragged toward the vacuum.

When it's over, a soft pop, then silence. David lets me go, and I crawl to the other corner, stomach heaving.

Someone far stronger than David grabs me and closes my mouth. "There'll be no vomiting on Gideon's floor, understand? Swallow it or choke on it. Your choice."

Tears squeeze from my eyes as I nod. One of the rat-faced guards lets me go, and I gulp the smoky air, hacking and belching.

"That," Gideon points to the place Elizabeth died, "never happens to a human. Plane-crash victims might be pulverized to almost nothing, but if you look hard enough, you can always find a tooth, a smear of entrails. Their bodies exist somewhere, even if they're fused with a hundred other bodies, or with concrete and steel. But Elizabeth is nowhere. She's nothing."

I stare at the pile of clothing and jewelry left behind, and suddenly notice they bear no stains. I examine my own clothes—clean. A minute ago they were spattered in blood. Even my hands bear no trace of Elizabeth's fluids.

"Nothing," Gideon repeats. He leans forward. "Now do you understand fear, Ciara?"

I clutch my knees, feeling a cold sweat trickle down my back. Shane's fangs, Regina's glare, even Travis's re-animation were one thing, but this—this is a whole other realm of wrongness.

Something can't just turn into nothing. Can't. Happen. But it just did. What else could happen? There are no rules, no boundaries, nothing for me to cling to. For a moment I feel like the panic will shatter me, and what's left of my body will soak into the soil a hundred feet below the ground.

"You may all go now," Gideon says to David, then turns to me. "Except you."

My heart goes cold. I whimper a wordless protest. I don't want to be livestock.

"No," David says in a hoarse voice. "We won't leave her behind for you to drink."

"I won't drink her." He keeps his gaze on my neck as he says, "Not if you bring me proof that the campaign is over. At sunset tomorrow." He regards Travis like an artist with a finished canvas. "Or I'll do more than drink her."

I start to tremble all over. As much as I don't want to be livestock, I want even less to be a vampire.

"Absolutely not." David crosses his arms over his chest, looking a lot less pathetic than he did a minute ago. "I'll stay instead."

"You have important work to do back at the station," Gideon says. "Besides, in your state, you'd be inclined to foolishness toward me. Just the girl."

Jim pushes past David to stand next to me. "I'll stay with her." He reaches down, takes my elbow, and helps me to my feet. I look at him, amazed and a little confused.

A smile slides over Gideon's face. "Yes, I think you could be useful."

Lawrence jerks his chin toward the door. "Upstairs."

I follow him and Jim into the hallway, then take a last look back at David's tearstained face. "Have Spencer drive you home," I tell him. "You don't look so good."

"Ciara—"

"I won't do anything stupid." I consider the events of the last ten minutes. "Anything else stupid."

Jim and I are being held in an empty "guest" room, the furnishings of which consist of a full-size bed with yellow-white posts and a matching nightstand. One wall is paneled with laminated wood and the rest painted a dusty pink.

Jim is sprawled across the bed, staring at the ceiling and tapping his fingers in a slow rhythm against his chest. I'm huddled on the floor in the far corner, every muscle taut. It's been ten minutes since Lawrence locked us in here, and we have yet to speak.

Jim starts humming a familiar tune. After a few bars, I realize it's "Norwegian Wood" by The Beatles.

"Get it?" he says finally. "There are no chairs in this room, like in the song."

"Ha." I stare at the white wooden door, as if I can hold it shut with my eyes.

"I wouldn't have let that chick laugh at me."

"Who?"

"In the song. She leads him on and laughs at him."

"Oh." I blink for what feels like the first time in minutes. "I thought she was throwing herself at him and he turned her down."

"Why would you think that?"

"Because he sits on the rug instead of on the bed with her."

"She's not on the bed, she's on the rug."

"But she doesn't have any chairs because she wants him on the bed."

"She doesn't have chairs because she lives in a cruddy flat with cheap pine board." His voice drips with scorn. "That's what Norwegian wood is."

"Oh." I can't believe I'm having this conversation right now. "So it's just a song about a guy who didn't get laid? My version's more interesting."

He scoffs. "Tell that to John Lennon."

"John Lennon's dead," I state, with emphasis. "You know that, right?"

Jim lets out a long sigh through his nose. "Yes. I know that." He sits up suddenly. "You know what's interesting? What's interesting is why you interpreted the song that way, what it says about you." He tilts his head. "Have you scared a lot of men with your sexuality, Ciara?"

"No." I look away and rub my cold hands together. "Define 'a lot.'"

From the corner of my eye I see him staring at me. "Gideon can probably hear your heartbeat from all the way down in his cave."

"Great. Thanks for the info."

"What I mean is," he digs in his jeans pocket, "you need to calm down. And I've got just the thing." He unfolds a plastic Baggie containing a pair of rolled joints.

"No thanks." God only knows what those things are laced with. "I'd like to keep my wits about me."

"So you can do what, make a break for it?" He lights one of the joints and takes a hit. "Sometimes, Ciara, one must accept when one has no control over a situation. This is one of those times."

The door opens, and Gideon enters, as if to prove Jim's point. A chill breeze seems to precede him. Lawrence and the other two lackeys follow, one lugging an old-fashioned Baroque-looking radio, the kind that sat in everyone's living room back in the early fifties.

Without looking at Jim, Gideon crosses the room toward me, soft and deliberate as a lion. He takes my arm and leads me to the bed. His touch is cold, and though his fingers are well fleshed, I can feel the bones through them, as if they were talons. He sits on the edge of the bed with me and nods to his radio-carrying minion.

The guard sets the contraption on the floor with a thud. He adjusts one of the knobs until we hear the haunting strains of an early Cure song. The radio's single speaker turns the notes flat and hollow, making our surroundings feel more alien than ever.

"Whoa," Jim says. "The station's signal is a lot stronger than it used to be."

Plus we're on top of a hill, I realize but don't say

out loud. Gideon's touch makes my throat too tight to speak.

I hate this guy. Not just for killing Elizabeth; he may have had his own reasons for doing that. I hate him for killing Elizabeth as an answer to my words. If I had just kept my mouth shut, maybe this wouldn't have happened.

The song fades, and rather than Regina, it's Shane who comes on the air. "94.3 WVMP. Twenty minutes past midnight. Evening, *Drastic Plastic* listeners. Regina's gone on a bit of a bender, so I'm taking over early for her tonight. Letters of complaint can be sent—hold on, where, Regina? Oh, right. Up your own ass."

I admire his ability to hold it together on the air. It's like an act of defiance. I want to reach out and touch the speaker, connect with him through the low vibration of radio waves.

"Anyway," he continues, "it appears that some people out there, and you know who you are, are taking this vampire gimmick too seriously. Our situation's gotten a little 'stalky,' as the kids today might say. At least I think they might. So for everyone out there listening: once and for all, we're not—" He clears his throat, which I've never heard him do on the air. "We're not vampires. Okay? Moving on. This first song isn't from my time, but it's by a guy many call the 'godfather of grunge.' It was a favorite of a friend of ours who is no longer with us."

The first quiet strains of Neil Young and Crazy Horse's "Running Dry" trickle over the airwaves.

"Great song," Jim says. "Bet it was David's request."

I speak to Gideon without looking at him. "We can go now, right? He's made the announcement."

"It's a promising start. But I need proof of a more permanent commitment." He finally lets go of me and stands up. "I'll return before sunrise. I suggest you sleep." His fingertips graze my chin, bringing ice to my veins. "Tomorrow night might be a long one for you."

Gideon and the three guards exit, leaving the radio on.

Neil Young's slow, reverberating guitar mourns with a keening violin. They hold each other up like siblings at a funeral.

I used to think that this song's subtitle, "Requiem for the Rockets," was for people who had died. But Shane told me the Rockets were the band that eventually became Crazy Horse. Their "Requiem" meant abandoning what they used to be and moving on to a new beginning.

Which means that there's more than one kind of death in this world.

I try to take Gideon's advice, but I can't sleep. Despite having consumed both joints, Jim is anything but calm. He paces the floor, rubbing his cheeks and eyes and mouth, a sure symptom of bloodthirst. He glances over at me, lying in bed.

Great. He's got the munchies.

"Don't even think about it," I warn him. The secondhand marijuana smoke is the only thing keeping me from a fear-induced aneurism.

"I can smell them." He points to the air-conditioning vent in the ceiling. "The others are drinking, everywhere. But not me." He rubs his hands on the sides of his jeans. "It's like that time before I died, when I tried to go vegetarian to impress a girl, and all my friends were still eating burgers and steaks."

The doorknob rattles, then turns. The door opens to reveal Lawrence standing next to a short plump redhead. I recognize her as the cigarette girl from the party upstairs.

She beams up at Jim. "Room service?"

"Thank you," he groans in Lawrence's direction. He yanks the woman into the room and drags her to the bed.

"Hey!" I leap out of the way of their bodies and retreat to my original corner. Lawrence sends me a grin on his way out.

The room fills with moans of pain and pleasure. I crawl to the radio and turn up the volume, then lie on the floor beside it, folding my arm into a hard pillow.

Shane's voice is the lifeline I cling to as the scents and sounds of sex and bloodshed surround me. He must know I can hear him, because he plays every one of my "last songs" in order, starting with "Hard to Handle" and going through the summer, twenty-some tunes from the late eighties and early nineties. "I'm No Angel" by Greg Allman, Matthew Sweet's "Girlfriend," Cracker's "Low."

In the middle of Springsteen's "Human Touch," the room goes quiet. The door opens. I yank my mind out of my musical sanctuary.

Lawrence comes in and lifts the semiconscious girl from the bed. As he exits, Gideon enters, alone.

I stand and move behind the bed, as if Jim—naked, stoned, and satiated—can somehow protect me.

Gideon shuts the door. "Sit."

His will is like a hand reaching out. I sit on the bed and cover Jim's, uh, self with the bloodstained sheet. He stirs and shifts, then his eyes move behind his lids in REM sleep. So much for my knight in tie-dyed armor.

Gideon sits at the end of the bed, for once not trying to overwhelm me with his physical presence. I rub my arms to ward off the chill.

"Admit it," he says. "We fascinate you."

I can't speak and look at him at the same time, and right now his shadow-eyed face glues my gaze.

He grunts and continues. "You wouldn't be working at the station if we held no attraction. Haven't you ever wondered what it would be like to be one of us?" He holds up one finger. "Before you answer, you should know I can read a lie even better than you can."

Of course. He can hear my heartbeat, probably feel my body temperature rise and fall.

I clear my throat and look away. "Of course I've wondered. Everyone does, even people who don't believe in vampires." With an effort, I speak to his face, though not his eyes. "But I don't envy you. I like sunshine, I like food. Plus, I wouldn't want to outlive all my friends and family."

"Family?" His dark gaze sharpens. "You're close to your family?"

"Not now. But maybe someday. If I were a vampire, I'd have to leave them behind forever."

"No." He stands and begins to pace, slowly. "My father was a vampire. Rather than abandon his children, he turned each of us at the age of thirty-three. For me it was 1918." He smooths his brown, pinstriped waistcoat, regarding it like a window to the past. "Later that year I did the same to my son. He took ill with the Spanish flu and within a day was at death's door. It was an easy choice. He was only fifteen, with his whole life before him."

"Is your son here with you?"

Gideon slides his hands into his trouser pockets and regards the floor. "He was always intractable, especially after death. I tried to teach him to keep out of humans' way, and for several decades he stayed at my side, though never satisfied. Ten years ago he left me, headed west, and began hunting people indiscriminately, like a rabid animal."

Gideon turns the radio volume down to near silence. "The Control and I came to an agreement, that upon his capture, they would bring him here, where I would deal with him. In exchange I allowed them to inspect my compound to ensure I wasn't harming humans."

His hands form fists inside his pockets. "Naturally the traitorous worms double-crossed me. One of their agents staked Antoine in Memphis."

Antoine? My heart gives a sudden pound. *Memphis?* David said Elizabeth's maker was a teenager in human years. It couldn't be . . .

Gideon pauses, examining me, then begins to pace again. "They claimed it was a rogue agent going against orders, but they wouldn't give up the man's name, so I could never confirm their story. I had no choice but to believe it a sanctioned assassination." He stops and looks at me. "Now you know why I staked Elizabeth, why I lured her here in the first place."

He knows who she was. He staked his own—what, granddaughter?

I try to stay calm, keep bluffing. "I thought you brought us here to threaten the station into anonymity." Fear makes my lips flub the last word, so that it comes out "anemone."

"That as well. I've ended your silly and dangerous campaign, and avenged Antoine's death. You could say I've killed two birds with one stake."

I lower my gaze, my mind racing. So he murdered Elizabeth because she was a Control agent, not because of her relationship to his son, which he doesn't seem to know about.

But he could find out. I have to warn David. He and Elizabeth wouldn't have come here if they'd known Gideon was her maker's maker. Someone in the Control's upper ranks got careless or arrogant or both.

"Penny for your thoughts," Gideon says softly.

I shiver, but keep staring at the floor at my feet. "I was just thinking, I didn't know vampire lives could be so dramatic. It's terrible what happened to Anthony."

"Antoine."

"Yes. I'm sorry."

Gideon's silence seems to consume all the air in the room. He moves toward me, closer and closer, until his shoes enter my line of sight, less than a foot away.

When he speaks, his voice is low and soft. "Today you will learn that with a few exceptions, we are not so monstrous. Perhaps you will decide to stay." When I don't respond, he turns for the door. "And Ciara. Should you entertain any thoughts of escape, know this: If I don't find you in your room at sunset, your gentleman friend here will be staked. Slowly. Have a pleasant day."

As soon as the door shuts and locks, Jim sits straight up in bed.

I yelp and nearly choke on my own breath. "I thought you were asleep."

"I was faking it to maintain the element of surprise."

"It worked. On me."

"Besides, that girl was so coked up, I may never sleep again." He runs shaky hands through his curls. "We're in deep shit, aren't we?"

"Do you think Gideon knows who killed his son?"

"No, but the fact that your pulse skyrocketed when he said Antoine's name probably made him suspicious."

"I couldn't help it. What are we going to do?"

He looks around. "First we're going to find my pants."

I retrieve them from the corner and turn away to look for his shirt while he puts them on. I find it under the bed—a VMP Lifeblood of Rock 'n' Roll T-shirt.

"We'll have to stop selling these." I hand it back to Jim as he zips up his jeans. "T-shirts, bumper stickers. It's all over."

"But now that Elizabeth's dead, at least she can't sell to Skywave." Jim pulls the shirt over his head. "Right?"

My stomach plummets to the vicinity of my knees. "Elizabeth told us she decided not to sell."

"Did she tell Skywave?"

"I doubt she had the chance yet. It sounded like she'd just decided tonight." I sink onto the bed and put my head in my hands. "If she's dead, with no next of kin, then the business will be liquidated and its assets auctioned off."

Shane's voice returns to the radio. "It's five fifty-four on a Tuesday. Thanks to everyone who called in to express support—"

"Liquidated?" Jim says to me. "You mean it would be—"

"Turned into cash. Hold on, I want to hear this." I go to the radio and turn up the volume.

"—asked about VMP merchandise," Shane continues. "Sorry, but we won't be selling any more, so hang on to what you have. You got yourselves some sweet collector's items."

Jim seizes my shoulder. "The station'll be sold for parts? Like a broken-down car?"

"Pretty much."

He curses and starts to pace. I lean closer to hear Shane over Jim's muttering.

"—official press release later today detailing the disturbing incident that made us decide to end the campaign. So look for our pretty faces on the evening news."

"All these years I put in," Jim huffs. "I'm not a fucking asset!"

I turn to glare at him. "You're less than an asset, you're an employee. Now would you shut up for two seconds?"

Jim's rant grows louder. I press one ear against the speaker and plug the other with my finger.

"This last song goes out to those of you who greet this morning wondering if this could be your last sunrise. I've been there, many times. Parents, preachers, and politicians think rock music is the source of young people's despair. They don't understand it's just a reflection. They also forget that music can be a source of hope, a reason to live."

"I gotta get out of this place." Jim rattles the knob, then pounds on the solid wood. "Hey! Open the goddamn door!"

I press my ear against the speaker. What if it's my last "last song"? I think about falling asleep in Shane's arms last night, and a ball of anger forms inside me. If I die and miss out on sex with my hottest boyfriend ever, I'm going to be so pissed.

Jim slams the door again and again with his shoulder. I close my eyes and soak in the voice from afar.

"—music still has any power left in the world, I hope it can bring you strength. Good morning, and good—"

Jim picks up the radio, yanking the cord out of the outlet, and hurls it against the door. The radio shatters, but the door stands solid.

I stare at the silent, splintered pieces of what used to be my lifeline. "You are such an asshole."

Jim cracks his knuckles and nods, his breath slowing. "But I'm an asshole who feels better now."

"You couldn't wait ten more seconds?"

"Sorry." He sighs and sits heavily on the bed. "It's not so bad, you know. Being a vampire. It's actually pretty far out."

"Did you do it on purpose?"

He stares at the ceiling. "Hard to say. It just kind of happened, and I went with the flow, you know?"

"How much do you remember?"

"I remember the Doors were playing onstage. It took the whole set for me to die. They took their time with me. They took turns."

"The Doors?" I had no idea.

"No, the vampires."

I hold my wrists in my hands, feeling both pulses. "What's it like to die?"

"For me it was really psychedelic. But it's probably like any trip—you get out of it what you put into it. Spiritually, I mean." Jim regards me with an inscrutable expression. "If it happens, I'll make sure you don't get hurt."

I give a bitter laugh. "Not hurt. Just killed." He seems dismayed, so I add, "Thanks for staying with me."

He waves off my gratitude. "What you said down there to Gideon, about all of us being people—did you mean that, or was it just a speech?"

"I meant it, but after what happened to Elizabeth I don't know what's true anymore. Maybe I was talking out my ass."

The idiom seems to confuse him. "Anyway, thanks for sticking up for us." He thinks for a moment, then furrows his brow. "So you're not really a crappy poker player?"

23

You Can't Lose What You Ain't Never Had

"Welcome to Gideon's Lair! You must be Ciara. I'm Ned, Ned Amberson. Welcome to Gideon's Lair. Did I say that already? That's because you're welcome."

The bald young man with sapphire eyes is still shaking my hand. His grip is warm, self-assured, and definitely human. Lawrence stands with him outside my room.

"Tour time!" Ned gestures for me to precede him down the hallway. Lawrence casually shoves Jim back through the door like a bouncer with an insufficiently cool patron, then locks it, muffling the younger vampire's protests.

Ned continues chattering as we pass a series of closed doors. "I've heard so much about you. I really think you'll fit in. So what did you do before you came here?"

He speaks as if my joining the cult is a done deal. Typical sales talk: act like the customer's already bought the product—and had a choice in the first place. I glance back at Lawrence, who follows several paces behind.

"Oh, don't worry," Ned says. "He won't be able to come all the way up with us. It's well past sunrise. Here, you probably could use one of these." He leads me to a door with a familiar sign: LADIES. I rush in, grateful.

When I come out, Ned begins the tour, walking backward as he speaks. "On this level, as you know, we have our guest rooms. Singles on the west end—" He points behind him. "—couples and families to the east."

"Families?"

"Children are welcome, as are pets, as long as they don't cause trouble."

"The pets or the children?"

Without answering my question, he opens a door on my left. "By earning points, guests can work their way up to better living quarters."

I peer in to see what looks like a tastefully decorated hotel suite, four-star accommodations compared to the rattrap I share with Jim. "What do you mean, earn points?"

"For the nourishment we provide, as well as other services, such as laundry, groundskeeping, child care."

"Sounds like a commune." Or a prison. I wonder which "guests" get to make license plates.

Ned nods as if I've said something profound. "Very much like a commune. The guests help each other and help the vampires in exchange for a place to stay and a meaningful life."

I step back into the hallway. "Can a guest lose points?"

Ned's serene composure flickers for a moment. "Of course," he says. "Some need carrots, others need sticks."

I wonder what happens when one's points dip below zero, but decide not to ask. If I can keep this Ned guy on my side, he'll reveal more information—maybe something I can use to get us out of this mess.

We reach the staircase. To my relief, we go up instead of down, but Lawrence still follows us.

"Where do the vampires sleep during the day?" I ask Ned.

"On the bottom level. That's not part of the tour."

The wide-open basement appears at the top of the stairs. On the love seat, a man about my age lounges in the arms of an older woman with heavy red lipstick.

"We'll move on," Ned says. "Someone's having a bedtime snack."

The woman dips her head to the man's neck, and I realize it's not lipstick darkening her mouth. Rather than cry out, the man just sits there watching *Regis and Kelly* on the black-and-white TV. He might as well be donating blood at the Red Cross.

As we climb the next staircase, Lawrence stays behind. The last thing I see is him stalking toward the love seat, fangs out.

Ned hurries me to the top. Just before the door shuts, a pair of screams ring out from the family room below.

My skin jumps. "What was that?"

Ned shrugs. "That was rank having its privileges. Want some breakfast? Might as well eat food while you can still enjoy it."

My stomach lurches, telling me I've already had my last enjoyable meal.

He leads me into a bright kitchen, where a thirtyish woman and a teenage boy sit at the breakfast bar. They stare at me apprehensively, then grab their plates and head for the back porch.

"Don't worry, people will be more polite once you're here for good. Not that they'll have much choice." Ned opens the refrigerator with a flourish. I haven't seen a fridge so crammed with food since the turn of the century—the last Thanksgiving at my foster parents'. "We grow most of our own food," Ned says, "to minimize trips to the all-night supermarket down in Frederick. The vampires escort us whenever we go off-site." He sidles to the counter and whips a cloth napkin off a plate. "We even bake our own bread."

On the plate sits a foot-high stack of bagels. Ned grabs one and starts tearing it in half crosswise with his fingers. No knives here, apparently. I wonder if it's to prevent suicide or homicide or both. Ned's blue polo shirt covers the waistband of his khakis, so I can't tell if belts are disallowed.

He examines me as he rips. "I sense a lack of enthusiasm on your part. Tell me your concerns."

"Well . . . there's the whole becoming a vampire thing. Not my wish."

"Not yet." He stuffs the bagel halves in the toaster. Their ragged edges prevent them from slipping in, so he crams them down with a wooden spoon. "It's a privilege to be made by Gideon."

"I saw the last vampire he made. Gideon left him to starve, tossed him away like a used tissue."

"His three bodyguards," Ned continues, as if he hasn't heard me, "Lawrence, Wallace, and Jacob. All his progeny."

"So?"

"You saw what happened downstairs a minute ago. They can take whomever they want, whenever they want, as long as it's within the rules."

"The vampires have rules, too?"

"If they didn't, they'd run out of food very quickly." He counts off on his fingers. "First, to keep us healthy, the same guest can't be drunk more than once every two weeks. For those two weeks, we wear something to keep them away." He pulls a gold cross from under his shirt collar. "The Jews wear a Star of David, the Muslims a crescent moon. The Wiccans—we have a lot of those— wear pentagrams."

"What about nonreligious people?"

He laughs. "Haven't you heard the saying, 'There are no atheists in foxholes'?" He goes back to counting the rules. "Second, after those two weeks, if a guest still doesn't feel up to it, they can request an extension, review-able on a case-by-case basis. One of the vampires used to be a doctor."

"But if you don't let them drink you, you lose points."

A buzzing comes from the toaster—the bagel is stuck. Ned leans over and jiggles the handle until the bread pops out, singed around the edges.

"As I was saying, you've been given a real honor. Many of us dream of becoming vampires." He puts the bagel on a small plate and opens the refrigerator. "Takes a long time to build up that many points. In the five years I've lived here, no one's ever done it."

"Can the guests leave whenever they want?"

"Regular or chive and onion?"

"Huh?"

"Cream cheese." Ned's head pokes up from behind the fridge door. "For your bagel."

"I don't want a bagel."

"But I made it for you. Why didn't you tell me you didn't want one?"

"I thought you were making it for yourself."

He looks insulted. "That would have been incredibly rude."

"Can the guests leave when they want?"

"Of course." He closes the refrigerator door. "But no one ever wants to." He smacks the counter. "I know. How about some coffee? We have a fantastic Nicaraguan blend."

"I don't want anything."

"Oh, I get it." Ned grabs a mug and pours himself a cup. "You think it might be poisoned." He takes a long sip and smacks his lips. "Mmm. Bottled water makes all the difference. Especially out here in the boonies—you never know what's in the wells."

I peek out the sliding door to the back porch. I can almost taste the sunshine.

"Let's go outside." Ned carries his cup to the door. "Could be your last chance." He grabs a Chicago White Sox baseball cap from a peg. "The thing I'd like most about being a vampire is not having to worry about skin cancer of the scalp." He slides the cap over his head and opens the door.

The morning's mugginess blankets us as we cross the small wooden porch. The woman and teenager from the kitchen are sitting at a round white wrought-iron table. They avoid my eyes, but I can feel their gazes burn into me as I step off the porch into the large backyard.

"Ellie's friendlier." Ned gestures to the playground, where a young woman is helping a small boy navigate the monkey bars.

Ellie waves to us, then claps wildly as the child reaches the end of the row of bars. "You did it!" She sweeps him into a hug, then lowers him to the ground. His orange T-shirt hikes up over his waist as he slides against her, and I can't help but check for bite marks. "Now go play in the sandbox while Mommy talks to Neddy. Try not to get sand down your pants this time."

Ned introduces us. Ellie shakes my hand. "New recruit?"

"Of Gideon's," Ned says to Ellie, with emphasis on the vampire's name. He turns to me. "Ask her anything."

I search for a diplomatic yet productive question. "How did you come to be here?"

"I was on welfare." She tucks a blonde curl back into her elastic ponytail holder. "Actually, I was about to get kicked off welfare, but I couldn't find a job. I was selling my blood plasma for grocery money. That's where Gideon's folks found me." She grins at her surroundings. "Now I get room and board, a safe place to raise my kid, and a purpose in life. Plus free hepatitis shots."

"A purpose in life? Feeding vampires?"

"Being part of a community. Contributing."

Ned sips his coffee. "Ellie teaches our homeschool."

My mind spins. "You have a homeschool here?"

"We can't let these kids grow up like animals," Ellie says with a laugh. "Though they'd have more fun that way." She looks over at her boy. "Trevor's still too young, but we have six other children, ranging from seven to fourteen."

"What happens when they grow up?" I ask her. "Do they become . . . guests?" I look at Ned, suddenly tired of hiding my hostility. "Or does Gideon even wait that long to start drinking them?"

Ned folds his hands around his coffee mug in a prayer-like posture. "Gideon has great respect for family." He bows his head slightly. "He said he told you about his son Antoine."

I notice he hasn't answered my question. "What's that got to do with these kids?"

"Ciara." Ellie sticks her thumbs in her belt loops and gives me a benign regard. "It's in Gideon's best interest to keep us happy and healthy."

"Because you taste better that way. Like organic chicken."

They don't even blink. They just keep smiling, though now their grins are tinged with pity.

"You'll come to understand," Ned says.

I turn away before another insult can leave my lips.

The woman and teenager have left the porch, but a tall thin man stands just inside the sliding door. He turns quickly and disappears into the shadows of the house, allowing me to glimpse nothing more than a head of thick white hair.

I turn back to Ned. "Who was that?"

He looks past me, then shrugs. "I didn't see anyone."

"Me neither," Ellie adds in a tight voice. "Could be one of the ghosts." She laughs. "Don't worry, they don't bother anyone, especially not the vampires."

I stare back at the door. Ghost or not—and my money's on *not*—this one bothers me.

*   *   *

After lunch—which I didn't eat—and the world's most surreal game of badminton—which I didn't play—Ned deposits me back in my room.

I find Jim sleeping on the edge of the bed facing out, leaving me plenty of space on the other side. I should suspect this sudden courtesy, but fear has exhausted me. I'll just rest a few minutes, then move back to the floor.

I lie on my back and feel my limbs sink into the soft mattress. My eyelids sag. Maybe if I doze for a bit, I'll be more alert later when I need to—

I jerk awake to see Jim staring at me. He's lying on his side with his head on his hand, elbow crooked. I suppress a yelp.

"What do you want?" I say in as steady a voice as I can manage.

"I was thinking." He runs his fingers and thumb over a fold in the bedspread between us, his eyes never wavering from mine. "If you have to become a vampire, I could make you. Right now."

I force my muscles to hold still. "That's okay, really."

His dark eyebrows pinch together. "You'd choose Gideon over me?"

"No." Probably not. "I'd choose life, hokey as that sounds."

"But what if David doesn't come through with the proof, or what if Gideon doesn't accept it?"

"I'll take my chances."

"Okay." He drops his gaze for a second, but before I can look away, he lifts it to meet mine again, mesmerizing me. "I've done it before."

"How many?"

"More than I can count."

I fight to keep my breath steady and deep. "Were they all voluntary?"

He glances at a spot of blood on his pillow. "Sometimes when I drink," he whispers, "I get a little . . . greedy." He pauses to let that one sink into my horrified mind. "Then I have a choice—I can either turn them, or I can let them die."

"How do you decide?"

"Whatever feels right." Jim takes my arm and turns it over to reveal its pale underside. I want to rip it out of his grip, but I remember from Shane what fighting back will get me.

"Don't do that."

The firmness of my voice seems to surprise him. He lets go but doesn't apologize.

Without taking my eyes off him, I slowly slip out of bed.

"What's wrong?" he says.

"I'm afraid."

He stretches one bent leg into the space I left behind. "Afraid of me?"

He wears a veneer of innocent surprise. I think of how he became a vampire while Jim Morrison sang onstage. Now he seems to be channeling the Lizard King himself.

The door swings open. I've never been so glad to see Lawrence.

"Six o'clock news," he says.

He marches me and Jim quickly down the hall, then up the stairs to the basement level. The television is in commercials when we get there. Ned waves to me from the other side of the room. I look for the white-haired man I saw behind the porch screen this morning, but as far as I can tell, Ned and I are the only humans among the dozen or so beings gathered around the TV. In addition to Lawrence, there's the woman who drank from the man on the love seat this morning, as well as Jacob and Wallace, Gideon's two other bodyguards.

But where's—

"Good evening."

I jump. Gideon's standing right behind me. He must have followed us up.

"I trust you are well rested," he says.

I try not to shrink as I step away from him. Jim loops a protective arm around my shoulders, an almost brotherly gesture. A few minutes ago I would've queased at his touch, but compared to the rest of them (even Ned), Jim seems quite human.

The commercial ends, and the news anchors turn from their phony camaraderie to face the audience. I squint at the tiny screen to see the blonde on the left—Monica something or other—deliver the latest:

"They said they were vampires, but now they're changing their tune. Last month a local radio station brought a unique twist to the airwaves. WVMP, the Lifeblood of Rock 'n' Roll." Footage of Spencer playing at the Smoking Pig party appears as she continues. "The disc jockeys, who each host a show from a different era, claimed to be real vampires. Michelle Sims is live in Sherwood."

An establishing shot of VMP's radio tower puts a lump in my throat. The camera pans down to show the news correspondent standing outside the station with David. "Thanks, Monica. I'm here with WVMP general manager David Fetter. Mister Fetter, you've decided to end the vampire promotional scheme at the peak of its popularity. Why?"

David focuses on the correspondent. "We had a few fans that took the endeavor a bit too seriously. We appreciate their enthusiasm, but when they started stalking our DJs and shaking stakes at them, we felt it was time to stop. Safety is paramount." Despite his ironic smile, his voice sounds hollow, and not just from the TV's ancient speaker. Less than a day ago, he pulled a stake out of the woman he loved.

The correspondent points at the bright sky.

"Can you prove they're not really vampires?" She flashes an impish grin at the camera. "Can you bring one outside to interview?"

David shakes his head. "Right now they're busy with production work. There's a lot more to being a DJ than talking on the radio for a few hours."

"This'll only take a minute. Let's bring one out." She beckons the camera operator to follow her toward the front door.

David's gaze goes sharp, then sly. "Wait." When Michelle turns back to him, he tilts his head as if to tell her a secret. "Do you want to know the truth? The real truth?"

"Of course," she says, eyes gleaming.

"We're not being threatened by stake-toting slayer wannabes. The real menace is a rival gang of vampires who live in a bunker near Camp David. They think our promotion threatens the anonymity vampires need to survive."

My jaw drops to form a capital O, as in, O Holy Shit. I don't dare look at Gideon.

The correspondent blinks at David for a moment, then chortles. "Fascinating." She mugs for the camera. "Tell us more."

"I'm afraid I can't," David says, "not without endangering us all. Believe me, you do not want to mess with these folks."

He steps away to end the interview. Michelle catches his sleeve.

"Wait, what about—"

"No more vampire talk. It's been fun, but now it's time for them to go back in the coffin." He gives her a smirk and what looks like a wink.

She laughs as she turns back to the camera. "There you have it: a vampire Mafia headquartered near Camp David. In Sherwood, I'm Michelle Sims."

"Thanks, Michelle." The anchorwoman raises her eyebrows at her cohost. "So would that be the jurisdiction of the FBI or the Secret Service?"

"More like the *National Enquirer*," he says. They share a lively laugh. "Now for the weather, let's see what—"

Ned switches off the television. All eyes turn to Gideon. He strokes his chin, staring at the blank gray screen as if he expects it to give him more answers.

I clear my throat and start to sidle away. "Well, that was good for a laugh."

Fast as a cobra, Gideon snatches the back of my neck and yanks me close. Jim reaches out to stop him, but Wallace and Jacob seize his arms.

Gideon lifts me until I'm standing on my tippy toes near his pale, perfect face. My knees turn to water, and only my state of total dehydration keeps me from losing bladder control.

He places a smooth finger against my lips. "Don't speak," he whispers. "I'm thinking."

He begins to pace, dragging me along. I fight not to stumble, for fear he'll jerk me up and snap my spine in the process.

"It's either stupid or brilliant," Gideon mutters. "But which? Perhaps both. They laughed, they all laughed. But they were already laughing, and even if ninety-nine people laugh, the hundredth person might wonder, might come looking . . ."

None of his henchmen speak up with advice or insights. He's surrounded himself with yes-men. If he turns me, will I be another blind disciple?

He continues to mumble, his grip on my neck pulsing. I can feel the anger building in him with every step, every incoherent word. His movements get jerkier, his pace faster as he hauls me with him, until I have to run to keep my head attached to my body.

He stops suddenly and looks at me. No, not *at* me—*inside* me. His black gaze starts at my temple and slides down my neck to my heart, the way Regina's fingernail traced Lori's blood vessel. My veins seem to constrict under his cold glare, as if they know they're under assault.

I am prey.

Gideon sways a little to the rhythm of my pulse. Slowly he pulls me closer, his huge hand tilting my head, fingers threading through my hair and exposing my neck. My dry lips emit a soft, "No."

"Shh." When he speaks, I can see his fangs. "It hurts less if you don't struggle."

His lips graze the skin just below my ear. Instinct takes over, and I push against him, but it's like trying to shove a Clydesdale. Gideon's other hand slides up my waist and tightens around my lower rib cage.

"Be still," he whispers again.

My body obeys, even as my mind screams a thousand protests. I'm going to die now. I think of Shane, and my parents, and Lori. A tear slips out of each eye.

"Don't!" Jim shouts, and I hear a struggle behind me.

"Another move," Lawrence growls at him, "and you're staked."

Gideon's tongue flicks over my neck, like a snake smelling its food. Halfway down, it stops. The heat of his breath and the heat of my blood strain for each other, burning my flesh between them. Against my skin I feel his mouth open wide.

"Uh, sir?" comes a small, clear voice behind me.

Gideon's grip tightens on the back of my neck. "Yes, Ned?" he hisses.

"Feel free to correct me, but it might help to consider the big picture here. Keep our eyes on the prize, as they say."

Gideon goes still as a stone. "Explain. Carefully."

"Think about what's most important to you, how you plan to accomplish it, and how killing the girl might complicate those means and, ultimately, hinder those ends."

Gideon's fingers twitch and tremble, squeezing me tighter. I wince as my flesh bruises between our bones. My ribs feel ready to snap.

He gives a feral grunt and shoves me to the floor. My hands barely rise in time to keep my face from hitting the rug. I scramble to crawl away, even though there's nowhere to go.

Someone grabs me. My hand lashes out, but Jim

catches it. He helps me to my feet and puts himself between me and the other vampires.

Gideon advances on Ned, who, instead of backing down, beams at the vampire's approach as if it's a visit from the pope.

"Get me another," Gideon growls. "Now."

Ned reaches inside his shirt and pulls out his cross. Gideon pauses. Ned yanks the cross's chain to break it. Gideon nods, then seizes his shoulder and drags him toward the stairs.

Before he descends, the vampire turns to me. "You think you want answers." He gives me a blood-freezing glare. "You don't want these answers."

As Ned's taken away, a beatific look on his face, he tosses the cross in my direction. On reflex, I reach forward and grab it before it hits Jim.

After a few moments, the others follow Ned and Gideon, except for Lawrence, who sits on the couch and opens an old edition of *Life* magazine.

"Why did Gideon let me go?" I ask him, my mouth drier than ever.

"You heard what he said." Lawrence flips a page. "Better not to know some truths."

I can believe that, and I'm not about to look this gift life in the mouth. I open my hand to see Ned's gold cross with its broken chain. Should I keep it? Maybe it would be rude not to. The man did save my life.

I think back to the moment I almost died, and everything that passed through my mind. The people I loved, the things I never got to do.

Jim heaves a relieved sigh and moves for the closest chair. I tread behind him and hold out the cross like a weapon. When he turns to sit down, he starts a little at the sight of the symbol, then relaxes.

"Man, you scared me there for a second." With a nervous laugh, he takes my wrist and draws my outstretched hand to the hollow of his neck, where the T-shirt ends. The cross presses his skin with no effect.

I drop the necklace on a bookshelf, realizing there was one thing that never joined the memories and regrets in my panicky, verge-of-death brain.

A prayer.

24

At Last

Franklin, of all people, picks me up. Lawrence waves good-bye to me and Jim from the porch, with a subtle smile that says he'll be seeing us again sooner than we'd like.

"I'm going back to the station." Jim gestures to his car. "Got a show at three." He fumbles in his jeans pocket for his keys.

"Thanks for staying with me," I tell him. "I think."

Jim shrugs, then turns and slouches back to his Charger. He glides his hand over Janis's roof, as if to reassure her that everything's okay, Daddy's home now.

Franklin watches him leave, then turns to me. "You all right?"

I shake my head. "But I don't want to talk about it."

"Good, because I don't want to hear about it." He opens the truck door and points to a plastic shopping bag on the floor of the passenger's seat. "Thought you might be hungry and thirsty."

I tear open the bag and find two bottles of water, a turkey sandwich, and half a convenience-store aisle's worth of snacks.

Let no one speak evil of Franklin in front of me. Ever.

He places a short call to David to let him know I'm out of danger, yet not quite ready for a full debriefing. After several miles and several minutes' worth of face stuffing, my mind finally turns from the trauma of the recent past to the dread of the near future.

"What's going to happen to the station?"

Franklin frowns. "Elizabeth didn't have a will in her office. Tomorrow night David wants to search her apartment in Rockville."

"Why not during the day?"

"If there's a safe, he'll need Shane to crack it. Hopefully it'll contain papers that'll help us keep the station in the event of her death."

"But she was already dead."

"It wasn't so long ago that she had to get a new identity. As far as the IRS is concerned, she's still alive. Sooner or later, some business contact or creditor—someone other than us, in other words—will report her missing."

"Then come the cops."

"The first place they'll look for her is the station."

"Including the vampires' apartment." I wipe my hand over my face. "And we can't report her missing without losing the station. It'll be sold for parts, like Jim said."

Thinking of Jim reminds me of Gideon's visit to our room. I suck in a sharp breath, almost choking on a corn chip.

"I need to call David back. Now."

Franklin flips open his cell phone, hits a speed-dial number, and hands it to me.

Halfway through David's hello, I blurt, "Antoine was Gideon's son."

Franklin curses, swerving the truck almost across the broken yellow highway line.

David, on the other hand, is silent. I pull the phone away from my ear to check the reception. Three out of four bars. "David, you there?"

"You're fucking kidding me."

"Not just his son. His progeny, too."

Another long silence. "I don't believe this."

"I don't think he knows you killed Antoine, or that Elizabeth was connected to him."

"He wouldn't have staked her if he'd known. They don't hurt their own blood."

"He didn't mind hurting Travis."

David ignores this point. "What else did Gideon say about Antoine?"

I repeat everything the ancient vampire told me, about Antoine's spaz attacks and the Control's double cross.

"They knew." David's voice goes cold. "The Control knew all along who Gideon was and didn't tell us." He breathes hard. "If we'd known, we wouldn't have gone there, and Elizabeth would still exist."

I have no response except, "I'm sorry."

"It's not your fault."

"If I hadn't mouthed off—"

"He wanted an excuse to kill her, to declare war against the Control. So what else happened?"

I tell him about my almost-death at the fangs of Gideon, and the calmness of my voice shocks me. It's like it happened to someone else.

"Sorry about the interview," he says. "I panicked

when that reporter wanted to bring the DJs out into the sun."

"You do need some thinking-on-your-feet lessons, but Gideon's so irrational, he might have bitten me no matter what you said." We enter another valley. The connection crackles. "David, we're about to get cut off. Call Shane and tell him I'm okay."

The phone goes dead. I hand it back to Franklin.

He gives me a bitter grin. "I can't wait to see how this could get worse."

It's past ten thirty when Franklin drops me off at my apartment. I grab my convenience-store feast, wave good-bye, and turn toward my door.

Shit. I left my purse—with my keys and phone—in Elizabeth's car two nights ago.

"Wait!" I run down the block after Franklin's truck, flailing my arms. But it's too late.

Groaning, I turn back to my apartment. Maybe by some miracle I left the door unlocked, or maybe my landlord is working late at the pawnshop.

Someone opens my door from the inside and steps onto the sidewalk.

"Ciara."

Shane says it softly, perfectly.

I drop my precious cargo and sprint down the block into his arms. He lifts me off my feet and holds me tight, and for a long time we say nothing.

Finally he whispers, "I thought I'd never see you again."

I pull back to take in his face in the glow of the streetlight. "You will."

Without putting me down, he opens my door and slides inside, then locks it behind us. He carries me up the dark stairwell.

I tighten my arms around his neck. "I know this sounds incredibly dorky, but I missed you."

"Then you should've sent a postcard."

It feels good to laugh. It feels good to hold him. It feels good to—

To do anything we're about to do.

Shane brings me into my bedroom, where one soft lamp is lit and my stereo plays disc two of *The Essential Leonard Cohen*, an album whose apocalyptic melancholy usually shreds my soul, but tonight feels right somehow.

He lays me on the bed and stretches out beside me. His hand strokes my neck and arm, then passes over my waist and hip, his gaze following it like he can't believe I'm really here.

Finally his hand and eyes return to my face, which he studies for several moments. I wait for him to ask if I'm too tired or scared or traumatized, but he seems to find the answer he's looking for.

He grasps my face and kisses me, and it's my turn to reach and touch all of him, everything I thought I'd lost.

I unbutton his shirt. Beneath it the smooth flesh of his chest is hot. I try not to speculate which donor he visited tonight.

"I raided our fridge," he whispers, "if you're wondering why I'm warm."

I smile against his skin. "I hadn't noticed." The muscles of his stomach tense when my lips pass over them. No surprise that he's ticklish.

We undress each other as slowly as we can stand it.

Naked, Shane looks and smells and sounds and tastes like a man. Like a human.

Limbs tangling and twining, we lie on the bed together as the room fills with notes of doubt and longing. I trace the spot on his chest that covers his heart. A vision of Elizabeth's death crashes my mind like an unwanted party guest.

I push Shane onto his back and crawl on top of him, shielding him from all the world's bad guys. They'll have to go through me first.

He slides his hands through my hair and lets it cascade over his face and neck. "I've dreamed of this, too, your hair falling down as you lie on top of me."

"What else did you dream about? Besides my hair."

"This." One of his hands cups my ass, fingertips venturing around and between my legs. "And this." His other hand fills with my breast, bringing it to his mouth.

I moan at the electric shock of his tongue. Before my mind can blur too far for speech, I say, "But you'd seen it all before. You got me naked that first night, remember?"

He lays his head back on the bed. "I saw you, but it was through a red haze of bloodlust." His thumb traces my nipple. "Now I see you clearly."

My muscles tense. I want to tell him that no one ever does, that if he did see past my layers, he wouldn't want me. But he knows what I was, knows what I did, and he doesn't care.

Or maybe he just doesn't want to care. Maybe he's lying to himself. He's never really seen that part of me, after all, the part that reduces everyone to a playing piece, a token to move however I need to win.

The bliss drops from his eyes. "What's wrong? And don't say 'nothing.'"

"Nothing's wrong." I tilt my hips to guide just the barest tip of him inside me. His chin lifts and his mouth opens in anticipation. I take his lower lip between my teeth, pause for one moment, then take him deep within.

His breath catches so hard, for a second I worry that the whole thing is about to end. But then he arches his back and plunges farther inside me, making us both cry out. My control shatters, and I grind against him, greedily, as his hips roll under me in perfect rhythm. For the first time since I've known him, Shane breaks a sweat.

Suddenly he turns his head to the side, covering his mouth with his arm. But it's too late.

"Don't hide them." I put a hand to his cheek and coax his mouth open with a thumb. "I want to see, up close."

"Careful." He breathes hard. "They're sharp."

His two fangs curve like rapiers, ending in thin, sharp points. "They're not what I imagined. They're not like dog fangs."

"I'm not a werewolf."

"Are there such things?"

He smirks and squeezes my thighs. "Now you're being silly."

"They're more like cat fangs." I run my thumb over the front edge of the left one. "That makes sense. Dogs take their prey by tearing it apart. Cats puncture the spinal cord nice and neat."

"Wow, Ms. Discovery Channel, you sure know how to talk sexy." He sways his hips against mine, studying my face to find just the right spot that will send me over the edge.

"Shh. Hold very still." I lean close and kiss the left fang, then the right.

He pulls in a long, slow breath, then lets it out, never breaking our gaze. "Now what?"

I know suddenly what I need to feel safe. "Shane, I don't want you to bite me. Ever."

"I know that."

"But, if you can, if it's not too much—I want you to pretend."

"Pretend to bite you?" His pupils dilate so quickly they wipe out most of the blue. "Are you sure?"

"I'm sure."

His muscles coil, and he flips me onto my back so fast it knocks my breath out. He seizes my wrists, pinning them above my head, and drives himself deep inside me. His eyes are pure animal now, dark and fierce.

Instinct makes my body buck, frantic to fight him off, but he takes my desperate rhythm and makes it his own. Holding both wrists in one hand, he reaches back and seizes my leg behind the knee, then pulls it forward into the crook of his elbow.

Shane has complete control. He could break my bones, bleed me dry, like Gideon almost did. I slam my mind shut on the memory, close my eyes against the image of Shane's savage face.

His head pushes mine aside to burrow into my neck. His mouth brushes my throat. Instead of growing cold with fear, my skin heats so fast it feels like I could singe him. I hear myself hiss the word, "Yes."

He pulls away suddenly, and I wonder if I've taken the game too far, if he has to flee to keep from biting me. But his eyes hold no fear.

Shane flips me onto my stomach, lifts my hips, and enters me with one long thrust.

I scream.

I didn't mean to scream.

He plunges deeper, and I scream again. I squirm and writhe beneath him, exactly like prey, but I can't help it. Every sound and motion releases the waves of energy slamming through my body. To be still and quiet would rip me in two.

When Shane's teeth touch the back of my neck, I know he wants to sink them through my flesh. But he won't, and this feeling of safety turns me on more than any danger ever could. I move with him, surrendering to the terrifying trust.

The music ends. No sounds now but our ragged moans and the shifting of skin against skin.

Shane's hands find mine, clutching the edge of the mattress. He slides his palms over them, interweaving our fingers. "I'll never hurt you. Ciara . . ."

Before I can return the promise—which I can't—he quickens his rhythm, carrying me with him up and over the last, highest peak. His groan lengthens into a feral howl, and my final scream is a vague approximation of his name.

He collapses on the bed beside me. I turn my head to see him gasping for breath, face damp with sweat. His eyes squeeze shut, and his body, like mine, shudders with the aftershocks. When he opens his eyes to look at me, I realize where I've seen that expression of happy gratitude: after he drank Deirdre.

No, that's not fair. There's something deeper in his gaze now, more than a hunger satisfied. I wouldn't dare call it love, but maybe he would.

Lacking the breath to speak, we say nothing, just stare

at each other from our respective pillows. Finally Shane reaches out and tucks a lock of hair behind my ear, then lets his hand drop onto my shoulder. "Was that what you had in mind?"

"Pretty much exactly." I roll from my stomach onto my side. The motion makes his hand slip off me. I put mine over it so it doesn't seem like I'm pulling away. "Was it hard not to bite?"

His other hand wipes the damp hair off his cheek. "I had other things to think about besides blood."

"But isn't there some vampire equivalent to blue balls?"

He laughs. "It's called thirst. But I told you, I drank before I came here."

"Your fangs still came out."

"Sometimes they have a mind of their own." He runs his tongue over his now human teeth. "But it's no harder for a vampire not to bite someone than it is for a man not to force himself on a woman. It's not something a decent vampire would even consider."

"And you're a decent vampire."

"No. I'm a damn fucking good vampire." He reaches over and drags me into his arms. I let him, even though it's too hot. His eyes turn serious. "David told me you almost died."

"If it weren't for that flack Ned Amberson I'd be dead or undead right now. I don't understand what he meant by the big picture and what it has to do with me. Gideon said I didn't want to know."

His arms tighten around me. "I'll kill him if I ever get the chance."

"Have you ever seen a vampire die?"

"No."

"You don't want to. I wish I could forget I ever saw it." My gaze hops over his shoulder to the far nightstand. "Hey, that might help."

Shane rolls on his back and grabs the bottle of red wine. "I brought it because I thought you might need to relax."

I let out a long sigh. "My limbs are pretty much jelly now, thanks to you, but the wine'll finish me off nice."

He kisses me and heads for the kitchen with the bottle. It turns out, the sight of him walking away is just as nice without jeans.

I get up to put in a new CD, deciding to expand Shane's horizons with a little Fiona Apple. As I place the Leonard Cohen disc back in its case, a wicked curiosity creeps through me. I insert the disc in the wrong place on the shelf, after Counting Crows, then slip off to the bathroom.

When I come back, Shane is lying on the bed, staring at the ceiling, with his hands behind his head and the sheet pulled up to his waist. The lamp is off, and candles on either side of the bed are lit (sandalwood, not sausage pizza). As I return to bed, I glance at the CD shelf.

Leonard Cohen's back where he belongs, between Chumbawamba and Coldplay. The shame and sorrow make me stumble. I slip under the sheets, wanting to pull them over my head.

"Did you do that on purpose?" Shane says without looking at me.

"I'm sorry."

"Why?"

"Why am I sorry?"

He pauses. "Okay, we'll start with that and work our way back to the other 'why.'"

"I shouldn't test you. You're not a lab rat."

"Then why did you do it?"

"To see if you had changed. You learn new things, and you have hope for the future."

"Because of you." Now he looks at me. "But you can't cure everything overnight. Some things you may never cure. It doesn't work that way."

"What doesn't?"

"Mental illness."

The sound of the words from his mouth make my eyes hot. "Don't say that."

"It's true. I know a lot of vampires have weird obsessive-compulsive behaviors. The world changes faster than we can understand, so we find something to control, some way to put things in order." He laughs softly. "It's the only way to feel sane."

I touch his arm, but he pulls it away to reach for the glasses of wine. "Don't pity me, Ciara. That's one thing I can't stand."

"What are the other things? Just so I know."

"I'm not giving you a list." He hands me a glass, and I sit up to take it. "That's one of the joys of relationships, finding out what drives the other person batshit." He clinks his glass against mine. "Tell me one thing you can't stand, and we'll be even."

"Licorice."

"Two things."

"Licorice and religion."

"Religion, because of your parents?"

"Yes. No. That makes it sound like they're responsible

for everything I am. I've thought about religion, even studied it in school, and come to the conclusion that it's pointless and dangerous. I don't get why people need it to give their lives meaning. Isn't life enough?"

"You're asking a dead guy?"

I take a sip of wine. "This is all just my opinion, of course. What about you? Before you were a vampire—"

"I was a Catholic."

"Oh." I wonder if now is the time to ask him about his story. "But when you become a vampire, you end your life. Isn't that kind of a no-no in Catholicism? Suicide?"

His face goes sad, sending a stake of regret through my heart. I feel like I'm about to meet Elizabeth's fate, inverting and twisting into a hole that will swallow me up. "You don't have to talk about it," I say. "I shouldn't have asked."

"Yes, you should have." He lays his hand over mine. "And no, I don't."

He continues to drink the wine. I wait for him to continue. After the first minute I sit back and take a few sips, waiting. After five minutes I realize there's no winning the waiting game with an immortal creature.

"You don't what?" I ask.

"Have to talk about it."

He doesn't look mad, but he doesn't look happy either. He just sits and drinks, as if I've left the room. Great. First I play games with his brain, then I accuse him of being a bad Catholic. How else can I demean him today?

A change of venue might break my streak of asininity. "Hey, you know what I could go for? Ice cream."

This snaps him out of his meditative state. He looks at me, smirks, then sings the first line to "Mean Woman Blues."

I cover my face. "I forgot you can't taste food. Never mind."

"It's okay." He sets his empty wineglass on the nightstand. "You've had a bad day, you deserve ice cream."

We dress in silence on opposite sides of the bed, though we might as well be on two sides of a wall. I remember how I opened myself completely to him, let him do whatever he wanted with my body and my life. What do I have to do to get that kind of trust in return?

Besides not being a total shitheel, I mean.

"My car's at the station, so we'll have to walk." I sift through my jeans pockets for change. "And my purse is in Elizabeth's car, so you'll have to buy. Sorry."

He looks up at me from the bed, where he's tying his shoes. "Come here."

I sidle over to him. "You want to extract payment in advance?"

"No." He takes me in his arms and kisses me softly. "Ciara, I promise one day I'll tell you my story. But I don't want to ruin this night."

My dread dares to thaw around the edges. I attempt a nod and a smile, and we head out for ice cream.

I know there are other reasons why he won't tell me. Some are about me, and some are about him. To get past all the reasons at the same time could take careful choreography, an endless emotional negotiation.

This is why I don't do boyfriends. Too much work.

The diner glows purple, inside and out. The Baltimore Ravens are in town for summer training camp, so every business drapes themselves in the team colors to draw in tourists. It might be fun one afternoon to go see the team practice, get some autographs. I turn to Shane to suggest it, then remember we can't ever have a daytime date. Oh well. He's a Steelers fan, anyway—or "Stillers," as he would pronounce it.

We stand in the lobby holding hands, just like any normal couple out for a postcoital midnight breakfast, in search of caffeine and carbs to keep the energy up.

A young waitress with a drooping brown ponytail shows us to our booth. Shane sits across from me as she dumps the menus on the table. We order black coffees and a banana split.

When she walks away, Shane props his feet on my bench, one on either side of me. I sit back and rest my elbows on the toes of his boots. The diner's harsh fluorescent and neon lights accent the feeling of otherworldliness about this evening, the sense of time out of time. Tomorrow—later today, I mean—we'll have plenty of problems to sort out. Right now, I sign a truce with life.

I run a thumb over Shane's left sole. "Are your feet ticklish, too?"

The corner of his mouth twitches. "No."

"Liar. I'm going to play with them when we get back in bed."

"Only if I can do the same to you."

I shrug. "I'm not ticklish at all."

"That's because nothing ever surprises you."

Was that a dig at my conniving nature? "'Surprise' is just another word for disappointment."

The waitress arrives with our order. I nudge aside the maraschino cherry and dig in. "They use real whipped cream here, not that canned stuff." I lick my spoon and mentally catalog the places on Shane's body I'd like to apply the condiment. Maybe I can get some to go. "Please, try it."

He nabs half a spoonful of mint chocolate chip, takes a tentative bite, then shoves the spoon back into the bowl. "Tastes like Maalox."

"Darn, I guess it's all mine." I pull the split to my side of the table and keep eating. "My parents used to buy me ice cream after a revival show. I'd always get as exotic a flavor as I could, because I knew the next town might only have chocolate and vanilla."

"So it wasn't all bad, then, your childhood."

"Not at the time."

He pulls his feet off my bench and leans forward. "What were some of the other things you liked about it?"

I eye him carefully. "I don't want to go there right now."

He slides the banana split toward him, out of my reach, then picks up his spoon. "For each good thing you can remember, you get one bite."

"It'll melt."

"Then you'd better hurry."

"Passing out fliers."

He hesitates, holding back the spoon. "Explain."

"In little towns I'd stand on street corners, or go from shop to shop, telling people about the revival. Sometimes the shop owners would give me candy or a flower or a bag of chips, because I was so cute and holy."

"Good." He feeds me a large spoonful, consisting of banana, chocolate almond ice cream, and whipped cream. "Next?"

"The carnival atmosphere."

"Good. You get a bite for each detail."

"The barkers, selling Bibles and tambourines and prayer books." Another bite, this one from the mint chip side. "The roadies and the local guys working together to put up the big tent." Ditto, this time a bit of each ice cream. He's got the hang of it now. "People from the town setting up booths to sell lemonade or homemade crafts or funnel cakes."

"I remember funnel cakes." His mouth opens, moist inside, as he spoons me another bite. "Add that to the list of things I miss tasting. Go on, what else?"

"Testimonies."

"What's that?"

"People would stand up and talk about how they were healed, or how they used to be sinners until they discovered grace and shit." I take another bite. "Some of them were shills, but some were believers."

"What's a shill exactly?"

"It's the grifter partner who plays the bystander. In a game of three-card monte, it'd be the guy you see winning. It makes the mark feel more secure. The herd instinct. Do I get a free bite for my lesson?"

He sighs and scoops another spoonful. "Only because of my undying love for you," he mumbles.

"What?"

He looks up. "What?"

"Your un-whatting what?"

"Huh?"

My eyes narrow at him. "What did you just say?"

"When?" He holds out the spoon. "Come on, it's dripping."

I accept his offering, my whole body running hot and cold. My memory flits back to his remark that nothing ever surprises me.

"So what else?" He digs the spoon into the bowl. "We've still got half a banana split here."

I collect myself in a hurry. "I remember . . ." What else? Counting stacks of money at the end of the night? Watching the dupes return to their ramshackle homes with empty wallets? "The hope in people's eyes."

"Sounds big. Give me more."

"They'd come to the revival so beaten down, by the bad crops or the factory closings. After a couple hours of listening to my parents shout and sing, and watching their neighbors be healed onstage, they'd go home believing anything was possible."

Shane feeds me. "Your folks, they were something, huh?"

"My dad, he was the best in the business. Charming, fast-talking, great-looking. He worked like a magician, full of misdirection and illusion. But he would've been nothing without my mom. They were like Fred Astaire and Ginger Rogers. Like two halves of the same person."

When the next spoonful comes, I turn my head away. "But maybe even their marriage was just part of the show. He hasn't called or written her in two years." My stomach tightens around the last bite of ice cream. "He's never called or written me. Fucking asshole creep pig-weasel."

Shane puts the spoon back in the dish. "Are you sure he's still alive?"

"They would've told us if he died, as his next of kin. They would've told me if he were paroled. I testified against him, after all."

"They think he might come after you for revenge?"

"I would if I were him."

Shane moves to join me on my side of the booth, bringing the bowl of ice cream. "Here, you've earned it." He sits close to me and sips his coffee while I consume the banana split with renewed urgency.

To distract myself from thoughts of my parents, I turn to a slightly less odious topic. "The station is screwed."

"Yeah. Our only hope is to find a will that says Elizabeth left everything to David. But then we'd have to prove she died, which is hard to do without a corpse."

I grit my teeth at the unfairness. "She was going to make it work. If Gideon hadn't staked her, she could have canceled the deal with Skywave."

He frowns into his mug. "When she doesn't show up for that meeting on Friday, they'll know something's up. Sooner or later there'll be an investigation. We should start looking for a new home."

"We can probably postpone the meeting, but that'll just be a temporary—" Breath stops in my throat. My spoon clatters to the table, then the floor.

Shane picks up his own spoon and holds it out to me, but my hand is frozen. All of me is frozen but my mind, which spins like a gyroscope.

"Ciara, you okay?"

I grab Shane's wrist, spilling his coffee. "I know how to save the station."

25

I'm Not Like Everybody Else

When devising a long con, the first revelation comes as a spark, a firecracker of an idea. The rest takes time and planning to perfect the entire game. Every player must learn his or her part, every loophole must be tightened, and every possible setback must be accounted for. This process often takes weeks.

I don't have weeks. I have until the day after tomorrow.

David and I sit in Elizabeth's office, searching for scraps of information about Friday morning's phone meeting between her and Skywave. Luckily, her files are well organized, and her ancient computer has no security, since she was using Windows 95 as an operating system.

"Let's see if we can buy some time." I hand David a piece of paper with a name and number on it. "Call Skywave and ask if we can postpone Friday's conference call until next week. Tell this guy's assistant that Elizabeth is ill."

I sit back in the chair while David navigates the labyrinthine phone tree to reach the Skywave head office.

After a short conversation, he punches the hold button. "The soonest they can reschedule is in a month. But by then someone else might figure out she's missing, and this charade won't play."

"Then tell them never mind."

He puts the phone back to his ear. "Rather than postpone, Ms. Vasser would prefer to keep the meeting as scheduled." He listens for several moments, then his eyes widen. "Oh, no. I mean, no, I'm afraid that won't work."

"What won't?" I whisper.

He shakes his head vigorously.

I lean forward. "What won't work?"

He holds up a finger. "One moment, please," he says into the phone. He puts them on hold. "They want to meet in person," he tells me. "They have something they want to show Elizabeth. Obviously we can't do it."

"Why not?"

His jaw drops, then his head shakes slowly. "No, Ciara. We can't do what you're thinking."

"Maybe we can. Tell them we'll call back."

As soon as he's off the phone, I grab it and dial the vampires' extension, which rings several times.

Shane picks up with a groggy tone. "Yeah?"

"Hi."

"Hey." He lets out a sigh like the one I heard as I fell asleep with him curled around me. "How are you?"

"Overcaffeinated. Is Travis there?"

He hesitates. "You called to talk to Travis?"

"I'll explain in a minute. Stay by the phone."

"Here he is."

"Yes, ma'am?" Travis's voice is steadier and warmer than I expected.

"It's Ciara." I congratulate myself for not adding, "The woman you tried to kill."

"What can I do ya for?"

"Lots. First, I need to know if any Skywave execs ever met Elizabeth face-to-face."

"Not that I know of, but it's hard to prove something didn't happen."

"Those photos in your camera, were they the only ones you took?"

"I downloaded a bunch to my laptop, but I haven't shown them to Skywave yet. I was just about to give them a report when I was, well, butchered." His voice dips for a moment, then picks back up. "Do you still have my camera? I want it back."

"Feel like taking a trip to Rockville?"

"Do I have a choice?"

"Afterward, we'll stop by your office and collect everything you need. I see no reason why you can't stay a detective just because you're a vampire."

"I was hoping to be a DJ. I could start a new country music program, call it—"

"We'll discuss that later." During intermission of an ice hockey game in hell, if David has any say in the matter. "Can you put Shane back on, please, and give him some privacy?"

Travis chuckles suggestively and hands the phone over. Shane says, "So what's next?"

"Can we trust Travis?"

"I think so. We took care of him in his first few hours of death, fed him and gave him a home. The transition period is really rough, and we were there for him. It's like when baby ducks take after the first person they see, what's that called?"

"Imprinting."

"Yeah. We're his mom and dads now, especially after Gideon rejected him. But what does he have to do with your plan?"

I outline a quick rundown of the updates, most of which come to mind as I speak. David stands in the middle of the office, jaw slackening as he listens.

After I finish, Shane lets out a low whistle. "Remind me never to piss you off."

"We'll meet you here after sunset. Sleep tight."

"The sleep of the dead."

I set down the phone. David plants his hands on the other side of the desk, looming.

"We can't do this," he says. "It's one thing to impersonate her over the phone. You're talking about identity theft."

"Why not? As a vampire, Elizabeth made sure there were no photos of her in the press. She wouldn't even talk to the reporters at the Smoking Pig party."

"I don't understand why we can't just decline the buyout with a phone call or an e-mail."

"Because they'll get suspicious and pushy. They'll think we're holding out for more money. Unless Elizabeth looks them in the eye and tells them she absolutely won't sell, they'll never stop until they get what they want."

His shoulders droop as he realizes I'm right. He sighs and heads for the door. "I'll double-check the Internet and my old press files, make sure there are no pictures of her anywhere." He slides his hand over the wall on his way out, as if it still bears her essence.

I sit back in her leather chair, feeling like an empress on a throne. Its soft surface reminds me of her Mercedes.

I pick up her keys from the desk. The car will be lonely without her.

Shane sings R.E.M.'s "(Don't Go Back to) Rockville" as I drive Elizabeth's car into the sprawling suburban city. David sits in the passenger's seat, with Travis behind him.

"Do you think Gideon is biting the children in his compound?" David asks me.

"I didn't see any evidence of that. But then again, I didn't see anything they didn't want me to see. Their smiley representatives made everything seem tightly controlled. Like Disney World." A memory sparks. "Except there was one guy I don't think I was supposed to see."

"Who?"

"Some human with white hair, too far away for me to see his face. The others said he was a ghost."

"A ghost? Hmm. Maybe the spirit of someone Gideon killed."

"Now you sound like Lori."

"So you believe in vampires but not ghosts?"

"I've seen vampires." I meet Shane's eyes in the rearview mirror and mentally add *gloriously naked*. "Now that we know Gideon was the cold presence in the parking lot, I'm even less inclined to believe in ghosts."

David silently ponders. "Something about that bothers me. Why was Gideon stalking you that first night? We hadn't even started the campaign."

"Noah made the same point. Maybe there was another vampire senior citizen following me."

Shane stops singing. "Let 'em try to touch you. I'll kick their ancient asses." He returns to the third verse.

I glance at him, then lower my voice to David. "Something odd about Gideon and the other vampires. They didn't seem to have compulsions like ours do."

"Their environment is so regimented, they probably don't need those sort of coping mechanisms."

"It's not like they were normal. They were really faded, kind of robotic. But not, you know—"

"Bonkers," Shane says. He shifts into a version of Van Morrison's "Crazy Love."

I pull up in front of Elizabeth's swanky apartment complex. David grabs a few empty duffel bags from his trunk. As we walk to the door, Shane keeps himself between the humans and the jittery Travis, who watches us like an Atkins dieter with a stack of pancakes. But without the strength of desperate hunger, he's no match for Shane, so I feel safe around him, if not particularly happy.

Elizabeth's basement condo looks like that of any other up-and-coming venture capitalist: leather furniture, stainless steel kitchen appliances, and hardwood floors begging for a good game of sock hockey.

"Wow," David says. "She never made enough working for the Control as a human to afford a place like this."

A thud comes from the kitchen, making us all jump. A large white cat struts into the living room and says *prrrow*.

David breathes a sigh of relief. "I didn't know she had a pet."

Shane squats down and makes little *puss-puss* noises to

get the cat to approach him. He picks it up and checks the tag.

"What's its name?" David says.

"There's no name. It's just a rabies tag." He quickly slides the blue collar and tag off the cat, avoiding David's eyes.

"Let me see the kitty," Travis says.

Shane turns away. "No, you'll bite him."

"I will not."

"Believe me, I was your age not too long ago. You'll bite anything that bleeds. Speaking of which." He nods at the insulated canteen on Travis's hip. "Meal time."

"Oh. Yeah, thanks." Travis pulls a fast-food straw from his shirt pocket and yanks off the wrapper.

"Give me the cat." David eases the beast out of Shane's arms. "I'll take him home with me. First let's get him some food."

I flip through a pile of mail on the dining room table. "Travis, what are we looking for?"

He jolts a little at being spoken to, especially in the middle of a drink. He bobs the straw in the canteen and wipes his mouth with a napkin. I look away from the red smear on the white paper.

"Uh." He smooths down the front of his shirt. "She probably keeps her important documents in a fireproof safe. Let's try the closets."

We open the coat closet across from the kitchen, where David and Shane are searching for cat food. I hold the flashlight for Travis, who seems calmer now that he's had a snack.

"Should we be wearing gloves?" I ask him.

"Naw, no one'll dust for prints in here. It's not a crime scene."

I look behind me into the kitchen. "It will be if David and Shane don't leave that thing alone and come help us."

Travis snickers. "You don't like puddy-tats?"

"I'm more of a dog person. But I admire cats and their ability to take so much while giving so little."

"I had a dog. Ex-wife took him, and the house."

"Is that why you like country music?"

He eases himself out of the closet. "Huh?"

"Just a joke. Sorry about your dog."

"Yeah, well—" He scratches his stomach. "—don't suppose I'll get another one any time soon. Let's try the bedroom."

Shane overhears and joins us. "Nothing personal, Travis, but we don't leave new vampires alone with humans."

The detective just sighs and sips his breakfast.

Elizabeth's walk-in closet would make most women swoon. I, however, could really give a shit how many pairs of—

"Oh my God." I kneel before the hottest pair of red pumps. "These would look so amazing on me." I check the brand. "Ferragamos! I always wanted a pair of—fuck, they're the wrong size." I hurl the shoe on the floor. It bounces under a row of skirts and hits something metallic.

Shane shoves apart the skirts to reveal a foot-high combination safe. "Excellent."

Before he pulls it out, he eyes me clutching the other red pump. I toss it aside, chagrined at my estrogen outburst.

"You didn't see that."

Shane drags the safe out of the closet and carries it to the bed. While Travis and I watch, he kneels beside the safe and pulls a pencil and a sheet of graph paper from his back pocket.

"What's that for?" I ask him.

"I'll show you when I'm done." He looks at his unwelcome audience. "It's tedious and takes forever. Go do something else, quietly."

We obey. In the living room, David is inspecting the bookshelf under the long, high window, which is covered in heavy room-darkening curtains. He pulls out a few volumes that look like Control manuals. "In case the police come," he tells us as he stuffs them in a duffel bag.

I approach a large wall-mounted cabinet on the far side of the dining room. I fish Elizabeth's keys from my purse and unlock it. "Whoa."

The cabinet contains an arsenal of anti-vampire weaponry: crosses, sharpened stakes, a long sword, a crossbow.

And at the bottom, a gun shaped like a prop from a 1940s alien invasion flick.

Travis approaches, giving the stakes a wary eye. "I never saw a piece like that before." He picks up the gun. "What kind of—"

"Don't touch that!" David shouts.

Travis drops the gun. I leap back, expecting it to go off. Instead of a heavy thud, it makes a hollow *whap!* against the floor. I bend down and pick it up.

David stalks over to me. "It doesn't fire bullets."

"It's plastic." I heft it in my hand. "Like a water pistol."

"It *is* a water pistol."

I look at the two bottles of holy water in the cabinet.

A box of latex gloves sits next to them, presumably for Elizabeth's safe handling.

I scrape the gun's rough surface with my nail to reveal bright pink. "Aren't there laws against painting water pistols black?"

"They need to be camouflaged for night ops," David says. "And a Control agent would never carry a pink-and-yellow weapon. It's a macho thing."

"Can someone kill a vampire with this?" I point the gun at Travis. "Like the vampire who tried to rip out my throat the other night?"

The detective puts his hands up, paling. "I said I was sorry."

"Actually, I don't think you did."

David steps between us. "It won't kill him, but it would burn him badly."

"It's empty." I flip the gun to David, sending Travis a wicked grin. "Besides, sacred weapons don't work in my hands."

"Holy water's different from crosses." David checks the pistol, then picks up one of the empty duffel bags he left on the table. "It's intrinsically powerful because it's been blessed. Most crosses, on the other hand, are just profane pieces of jewelry made in a factory. They have no power unless they're wielded in faith." He crams the gun, the holy water, and a small funnel into the outside pocket of the duffel bag. "Also, a vampire never completely heals from a holy water burn. It leaves permanent scars."

"Then I won't use it to give Shane a sponge bath." I lift the sword from the cabinet and unsheathe its long curved blade. "Ooh, nice machete."

"It's a katana." David takes it from me, reverentially,

both hands on the hilt. He steps into the open area between the dining room table and the living room sofa. "Considered by many to be the perfect fighting weapon." He assumes a defensive stance, eyes narrowed, ready to strike an unseen foe. "It provides range, control—" He swings it in a whistling arc. "—and power."

"What's it for?" I ask him.

He blinks himself back into our world and lowers the sword. "Beheading vampires."

We look at Travis, who's turned even paler. He waves his thumb at the hallway. "I better go help Shane with . . . stuff."

When he leaves, David resheathes the sword and places it carefully in the duffel bag. It's too long, so the hilt hangs out of the opening.

"Do you miss it?" I hand him as many stakes as I can hold. "The slayage?"

"No," he says, too quickly. "I like what I do now. I want to keep doing it."

Last come the crossbow and quiver of arrows. "Why would she keep these weapons here, when they could be used against her?"

David takes the crossbow. "She wanted to make the world safe from vampires, not the other way around."

"So why would a self-hating vampire start a radio station?"

David stops, still holding the crossbow. "Because I wanted it," he says without looking at me. "She felt bad for almost ending my life." He runs his finger over the trigger. "It was complicated."

"Yeah!" comes a voice from the bedroom.

David stuffs the weapon in the bag. We hurry to the

bedroom as Shane opens the door. He shakes the graph paper, which is full of lines and circles.

"Jackpot," he says and makes a grand gesture to the bed, where the safe sits wide open.

Travis is sifting through a pile of papers. He smiles and hands them to me. "Birth certificate, Social Security card, PIN numbers, passwords. Everything you need to become Elizabeth Vasser." He looks at David. "Didn't find a will, but maybe Ciara can get a copy from Elizabeth's attorney. Just in case, I'll check the other room." He heads into the hall.

"Nice work." I notice Shane's holding a small black jewelry box. "What's that?"

"Oh, it's just—" He hands it to David. "Sorry."

David opens the box. His face goes slack. "She kept it." He sinks onto the bed. "I can't believe she kept it."

"You two were engaged?" I ask him.

"For about a week." His thumb curves around the corner of the box. "Before she turned."

"You must have meant something to her if she kept it." I sit beside him. "I think she'd want you to have it."

He takes the ring out of the box and holds it up to the light, which sparks like fire off the diamond and rubies. "What would I do with it?"

"I could get you a good deal at Dean's."

He looks at me as if I've drowned the cat. "You want me to pawn her engagement ring?"

"Be practical. You could be out of a job." I hold up the documents. "Elizabeth's going to help the station from beyond the grave. Let her help you, too."

David examines the ring in his palm. "I haven't been able to afford a vacation in years. Even just to Florida to see my mom would be nice." He shakes his head hard. "What am I saying? If Elizabeth wanted me to have the ring, she would've given it to me." David puts it back in the box, which he tosses in the safe. He slams the door shut and turns the lock, then stalks out.

Shane carefully sets the safe back in the closet and arranges the row of skirts to hide it.

I follow him in and point to the graph paper in his hand. "What's all that mean?"

He unfolds the paper. "It's complicated, but each number of the combination corresponds to a wheel in the mechanism. This one has three. After finding the contact points—"

"By listening?"

"Right, like in the movies." He explains the process, showing me the click points on the graph paper. I don't catch most of it, but I notice the three numbers: 12, 43, and 61. He's crossed out the first two permutations, leaving four others.

"Fascinating. You'll have to teach me more some time, and I'll show you how to do a pigeon drop." I sift through the closet. "They'll never believe I'm Elizabeth in my Kmart cast-offs." I pull out an ice-blue suit and hold it up in front of me. "Flattering?"

"Very." He nods approvingly at the short hemline of the skirt. "You're going to steal it, aren't you?"

"I'm borrowing it for the meeting. First I have to try it on."

"I'm not talking about the suit." He holds up the graph paper. "I could just tell you the combination, or I could open it for you if you want the ring that bad."

Foiled. I give him an indignant glare. "Why would I steal the ring? I'm not a thief."

He brushes his hand against my arm. "I get it, okay? Running a con makes you feel more alive than anything. You feel powerful, smart, superior."

"That's not—"

"If you want to go back to grifting, I won't stand in your way." He steps back. "But don't ever lie to me, Ciara. Don't play me."

He leaves the closet and shuts the door behind him.

I mull his words as I whip off my clothes. I can run a con and still be a good person, right? I'm pulling this scam *because* I'm a good person. How dare Shane get all judgmental when it's his ass I'm trying to save. He needs a home, he needs his music, he needs a purpose in life.

And David needs a vacation, I tell myself as I open the safe.

After I'm dressed—minus the shoes, tragically—I find the men in Elizabeth's office examining a wall map of the United States.

Shane looks at me. "And you thought *I* was weird."

Each state has a silver coin taped to it. "So she collected state quarters. Lots of people do that." I feel sad that she only made it to Idaho before getting staked.

David hands me a Polaroid photo. It's a nighttime flash shot of a U-Haul truck. On the side of the truck is a picture of racehorses under the word "Kentucky." Scribbled underneath in neat Magic Marker are the date and location of the sighting.

I look up to see rows of U-Haul state design photos pinned to the wall next to the map.

"Okay, that's weird."

The doorbell rings. We all gape at each other for a long second, flatlining from panic. The cat leaps out of David's arms and scampers down the hall.

"The weapons." I dash for the dining room in my bare feet. The jingle of keys comes from the other side of the door. I grab the duffel bag from the table just as the knob turns.

The door swings open to reveal a tall, well-built bald guy in a black uniform. He looks unsurprised to find me here. "Evening, ma'am." He turns and nods to someone behind him in the hallway.

Through the door steps the white-haired man from Gideon's complex. He gives me a wide smile.

"There you are, Pumpkin."

My vision clouds, and I feel my face crumple. My throat, tight as a fist, can squeak only one word.

"Daddy?"

26

Crucify

He holds his hands toward me, palm up. "Look at you, all grown up. In a suit, no less."

All I can do is clutch the straps of David's heavy duffel bag. Instinct tells me to keep the table between myself and this—impersonator.

As if reading my mind, he says, "It's really me. The prodigal father."

I back up, still holding the bag. When it slides off the table, its weight tears it out of my hands and sends it crashing to the floor, wood and metal clattering.

I rub the pulled muscle in my forearm. "Dad, what are you doing here?"

"It's a long story. Can I get a hug first?"

David and Shane come up next to me, one on each side.

"Major Lanham?" David says to the first man, the one who's not *my freaking father*.

"It's Lieutenant Colonel now," the man replies, pointing to something silver on his shoulder. "Good to see you, Fetter."

I turn to David. "You knew about this?"

"No." He holds up his hands. "Okay, I knew we had to hire you as a favor to someone in the Control. I didn't know who or why."

"Ciara."

At the sound of my father's voice, I turn to him.

"Is that all you have to say after eight years?" He opens his arms. "I missed you, Angel."

My throat clogs up. I don't want to move toward him, but I can't help it. His red-gold hair has faded to a shocking white, but the glint in his wide blue eyes is the same one he always had, reading me a bedtime story or gazing at my mom across a crowded revival tent.

He meets me halfway and takes me in his arms. His cozy plumpness is gone, and I can feel his collarbone and shoulder blades through his soft cotton shirt.

I start to sob. None of the questions or accusations matter right now. They feel like they might never matter again.

He passes soothing strokes over my back. "It's all right," he says, "we're here now. No one's going to send me away this time."

I cling to him even after his arms slacken to signal the hug's impending conclusion. Finally he draws me away and wipes the tears from my cheeks with his thumbs. "Don't cry, honey. Everything's going to be okay."

"But—but, why?"

Colonel Lanham gestures to the living room. "Perhaps we should all sit down."

On numb legs I walk to the center of the couch. After

I sit, my father joins me on my right. To my relief, Shane sits on my other side. He extends his hand across me.

"Shane McAllister." His tone is cordial but chilly.

"Ronan O'Riley." Dad shakes his hand and beams at him. "You're a vampire, aren't you? I haven't seen many as young as you. You pass very well."

Shane gives him a nod of acknowledgment. When he sets his hand on the cushion beside me, I place mine over it. Just so things are clear from the start.

The touch of his skin returns my equilibrium. I shift away from my father, ostensibly so that I can see him better. "Start from the beginning."

He opens his mouth, but Colonel Lanham speaks instead.

"Your father has been working undercover with the Control at Gideon's compound for two years." He sits on the edge of the recliner, ramrod straight, as if balancing plates on his head. "We offered him parole from federal prison in exchange for information and his help in this project."

"It was either that or the Witness Protection Program." Dad nudges me with his elbow and winks. "This seemed like more fun, no?"

"What information?" I ask him.

His smile fades, and he lets out a heavy sigh. "I never told you much about my family. That was for your protection. You've heard of the Travellers?"

"Aren't they like gypsies or something?"

He shakes his head emphatically. "They hate that word, 'gypsy.' They're Irish itinerants, folk who travel from place to place in the South and Midwest, selling their wares."

"They're crooks, aren't they?"

"Most of them, no. But my family was one of the best." He looks at Lanham, who frowns. "One of the worst, I mean. I left them when I met your mother. But I kept in touch with them over the years, sent money when they needed it, on the condition that they leave you and your mom alone, which they were happy to do, since you were outsiders—'country folk,' as they'd say."

As he speaks, I notice the wrinkles in the corners of his eyes and mouth, and the way his hands quaver as they illustrate a point. More than his hair has changed in eight years. But not his inherent swagger.

"Anyway," he continues, "I knew enough about my family's activities and whereabouts to help the feds win a racketeering case against them."

Colonel Lanham clears his throat. "We thought this opportunity would appeal to your father, since it gave him a chance to be near you and the possibility of contacting you in the course of the operation."

"And here I am." Dad spreads his hands in one of his trademark expansive gestures, flicking his fingertips upward as if he's conjured himself out of nothing.

"What about Mom?" I ask him.

"What about her?"

"She's still in prison, right?"

"Of course. I always shielded her from any knowledge of my family, so she had no information to offer the FBI."

"But why couldn't you bring her with you?"

A corner of his eye twitches, and he glances at Lanham. "We'll talk about that later."

"Hmm." David is leaning against the wall, arms crossed over his chest. "Mister O'Riley, how—"

"Please, call me Ronan."

"Ronan. How did you escape Gideon's compound?"

"We extracted him," says Colonel Lanham. "Earlier today."

A rush of heat runs up the sides of my neck. "If you could get him out, why not me? I almost died."

Without moving his head, Lanham gives the impression of a nod. "Your father's extraction was a coordinated, covert operation planned in advance. In a cult situation such as Gideon's, a surprise raid to rescue you could have triggered a mass murder or suicide. We didn't want another Waco on our hands."

I consider this, wondering what would happen to Gideon's guests—especially the children—if the Control stormed the compound.

"We can explain more later." Colonel Lanham rises with a sharp exhalation. "Once we get you to the safe house."

"What?" I think of all I have to do for Friday's meeting. "I can't go to a safe house. I have to work."

"Just for a couple nights, Sweet Pea." Dad squeezes my hand. "They'll take you to the station in the morning, make sure it's safe. Besides, this way we can catch up in private."

The flood of questions comes surging back. "First I need to talk to David and Shane." Without looking at my father, I get to my feet and head for the bedroom. Shane walks with me.

Behind me I hear David say to Lanham, "Watch this one. He's new."

In response, Travis mumbles, "No respect."

David joins us in the bedroom. He shoves his hands

in his pockets and gives me a rueful look. "I swear I didn't know your father was involved."

He doesn't seem to be lying. "But this Lanham guy, can I trust him?"

Shane scoffs. "I wouldn't. He's Control."

"He won't hurt you," David says, "but don't think for a minute he has your interests in mind. Everything's a means to an end with these people."

"Then my dad's found kindred spirits."

David frowns, then touches my shoulder. "You've been given a second chance with your father. Don't waste it." He leaves and shuts the door.

I turn to Shane. "So that's my dad."

"The guy who last night you called a 'fucking asshole creep pig-weasel,' if I remember correctly."

"Because I thought he'd abandoned us."

"And now?"

"He looks so old." I stare at the floor. "I did that to him."

"He just seems old because you haven't seen him in so long. Humans age."

"Not like that. Not unless they're in prison, or a vampire farm." I rub my face. "If they've drunk him every two weeks for two years, that's fifty-two times. No wonder he's so thin. You think he's sick?"

"He doesn't smell sick."

"You can smell it?"

"Of course, just like an animal can. It used to help vampires find easy prey. Anymore, we use it to avoid fatal bites." He reaches for my hands, but I pull away. "What?"

"Nothing, it's just—now would be a nice time for you to be normal." I wince as soon as I hear my words. "Sorry."

Shane puts his hands on my shoulders and turns me to face him. "I'm not one for giving advice, but here I'll make an exception." His eyes are cold blue and serious. "Just because someone gives you life doesn't mean you have to give it back."

I nod, wondering if he learned that from his own parents, or Regina, or both.

We head back down the hall. David is in the kitchen, gathering cat supplies. My dad stands in the dining room, examining the tag on the collar Shane left on the table. The white beast rubs against his ankles. Dad looks down and smiles.

"Hey there, Antoine. How's a kitty?"

David drops the bag of cat food on the kitchen floor. It bursts open, scattering kibble across the stone tile. He steps forward, crunching. "She named him Antoine?" He glares at the collar, then at Shane. "You knew. You said it was a rabies tag."

"I didn't want to upset you," Shane says in a low voice, glancing at Lanham and my father. "Besides, I thought you might not want him if you knew his name. The cat needs a home, and he wouldn't last a day at our place."

Impressed as I am by Shane's conniving compassion, I keep my attention on my father. He's squatting down petting the cat, but his eyes are on David, evaluating him.

I know that look. It seeks weakness.

Dad's gaze trips between the animal and David, and I can almost hear the calculations running through his head. He must know who Antoine is to Gideon. But does he know who Antoine is to David? How long will it take him to figure it out? It might not matter, but I can't take that chance.

"Ready, Daddy?" I pipe up to distract his thoughts.

His eyes light up in my direction. He straightens with a grunt and offers his arm in a gallant gesture. "Let's go, Pumpkin."

He always was a sucker for the "Daddy" thing.

Due to Colonel Lanham's presence, my father and I keep the conversation casual on the way to the safe house. I tell him about school, the basics of my job, and he tells me about life in a minimum security federal prison. It sounds a lot like Gideon's lair, minus the bloodletting.

We pull up to a split-level home on a tree-lined street in Silver Spring, a suburb that is neither silver nor springy. The garage door opens as we approach.

I admit, I'm a little disappointed that the "safe house" isn't surrounded by armed guards with radioactive Rottweilers. I hope it's more secure than it looks.

Lanham opens the car door for me. "The bedroom on the top floor should have everything you need."

I pass through a family room, then up a short stairway to the cozy, inviting kitchen. Another turn brings me to another staircase. I grab the railing and bounce up, buoyed by the novelty. The only house I ever lived in was my foster parents'. Before that was mostly motels; after that was dorms and apartments.

On the top level is a large, neat room with homey-looking furniture. The bed is wide and low and bears a faded patchwork quilt. The air's a bit stuffy, so I switch on the wicker ceiling fan, then exchange Elizabeth's suit for a T-shirt and pair of jeans I find in the closet.

As I head downstairs, a man in a black shirt and pants

slides back into the shadows of one of the bedrooms. I wave to him.

"Evening, ma'am." His clipped voice says he doesn't want to chat.

I grab a soda and an egg salad sandwich from the fridge and go down to the family room, where my dad is watching Jay Leno and eating a bowl of cereal.

He beams at my casual clothes. "Now you look like the Ciara I knew." He pats the sofa next to him.

Instead I sit in a chair across the room. I need distance for what I'm about to ask. "You said you'd tell me why you didn't take Mom."

His head jerks back in surprise. "What did we teach you about small talk? When did you get so direct?"

"Just tell me." I try a smile. "Please."

He scoops the last of his cereal into his mouth, then wipes his face with a paper napkin and sets the bowl on a side table. "First, you should know that this place is bugged."

I take a bite of my sandwich, pretending the surveillance doesn't bother me.

"But don't worry," he says. "The Control already knows everything I'm about to tell you." He mutes the television, then sits back on the cushion with a sigh. "I couldn't take your mother into Witness Protection because she's not my wife."

The sandwich goes dry in my mouth. "You got divorced?"

He puts a hand to his chest, as if my words are more shocking than his. "Divorced? No. My goodness, no. We were never married."

"*What?*" I brandish my sandwich at him, still chewing. "Are you fucking kidding me?"

His eyes widen. "Language, Ciara."

I struggle to swallow. "Am I really your daughter? Am I Mom's daughter?"

"Of course you are." He holds up both index fingers. "Let me explain. When I was eighteen, I married another Traveller. It was an arranged thing, the way marriages often are among my people. She was only fifteen."

"Yuck."

He ignores this. "Your mom and I met when we were twenty-two. Her grandmother was a, er, customer of mine."

"A mark, you mean."

"The usual scam." He dramatizes the process with almost hypnotic hand gestures. "Go to an old person's house, convince them their roof desperately needs fixing, offer to do the job, then disappear with their cash deposit." He grins. "Your mom tracked me down on my way out of town and . . . well . . ."

"Kicked your ass?"

"In a sense. A week later, I left everything to be with her—my family, my religion, my home." He gives a sly smile and flicks up his fingertips. "After I fixed her grandmother's roof."

"Why didn't you just divorce your first wife?"

"Even if I'd asked, she would have refused. The Travellers are strict Catholics." He heaves a sigh. "It's the way we were brought up. Divorce is a terrible sin."

A fuse just blew in my head. "More terrible than adultery?"

"Yes. I would've been excommunicated."

"But you just said you changed religions for Mom, so why would you care?"

"When you're born a Catholic, especially among my

people, you're part of a body. Being cut off from that body is like losing a piece of yourself."

"I don't get how that's more important than marrying the woman you love."

"I don't expect you to understand. We raised you as a Pentecostal, like your mother. For you, and for most of the people who came to our revivals, living in sin is worse than divorce. That's why we never told anyone."

I wave my hands. "Don't assume anything about what I believe. As far as I'm concerned, the lies are the worst part of it." At least until the next thought hits me. "Do you have children with this woman?"

"I do not."

I squint at him, wishing I could play back his reply to search for the deception. "Four years and she never got pregnant? I'm assuming no birth control, of course, since that would be a sin."

He scratches his ear, face reddening. "That's more detail than I want to discuss with my daughter."

"Why didn't you tell me the truth when I was a kid?" As soon as the question leaves my mouth, I know the answer. They figured I'd blab to someone, and they'd be exposed as sanctimonious hypocrites.

"I'm sorry we never told you. It came out in the trial, but you were only allowed in the courtroom long enough to testify." His pause swells the tension. "Since you were the key witness against us."

I take a sudden renewed interest in my sandwich. "They made me testify. I couldn't lie on the stand."

I feel his gaze on me as I pick the flaxseeds off the crust of the multigrain bread. For some reason they've always bothered me.

My father doesn't speak, and in his silence lies the accusation I can't deny.

I wasn't just the key witness; I was the fink. I gave the cops the anonymous tip that started the entire investigation.

If I could reach the remote, I'd un-mute the TV to crack the oppressive hush. There's a band on the *Tonight Show* I don't recognize, with a female lead singer in a red muumuu.

I can feel my father watching me, waiting for my confession. Now I know why Shane's silence last night tore up my insides. I'm tired of being on trial.

I turn to look him in the eye. "Are you going to do this for the next eight years, too?"

"Do what?"

"Not talk to me."

He shifts his weight. "I've been undercover. I haven't talked to anyone on the outside."

"For two years. And the six years before that, you were in prison, not calling me. Not writing."

"Not being called. Not being written to. Not being visited by my own daughter."

My stomach twists at his victim voice. "Illinois is a long way from here."

"Your foster parents were an hour's drive from the prison, and I know they offered to bring you." His voice rises, bludgeoning the air between us. "In the eighteen months before college, you never came to see me. Not once."

"Because you never called."

"Why was it my job to call you? You were the one who put me there."

"And that's why I needed you to call me. To tell me I was forgiven." My voice cracks on the last word.

He looks away. He can't say it.

My throat grinds out a whisper. "Mom forgave me."

His jaw clenches. "Yes, she was good at that. Not like you and me."

I enunciate each word. "I'm not like you."

He lifts his head to meet my gaze. "You're exactly like me. We hurt people even when we don't mean to. And when we do mean to . . ." His smile is both proud and diabolical. "The Control told me all about your last con. A masterpiece."

My hand clenches around the sandwich, squeezing egg salad over my fingers. "I needed money for college."

"So did that man's children."

"Stop it."

"Ciara, we do what we have to do." He comes over and sits on the arm of my chair. "That man was greedy, like all marks. He wanted to get rich quick. He was cheating on his wife, for heaven's sake. He deserved everything you did to him." Dad sighs and rests his hands on his knees in a posture of defeat. "I only wish you hadn't compromised your virtue to make the score. Your mother and I raised you to be decent."

I lean away from him and scoff. "What does sex have to do with decency?"

He doesn't answer, just cocks his head as if I'm speaking Swahili.

I glare at him. "I spent my childhood watching you steal from people who weren't greedy, just gullible. How is that raising me to be decent?"

He stands and moves away, waving his hand dismissively. "Regardless, I don't think you should be dating a vampire."

My brain goggles at the rapid change in subject. "What?"

"I've lived with them for two years. They only care about feeding their needs."

"Shane's different."

"Maybe now he is. But it's just a matter of time before he decays into a monster."

"Not if I can help it."

"And you can't."

I won't have this argument with him. "I'm only twenty-four. I'm not looking for a husband."

"And one day when you hurt him, he won't crawl away quietly like your last boyfriend did."

"This isn't about the mark, and it's not about Shane." I stand and face him. "Say it, Dad. I betrayed you. But you just did the same thing to your own family."

He eyes me up and down, coldly. "Yes, I learned about loyalty from the master."

My chest tightens. I shouldn't let him do this to me. I shouldn't feel guilty. I shouldn't care how much I've hurt this lying, scheming sociopath.

The tears come anyway. Immediately my father's at my side, his arms around me.

"Ciara, I'm so sorry. I didn't mean it." He strokes my back in soothing circles. "Angel, please don't cry." His voice is rough around the edges, like he'll break down himself any moment. "It's not your fault I'm a crook. You just did what you thought was right."

"I didn't know they'd send you away." I pull back and wipe my face. "I thought you'd get a fine or maybe a few days in the local jail. I just wanted you and Mom to stop so we could have a normal life."

"I know. You didn't realize you were knocking down such a big house of cards." He picks up a tissue box from the side table and hands it to me. "You didn't know about the rest of it: the insurance fraud, the phony investment schemes, the identity thefts."

His last words stop the flow of my tears. I drag the tissue over my eyes, so hard it pulls my lashes. Time to wrestle my brain back to business.

I glance at the clock. "I'd better get to bed. I have a lot of work to do tomorrow."

"Ciara, have a seat for just a minute longer."

I sit, this time next to him on the couch, though not close enough to touch.

He folds his hands. "I want to help you."

"Help me what?"

"I know why you and your friends were at that apartment."

My face stays straight, even as my mind is screaming *Oh shit!* "We were just cleaning up."

"And gathering her papers so you could pose as her."

"We weren't." I remember the bugs. "And keep your voice down."

"The Control knows about your plan, and they don't care. It's not their jurisdiction."

"They wouldn't care if I impersonated one of their agents? Not that I am."

"In the short term, all they care about is getting Gideon. I've given them enough evidence against him to ensure my freedom—and yours—for a long time."

"What kind of evidence?"

"Photos. Documentation." He tugs on the end of his sleeve and looks away. "Physical evidence."

I wince. "Were you bitten a lot?"

"The usual two-week rotation. I'd feel sick and tired the day after, but the rest of the time it wasn't half-bad."

I decide not to undergo the does-being-bitten-feel-good discussion with my father.

"So tell me your scheme," he says. "Friday's the big day, huh?"

"How do you know all this?"

"Elizabeth's office is bugged. So are her phone lines. And no, David doesn't know."

I hesitate. He already knows about the scam, so I wouldn't jeopardize it by telling him. And I could use his help. I'm sure I haven't thought of all the angles. Saving the station is more important than my pride.

Speaking of pride, the criminal's kryptonite, a not-so-small part of me wants to flaunt my work, to show my father what I've learned. Show him what I've become.

"All right." I pick up my sandwich, suddenly hungry again. "Here's the deal."

27

Everybody Wants to Rule the World

August 2
8:00 a.m.
An anonymous Control agent drives us to the station. It feels odd planning a crime under the watchful eye of a man in uniform, but what my dad said makes sense: outmaneuvering a communications conglomerate is small potatoes next to capturing Gideon. Actually, the scam is big potatoes, but the Control doesn't eat potatoes. Anyway . . .

The station's front door is locked as always. I knock.

"Go around," says a voice I recognize as Shane's.

I lead Dad to the cellar door at the back of the building, the door that connects via a closed corridor to the downstairs lounge. "So they don't fry," I explain.

We come upstairs to find Travis at my desk with his laptop, color printer, and binding machine. Shane and

David stand behind him, and Franklin sits at his own desk with a cache of sharpened pencils within reach.

Shane steps forward. "Ciara, what's he doing here?"

I walk over to him. "Dad's going to help us with the con."

"You told him?"

"He already knew." I look at David. "The Control bugged Elizabeth's office and phones."

David grimaces and lets out a sharp exhale. "What about my office? What about downstairs?"

"I don't know," my dad says, "but I could check if you like."

David's shoulders sag in relief. "Thank you. Let's start in the lounge."

When they're downstairs out of hearing, I turn to Shane. "You could be a little friendlier to my dad."

"He looks at me like I'm a circus lion about to turn on my tamer."

"Ooh, I'm your tamer?" I tug his shirt collar to bring his mouth to mine. "Let me get my whip and chair."

Travis clears his throat. "When y'all get your tongues off each other's tonsils, I'll show you the file." With a few swift mouse moves, he displays a two-page print preview. One page contains a surreptitious photo of the real Elizabeth, followed by a list of fun facts about her. "All we gotta do is replace the information with disinformation."

I pull his digital camera out of my lower drawer and turn to Franklin. "I'm ready for my close-up, Mister DeMille."

In the parking lot, Franklin shoots me doing mundane things like walking to my—I mean, Elizabeth's—Mercedes. To simulate candidness, I pick my teeth in the rearview mirror.

Soon David and my father join us. Franklin starts snapping shots of David. I scan the woods for the Control agents I know are patrolling, but even in the morning light I can't see them in their mottled green daytime uniforms. I doubt Gideon would send a human to do his work, anyway, so we're probably safe until dark.

Dad stands next to me, chin in hand, examining David.

"Hold everything," he says suddenly. "I have an idea."

David stops his charade of casualness and turns to my dad as if awaiting orders from General Patton.

"I know what this con is missing." Dad takes a dramatic pause. "Emotion."

I ask him to explain, knowing I'll regret it.

"These Skywave folks," he says, "won't believe Elizabeth has changed her mind just for the money. After all, the whole reason she was improving the station was so she could sell it." He points at David. "What if she has a better reason to keep it?"

"I don't get it," I say, though I actually do. I just don't want to be the one to explain it to my boss.

"Hear me out." Dad slips into sales mode—not that he was ever much out of it. "A relationship gives Elizabeth a plausible motive for keeping the station. After all, she wouldn't put her ever-lovin' honey out of work."

David looks at him, then me, with more than a touch of trepidation. "So we pretend we're going out."

I gasp. "No, more than that." I reach into my—I mean, Elizabeth's—purse and pull out the tiny black jewelry box.

David advances on me. "You stole the ring?"

"I was going to give it to you, once you'd wised up enough to take it."

He snatches the box from me and opens it, looking relieved it's not empty.

"A good con is all in the details." I reach forward and pull out the ring, then slip it on my finger. "We get a picture of me wearing this and maybe us holding hands."

"That's brilliant, Pumpkin." Dad beams at me. I feel my face flush with pride. "But better yet, wait until the meeting tomorrow to show the ring and announce the engagement. It'll create a distraction." He waves a hand between me and David. "You two should kiss for the photo."

My smile fades. "But he's my boss."

"No, you're his boss, in our new reality."

"*Our* reality? When did this become your con?"

"When I improved it." He tilts his head toward the station. "I'm sure the corpse will understand."

My jaw drops as I realize he's referring to Shane. For a moment I can't find my voice.

Finally I raise a trembling hand and point to the station. "Go."

"Honey, I didn't mean—"

"Now." I turn my back. I can't even look at him.

The sound of crunching driveway pebbles fades as he walks away. I look up at David. "I'm so sorry."

"Why?"

"For what he suggested. I know why he did it. He doesn't want me with Shane, so he thinks he can push me into another man's arms. I'm not some gypsy wench who'll let Mum and Da choose her husband."

"I'm sure your father just wants you to be happy." He puts his hands in his pockets. "So how do we do this?"

"Do what?"

"Kiss."

I snort. "We don't. It's stupid."

"It's not. You said, 'It's all in the details.' A sneaky candid of us kissing will make the engagement a lot more credible. It'll already be established in their minds that we're a couple—that Elizabeth and I are a couple—so it won't come out of the blue."

I rub my temples and wish he were wrong. I should have figured it out myself, and probably would have if I weren't so pissed at my dad.

"You're right." Determined to be a professional, I move to stand beside Elizabeth's car. "Let's get it over with."

David joins me, and we stand there looking like idiots for a few moments. "I'll ask again," he says. "How do we do this?"

I shrug. "Close our eyes and think of England?"

"Are we done yet?" Franklin yells from the other end of the parking lot.

"Keep shooting until we tell you to stop," I call to him, then turn back to David. "Pretend I'm Elizabeth."

His dark green eyes droop at the corners.

"But don't look sad," I add. "Remember, we just got engaged."

I hold my hand up to display the ring. He takes my fingers and runs his thumb over the diamond, a dozen emotions playing over his face. The breeze suddenly drops to nothing. Along with the distant *click-whir* of the camera, I swear I can hear my own pounding pulse.

"I really loved her," he murmurs.

"I know you did." I stop myself from asking why.

"But it's time to put away the past." He covers the ring with his palm, then shifts his gaze to meet mine. "Can you help me?"

I want to look away, break the connection our all-too-human eyes are forming. "Depends what you mean by 'help.'" I pull him closer with the hand he's holding. "If you mean, can I give you one last moment with her, one chance to say good-bye the way you wanted to, then yes."

He draws the back of his fingertips over my cheek, then leans in close. "Good-bye," he whispers.

I expect the kiss to be tentative, awkward. Instead, David's mouth meets mine with a familiar conviction, as if we've done this a thousand times. As the kiss deepens, his longing makes me dizzy, a wave pulling me under. It feels like it could drown me.

He pulls me tight against him. I can't push him away, can't even wedge a hand between our bodies, so I respond the way Elizabeth should have, returning his passion and making him feel, for a moment, that he's not a heartsick fool. As he presses me against the car and his fingers tangle in my hair, I find myself hoping—and fearing—that I'll never be the object of such a love, one that could bring a man to his knees and never let him stand again.

His mouth tenses suddenly, and he draws in a sharp breath through his nose. He pulls away, eyes glistening.

"Okay?" I whisper.

"Yeah." He passes a hand over his mouth, then clears his throat. "I think that went well."

"Me, too," I try to chirp, hoping to ease the terrible weight of the moment. My face feels like it's been in a sauna.

I signal to Franklin, promising myself I'll never think about the kiss again.

David says, "Um . . ."

"No." I put up a palm between us. "No 'um.' Let's just—leave it."

He nods quickly. "Good idea."

A car is rumbling toward us down the gravel driveway, sending a cloud of dust into the trees.

Lori.

She doesn't even pull into a parking spot, just shuts off the engine in front of me and leaps out.

"Where have you been? I've been calling you for three days." She slams the car door. "I went to your apartment and some goonie-looking guy told me to mind my own business. What the hell's going on?" She steps back and scans me. "And why are you wearing a suit?"

I take her hands. "I'm so sorry about the phone. I was held hostage, and then the battery ran out and I didn't have time to charge it."

"Hostage? Are you okay? And again, what's with the suit?"

I hesitate. She knows about the vamps, but nothing about my past. "I have a big meeting tomorrow."

"Oh." She looks at David, then at Franklin, who just walked up to us. Her voice lowers. "Does it have anything to do with, you know . . ." She makes fangs with her middle fingers.

I look past her shoulder to see my dad striding toward us. I seize Lori's arm and drag her toward Elizabeth's car. "Tell you what, I'll explain it all over lunch."

"Isn't it a little early—"

"Greetings!"

Lori turns and smiles at my father's approach. "Hello."

"You must be one of Ciara's college friends," he says to her in a snake-smooth voice.

Lori shakes his hand and introduces herself as I stand there hoping the earth will swallow me as a midmorning snack.

"Pleased to meet you," he says to her, "I'm Ciara's father."

Lori's face goes blank for a moment. "Oh, you mean her foster father."

He turns to me. "Pumpkin? What did you tell her?"

"That you were dead."

Lori gapes. "Wha . . . ?"

I take her arm to lead her inside. "David, I'm taking a very long coffee break."

"Wait," my father says. "Lori, do you have any acting experience?"

9:45 a.m.
My best friend Lori, innocent little cutie-pie Lori, the one uncorrupted element in my *entire fucking life*, has turned into a monster.

I stand in the parking lot with my father, watching her pretend to be me. She hikes her miniskirt into microskirt territory, flirts with David, jams in my driver's seat to an imaginary song on the radio, and generally acts like a dork.

Dad thought it would be a great idea for Elizabeth's marketing director Ciara Griffin to come to the meeting with her tomorrow. I admit a bigger staff makes Elizabeth look more impressive, but despite Lori's enthusiasm for the role of yours truly, she's a novice. And despite Dad's qualifications, I'm beginning to resent his enhancements to my operation, like I'm a kid who needs help with her science project.

I glare at him. "If she gets in trouble because of this—"

"It's her choice. And look how jazzed she is."

He's right. After an initial flurry of indignation that I'd hidden my darkest secret from her, Lori adjusted rather well to my criminal past and present. If I were a mugger or a bank robber, she'd feel different, but people think con artists are cool.

Mostly because we are.

10:15 a.m.

"This was your dad's idea?"

"Yes, although I had to agree it was an improvement on the plan."

Shane glowers at the empty chair behind David's desk. I brought him in here so we could speak privately about The Kiss, away from the mockery of Travis and Franklin. "Where's your father now?"

"Outside, directing Lori on the finer points of being Ciara Griffin. I couldn't watch anymore. Besides, I wanted you to hear about this from me."

Shane's face is set in a stony pensiveness, his posture closed, arms folded over his chest. He flicks an icy glance at me. "Why? What's the big deal?"

"No. None big deal. I mean, it was nothing." I drag a hand through my hair. "If I seem nervous, it's not because it affected me. I just didn't know how you would react."

"You think I'm a jealous man?"

"Kinda, yeah."

"Insecure?"

"No," I hurry to say. "Just sensitive."

He takes a step closer, backing me up against the desk. "Do you want me to get mad?"

"No."

His lips curve in a crafty smile. "Good. Because it'll be a lot more fun to get even."

11:15 a.m.

I stare at the Gallery of Me, both genuine and pretend, on Travis's computer screen.

"Am I really that obnoxious?" I ask Lori over a box of doughnuts at my desk.

"Yes," Franklin answers.

"But now you know where I get it from." I glance at David's closed office door. My dad is in there ingratiating himself with my boss. In just a few hours they've become good buds. David's probably hungry for a substitute father since his own died so young. As for my dad, he wants to be everyone's friend, just in case he needs to take advantage of them one day.

At least it keeps both of them out of my hair.

I click and drag the best picture of Lori/me into the box in Travis's report. "We'll print and bind this, then have it messengered to Jolene's boss right at five o'clock."

"What about Jolene?" Lori flips through the pages of the report. "Won't she recognize us at the meeting to-morrow?"

I check my watch. "Travis had agreed to get the report to Jolene this afternoon. Of course, that was back when he could still do daylight. He's probably called her by now to tell her that, A, there were some late developments that had to be added to the report, thus delaying its produc-tion, and, B, his car broke down and she needs to meet him at five at his office, where his curmudgeonly associate

Leonard—played by Franklin—will be waiting with the original report."

Franklin nods. "For some reason Ciara thought my personality would mesh well with Jolene's."

"Well enough to have a drink while waiting for Travis to walk back from the print shop with the addendum she wants. She sees the original report—the one that shows the real Elizabeth and the real Ciara—inserted in that envelope."

Franklin holds up exhibit A.

"So what's this addendum she's waiting for from the printer?" Lori asks.

"Travis has promised her some serious dirt on yours truly." I lean back in my chair. "See, the key to conning someone is to exploit their weakness. Jolene's weakness is me, or more precisely, her hatred of me."

"You ruined her bachelorette party," Lori says. "But how long is she going to sit around waiting for Travis before she takes the original report?"

"As long as it takes her to pass out." Franklin shakes a bottle of prescription sedatives. "It'll help time go by faster for her."

"How much time?" she asks me.

"Until after our meeting tomorrow."

"You're going to drug her for over twelve hours?"

"David will be there all night to monitor her vitals. Shane'll stand watch so David can get some sleep before our big meeting."

She holds up a photo of The Kiss. "Shane and David, together all night? I'd love to be a fly on that wall."

I take the picture from her. "That issue's been settled to everyone's satisfaction."

"So then what happens at sunrise?"

"Franklin will be there when she wakes up. Only he won't be the same man."

"Hi, I'm Frankie!" Franklin slips seamlessly into *La Cage aux Folles* mode. "I am *so* sorry about my brother Leonard's party. My gracious, they get out of hand sometimes. You're lucky no one called the cops. Let me fetch you some coffee. Do you need Sweet'n Low?"

I fill in the part of the groggy Jolene. "Whah? What happened? Why are you talking like that?"

"I guess you had a leeeetle too much butterscotch schnapps, judging by the photos."

I cross to Franklin's desk. "What photos?"

He hands me the digital camera. I pretend to flip through the pictures, then gasp. "Oh. My God. Is that me? Who's that guy?"

"I don't know, but my goodness, he has a nice butt. Did he mention my name at all?"

"You drugged me!" I mime hurling the camera against the wall. "That's what I think of your stupid tricks!"

"Hey! Do you know how much that camera cost?"

"Not as much as a lawsuit will cost *you*."

Franklin flips his hand. "You can work that out with Travis when he gets back. Since he already downloaded the pictures, I imagine there'll be some negotiation." He looks up through his lashes. "Unless you have somewhere you have to be."

As Jolene, I look at my watch. "My meeting! Just give me the report."

"You sure you don't want coffee? I found this to-die-for Costa Rican blend."

"Leonard, cut the evil twin bullshit and give me the fucking report!"

Franklin hands me a different envelope—identical to the one containing the original report—and waggles his shoulders in indignation. "Aren't you the fussy little queen bitch this morning?"

"And . . . scene." I bow, then speak to Lori in my own voice. "Without opening the sealed envelope to look at the report, which is mostly blank, she runs to her car and drives away like a maniac. But the night before, Noah siphoned off most of the fuel, and Jim tampered with the fuel gauge serving unit so that her needle stays on half a tank. When she runs out of gas, somewhere on a country road between here and the next town, she tries to call the office, but alas, her cell phone battery is dead, due to the fact that it's been used all night to play Tetris and check the local weather in Hong Kong. Oddly enough, her phone's car adapter has vanished."

"Back up a second," Lori says. "Why does Franklin need to act like he's his own twin?"

"Just to disorient her, then piss her off. The more emotional she is, the faster she'll get out of there and the less likely she'll look at the blank report."

Lori nods. "So she misses the meeting."

"She misses the meeting and probably gets fired. Travis and his detective agency have packed up and disappeared that morning, so she has no legal recourse. Since he has naked photos of her, she'll drop the whole thing to protect her new marriage."

"Wow." Lori sets down her half-eaten doughnut. "You're really going to screw her over, aren't you?"

"Uh-huh." No point in showing remorse I don't feel. "But it's screwery in self-defense. She can't wait to fire us all after the takeover."

Lori looks nauseated. "And that makes it okay?"

"Yes, it does." I cross the office and pull my chair to sit next to her. "I've done a lot of bad shit in my life. This summer, for the first time, I've done really good shit. These vampires are finally questioning the so-called fact that their future is nothing but an endless fade. They're starting to live in the Now. I won't let anyone take that away from them. And no one is going to take away the one good deed of my life." I pick up another doughnut. "Especially not some horse-faced twat like Jolene."

My phone rings. It's Travis, who reveals that he phoned my nemesis about the report's delay. Jolene was predictably pissed but heartened when she heard that the reason for said delay was information that could hurt me.

I hang up and turn to Lori. "I'll understand if you don't want to be a part of this, but I need to know now. Are you in?"

She stares at the picture of her/me in Travis's report, then swallows hard. "I'm in." She sets the report aside. "So who's the 'nice butt' guy in Jolene's naked pictures?"

Franklin snickers. "Let's just say Shane will have his photographic revenge tonight."

12:00 p.m.
David, Lori, and I grab a table at the local diner and go over the script, with my dad's semi-unwelcome assistance. David and I are the two major players, with Lori supporting us as a shill, there to help create our reality—or our "truth," as she calls it. She seems to relish the opportunity to put one over on The Man.

The Man, in this case, consists of Alfred Bombeck and Sherilyn Murphy, the Skywave executives overseeing the

WVMP takeover. Travis's research gives me a few personal details I can use: Murphy has "adopted" a wolf pack in Yellowstone National Park, and Bombeck thinks the New York Yankees are evil incarnate.

Elizabeth's notes and e-mails reveal Murphy and Bombeck as a good-cop/bad-cop team. One of them (Bombeck) lays on the fear tactics, trying to railroad the young station owner into parting with her holding. Meanwhile, Murphy plays on Elizabeth's need for economic security and the knowledge that the station will be able to grow and blossom in the best possible hands.

They're con artists even if they don't know it. But I think they know it.

1:30 p.m.

I wait in line alone at Motor Vehicles, ready to commit my first identity theft. I think about the credit card commercials that portray such bandits as sadistic hedonists, cackling over the booty they've bought with their victims' good names. I tell myself I'm not like them. I tell myself this theft serves a noble purpose. I tell myself there's no other way.

I convince myself. It's not hard.

"Next?"

I approach the counter and grimace at the ennui-ridden clerk. "I lost my driver's license."

"Was it stolen?" she asks. Her tone suggests she doesn't care.

I sigh and conjure a blush. "No, I was bungee jumping yesterday, out in Washington County? You know, where that big gorge is?" The clerk blinks. "Anyway, my license was in my shirt pocket. It never bounced back up with me. It's probably halfway to the Chesapeake Bay by now, if a trout hasn't eaten it."

She's already torn off a number. She pushes it and a blank form across the counter at me. I thank her, glumly, and move to the waiting area. An electronic marquee announces the latest news and offers the occasional music trivia, the inanity of which would make the DJs snarf their blood cocktails.

My number dings. This clerk, an athletic-looking brunette in her thirties, appears to have taken her happy pills today.

"Good morning! What can I do for you?"

I tell her my sad bungee story, and she relates her own extreme sports experiences while typing in the information from Elizabeth's birth certificate and Social Security card.

"I just can't get enough of that adrenaline rush," she coos. "Of course, you know what I mean."

My heart pounds in my ears, and every sense is amplified times ten. "Absolutely."

When requested, I hand her several more proofs of residence than she needs, plus a twenty-dollar bill for the fee.

"Stand up against this wall and smile, okey-doke?" She hums along with the Blue Öyster Cult tune piped in over the speakers. "Ready? Don't say 'cheese,' say, 'Tomorrow's Friday!'"

Five minutes later, I pick up Elizabeth's new driver's license, featuring a picture of me looking as if I just swallowed a turkey bone.

I'm in the game again. I give the clerk a wave and a broad smile. "Tomorrow's Friday!"

* * *

2:15 p.m.
I use Elizabeth's debit card to buy a decent pair of shoes to go with her suit. For the meeting, of course.

5:45 p.m.
The Control robo-dude drives me and my dad back to the safe house.

5:52 p.m.
Franklin text-messages me:

    BOTTOMS UP

28

Money For Nothing

August 3
5:54 a.m.
I wake to the sounds of Jim signing off with the Stones' "It's Only Rock 'n' Roll." The song gives me the soul-deep inspiration I need to jump out of bed and begin the Day of Triumph. In the shower I wail it three times over, full volume.

I put on Elizabeth's ice-blue suit, then bop down to the kitchen, where my dad sits with a cup of coffee and yesterday's newspaper, still in his robe and slippers.

"Wish me luck?"

"You don't need it." He looks at me over his reading glasses. "I wish I could be there."

I breeze past him to the refrigerator. "What are your plans for the day?"

"Gideon issues."

"I hope they hurry up and neutralize that motherf—uh, that guy soon. This place is nice, but I want to go home." I pull out the orange juice and the package of English muffins. "Ooh, honey wheat. My favorite."

"It'll all be over before you know it."

"Then what? Will you stick around, or will the Control move you somewhere else?"

"Hard to say. Ciara, I've been meaning to ask, what church do you go to now?"

I put the muffin in the toaster and push down the lever, harder than I have to. "I don't go to church."

"So you have a purely private relationship with Our Lord?"

I snort. "Come on, you don't really believe all that shit, do you?"

"Hey! What did I say about your language?"

"Goddamn it, Dad, your preaching days are over. Drop the act."

"It's not an act."

"Have you forgotten? All those years, you and Mom weren't really healing people. You were fooling them."

"Their faith was real," he says, "and that's what healed them."

"But yours wasn't."

"Maybe not at first." His voice lowers and sobers. "But if you play a role long enough, eventually you become it."

"In other words, fake it till you make it? I'll try that. One day I'll be a rich vampire owning a radio station. Maybe I'll even get taller." I pop the English muffin from the toaster, even though it's not done. I just want to get out of here.

"Ciara, I know you're bitter over the lies you think your mother and I told—"

"That I *think* you told?"

"—but don't take it out on God."

"Can we talk about this later? I need to keep my head in the game."

"Sure, honey." He sits back in his chair, folds his paper, and sets it aside. "I want you to know, whatever happens, I'm proud of you."

I turn toward the counter and fumble with the butter dish. My vision's gone cloudy, and my knife misses the muffin and spreads butter on my thumb. "Tell me again at the end of the day, okay? Assuming you're not bailing me out of jail."

I blink back the wetness—for the sake of my mascara, of course—and finish buttering the English muffin. Then I set it in front of him on the table.

"Here, you're too skinny." I bend down to kiss his forehead. "I'll call you when it's over."

He grabs my hand as I move away. His face is strangely solemn. "Good luck, Angel."

"Thought you said I didn't need it." I wave at him on my way to the garage, where my Control chauffeur awaits. Something makes me want to look over my shoulder at my father one more time, like a kid on her first day at kindergarten.

But I keep moving, straight ahead, a woman on a mission.

*   *   *

8:25 a.m.

Skywave's regional headquarters looms like a glass Godzilla over the skyline of its Virginia suburb. As I walk toward it, followed by my entourage—and the Control goon at a discreet distance—I resist the urge to gawk at its gleaming façade like a tourist at the Empire State Building. I'm supposed to be here, after all, and I have to act the part.

My name is Elizabeth Vasser. I was born in Evanston, Illinois, on July 19, 1970. I graduated *magna cum laude* from the University of Chicago in 1992 with degrees in psychology and criminology. I play racquetball, poorly, and once won a Skee-Ball contest on the boardwalk of Wildwood, New Jersey. Pet peeves: men who curse in public and people who use the word "schizophrenic" to mean "of two minds."

My name is Elizabeth Vasser.

8:30 a.m.

"Good morning, Ms. Vasser. Welcome to Skywave." The young blond assistant holds out his hand in greeting as he strides across the lobby's marble floor.

"Thank you so much." I shake his hand with a warm, dry palm. "Let me introduce my staff. This is David Fetter, my general manager, and Ciara Griffin, our marketing director."

His regard lingers on the latter for an extra moment before turning back to me. "I'm Jonathan, Sherilyn Murphy's assistant. You can call me Jon," he adds in Lori's direction. "Ms. Murphy asked me to bring you up to the conference room."

He leads us down a hallway lined with gold and platinum records on the wall. I catch Lori checking out Jonathan's butt and give her a warning glare. It's not as if they can go out, considering he thinks she's me.

The brass-railed elevator displays a television screen running a music video by a new country/western band. On the top floor, we enter a lavishly decorated conference room, the walls of which are filled with autographed photos of recording artists.

Two executives await us, flanked by what looks like stacks of contracts. Between them sits a single windowed envelope.

A sharp-dressed brunette in her late thirties stands to greet us. "Good morning, I'm Sherilyn Murphy. We've spoken on the phone many times." She points to my lapel. "Hey, great pin."

I finger the silver brooch. "Thanks, I just love wolves."

"Me, too. There's something magical about them, don't you think?" She gushes as if wolves are a rock star she would sleep with if she could.

A gruff, balding man in his fifties joins us. "Alfred Bombeck. Glad you could be on time."

"I almost couldn't get out of bed this morning." I rub my eyes and smile at David. "We were up late watching the White Sox beat the Yankees in extra innings."

Bombeck's face lights up. "How about that bottom of the fourteenth?" His eyes narrow with sadistic pleasure. "I loved watching those bastards in the bullpen get pummeled."

Jonathan offers us coffee and Danish on the credenza. I resist the free food, taking only a small cup of coffee before I sit. Near the contracts, three expensive-looking pens are lined up like a military color guard.

"Your station has acquired a bit of notoriety this summer," Murphy says. "The vampire gimmick was very successful."

Bombeck clears his throat. "Odd, but successful."

"We've talked to our marketing folks," Murphy says, "and they want to continue the vampire theme after the takeover. With our own radio personalities, of course."

I give them a sweet smile to mask my utter hatred of everything they stand for. "Rather than waste your valuable time, I should be frank. We've decided to decline the buyout offer. I don't want to sell the station."

The Skywave folks gape at me. Bombeck sputters. "What? Just a week ago you couldn't wait to take our money."

"If circumstances have changed," Murphy purrs, "I'm sure we can work something out."

"Circumstances have changed." I beam at David. "We want to leave the station as a legacy to our children." I pull my left hand from under the table. "David and I are getting married."

"Oh my God!" On cue, Lori squeals, rolls back her chair, and rushes around the table to hug David, then me. "I'm so happy for you!" She yanks my hand closer to her face. "I saw this ring earlier but didn't want to say anything. I thought maybe it was one of those 'pre-engagement' rings guys give when they're not ready for commitment but don't want to lose the girlfriend." She hugs me again and whispers, "How am I doing?"

"Perfect," I whisper back. In my regular voice, I say, "Thank you, Ciara. It's wonderful to have your support."

Murphy coughs. "Congratulations. But I think we can offer your children an even better legacy."

"Given the recent popularity of the station, we've raised the offer a bit." Bombeck slides the envelope down the table to me. Through its plastic window I see the words, "Pay to the Order of Elizabeth Vasser."

"Thank you, but no." I try to slide it back, but Bombeck's hand stops its movement.

"Please at least look at the amount," he says. "You don't want to walk away from this deal with your eyes closed."

My hand wants to open the envelope, just to see, but my better judgment says, *Don't even think about it.* It makes my hand push harder. "I'm sorry, but the station is priceless to me."

Murphy cuts in with a strained smile. "We understand that, but if this deal breaks down, our bosses will want to know that we made every effort to convince you. If we tell them that you never even looked at the figure, it could make things difficult for our jobs."

I calculate the risk of seeing the check versus that of pissing them off further. If I get them in trouble, they might investigate Elizabeth's change of heart. "Just tell me how much."

"It's on the check," Murphy says evenly.

I know where this is going. Seeing a check with Elizabeth's (my) name on it will have more impact than hearing an abstract number out loud. I'll imagine what I could do with all those zeros and commas. I want to push it away again.

More than anything, though, I want to get out of here. Things are running too smoothly. A con without a hitch is a con waiting to implode. Maybe the check is the hitch, just a speed bump.

A piece of clear tape holds the envelope shut. It pops off easily. The check is a lovely mottled pink that complements the rubies on my ring.

$10,000,000.00.

I am Elizabeth Vasser. By the end of the day I'll have a passport in her name with my picture on it. By the end of the weekend I'll be in New Zealand. By the end of next week, the check will have cleared into a new offshore account, and I'll never have to work again. No more ramen noodles and piece-of-shit cars and shoes with holes in their soles.

I'll set up the DJs in fine fashion for years. Maybe they could start a new radio station. I'll get Lori her Sherwood ghost tour business. I'll support my dad, and my mom when she gets out of jail, and they'll never have to cheat anyone again. The world's overall misery level will actually drop.

My hands begin to quiver. I blink hard to break the spell the money is casting over me. My hesitation only weakens our position. If Skywave thinks Elizabeth can be bought, they'll never stop trying.

Beautiful New Zealand. Land of *Lord of the Rings*.

And then it hits me. Taking this check means getting something for nothing, the mark's dream. Who's the sucker now?

Unless . . .

An angry voice echoes in the corridor outside the conference room. The door bangs open, letting in a bedraggled ball of fury.

Jolene.

She points at me, hand shaking like she has the DTs. "Ciara Griffin, I'm going to kill you." She reaches inside her bag and pulls out—whew, not a gun, but the detective's report.

I look at Lori, whose face has locked into panic. I knew she wasn't cut out for this. I stand and speak to Jolene. "I'm sorry, miss, have we met? Why are you calling me Ciara?"

Jolene stares at me. A lock of unwashed hair flops across her right eye. "What are you—? Of course we've met. You stole my shirt." Her voice pitches into hysteria. "I bet that guy Leonard or Frankie or whatever is a friend of yours. He broke into my detective's office to drug me and take naked pictures. You had him screw up my car so I'd miss the meeting. I bet you didn't count on me running out of gas in front of a gas station."

David rises and places a protective arm around me. I send Murphy and Bombeck a helpless look. "I'm afraid I don't know what she's babbling about. Does she work here?"

Lori gasps and grabs my hand. "That's the woman I told you about, the one who's been following me." She stands and glares at Jolene. "Stop stalking me or I'll call the cops."

Jolene's sedative-fogged expression drifts from indignation to bewilderment. "You're not Ciara, you're that barmaid. Why are you pretending to be her?"

"No one's pretending anything here but you, apparently." I put my purse on the table and retrieve my wallet. "I have identification." I hold out Elizabeth's new driver's license to the Skywave executives.

Murphy waves it off. "That's not necessary. Jolene,

please go back to your office. We'll discuss this matter after Ms. Vasser and her staff leave."

"But that's not Elizabeth Vasser!" Jolene plops down the padded envelope and tears it open, showering the table with fuzzy gray packing material. "See? Read this. It tells the truth."

Murphy gives us a nervous glance and tells Jolene in a low voice, "I already received this yesterday."

"What?" Jolene shoves the thick document toward her boss. "No, this is it. I hired the detective, why would he send it to you?"

"Maybe because I sign his checks?" Murphy licks her finger and pages through the report. She puts a hand to her head like she's got the world's worst migraine, then slams the report shut. "There's nothing here."

"I saw it yesterday." Jolene grabs the report and turns the pages so hard, some of them rip. "How can it be blank? It was all there, the real Elizabeth, the real Ciara—where is it?" Her face flushes an even deeper red.

"Wait a minute." David stalks over and flips the report to the front cover. "You hired someone to spy on us? What kind of shady company are you?"

"It was all legal, I assure you." Bombeck looks at Murphy. "This PI of yours was fully licensed, right?"

"That's what I was told." Murphy turns a glare on Jolene. "But I think I was told a lot of things that weren't true."

Sounds like my exit cue.

"I can't believe I almost let your company buy my station." In a fit of fake melodrama, I tear the check into tiny pieces and shove it back in the envelope, which I crumple in hands that shake with rage. "Good day."

Jonathan stands quickly to escort us out through the other door, the one Jolene isn't standing near. We head down the corridor, and I steel my legs not to run.

A voice echoes down the hall. "This isn't over, Ciara!" Jolene yells. "You hear me? It's not over!"

Lori huddles closer to me. "Elizabeth, that lady scares me."

Jonathan shades his eyes, as if the embarrassment blinds him. "I'm very sorry. She's new here and obviously hasn't learned the Skywave standards of client relations." In a near whisper he adds, "I doubt she'll be here by the end of the day."

I tuck the crumpled envelope into my purse and keep my tiny smile inside my head where it belongs.

29

Wicked Game

"A toast." David raises his beer bottle over the center of the picnic table. "To Ciara."

Everyone but me—that is, the six vampires and the three other humans sitting on David's back deck—smashes a raucous clink. We even convinced Franklin and Monroe to join our party. My Control goon, however, insisted on sitting by himself out front to keep watch for trouble.

"No." I lift my beer and look at David. "To Elizabeth."

His smile is tinged with pain and gratitude as he clinks, then drinks.

"To all of us." I raise my voice. "We rocked."

Cries of "Hear, hear!" "Right on!" and "Fuck, yeah!" resound over the backyard, which is shaded in a deep twilight. Through the sliding screen door we can hear Noah's reggae show on the stereo. The lilting, bouncing music matches the mood of the celebration.

The closest neighbor is a farm several acres behind David's house, so we can crank it up.

The four of us who eat are bedecked in napkin bibs, to ward off the guts of steamed crabs. Shane seems to enjoy taking a wooden mallet to the bright red shells. From the seat on my right he slips me another piece of moist white crabmeat. I push it around my plate without eating it.

"I thought it was all over when you opened that check," David says to me over his beer.

Lori claps her hand to her chest. "My heart stopped. I could almost hear your thoughts, Ciara: Take the money and run!"

David wipes his hands. "Now that we're all here, care to tell us how much it was for?"

I shake my head. "Never telling."

"Two million?"

I brandish my teeny fork at him. "I won't play this game."

They all put their beers on the table and stare at me, waiting.

"Five million," I tell them.

Franklin whistles. "And you just walked away. You have Elizabeth's identity, you could've kept the money." He looks around the table. "After giving us a cut to buy our silence, of course."

I nod. My thumb draws trails in my bottle's condensation, but my churning stomach won't let me drink any more. I can still see the check in my hands, begging me to give it a good home.

David stands and clears his throat. No more toasts, I hope.

"Ciara, in honor of the job you've done this summer, I'd like to give you this, if you'll accept it." He hands me a narrow black box, the hard vinyl type found in gift stores.

My nausea surges as I lift the lid. "David, this really isn't—"

A nameplate sits inside the box. CIARA GRIFFIN, it reads, then in smaller letters, MARKETING MANAGER.

"I don't get it." I look at David. "What's this for?"

"For your desk."

"Shouldn't it say, 'Marketing Intern'?"

"Not if you take the full-time job I'm about to offer you."

I gape at him. "What about school?" My voice goes raspy. "I still have a year left."

"You can take classes part-time, even during the day if you need. I'm sure Elizabeth would be happy to start a tuition reimbursement program, wouldn't she?"

A real job. A steady boyfriend. Stability. The rest of my life closes in like a velvet vise. I can't breathe.

"So what do you say?" David asks.

"I—" The letters on my nameplate blur and clear and blur again. Who the fuck is Ciara Griffin, anyway?

Everyone around the table watches me with anticipation. Lori's grin beams in the porch light. I can't look at Shane.

"I have to think about it." I spy my cell phone on the table. "Hey, we should invite my dad over."

"Why?" Shane says.

"That's a great idea." David gestures to the pile of crabs. "Plenty of food. I can't believe I didn't think of it earlier."

"I'll go inside where it's quieter." I grab the phone and stand up.

"I'll come with you," Shane says. "We need more beer, anyway."

"The extra case is downstairs in the storeroom," David says. "End of the hall."

Shane follows me in to the dining room/living room area, then to the stairs. I wait until we hit the landing of the split foyer to turn on him.

"It's bad enough I've got that Control goon following me around. Now you. Don't you trust me?"

"I trust you. I just don't trust your dad."

"Neither do I."

He gives me a skeptical look. "You've been acting strange tonight. Not eating, hardly drinking. What's going on?"

I look away. "Leftover nerves, that's all."

Shane studies my face, his own turning stony. He knows I'm lying, something I've never done to him before. But I can't tell him what I've done, especially when I haven't decided to follow through on it yet. Calling my dad will help me decide. I think.

"I've gotta get the beer." He trots down the short stairway from the foyer into the basement. I follow him, opening my cell phone and searching my contacts list for Dad's number. Adding him to speed dial will be a big step in our renewed relationship.

Shane turns down the dark hallway. I have to switch on the light to see. A flash of white startles me, until I realize it's just Antoine the cat. He trots ahead of me.

At the end of the hall Shane opens a door to a room with concrete walls and floor. The cat slips in around his ankles. I find Dad's number and hit "Send."

The storeroom holds the furnace and a series of well-organized shelves that contain mostly home improvement supplies—paints, tools, gardening equipment. They might as well be museum exhibits for all their familiarity to me. Shane finds two cases of beer under a workbench.

My foot hits something soft that clanks. A familiar duffel bag.

Dad finally picks up on the fifth ring. "Ciara?"

"Hi Dad."

He makes a muffled noise, like he's switching the phone to the other ear. "What do you want? I mean, how's my girl?" Sounds of traffic rush in the background.

My thumb runs over my back jeans pocket, tucking in the piece of paper. "Where are you?"

"Oh." His voice pitches a bit higher. "On the road."

"Get your Control bot to bring you over here. We're having a party."

Shane slides the cases of beer across the concrete floor.

"A party, that's nice," my dad says. "At the station?"

"No, at David's house."

"David's house?" he blurts. Tires squeal in the background.

"Yeah. You like steamed crabs, right? We've got—"

"Ciara, get out of there!"

"Why?"

"Gideon's coming."

My stomach turns cold. "Gideon's coming after me now? Here?"

Shane jumps up and shuts off the light. He motions for me to get down, then creeps to the ground floor storeroom window, the one facing the front yard.

My father's voice is breathless. "Not you. He wants David."

"Why?" I whisper.

"Because of Antoine."

A cold horror creeps up the back of my legs. I force myself to speak slowly. "How does Gideon know David killed Antoine?"

"David told me." My father's voice tightens. "I told Gideon. I'm sorry, Angel."

A tear slips out of my left eye. "Daddy, no . . ."

"Please get out now. Run."

Shane strides from the window and grabs the phone from my hand. "Ronan, they're here. Gideon and three others, all armed. Call the Control."

He slaps the phone shut. "They're in the driveway," he whispers to me. "One of them's heading for the front door, the rest around back toward the deck."

"The Control agent is out front. He'll—"

A loud clack rings out from that direction, sounding like a staple gun. The cat streaks behind the furnace to hide. Shane motions for me to stay on the floor while he returns to the window. A shadow sails by, and Shane leaps to the side out of sight.

He peers out the window at the retreating figure. "I think one of the vampires just shot your guard. Now they're all around back."

I turn to the windowed door leading to the backyard. Three figures dash by, then another. I hear shouting, then the pounding of feet up the stairs of David's deck.

Lori screams. I suck in a breath and try not to echo her.

Shane puts a finger to his lips and goes to the back

door. I hear the door to the deck slide open, and soon the feet are on the floor above us.

"They're herding everyone inside." He grabs the duffel bag and unzips it. "You should go out the back door now before they search the house."

"No way, those are my friends up there."

"Need something long-range," he mutters, then pulls out the stakes and sets them aside, careful not to let them rattle against the concrete floor. "Here we go." He lifts out the crossbow.

I open the outside pocket and pull out the Holy Water Super Soaker. "Is fifty feet long-range enough?"

He nods and sets aside the crossbow. "And no human collateral damage."

I grab the funnel and turn away from Shane to load the gun's reservoir. I remove the cap on one of the glass bottles and begin to pour.

Another clack sounds from above, followed by another scream. I fumble the holy water bottle, spilling drops on my bare knees. Shane reaches out to grab it, then draws his hand back just in time. I scoop it up from the floor before it empties.

Two sets of footsteps pound down the stairs. A crash and a cry of agony come from the hallway outside the storeroom. I pour the rest of the spilled bottle into the reservoir, then quickly dump in the other one. It's only enough for two, maybe three shots, none of them deadly. But with the crossbow I'd be as likely to hurt David as Gideon.

Shane stands and unsheathes the katana sword. The blade reflects the golden glow of the porch light filtering through the back window. He looks down at me. I nod. Our battle plan is clear.

I pull back the pump handle twice to fill the pistol's reservoir. The hallway is quiet now. Silently, Shane turns the knob of the storeroom door. I hold my breath as it swings open, waiting for the hinges to creak and give us away. When I peek around the corner, I realize it doesn't matter.

At the bottom of the stairs, at the other end of the hall, Gideon has David pinned to the floor, his mouth to his neck.

Gun raised, I step into the hallway and aim. Gideon's eyes flash up at me, his dark hair disheveled, the lower half of his face soaked in David's blood.

I fire.

Gideon's howl mixes with the hiss of steam. He swipes at his face, which blackens and smokes like a marshmallow in a campfire. Blinded, he jumps to his feet and rushes me, slamming his shoulder into the wall. Shouts echo from upstairs. I pump wildly to reload.

Shane jumps between us, but my finger is already squeezing the trigger. This time the scream is his. He draws back his sizzling arm to raise the sword, then strikes.

Gideon raises his own arm in time to block the blade, which slices clean through at the elbow. The severed limb hits the floor as Gideon spins to grab Shane by the neck with his remaining hand.

He pins him to the wall and starts to squeeze. With his strength, he could rip Shane's head off in one motion.

I fire one last shot.

When the water hits his face, Gideon hisses and falls

to his knees, still throttling Shane. The stump of his left arm is closing up already.

Shane slams his elbow onto Gideon's arm, loosening his grip enough to slip out. Gideon roars and flails one-handed for his opponent, but Shane is already lifting the sword.

From the stairway behind him steps Gideon's body-guard Lawrence. In one hand he holds a pistol; in the other, a sharpened stake. He raises both.

The sword screams through the air. Gideon's head drops to the carpet, bounces against the wall, rolls once, and comes to a stop. His eyes shine white at me from his charred face.

"No . . ." Lawrence clutches his own chest and falls to his knees as Gideon's body thuds the floor, slump-ing on its side between his severed arm and head. Blood spouts from his neck in two arcs against the white walls, splashing onto my feet and ankles before I can leap out of the way.

Shane whirls on Lawrence, ready to strike. Seeing his opponent defenseless, he lowers the weapon and stares down at the vampire's writhing form. From upstairs come three distinct thumps.

I toss away the water pistol and run up to him. "I burned you. Are you all right?"

"I'll live." He kicks Lawrence's weapons out of reach. "David looks bad."

Blood streams from the wound in David's neck, soak-ing the carpet beneath him. Before I can react, Franklin and Spencer are rounding the stairs, the latter holding David's red EMT bag.

Spencer kneels beside David and opens the bag.

He rips open several packets of gauze and presses them against the wound.

"Put his feet up," he tells me, then examines the wound briefly before pressing the gauze against David's neck again. "Looks like Gideon maybe grazed the internal jugular. Lucky. Another inch would've taken his carotid. If we stop the bleeding and get him to the hospital, he should be all right."

"I'll call an ambulance." Franklin pulls out his cell phone.

"No," David wheezes. "No ambulance."

Franklin looks around at the blood-spattered scene, one that would surely launch the biggest police investigation in this county's history. "Is it safe for me to drive him?"

Spencer nods. "I'll go with you. We can move him as soon as I control the bleeding."

Franklin leaps up and heads for the stairs. "I'll pull the truck up to the front door." He takes one last glance back at the carnage. "This is why I never come to vampire parties."

As he goes up the stairs, Jim passes him coming down, holding a long metallic-looking cord.

"Monroe and Regina are tying up the other two bodyguards. They dropped like sides of meat." He looks at the pieces of Gideon, then at Shane. "I knew you had it in you." His foot nudges Lawrence, who's still trembling and looks nearly unconscious.

"What's happening to him?" Shane asks.

"Same thing that'll happen to you when Regina bites the dust." Jim drags Lawrence's arms behind his back and starts to bind his wrists with the cord.

"They must have all been Gideon's progeny," Spencer says.

"They were," I tell them. "But why hasn't he been sucked into the void yet?"

"The heart's got to drain," Spencer says. "With a staking it's mighty quick, but a beheading can take a minute."

I stand slowly and move to Shane's side. Gideon's blood has stopped flowing. As we watch, his body starts to turn inward, folding into the stump of his neck.

I cover my face. "Shane, you don't want to see it."

"I have to," he whispers. "I did this."

"That's exactly why you shouldn't see it." I tug on his arm, but he resists. At our feet, Lawrence starts to moan and shake. His cries are echoed upstairs. "Shane, please."

"Go if you want." His gaze is fixed on Gideon. "I'm staying."

Gideon's head starts to slide across the floor, drawn into the vortex of his corpse.

From above, Travis begins to shriek. The sound isn't human, isn't animal, isn't even something in-between. It's the sound of hell. I cover my ears and lurch up the stairs.

In the middle of the living room floor, the detective lies in the fetal position, ripping at the front of his shirt and emitting a high, rusted screech. Monroe kneels beside him to grab his wrists, murmuring low, soothing words to the young vampire. I notice his own leg has a solid circle of blood—no longer flowing—perhaps the result of the other gunshot. Lori huddles in the corner, face buried in her arms.

Wallace and Jacob, Gideon's other two progeny, writhe and scream on their stomachs, hands bound behind their backs. Regina guards them, insufficiently armed with a pair of stakes. Two large pistols fitted with silencers sit on the dining room table. The radio is still playing, the peppy reggae tune oblivious to our drama.

Regina glances nervously at Travis. "Here comes the downside of killing Gideon."

Travis's eyes bulge, and his neck seems to contract around his throat, cutting off breath. He rolls on his back, spasming like a poisoned bug.

But the worst is what appears beneath his torn shirt. The skin above his heart twists and pulls as if an unseen hand is trying to tear it off. A great purple stain spreads across his chest, widening like a pool of blood under a murder victim.

Franklin opens the front door. His truck is parked on the lawn near the porch, engine running. I follow him back down to the basement, relieved to have a purpose.

Slightly more alert now, David groans when Spencer picks him up. As directed, I hold his head firm against Spencer's shoulder while Franklin keeps the pressure on his wound. I don't even glance behind me at Shane and what's left of Gideon. The popping, hissing, cracking sound is enough.

"Ciara . . ." David whispers as we carefully maneuver over the foyer landing and out the front door.

"Don't talk." We pass my Control guard, sprawled on his back in the bushes, the porch light revealing a neat hole in the center of his forehead. "Oh, no."

"What?" David rasps.

"Nothing you need to worry about," Franklin says.

I climb into the truck ahead of David and steady him as Spencer lays him on the narrow backseat of Franklin's truck.

David lifts a hand to me. "Do you want the job or not?"

"Now's not a great time to ask that." I place his hand back on his chest. "My dad ratted you out to Gideon."

He shuts his eyes. "Shouldn't have told."

"No, you shouldn't have trusted him. But everyone does. You're just the latest in a long line of—" I decide not to finish the sentence.

"Suckers," he whispers.

Spencer opens the door on my side and motions for me to get out so he can take my place.

I hop out, then turn quickly to David. "Hey, this means we can go back to being the Lifeblood of Rock 'n' Roll."

He gives me a weak thumbs-up as Spencer shuts the door.

As I move away from the truck, a sudden shivering movement from below catches my eye. I look down in time to see the blotches of Gideon's blood fly off my shoes toward the house. They squeeze through the screen and disappear within.

My knees weaken, but the sound of Travis screaming forces me to keep moving. I rush back into the house just as Shane comes up the stairs to the foyer, his face paler than I've ever seen it.

"He's gone," he whispers, then looks down to see the sword still in his left hand. I take it from him gently, avoiding the long black burns on his arms, and lead him upstairs.

Travis utters a long wail that seems to echo between the walls of the house even as it fades. He falls silent and still. After a few moments, he draws a sudden, sharp breath, then another, until he's panting wildly. Jacob and Wallace lie unconscious.

Regina kneels to examine them. "They'll be okay, unfortunately. I should have staked them while they were awake. Wouldn't be sporting now." A loud *thup!* comes from the bottom of the stairs. Regina looks down over the railing. "Hm. I guess Jim doesn't agree."

In a few moments, Jim saunters up the stairs carrying the crossbow in one hand and a blood-tipped arrow in the other.

He sees us staring at him. "What? I didn't like the way that guy pushed me around. Sue me for having pride." He reloads the crossbow at the top of the stairs and looks at Wallace and Jacob. "Should I waste these other two?"

"No," Shane says. "There's been enough death for one day."

"Not quite." Regina kneels next to Travis, who lies slumped on his side. "I don't think our little friend is going to make it. He's too young and weak to survive his maker's death."

"Unless . . ." Monroe lifts his dark gaze to me, then shifts it to Lori, who's still crouched in the corner.

I take a step forward. "Is there something we can do to save him? We should at least try."

Jim snickers. "You might change your mind when you hear what it is."

I look at Travis, gasping like a fish on dry land. "I know what it is." I close my eyes. "I'll do it."

The room is silent for a few moments, until Regina speaks. "You do realize it doesn't exactly involve a smoothie and a foot massage?"

"I know." I look at Shane. "Although I wouldn't mind that as a reward."

"Ciara, are you sure?" He comes to my side. "This is the guy who tried to kill you."

"He couldn't help it. And he's one of us now."

My words play back in my head. *One of us.* Am I one of us? It's been eight years since I've been one of anything.

"Just one condition," I tell Shane. "It has to be you who makes the—you know."

He takes my hand. "We'll do it in David's room." He looks at Travis. "Someone bring him. Hurry."

"I'll get him," Jim says.

"Uh-uh." I hold out my palm. "I'm never having so much as a hangnail in front of you." I look at Monroe without meeting his gaze. "Please."

30

Inside Out

"Lights on or off?" Shane says.

In reply, I pull the cord on David's bedside lamp. It emits a muted glow through a smoked-glass shade.

Shane lays a dark brown towel in place of one of the pillows. "To get the blood quickly enough to save Travis, I should do the neck. Is that okay?"

"Is it safe?"

"Sure." He touches my throat. "I'll nick the external jugular. It's small, right near the surface so there won't be much pain. No muscle to go through. It's safe as long as you lie down."

I nod, hoping I don't pass out. I lie down on my right side with my back to the center of the bed. "Gideon was going to bite my neck, but we were standing up."

"Really?" Shane stretches out facing me. "Interesting."

"Why?"

"I'll explain later. You sure about this?" he asks again.

Without gravity to keep it down, my heart has crept up into my esophagus. "No, but I'd be a real bitch to back out now." I touch his mouth. "Will you be able to, you know—"

"Get it up? Yeah. Fangs are like coughs—they can be voluntary as well as involuntary."

He draws back his lips, and there they are. I shrink back a few inches just as Monroe lays Travis on the bed behind me.

"Don't be afraid." Shane tilts my chin up. "Just breathe deep and slow, and look in my eyes."

I obey, and feel myself start to fall. Shane turns loose the same hypnotic power he showed that first night outside the library, when he was trying to convince me of his monstrous nature. Every moment since then he's been more than human with me. Now the blue of his irises holds an ocean that promises a trip to another world if I just dive in.

My pulse slows. My muscles slacken. My mouth opens. Shane leans in and covers it with his own, lips soft and full, tongue soothing rather than demanding. My skin grows warm with a languid desire, my body melding into his.

His lips leave my mouth, caress the edge of my jaw, and finally reach my throat. His tongue searches for the heat of my pulse, and I don't even flinch. I'm not afraid. I can do this. I probably won't even scream.

A sudden pain pierces my throat. Its electric echo shoots down my spine and up into my skull.

I scream, but just a little.

Shane's hand tightens on my hip to hold me still, while the other strokes the back of my neck. I focus on the touch of his fingers, letting my awareness shrink to those inches of skin, rather than those that are protesting this violation of flesh.

He groans deep in his throat, as he did when he bit Deirdre. I remember wishing I could make him make that noise.

His fangs withdraw. The pain subsides slightly. A trickle of warm liquid travels down my neck. Shane catches it with his tongue and gives a long, heavy exhale.

"You don't have to enjoy this quite so much," I remind him.

He glances at my face. "Sorry." He places his hand against my neck, below the wound—catching the blood, I assume. Then he reaches over me toward Travis. "Come on, drink." He sighs and pulls back. "He's too out of it." He nods to Monroe. "Sit him up."

Shane bends over my neck again. "I have to get it in him directly, like with a baby bird. Once he wakes up, he can drink on his own."

He puts his mouth to my throat and this time manages to hold back sounds of ecstasy. I notice he doesn't touch the wound itself, only the trickle of blood as it flows away.

Without swallowing, he sits up and leans across me, where Monroe holds Travis. He takes the semiconscious vampire's face in his hands and kisses him. His tongue moves in the other man's mouth, delivering the life-giving blood.

If it weren't my blood, it would be totally hot.

A few moments later, Shane breaks the kiss, then tilts Travis's chin up and strokes his throat. "Swallow, damn it."

Travis's lashes flutter, and his lips smack ever so

slightly. He swallows, then draws in a sharp breath. Monroe and Shane share a sigh of relief.

Shane tilts me to lie almost on my back. I feel the weight of Travis next to me on the mattress.

"Easy, son," Monroe murmurs. Cold lips touch the side of my neck, where the blood is dribbling slowly, like a broken water fountain. I wince at the pain the new pressure brings.

Shane squeezes my knee. "Back in a sec." He hurries to the bathroom, where sounds of mouth-rinsing ensue. I close my eyes and wait for his return.

"That was considerate," I say when he sits beside me again.

He shrugs. "I like to think of myself as a Sensitive New Age vampire." He checks Travis's progress, then says to Monroe, "You should probably go check on the others, make sure Regina and Jim haven't dismembered anyone."

Monroe leaves without a word. "It's weird," I tell Shane. "The two guys who saved me from Travis are helping him drink from me now."

"Oh, the irony."

I feel a strong desire for small talk. "So how's Deirdre?"

"Good, or so I hear. She's with Jim now. I told you last month I wasn't going to drink any more women."

"Only if I agreed to be your girlfriend."

"I preempted you."

"Oh." I would feel warm and toasty inside if a vampire weren't slurping my collarbone. "Did you get any good men out of your trades?"

"There's one really cool guy from Pittsburgh. We've scheduled a couple of visits when the Steelers play *Monday Night Football*. He's got cable."

"Is he cute?"

"He's sixty-three."

"Eww. I mean, oh."

The pain spikes, making my eyes water. I cry out.

"Hey!" Shane's hand flashes out and eases Travis's head away from my throat. "What did we teach you about sucking?"

"Sorry," Travis croaks, then goes back to licking my neck.

I wipe my eyes, resisting the urge to jump up and run away. "What's wrong with sucking?"

"It can damage the wound and make it more infectible."

My stomach flips over and my head goes sloshy. "Quick, tell me a story so I don't hork."

Shane lies beside me. I can't see him now without turning my head, which hurts to do, so I just look at the ceiling.

"I'll tell you about April 5, 1995."

My eyes widen. "I didn't mean *the* story."

"Do you want to hear it or not?"

I touch his chest. "If you want to tell me."

He takes a few deep breaths. "I didn't want to live," he says finally. "The reasons aren't important. Basically, my life sucked, and I was on the wrong medication. Same sad story of a million depressives."

I close my eyes and listen. It's like hearing his voice on the radio again, except this time his words really are just for me. Even Travis seems to swallow more quietly out of respect.

"Then I met Regina," Shane continues. "She understood how much I wanted to be released from this shitty world, from the pain that had become the only thing I knew. The same darkness was in her." He scoffs. "Or so I thought. She was a vampire, she had to be dark, right?"

"One would assume."

"I struggled with it. I hadn't been to mass in years, but I prayed for the strength to live, for a sign that I belonged here. I never got either. So I asked Regina to kill me." He runs his fingers through my hair, soothing the muscles at my temple. "Guess I should've picked a more reliable method."

"But as suicides go, it's kinda cool."

"And useful. Since I didn't need my blood anymore, why not give it to someone who did? Better than spilling it all over my living room and waiting for the old lady next door to complain about the smell." He pauses. "Besides, Regina had bitten me before. It felt incredible. I thought, what a magnificent way to die."

I wonder why vampire bites don't have the same effect on me. Maybe they're like any other drug—some people get high and others just get nauseous.

"That night," he continues, "Regina drank me deeper than ever. My heart felt like it was playing the drum solo to 'Wipe Out.' But I didn't care, because I was leaving my body behind. I was happy.

"Next thing I knew, her blood was gushing into my mouth. I tried to turn away, spit it out, because I knew what it meant. When I finally swallowed, everything changed. There was bright light instead of darkness, hunger instead of emptiness. I grabbed her, and I drank."

"Why'd you do it, if you wanted to die?"

His fingertips stroke the back of my arm. "Bodies want to live. Stomachs vomit poison. Wrists close up. It takes a lot to make the machine turn itself off."

I wonder how many times he tried. My life hasn't always been happy, but I never thought the alternative could be better.

"Maybe Regina planned all along to turn me, but she won't admit it. She claims she couldn't bear to watch me die."

I understand her impulse. After seeing Elizabeth and Gideon die, I plan to dress Shane in a Kevlar turtleneck. "She saved your life."

"I wanted death," he says bitterly. "She wanted a pet."

God, I fucking love this man. I'd do anything to keep him from entering that dark place again.

I open my mouth to tell him so, but Travis chooses this poignant moment to start snoring.

Shane looks over my shoulder. "His color's a lot better now. I think he'll make it after all." He reaches for the packet of gauze on the nightstand. "Thank you for your kind donation, ma'am. Please help yourself to juice and cookies before you leave."

"So what happened after you were turned?"

"Regina took me to a veteran donor, and I drank a human for the first time." He sits up, then tears open the gauze and presses it gently against my neck. "I felt better."

"That good, huh?"

"It was like I'd found everything I was ever looking for. Blood's a lot like drugs, but it makes you strong instead of weak. All the other vampire crap—never seeing the sun, not enjoying food, having to find, flatter, and fuck donors you don't even like—blood makes it all worthwhile."

I move his hand so I can hold the gauze myself and press more firmly than he would dare. "So you were happy, then, after you turned."

"Hell, no. Regina and her friends had to put me on suicide watch. They'd force-feed me blood, then nail me into a coffin before sunrise. A coffin, for Christ's sake." Still holding my hand, he stretches out beside me again, closer than before. "Finally the Control stuck me in one of their nursing homes for rehab. Two years later, David visited and offered me this job. They wouldn't let me leave, said I wasn't ready. So I escaped and refused to go back, because I finally had something to live for."

I tighten my fingers around his. "I'm glad Regina gave you another life."

Shane touches his forehead to my temple. "Me, too," he whispers. "Now."

He kisses my cheek softly. I slide my hand up his arm, then remove it quickly as I remember his burns. I look down and gasp.

"You're healed."

He sits up and rotates his smooth, unmarked arm in the lamplight. "Whoa."

"David said holy water always left scars."

"I know, but there's nothing." He stares at me. "It must've been your blood."

"But if blood could heal holy water burns, someone would've figured it out by now."

"I don't mean any blood, Ciara. I mean *your* blood."

The awe in his eyes makes me shiver. "What's so special about my blood?"

"Good question."

I check the gauze pad. The red spot looks normal to me. "If I'd known it would heal you, I would've let you drink me right away."

"Thanks." He marvels at his arm again. "I'll remember that next time you shoot me with holy water."

"Besides, it would've been so romantic, very Buffy and Angel." Now I know I'm delirious.

"Very what?"

"TV shows. After your life. We can rent the DVDs if you want to catch up."

"We'll have lots of time once the nights get longer."

Suddenly I can imagine the time. Cuddling in front of the TV with Shane and a mug of apple cider. Hanging with the whole VMP gang around David's fireplace—with the humans closest to the flames, of course—shooting the shit and arguing over who was the most talented Beatle.

This time, such a future doesn't feel like a vise or a straitjacket.

A knock sounds at the door. Shane lies down and shoves his healed arm under the covers. "Who is it?"

Regina opens it far enough to fit her face. "The Control's here. A bit late, but at least they can help clean up. You almost done?"

"We're done, we're just recovering." Shane peeks at the sleeping Travis. "He'll need to drink in another couple hours, but he'll survive, barely."

"Poor bloke." The sympathy in her voice sounds genuine. "How about the sunnyside? She make it?"

"I'm right here," I say, "and yes, I'm fine."

"Good. That colonel guy wants to see you."

In a few moments, Colonel Lanham's voice comes from the door. "Ms. Griffin, your father called us."

I close my eyes against a wave of dizziness. "Where is he?"

He hesitates. "I was hoping you'd know."

My eyes slam open. "He's skipped town?"

"I'm afraid so. When he phoned, we thought he was still with his guard, so we didn't trace the call." He moves next to the bed where I can see him without turning my head. "But we'll find him. One of our agents was killed here tonight. More humans might have died because of his treachery."

"Did he say why he did it?"

"No. Near as we can figure, he was acting as a double agent for us and Gideon. At some point he switched loyalties. Maybe Gideon paid him more."

My eyes grow tight around the edges. "He never switched loyalties. He just stayed loyal to himself." Nice game, Daddy.

"What about the station?" Shane asks him.

"As far as we're concerned, Elizabeth can stay alive. The Control will continue to support the mission of WVMP in keeping the six of you off the streets, as it were."

"Thanks," I tell him, wondering how long we can fool the IRS. "Can I go home now that Gideon's dead?"

"Certainly. With two of his top men in custody, we should be able to dismantle his compound."

"Don't count on it. Those people want to be there. There'll always be another Gideon."

"Nonetheless, we'll do our best to ensure your lives return to normal." He looks at the three of us sprawled on the bed and seems to hear his own words. "Relatively speaking."

31

Come as You Are

"You're getting really good at that."

"I'm an excellent driver," Shane says in his best Rain Man imitation as he shifts into first gear.

I look back at David's driveway, full of black vans belonging to the International Agency for the Control and Management of Undead Corporeal Entities. Luckily, out here in the country all this hubbub won't attract attention. Then again, if David lived in town it would have been harder to attack him in the first place. Location really is everything in real estate.

These thoughts, along with my lingering light-headedness, fail to distract me from the day's biggest devastation.

"Thanks for not saying 'I told you so.'"

Shane concentrates on second gear before answering. "I didn't have to tell you so. You knew."

"I thought I was being careful with my father, not giving away too much. But I never thought he'd take Gideon's side. It explains everything—why Gideon was stalking me that first night I came to the station, why he didn't turn me into a vampire."

Shane gives me a long look, then turns off the lane onto the country road. "He wasn't going to turn you into a vampire. He was going to kill you."

"How do you know?"

"You said he was going to bite your neck standing up. That can cause an air embolism that would've stopped your heart or given you a stroke. You wouldn't have lived long enough to be turned."

I grab the door handle, expecting a surge of nausea. Usually a phrase like "air embolism," even out of context, would make me need to lie down. But after a few deep breaths, I just feel glad to be alive.

"What was the last 'last song' you played for me, the night I was at Gideon's? Our, uh, reception died." I omit the reason, that Jim had smashed the radio against the door.

"I'll play it for you on my next show."

"Just tell me."

"That's not how it works. How are you feeling?"

I sigh at his change of subject. He'll do what I want, but in his own time. "A little sore when I turn my head. Otherwise okay."

"Good, but that's not what I meant."

Ahead of us, a rabbit darts halfway across the road, then changes its mind and springs back into the weeds.

"I feel stupid. I thought my father was lying about something, but I figured it had to do with his wife and whether they had any kids. I should have put all the pieces together."

"You had a lot on your mind with the con."

"I should have warned David about him. Dad has a talent for wrangling confessions."

"People feel better after they share their darkest sins. They feel lighter."

He's right. Now that my moments of adrenaline and heroism have passed, the weight of what I did earlier today sinks to the bottom of my stomach. I can undo that deed, but the knot in my gut won't leave until I tell Shane. Even if it means losing him.

My phone rings. Franklin.

"Figured you'd want to know," he says. "David's okay. He'll be in the hospital overnight, but he won't need surgery."

"What did you tell the doctors?"

"That David was attacked by a stray pit bull."

"Did they believe you? This is the guy who publicly claimed to run a vampire radio station."

"Just play those last three words back in your head. That ought to answer your question."

After two months of this job, sometimes I forget how ridiculous it sounds. "Can David talk?"

"He's asleep. Before he conked out, he told me to ask you if you're taking the job."

"I'll see you guys on Monday."

"That doesn't really answer—"

I hang up. "It's official," I tell Shane. "We saved our boss's life."

"Time for a raise."

We stop at the traffic light connecting David's road to the highway. In the red glow, I look at Shane's bandaged arm. Beneath it lies unblemished skin—we covered it so no one would see and ask questions.

"There must be a simpler explanation for your recovery. Maybe I have a rare blood type or Rh factor, whatever that is."

He glances at his arm. "The burn was so bad it only hurt for a second, then went totally numb. That's third degree. It should have taken weeks to heal and left nasty scars. But it's like it never happened. You did something."

"My father thinks people can be healed by faith—their own or someone else's."

"Maybe, but neither of us expected me to get better."

"Plus I have no faith." I point to the bumper sticker on the car in front of us. *Eternity, Your Choice: Smoking or Non-Smoking.* "Heh. As long as I'm already dead, I'll take smoking. Speaking of which, I could really go for a cigarette. Is that a side effect of being bitten? Someone should tell Philip Morris." I look at Shane, whose expression has sobered. "I'm just kidding."

"You really don't believe in heaven and hell?"

"No, I don't." I manage to scrub my voice of most of the scorn I feel. "I don't believe in any of—" I suck in a sharp breath. "Shane, that's it!"

"What's it?"

"It wasn't my faith that healed you. It was my *lack* of faith. I'm like a desanctifier. An anti-holy." This pleases me more than it should.

He laughs. "Wait. You're saying your skepticism is some kind of holy-weapon neutralizer? That's ridiculous."

"Never underestimate the power of the scoff."

He shakes his head. "Man, that's really heavy, as Jim

would say." The light turns green. We turn onto the highway, downhill toward Sherwood.

An even better thought occurs to me. "Maybe I changed you permanently, made you immune to sacredness."

"That would be nice."

"Then you could go to mass again."

"Who says I want to?" He looks at me, then back at the road. "Maybe on Christmas and Easter. But how would we find out it was permanent without burning me again?"

"Good point. I suppose we could hold clinical trials, put an ad for volunteers in the *City Paper*."

He laughs again, then goes silent. "I can't wear this bandage forever. The others will notice."

"Tough. I won't be a walking pharmacy for vampires. I didn't exactly get my jollies from being bitten."

"I know. It makes your sacrifice that much nobler."

"Please. I'm no saint."

"You're loyal to your friends, and that's good enough for me."

I don't answer, knowing I have evidence to contradict him.

We get home to my apartment, and I use my own key for the first time since Sunday. As I push open the door, its rubber bottom edge slides against today's mail.

"I'll get it." Shane picks up an envelope and hands it to me. On the front is my name written in a handwriting I wish I no longer recognized.

My dizziness returns, having nothing to do with shock or blood loss. I sink onto the bottom step leading to my apartment. Shane flicks the switch, and for the first time in months, the overhead light comes on.

I look up at it. "My landlord finally changed the bulb."

"Or maybe the Control guard got bored during his stakeout." Shane sits beside me. "You want me to read it for you?"

I shake my head and slide my thumb under the envelope's edge, feeling a strong sense of déjà vu from opening the Skywave check.

The letter looks scribbled in haste, perhaps on a vertical surface, as the pen seems to have run out of ink a few times.

> *Ciara,*
> *First, I never intended to betray you. In fact, my alliance with Gideon was probably all that prevented your death at his hands. But I'm sorry for the lies. Every one of them.*
>
> *They'll catch me soon, if they can. I'll go back to jail, perhaps for the rest of my life. In that event, please, please come see me. Forgive me.*

Those last two sentences are underlined so hard the pen poked holes in the paper. My rib cage seems to constrict.

The rest of the words are barely legible.

> *When you were younger, I told you about our family curse. I said it was salesmanship, that we could make anyone buy what we offered and beg us for more. It was meant as a joke, since the power of persuasion is usually a coveted gift.*
>
> *But every gift is a curse in disguise. Because eventually we run out of suckers, and the only fools left are the people we love.*

He must not have had time to sign it. It's folded un-evenly and wrinkled from being crammed in the enve-lope.

I hand the letter to Shane and rest my forehead in my hands while he reads.

When he finishes, he says, "You're not like him."

I look at him from the corner of my eye. "Remember when you said you wanted to peel back all my layers until you found the real Ciara?"

"On Lori's boss's desk. I remember."

I lift my head. "Have you ever thought, if you got past all those layers, you might not want me anymore?"

"How do you know I haven't already found the real you?"

"Trust me, you haven't." I take a deep breath and let it out. "But you're about to."

I reach in my back pocket and pull out another en-velope. I hand it to him in exchange for Dad's letter. He gives me a quizzical look as he opens it and withdraws the pink Skywave check.

$10,000,000.00.

I hold my breath as Shane stares at it.

"No . . ." He shakes his head. There's no triumph of cynicism on his face. His eyes fill with nothing but hurt and bewilderment, and that tells me everything. He be-lieved in me until now.

His voice is nearly a whisper. "David said you tore up the check at the meeting."

"I did tear up a check. I had Travis's paycheck in my purse, along with his expired license—evidence of Skywave's spying in case we needed them to back off. I switched the checks when Jolene came in." From my purse I pull the last envelope, full of crumpled paper. "I tore up a check for eight hundred forty-six dollars and fifty cents."

He stares at the ten million dollars for a long moment, then shoves it into my hand. "Go. I won't tell anyone." He sets his elbows on his knees, not facing me. "And I don't want a cut in exchange for my silence."

"Shane . . . that's not why I showed you."

He turns back, his gaze intense. "I can't go with you. I can't fly, I can't even chance a boat. We could get an inside cabin with no windows, but ships sometimes run fire drills in the daytime."

"If I could take you, I'd go—"

"And I'd just slow you down."

"—but I can't, so I won't."

"You deserve a new life." He stops. "Wait—won't what?"

"Go."

His eyes narrow. "You'd give up ten million dollars and a new life just for me?"

"Not just for you. I'm staying for my job, for the station and that whole dysfunctional family that makes the Munsters look like the Cleavers." I hold up my dad's letter. "Most of all, I'm staying for me."

"Just tell me one thing." His solemn voice chills me. "Did you plan all along to cheat us?"

I let out a deep breath. "No—except maybe in poker, just a little. For the big stuff, I was always on your side. I didn't even know they were going to give me a check at the meeting. But once it was in my hands, some terrible, evil part of me couldn't let it go."

"That part of you isn't evil. That part's a conniver, but

it's what saved the station." He takes my hand. "That part is why I love you."

My mouth drops open, and I forget how to breathe.

"It's not the only reason, of course," he says. "I also love the part of you that takes pity on stray dogs, and the part that makes my body feel like spontaneously combusting—in a good way, I mean."

I take his face between my hands and try to tell him with my eyes what it means that he loves me *because* of who I am, not in spite of it. In case the eyes aren't enough, I add the three words themselves, in alphabetical order, whispered between kisses and ragged breaths, repeated until they no longer sound strange coming from my mouth.

Shane wraps his arms around me. My skin feels raw and exposed, even under my clothes. I flinch, and his touch softens in response, hands gliding up my back, over the unbitten side of my neck, to my face, caressing me like I'm made of silk.

"Come on." He stands and helps me up. Unlike my knees, my brain feels strong and clear. As we ascend the stairway, I know what I have to do.

I stop at the doorway to my bedroom while he moves inside.

"You wanted to hear my last 'last song' for you," he says, "the one I played while you were at Gideon's." He goes to my shelves, blocking them with his body so I can't see which CD he pulls out. After a rattle of plastic, he taps the play button.

Applause, then a soft voice. "Good evening. This is off our first record."

The opening acoustic chords of "About a Girl" rumble forth, the first song we listened to together—before he bit me and I hit him. I laugh, having never been so uplifted at the sound of Nirvana.

He walks back to me, an ironic smile on his lips. "Did you expect something sappy just because you were in mortal danger?"

"Come with me." Carrying the check and my father's letter, I lead him into the bathroom. I pick up the matches lying next to the strawberry-scented candle.

"No." He takes Dad's note and tucks it into his shirt pocket. "Someday you'll wish you had this."

I nod, wondering if someday I'll hate it when he's right.

I open the matchbook. Sweat makes my hands slippery, and even the rough cardboard of the match is hard to hold, but I manage to light it.

I place the check in the dry sink and find myself unable to continue. Flame eats the flimsy cardboard stick, traveling down the shaft of the match so quickly it burns my fingers and falls smoldering on the edge of the sink. Shane waits.

The second match lights more easily. My hands are steady now, so steady they freeze when it's time to drop the match onto the check. I light the candle instead and stare at the trail of zeroes.

"It's freedom," I say to Shane's reflection. "The con to end all cons. With ten million dollars I could afford to be a good person for the rest of my life."

One side of his face crinkles into a smirk. "Fortunately, it costs nothing to be bad, and you're better at that." His fingertips brush the back of my shoulder. "Cut the drama and just burn the thing."

"Okay, okay." As the song heads into the last chorus, I

light the third match off the candle's flame and pick up the check in my other hand.

I feel on the verge of a freedom even ten million dollars can't buy. Who knows? Maybe only negative ten million dollars can buy it. A small price to beat a curse.

Match meets paper, which flares the colors of a sunrise. The crowd cheers again.

Author's Note

Visit the vampire DJs, listen to VMP playlists, and get your own Lifeblood of Rock 'n' Roll merchandise at www.WVMPradio.com. For the vamps' secret stories of how they were turned, check out www.jerismithready.com.

Read on for a sneak peek at

BAD TO THE BONE

the thrilling sequel to WICKED GAME.

Available everywhere in May 2009!

1

Whole Lotta Shakin' Going On

The things I believe in can be counted on one hand—even if that hand were two-fifths occupied with, say, smoking a cigarette, or making a bunny for a shadow puppet show, or forming "devil horns" at a heavy metal concert. The things I believe in boil down to three major categories:

Rock 'n' roll

Vampires

A damn good pair of shoes

Number Two came about when one bit me, in the middle of what could non-skankily be called an "intimate encounter." The third came later, when I gained the identity and thus the bank account of my dead-undead-dead boss Elizabeth Vasser, owner of WVMP, The Lifeblood of Rock 'n' Roll.

I'm two people only on paper. In real life, I'm just Ciara Griffin, underpaid marketing manager and not-paid miracle worker for a vampire radio station.

On nights like this, marketing is a miracle in itself.

The Smoking Pig is packed with fans who chose to spend Halloween Eve—aka Hell Night, Mischief Night, or Tuesday—in a bar with their favorite DJs, the ones who whisk them through time into another era, and into a world where vampires just might exist.

I lean back against the brass bar rail to avoid getting trampled by a couple dressed as Marilyn Monroe and Marilyn Manson. The guy in the Monroe costume can't be more than twenty-one, but he's twisting to a fifty-year-old tune with as much enthusiasm as his grandfather probably did.

Above me, the station's long black banner hangs on one of the rustic pub's long wooden crossbeams. Draped with fake cobwebs, it features our trademark logo, an electric guitar with two bleeding fang marks.

The two Marilyns jostle me again, and I reach up to check the status of my mile-high ponytail. Wearing a short floral dress as twenty percent of the Go-Go's (the Belinda Carlisle percent), I'm glad the crowd provides plenty of heat. October in Maryland shows no mercy to beach wear.

"Excuse me," shouts a voice to my left, straining to be heard over Jerry Lee Lewis's slammin' piano.

I peer over rosy-lensed sunglasses at a young man about my age and height—mid-twenties, five-eightish, with a lanky frame verging on heroin-chic thin.

"The bartender said I should speak to you," he says.

I examine his swooping bleach blond hair, skinny jeans, and faded Weezer T-shirt. The smudged black guyliner makes his hazel eyes pop out behind a pair of round glasses.

"Billy Idol meets Harry Potter. I like it."

He puts a hand to his ear. "What?"

"Your costume," I shout, my voice already raw after only an hour of this party.

He gives a twitchy frown and shifts the messenger bag slung over his left shoulder. "I'm Jeremy Glaser, a journalism grad student at University of Maryland. I came up to do a story on your station."

Oops. I guess it's not a costume.

Jeremy extends a heavily tattooed arm toward the rear wall of the Smoking Pig, away from the stage and the speakers. "Can we talk?"

I reach back to the bar for my ginger ale. "Interviews by appointment only. Give me your e-mail and—"

"It's a freelance assignment for *Rolling Stone*."

My glass slips, and I spill soda down my arm. "Whoa!" I shake the liquid off my hand and grab a bar napkin. "I mean, wow."

He gestures for me to join him at the back of the Pig. This time I don't hesitate.

We push through the crowd toward a dark corner, my espadrilles sticking in the booze puddles. I take the opportunity to rein in my galloping ambition and figure out how to play my hand.

Why didn't this guy call ahead? Either he's an imposter (always my first guess, due to my own former occupation), or he's committing journalistic ambush to see if we'll embarrass ourselves.

"So what's the angle?" I ask him over my shoulder.

"The first issue of the new year will focus on the death of independent radio." He turns to me as we reach the back wall. "You guys are putting up a valiant battle against the inevitable."

"Thanks. I guess." I hand him my business card. "Ciara Griffin, marketing and promotions manager."

"I know who you are." He examines my card in the light of a dancing skeleton lantern, then jots a note under my name. "*Keer*-ah," he mumbles, noting the correct pronunciation.

I keep my smile sweet. "Could I take a peek at your credentials?"

He pulls a handful of folded paper from his bag's outside pocket. "The one with the letterhead is the assignment from *Rolling Stone* editorial. The other pages are e-mails discussing the nature of the story."

I angle the paper to the light. "How does a journalism student snag such a major gig?"

"My professor has a connection." He adjusts his glasses with his middle finger. "Also, I can be pushy."

"I like pushy." I hand him back the papers. "In fact, I'd like to buy pushy a drink."

My best friend Lori swoops by with a trayful of empty glasses and "horrors d'oeuvres" plates. I reach out to stop her—gently, due to her momentum and the breakable items. She's dressed as another twenty percent of the Go-Go's, a small black Jane Wiedlin wig covering her white-blonde hair.

"Hey, Ciara." She sends her words to me but aims her perky smile at Jeremy.

"Lori, I know you're busy, but can you get this gentleman from *Rolling Stone*" —I emphasize the last two words— "whatever he'd like to drink? Bill it to the station."

"I can't accept," he says, impervious to her cute. "Conflict of interest."

"Put it on my personal tab," I tell her. "A drink between new friends."

She beams at him. "There's a dollar-a-pint Halloween special on our dark microbrew."

He hesitates. "Do you have any absinthe?"

"Um, I'll check." Lori tries not to laugh as she looks at me. "Another ginger ale?"

"Definitely."

Lori winks before walking away. She knows I always stay more sober than my marks.

I take the last sip of my flat soda to wet my drying mouth. Dealing with the press is usually the jurisdiction of my immediate boss, Franklin, the sales and publicity director. Despite great effort, he's never raised the interest of a national publication, much less *Rolling Stone*. And now they've fallen in our laps, waiting for me to fill them with fascination.

Jeremy crosses his arms and examines me, in a skeptical pose right out of *All the President's Men*. "So what gave you the idea to start this vampire DJ gimmick?"

"It's not a gimmick. They're really vampires." I offer an ironic smile. "They're each stuck in the time they were 'turned,' which is why they dress and talk like the people back in the day." I point to the stage, where a tall man with slicked-back auburn hair surveys his poodle-skirted, ponytailed groupies through a pair of dark sunglasses. "Spencer, for instance, became a vampire in Memphis in the late fifties. He was around when Sun Records discovered Elvis Presley, Johnny Cash, Carl Perkins, all those guys." He sends the girls a smile of false bashfulness as he arranges his stack of 45s. "Spencer was right there at the birth of rock 'n' roll. You could even say he was one of its midwives."

Jeremy looks at me like I've just recited my grocery list. He hasn't written any of this down. "My research says you came up with this Lifeblood of Rock 'n' Roll thing in a desperate effort to boost ratings."

"It was either that or get bought out by Skywave." I still have corporate-takeover nightmares, where my fanged friends are forced to spin Top Forty hits until they stake themselves in despair. "Something wrong with try-ing to survive?"

"No, it's genius." He checks out the Lifeblood of Rock 'n' Roll banner. "But how long can it last?"

"Well—" I scratch my nose to cover my wince. Despite our rabid fan base, ratings since the summer have tanked. The public at large is beginning to yawn and look for the Next Big Thing.

It doesn't help that the DJs don't look or act like stereotypical vampires. They wear blue jeans instead of capes. They'd rather guzzle beer, bourbon, and tequila than sip red wine. They don't brood, except about hav-ing to record promos for car dealerships and power vacs. They never attend the opera.

As much as the vampires enjoy their adoring audi-ences, they want to keep their real nature secret, to avoid the inevitable mass freakout and subsequent stake-fest. Survival is paramount, and without WVMP, our vampires would lose their sun-shielding home under the station. Not to mention their whole reason for "living."

The music.

"It can last forever," I tell Jeremy. "Rock 'n' roll will never die. Just like vampires."

A muscle near his eye twitches—the classic journalist *spare-me-the-spin* facial tic.

Lori arrives with our drinks. "Sorry, no absinthe. Hope beer's okay."

"Whatever." Jeremy accepts his drink and hands her two dollars. "Keep the change."

Ignoring his refusal of my generosity, I raise my new glass of ginger ale. "To the music."

He clinks and sips, then nearly spits the experimental dark microbrew back into the glass. There's a reason they sell it for a buck.

He wipes the foam from his mouth with a bar napkin. "I noticed that after the last ratings report you cut your advertising rates by ten percent. Sounds like you're having trouble holding the public's attention and it's hurting your bottom line."

"Every business has its ups and downs."

"But commercial radio is hopeless. How can you compete with downloads and satellite stations?" He raises his eyebrows. "What's next, werewolves?"

I ignore the jest. "We'll compete the same way radio stations always have—by providing a unique experience and quality entertainment."

Jeremy doesn't record those weasel words. I scan the bar, hoping to see David, our general manager, or another DJ—anyone who can impress this guy.

The front door opens, and in walks my savior.

"Come on." I beckon Jeremy to follow me. "Meet our star."

The reporter looks past me, and his jaw drops, transforming his face from cyni-cool to little-kid glee. "Yeah yeah. That'd be great."

Pushing through the crowd, I glance back to see Jeremy close behind, frantically flipping the pages of a small notebook.

By the time I get to the door, Shane is surrounded by a gaggle of college girls. Towering over them at six-foot-five, he greets with an easy grin, but when his gaze rises to meet mine, his pale blue eyes light up with such force, the groupies' smiles turn to scowls.

The women look over their shoulders at me. One is dressed as Courtney Love in a white baby doll dress, black combat boots, and smeared mascara—presumably to appeal to grunge-boy Shane. As I pass through the gauntlet, she gives me and my costume a glare that could melt Teflon.

I take Shane's hand, then pull him close to speak in his ear. "This guy's from *Rolling Stone*."

"You're kidding."

"I've never lied to you." He's the only one I can say that about. I turn to introduce the reporter. "Jeremy Glaser—"

"Shane McAllister," Jeremy says, then reaches forward and pumps Shane's hand hard enough to hurt a mere human. "I love your show. I listened to it back when I went to Sherwood College, in your pre-vampire days."

"Wow. I mean, thanks. I mean, good to meet you."

"Would you consider an interview?"

"Seriously?" Shane smoothes the front of his flannel shirt.

"He'll meet you over there in a sec." I look at Jeremy and point to the place where we were just talking. He salutes with his little notebook and hurries to the back of the bar.

Shane squeezes my elbow. "You look cute tonight."

"Tonight?"

"Always." He succeeds in sneaking a kiss. "So what should I tell this guy?"

"He says his angle is the struggle of independent radio, so give him your authenticity spiel and how radio should be all about the music." I hook my pinky into the belt loop of his faded ripped jeans. "You know, the stuff I find so adorable."

"Adorably naïve, right. What about the undead issue? The standard 'pretend to be a human pretending to be a vampire' routine?"

"Yes, with lots of wink-winks. Your usual ironic self."

He nods, then hands me his backpack of CDs before heading off to join Jeremy.

Bill Riley's "Flying Saucers Rock 'n' Roll" fades out,

and Spencer's honey-smooth drawl comes out of the speakers.

"Ladies and gentlemen, we got two hours left 'til Halloween. Time for me to say good night, but I'm gonna turn it over to my great friend, 'Mississippi' Monroe Jefferson." The crowd whistles and hollers, especially the older members. Spencer continues, "He'll play you some blues that I guarantee'll send a shiver down your spine."

He steps aside and adjusts the microphone down to the level of Monroe, who has appeared in the chair behind him, like in a magic trick. Another cheer. The stage light makes Monroe's suit glow white, setting off his smooth ebony skin and the lustrous scarlet of his acoustic guitar.

Monroe lets loose with a weepingly beautiful version of Robert Johnson's "Me and the Devil Blues." I smile at the choice; the story of his turning is well known by his fans. Like several legendary musicians of his place and time, Monroe supposedly went to the crossroads at midnight, to trade his soul to the Devil for the ability to master the blues. A vampire was waiting for him, and the rest is history.

The blues always makes me want to drink, so I head to the bar and signal to Stuart, the owner of the Smoking Pig, who is making a valiant attempt to look like Simon Le Bon of Duran Duran.

He slides a bottle of my favorite beer across the bar. "How's it going with the reporter?"

"Journalists are a lot harder to impress than the general public." I watch him light a cigarette. "Any luck on that smoking ban waiver?"

Stuart shakes his head in disgust. "I sent the state a photo of the sign hanging over our front door. I said, 'If you look closely, you'll notice that under the words 'The Smoking Pig' is an illustration of a pig with a cigarette. They didn't care." He takes a hostile puff. "Fascists."

"So what are you going to do?"

"Set up an outdoor lounge with space heaters. It'll cost a fortune."

"Hey, Ciara," comes a voice at my elbow. Lori sidles close and adjusts the poof of my ponytail. "I remember that guy Jeremy from my History of the Middle East class senior year. Smart, but kinda intense. He said he hoped the Iraq war lasted long enough for him to be an embedded reporter."

"A thrill-seeker, huh?" I watch him in the corner speaking with Shane, scribbling madly in his notebook. Shane maintains a casual posture against the wall, but his supernatural stillness creates a magnetic field that seems to have snagged the journalist. "I don't like it."

"Why not?" she asks me just as Monroe finishes his song to a rush of applause. "Don't you want the publicity?"

"I want fawning puff pieces about how cool it is to be a vampire. I don't want someone to find out the truth."

Lori hurries off to pick up an order as Monroe begins another song. I watch his fingers glide over the strings like a water bug skimming a pond. He makes it look so easy. Shane tried to teach me guitar last month—I stopped after two days and ten blisters.

A familiar arm slides over my shoulders. I lean into Shane and crane my neck to look behind him. "Where's the reporter?"

"Interviewing Spencer." He hesitates. "I think he wants to be bitten."

"Lori said he was weird. Are you sure?"

Shane nods. "A vampire can smell an eager donor a mile away."

"Do I need to forbid you to bite a reporter?"

He rolls his eyes. "I'm not that dumb. Anyway, I don't think he thinks I'm really a vampire."

"Because that's insane."

"I think he thinks I'm a wannabe."

Ah yes. In the "real" vampire subculture, some humans believe they need to drink blood to thrive, and there are people lined up to oblige them. Lacking fangs, they use razors or needles to bleed their "donors."

Some of those donors find their way to a *real*-real vampire, and if they can be trusted to hide the truth, the two form a symbiotic relationship. The donors exchange blood for money or sex or—most commonly—the masochistic thrill of serving a creature that could rip off their heads.

Not for me. The sensation of being stabbed with a pair of ice picks does nothing for my self-esteem or libido.

At a minute to midnight, my boy takes over the stage from Monroe, who tips his hat to the worshipping crowd on his way out. No one dares to follow. Like Spencer and the other older vampires, Monroe's charisma holds an edge of menace that sane people wisely avoid. It's why we ask them to wear sunglasses in public whenever possible.

Shane, on the other hand, exudes humanity, giving his admirers a friendly wave as he moves to the microphone. "Ladies and gentlemen, the time is twelve a.m. It is now. Officially. Halloween."

He hits a switch and a low, hypnotic bass emanates from the speaker—the opening moments of Concrete Blonde's "Bloodletting." The patrons writhe and vamp, reveling in the dark magic his music weaves.

Someone calls my name. I turn to see Lori leaning out of the kitchen, holding onto the edge of the swinging door.

"What's up?" I ask as I follow her into the kitchen.

She takes me behind the salad prep area, where an old boom box sits on a shelf. She turns up the volume. Above the clatter of pans and the sizzle of grease, I hear an angry male voice.

"—not participate in the unfruitful deeds of darkness, but instead even expose them, as Paul told the Ephesians." He lets that sink in. "Don't let the secular media and your children's public school teachers convince you that Halloween is harmless fun. Your *tolerance* is their greatest weapon in this culture war. Fact: Halloween is a pagan holiday that glorifies darkness and evil and everything God wants us to fight."

I glance past her at the chef/dishwasher, who's searing a pair of burgers on the grill, then at the ceramic white statue of the Virgin Mary above the prep table. "When did Jorge get born again?"

Lori shakes her head. "It's supposed to be WVMP."

"No, it's just mistuned." I twist the grease-encrusted knob, searching for the station. "The antenna probably got knocked."

"I already tried that. I was here when it happened, just now." She points to the wall clock, which reads a minute after midnight. "Regina was giving her usual creepy intro, then suddenly it was this guy."

I tweak the dial again and again, but there's no Regina, no Bauhaus, no Sex Pistols. Just a whole lotta Jesus goin' on.

"I better get David."

The kitchen door sweeps inward, banging into the stainless steel dishwasher. My boss stalks toward us, dressed as Bruce Springsteen circa *Born in the U.S.A.*, cell phone at his ear. As David passes me, I hear a woman's screech from the earpiece.

"I'll call you back." He shuts the phone as he stomps up to the radio, the bandana around his ripped blue jeans flapping with each step.

"She's not on," I tell him. "It's some guy nutting off about Satan."

David adjusts the knob up and down, only to get another dose of Ranty Man.

He curses under his breath. "Regina said she's flooded with calls."

"It happened exactly at midnight," Lori offers.

"Strange." David stares at the boom box. "It's like another station was just created on the same frequency."

"Isn't that illegal?" I ask him.

"Extremely." He rubs the dark, uneven stubble on his chin, a look he's been working on for a week (and, if I may say, has been worth the wait). "If it's a pirate operation, the FCC could slap them with a fine and confiscate their equipment, maybe even throw them in jail."

"Then what are we waiting for? Let's report them."

He gives me a patronizing glare, like I've suggested we call up Santa Claus. "Ciara, the FCC doesn't exactly have a twenty-four-hour emergency number. We'll have to file a report during business hours."

"What if it's not pirates?" I gesture to the radio. "It sounds too high-quality to be coming out of someone's basement. What if it's another real station?" My mind sounds the *cha-ching!* of a cash register. "Can we sue them?"

David turns away, dark brows furrowed. "If it's a real station," he murmurs, "I might be able to find out—" He looks at Lori. "Can I use your boss's computer?"

She points to the back of the kitchen. "There's Stuart's office. Sorry about the mess."

David speaks to me as he strides away. "Call Regina, tell her to get the location of everyone who can't hear us."

I head back to the bar, where Shane is onstage and on the phone. He pulls his head away from the phone, as if it's delivering electric shocks.

I weave through the crowd to the edge of the stage, then mouth the word, "Regina?" to him. Shane nods. Good thing his eardrums are as immortal as the rest of him.

I signal for him to hand me the phone. He shakes his head but obliges. "Be careful!" he shouts.

I move away from the speakers to hear Regina. Unnecessary. Astronauts on the International Space Station can probably hear her.

"Hey, it's me," I say as calmly as I can. "David says to find out the locations of all the callers who can't hear us."

"Don't you think I thought of that?" Regina's voice is even harsher than usual. "They're everywhere—D.C., Sherwood, Baltimore, Harrisburg, every town in between. This isn't some half-assed pirate operation. Someone is fucking with me."

"I doubt it's personal. It's probably just an anti-Halloween demonstration by religious wackos. David says he might find out who it is by looking on the Internet."

There's a long pause before her voice comes back, muted. "Really?"

Regina died in 1987, so her entire experience of the Internet consists of the Matthew Broderick movie *WarGames*. To her, the Web is omnipotent, able to produce tragedies and miracles with a few keywords.

"Go on with the show as if nothing's happened," I tell her, "and we'll be at the station after the bar closes at two."

She gives a tight sigh. "I wish I could figure out how to blame you for this."

I hang up the phone as Jeremy approaches me, notebook in hand. "Everything okay?" he asks.

"Of course. Why?"

"The way you and the station manager were running around, it looks like there's a crisis."

"Nope." I adjust my sunglasses. "No crisis."

"You mean, other than the fact that no one can hear your broadcast?" In response to my stunned look, he holds up his own phone. "My roommate just texted me."

Crap. How many other media outlets have noticed already? How many *advertisers* have noticed?

He steps closer, a new gleam in his eye. "Let me help you find the pirate."

"I don't think so." That's all we need, for him to snoop around and discover the real truth. "Thanks, anyway." I pat his arm and turn toward the stage.

"This could be a huge story," he says.

I stop. Visions of the station, the logo, maybe even Shane's face, on the cover of *Rolling Stone* form a slide show in my head. Visions of solvency. Visions of survival.

I turn back to Jeremy. "Give us a day to put our own people on it. I'll get you something Thursday morning."

"Exclusive?"

"Through the weekend."

"Good enough." He tucks his notebook back into his pocket. "I'm going to drive back home to College Park and listen myself. I'll call you Thursday."

On my way back to the kitchen, I wing Shane's cell phone toward the stage. He snags it with a deft maneuver.

In Stuart's dim office, I find David leaning close to the monitor, his worried face aglow in the pale white light. He gives me a distracted glance as I pick my way through the piles of papers and stacks of shrink-wrapped Halloween bar napkins.

"Found something odd." David points to the screen. "The FCC keeps a public record of every application. Here's one for a translator construction permit from earlier this month right here in Sherwood."

"A what construction?"

"Translator. It's a two-way antenna that takes a radio signal and transmits it way outside the station's original range. Let's say we wanted to broadcast in Poughkeepsie. We'd build translator stations to relay the signal, and then everyone between here and there could hear us."

"But we couldn't trample on another station's frequency, right?"

"Right. To stay legal, we'd have the translator change our frequency to one that's available in our target area. If we're 94.3 here, we might be 102.1 in Scranton."

I squint at the browser to see what looks like an application from a Family Air Network, Inc. "But these people didn't bother switching."

"No, they bothered." David highlights a box on the application. "Specifically requested our frequency." He rips off his Springsteen headband and glares up at me. "They're after us."

Not sure what to read next?

Visit Pocket Books online at
www.simonsays.com

Reading suggestions for
you and your reading group
New release news
Author appearances
Online chats with your favorite writers
Special offers
Order books online
And much, much more!